I0665654

Soul Rhapsody

G. C. Ellis

Soul Rhapsody is a work of fiction. Names, places, and incidents either are the products of the author's imagination or are used fictitiously. Any resemblance to actual events, locales, or persons, living or dead, is entirely coincidental.

Regarding the book cover and title page images: All photographs used are either in the public domain or are licensed under a Creative Commons Attribution-Share-Alike license. For detailed information on this subject, see the section titled "Image Attribution" in "About this Book."

This trade paperback edition was published in the United States of America by SageSerpent Productions. The SageSerpent logo and "SageSerpent" are trademarks of SageSerpent Productions. **ISBN 978-1-952094-06-4**

Soul Rhapsody Contents:

Soul Source

1: In the Beginning...

Nothing that I'm about to relate would have occurred if Albert hadn't been a mere angel-in-training. In fact, he was the most junior member of his class. Given that Albert had previously had an Earthly existence, that he'd been admitted to the program at all was something of a miracle. Certainly, the council of archangels had debated the decision fiercely. In the end, Albert had received their blessing, not because he was outstandingly capable or competent, but because, of all the candidates presented for consideration, he had the most positive spirit and the kindest heart.

When those who'd known him during his Earthly life heard the news, they were happy for him of course— happy, but with reservations... happy, but with concerns. You see, in life, Albert had been, well, a bit of a klutz, a well-meaning bumbler... perpetually trying his best to genuinely serve others but somehow always coming up a little bit short. I suppose I should give you an example or two so that you can appreciate what I mean.

Albert lived for most of his adult life at the Columban monastery known as Iona Abbey. He was there during the period from 807 AD to 814 AD when it was refounded as the Abbey of Kells, and he almost lived long enough to see the consecration of its church. Like most monks of his day, he did whatever tasks the Abbot ordered him to do— working on the farm, in the dairy, in the brewery, and so on. There were only two arenas in which Albert seldom worked—the kitchen and the scriptorium.

The Abbot kept Albert out of the kitchen because Albert had a tendency to cut himself accidentally when chopping meat and vegetables, and all too often, when he'd put loaves of bread in the oven to bake, he'd fall into a daydream, forget, and let them burn. After the third time the Abbot had to scrape charcoal off of his bread crusts at the evening meal, he decided that perhaps Albert would be better suited to scrubbing the chapel floor, polishing the sacramental vessels, or sweeping out the dormitory.

Now, the fondest and most fervent wish of Albert's heart was that, if only he could serve his brothers well, he might be allowed to work in the scriptorium. There, a select few of his brothers—the ones who could read and write—would toil day and night, by sun's rays and by candlelight, copying and illuminating manuscripts of sacred text. Unfortunately, Albert couldn't read or write. In those days, monks came from two social castes: members of the lower and middle classes who offered to serve God by whatever means they could—and thereby earn a place at the refectory table so to speak—and members of the gentry.

At this point in European history, primogeniture was alive and well throughout most of the continent. That is to say, the firstborn son inherited the lord's lands and titles, the second son most often went into some kind of military service, and the third son went into the church, either as a priest or as one of the monks who might ascend to become Abbot some day. Such monks generally had at least some education, and they could be put to work copying prayer books, hymnals, the Bible, and any other texts deemed worthy of preservation in that era before the invention of the printing press.

To show reverence for the texts they copied and to highlight key passages, monks would often draw and paint beautiful illustrations, ornamented capital letters, and gold-leaf-embellished designs in the margins. Moreover, a monk who was bored or who had a sense of humor might add small sketches of gargoyles, dragons, and other mythical beasts where space permitted. Albert saw his brothers' work whenever he was tasked with sweeping the scriptorium floor or cleaning up their work carrels, and although he was illiterate, he longed to participate in creating beautiful sacred books along side them.

Sometimes, late at night when he'd finished gathering up the scraps of parchment that had been cut from the edges of new pages, he'd steal a moment and try his hand at sketching small designs using a discarded quill and a borrowed inkstand. At first, he could see plainly that his efforts were quite crude when compared to those of his brothers. But with time and practice, Albert began to master some of the simpler motifs—Celtic knots, flowers and foliage, and thumbnails of farm animals and beasts of the field.

As it happened, Albert's luck changed because of his secret sketching. The dormitory afforded the monks no privacy, and one of his fellows spotted a scrap of parchment protruding from the edge of his sleeve. Assuming that Albert's effort would be primitive at best and eager to expose Albert's folly, the other monk snatched the parchment and ran laughing from the room, seeking out the Abbot to show him this discovery.

The Abbot took the scrap of parchment, unfolded it, and studied it carefully. To the other monk's disappointment, the Abbot didn't join in the joke and laugh at Albert's drawings. Instead, he looked up and exclaimed, "Bring Albert to my office." Taken aback, the other monk hastened to obey.

Albert entered the Abbot's office certain that he was about to receive a humiliating rebuke. Instead, the Abbot gestured for Albert to take a seat on the bench that faced the Abbot's work table. Albert eased gingerly onto the bench and sat at attention.

"You did this?" The Abbot held out the parchment scrap. Albert nodded. "Did you enjoy doing it?" Albert nodded again. "Brother Albert, we're about to begin work on perhaps the most ambitious project that our Abbey has ever undertaken, and we'll need all the help we can get to complete it in time for the consecration of our church.

"Given your background, I can't assign you a role as a scribe. But there are other valuable roles that you could fill. Will you accept whatever assignment I give you and do your best at it, even if it requires that you subordinate yourself to the good of the team?" Albert nodded enthusiastically. He felt as if his heart was about to burst with joy. "Good. Report to the scriptorium immediately after Matins tomorrow. I'll designate someone to show you what to do. Dismissed."

So began Albert's service to the monks who created one of the most magnificent manuscripts ever produced—*The Book of Kells*. Albert scraped lamb skins and prepared parchment. He cut the parchment into pages and carefully drew guidelines to help the scribes keep their lettering straight. He harvested feathers from geese in the barnyard and cut the feathers into quill pens. He followed recipes, pulverized pigments, and mixed gesso, inks, and paints. He replenished inkwells, replaced guttering candles, and trimmed wicks and scraped up spilled wax so that the precious pages wouldn't be damaged by smoke and oily residue.

At first, Albert's brethren grumbled at his presence in their midst. He did have a tendency to accidentally knock things off of tables if he turned around too quickly in the narrow aisles. Also, the loose, flowing sleeves of his cassock would catch on pages and inkwells left too close to the edge. The Abbot solved some of these issues by giving Albert the carrel at the very back of the room, immediately inside the door, so that he didn't have to pass by his fellows any more than was necessary. But soon, he learned to hug his arms to his short, slightly-chubby body whenever he delivered supplies so that he was less likely to slip up and damage one of his brother's efforts.

In time, he and his brothers learned to accommodate each other, and from dawn until long after dark, Albert would hear his brothers calling to him from their benches. "Albert, I'm almost out of ink!" "Albert, I'm ready for my next page!" "Albert!" His heart would glow with happiness, knowing that he was contributing to the creation of so much beauty, and he knew a few proud moments all his own, such as those when he carefully crafted brushes from strands of animal fur or rolled out tissue-thin foil of pure gold for use in embellishing the glorious full-page illuminations. The Abbot even let Albert return to the kitchen, where he learned at last how to separate egg yolks from the whites so the whites could be used to glue down the gold leaf to the gesso'ed areas prepared to receive it.

Whenever Albert uttered a personal prayer during this period, it was solely that he'd live to see *The Book of Kells* completed. He knew that his brethren were close to achieving that goal. The Abbot had contracted with a goldsmith to have a heavy bejeweled cover made. But alas, men may ask, and God always answers, but sometimes the answer is "No."

Before Albert could attain his heart's desire, an epidemic swept through the British Isles—not the ghastly pandemics of Small Pox or Black Death... Not every contagious illness turns into a disaster like the Plague that would later devastate Europe in the thirteenth century. No, Albert and his brothers found themselves facing a much more mundane disease, probably a variant of influenza, but it proved to be enough.

Villagers outside the monastery walls fell sick, and the monks, practicing genuine Christian charity, went forth to nurse them back to health. The monks then brought the virus into the monastery, and desperate to save the lives of the gifted scribes and artists that he served, Albert labored around the clock—bathing their fevered brows, spoon-feeding them broth and gruel, and holding pots beneath their mouths when they couldn't keep food down and vomited.

In the end, he saved them all. Then, exhausted and exposed unceasingly to all manner of noxious and infectious bodily fluids, he collapsed and quickly died. His death brought home to them as perhaps nothing else could have just how much they'd come to rely on him. Only when he was gone did they realize his true value. They buried him with honor and said many masses for the salvation of his soul, and the Heavenly Hosts answered their prayers by elevating him directly into a state of eternal blessedness.

*   *   *   *   *

Albert was astonished to find that he'd been admitted directly into Paradise. Church doctrine held that, because he'd perished before anyone could hear his confession, absolve him, and administer last rites, he'd passed on without being in a State of Grace. Consequently, given how imperfect he knew himself to be, he'd expected to have a lengthy stay in Purgatory. Instead, when he figuratively opened his eyes for the first time in his new abode, he was dazzled by brilliant light, enraptured by the songs of an angelic choir, and filled with such feelings of loving and being loved that he quite literally didn't know what to do with himself.

Fortunately, the Heavenly Hosts leave nothing to chance. They assign every newcomer a welcoming committee. The committee helps the new arrival connect with the spirits of friends, family members, and even pets who've predeceased him. One or more of these spirits will then take on the task of helping the newbie understand what to expect in the afterlife and get oriented in its timeless realm.

Albert was delighted to see his parents again, although their first conversation gave him yet another surprise. When Albert joined the monastic community, the Abbot (in a fit of unwarranted optimism) assured Albert that his parents had undoubtedly named him after Albertus, Bishop of Hereford, who'd died in 786 AD, not long before Albert was born. Now Albert's father felt honor-bound to correct this mis-impression. In reality, he'd named his first and only son after a close childhood friend who'd perished in his mid-teens from pneumonia. After Albert got over his surprise, he actually took the news quite well. To him, the Bishop of Hereford seemed a remote and rather awe-inspiring figure. He felt much happier knowing that his father had used his birth as a chance to honor someone that his father remembered fondly.

Albert and his parents communed for quite a while, catching up on each other's news. Albert even got to meet two sisters who had died before he was born, one immediately following childbirth and one from measles at the age of three. Eventually though, Albert's father suggested that he and Albert should go and see one of the angels.

Albert's father explained that souls had options. Those who regretted the sins of their Earthly life could request the chance to return to corporeal existence. If their wish was granted, they could try to do better, expiating past sins through repentance and righteous living. Likewise, if a soul had truly loved his Earthly life, or if he wanted to continue serving those souls trapped in bodies, he could ask to be sent back into flesh as an "old soul." Neither of these options felt right to Albert, and he said so, so his father described a third way to while away Eternity, assuming that Albert didn't want to treat it simply as a wonderful, unending vacation. Albert's father told him that one could apply for a job.

As accustomed to service as Albert had become, this option attracted him immediately. He asked what jobs were available. His father began listing them, and Albert felt his heart sink within him. He wasn't the least bit musically gifted, so joining the choir was out of the question. He felt that he was by far too limited in his understanding to take on the responsibility of being a "watcher" or a spirit-guide. He was beginning to think that here, as in the monastery, he would be hard-pressed to find a suitable way to serve when his father mentioned "soul management." Albert stopped short, baffled but intrigued.

"What's that?" he demanded.

His father smiled happily and explained. Every living creature, no matter how elementary, had a soul, and the angels welcomed the help of formerly flesh-bound spirits because so many trillions of creatures were constantly being created and each one had to be infused with soul-energy. When Albert asked what kinds of creatures, his father proudly revealed that he, a former subsistence farmer, had been entrusted with the job of infusing souls into archaea, bacteria, and even protozoans!

Albert shook his head in confusion. He had no idea what kinds of beings his father was talking about, but clearly, his father was proud to have such a job, and such jobs were obviously necessary to the fulfillment of God's plan. Albert asked his father to help him get such employment, and the two of them struck off across the infinite expanse of Heaven to track down Albert's father's boss.

Because time doesn't exist in the afterlife, it took them no time at all to find said boss. She was patiently instructing a sentient soul of non-Earth origin in the method for infusing soul-energy into germ cells of flowering plants. Albert and his father waited until she'd finished the lesson and watched as the alien being successfully performed the first few downloads. Then Albert's father coughed politely to get her attention.

She turned, recognized Albert's father and smiled. "Ah good! You've brought your son, I see. We've been watching him for a long time. Please tell me he's interested in taking a job."

Albert's father seemed to swell with pride. "He is!"

"Come with me." She transported the three of them through the Ether to what Albert was beginning to recognize as a work station. "Albert, at first you'll work along side your father. That way, you'll have someone familiar that you can ask for help if things become too confusing. We'll start you out on something simple, I think." She stroked her chin thoughtfully. "Ah yes, that should work quite well. We'll switch your father to working with insects and worms, and you can take over his former role with single-celled organisms." Albert's father beamed at this unexpected promotion. "He's done splendidly with them. Just do as he instructs, and you'll perform very well indeed."

With this assurance, the boss departed, and Albert's father began teaching Albert his new tasks. There was no doubt that infusing a being with soul-energy required finesse, but with his father's guidance, Albert quickly mastered the basics.

First, one opened the tiny portal that led to the cell in question. One had to be quick, reaching the cell just at the point of mitosis, budding, or whatever other reproductive process it might follow. Next, one infused the microscopic critter with just the tiniest possible smidgen of soul-force. Finally, before the soul-smidgen could escape back through the portal to Heaven where it would so much rather be, one had to close the portal—gently, but firmly—keeping the soul in place. Now the critter could be watched and tracked for as long as it lived, for not a sparrow falls but God is aware of it.

Albert came to love the work. More than anything he'd ever done before, this job had deep meaning, a Holy Purpose. He came to feel great fondness for each of the billion-trillion creatures that he infused—even for those pathogens that he'd formerly feared and loathed during his Earthly life. He began to glimpse a small fraction of the glory and perfection of God's plan, and he took pride in being an infinitesimal cog in that plan's vast machine.

* * * * *

Albert and his family did well in their respective roles. Albert and his father were promoted repeatedly—from microorganisms, worms, and insects to various sea creatures, fish, amphibians, reptiles, birds, and ultimately mammals. The so-called higher animal orders required greater judgement and care because the amount of soul-energy that had to be infused depended on the complexity and potential of the individual being. Albert's father did his work with a steadiness and insight that pleased the boss greatly. Albert occasionally made minor miscalculations, but he never erred so greatly that the boss had to take corrective action, so Albert was also deemed a success.

After completing each shift, Albert and his father would seek out Albert's mother. She and the daughter who'd lived to be three now served jointly as the guardian spirits for a nesting pair of California condors, an assignment that gave them both great satisfaction. The daughter who'd died in infancy had requested the chance to be born into flesh again, and whenever Albert's family looked in on her, she appeared to be making the most of her new existence as an old soul—a comparatively new old soul really, because her first stay on Earth has been so brief. In short, Albert and the souls he knew best were still a surprisingly cohesive group, a fact that both amused and bemused the angels around them.

Another source of angelic bemusement was the way that Albert and his family chose to present themselves. Most angels have never had an Earthly existence, so if they present themselves to others at all, they generally manifest solely as light. Occasionally, they will manifest as glorious choral sound heard faintly as if in the distance. Once in a great while, an angel will manifest as a feeling, such as the emotion of perfect warmth, love, and security. But all in all, whatever presentation an angel may choose, the common theme is that the manifestation will not include a particular appearance derived from a physical form.

Albert and his family, on the other hand, were definitely most comfortable with physical forms. His father appeared as he had in life: a short, muscular man with sunburned skin, work-roughened hands, unkempt brown hair, and merry brown eyes. Albert's mother appeared as a plump, comfortable matron. Her honey-blond hair curled in tight ringlets all over her head, and her chin and cheeks dimpled whenever she smiled. As for Albert himself, he maintained the outward form he'd always known—short like his father, plump like his mother, but sporting a bald, tonsured head with no more than a wisp of unruly hair surrounding his shining pate. From habit, Albert also wore a habit, or more accurately, an ankle-length robe with long flowing sleeves, belted at the waist with a length of knotted cord. Over his head he wore a cowl, and on his feet, sandals.

Albert's little sister was another matter. She felt no desire to return to Earth. She was too happy being with her family and watching the condors. But given that she'd only spent three years incarnate, she was equally happy to emulate the angels and present herself as a ray of light—a ray that would fan out into a vivid rainbow whenever she was particularly pleased with whatever she was experiencing.

Albert was also quite content living in the bosom of his family so to speak. On Earth, he'd avoided all the cardinal sins: pride, greed, lust, envy, gluttony, wrath, and sloth. He was by nature a humble, mild-mannered, diligent being whose only (quite modest) aspiration was to help those around him. Prior to his death, he might have had little scope to demonstrate any of the cardinal virtues— prudence, justice, temperance, and courage—but through-out his entire life, he'd practiced the spiritual virtues of faith, hope, and charity. So unbeknown to him, he was increasingly finding favor among his superiors.

Finally there came a proud day—proud in the most positive sense of the word... Albert and his father received a visit from their boss. She let them know that Albert's father was being promoted from his current position in "Shipping" to one in "Receiving." Henceforth, he would operate the portals in reverse, collecting souls that were exiting their bodies and welcoming them into the Heavenly realm.

This job was a huge responsibility because such souls must only be allowed to exit at the proper moment. Some individuals would have near-death experiences, yet for a variety of reasons, it would not yet be "their time." Instead, either through their own choice or through spiritual counseling, they must be allowed or induced to return to the flesh and continue their Earthly lives. And Albert's father had been deemed wise and compassionate enough to make such determinations and give such counseling.

Had Albert and his father still had the capacity to cry, they would have wept with joy at hearing this news. Albert's father rushed off to share his good fortune with his wife. Albert remained behind only to ask a question. He wanted to know if the boss thought he'd be OK performing his work alone going forward. He hadn't relied much lately on his father's guidance, but he'd been comforted by the knowledge that he could ask his father questions if necessary.

The boss was quick to reassure him. That's when Albert learned that she had good news for him as well. He'd been accepted into the angel-in-training program. There, his mentors would prepare him for a career infusing souls into human beings.

Albert was astonished. He could scarcely credit what he'd heard. Impulsively, he started to rush after his father to share *his* news with his family, but realizing the import of the moment, he stopped himself and returned to address the boss. "Thank you. Thank you! I promise. I'll pay attention and work hard. You won't be sorry you gave me this chance."

The boss smiled at Albert in a kindly way and patted him supportively on the shoulder. "I know you'll do your best. Just keep in mind as you do your duty that someone did the same for you once. Someone helped you come to life." Albert swallowed hard, looked up into the boss's shining face, and nodded.

* * * * *

At first, the boss conducted Albert's training personally. Just as she'd once stood at the side of the alien being, she now stood with him, coaching him patiently through the steps of infusing and awakening a member of his own kind. Even though Albert had awakened countless beings before, including members of sophisticated species like dolphins, gorillas, and chimpanzees, he was at first overwhelmed by the additional requirements for infusing a human.

For one thing, picking the right moment was more complicated. It depended on the religious beliefs of the parents and their community. Some held that the embryo was a person as soon as the egg and sperm joined. Others asserted that one must wait until the fetal heart began to beat. Still others refused to recognize the baby as a person until the moment of birth or even a few days thereafter, when the child's survival could be assured.

Albert was confused by the sheer number of conflicting views, many of which flew in the face of teachings he'd received from the Orthodox Roman Catholic Church. When he questioned his boss on the subject, she simply smiled a wistful, somewhat-enigmatic smile and said, "We try to respect the parents' ethical and philosophic stand, assuming they have one of course."

Another source of Albert's confusion was that human subjects, unlike any of the other beings he'd dealt with, had more options concerning their life-course. Albert had lived on Earth too early to hear the arguments regarding free will versus predestination. But now he became embroiled in the question.

The simpler species he'd previously served were motivated by fairly basic drives—the quest for sustenance, the need for rest and protection from the elements, the urge to find a mate and reproduce... Humans were a lot more complex, sublimating those drives into all sorts of secondary and even tertiary activities, many of them purely symbolic. And as trivial a decision as turning right instead of left on a city street could change the individual's life-course in dramatic, sometimes irretrievable ways.

So Albert had to deal with a huge variation in the quantity and quality of soul-force that he delivered. He had to work within the guidelines of God's Plan, but within those guidelines, there was scope for a degree of personal creativity that he'd never been called upon to express before. His subjects would be expected to "hit certain marks" during their lives, but how they traversed from mark to mark was entirely up to them, and sometimes, through prayer and angelic intercession, even those marks could be accelerated, delayed, or changed.

Thus, Albert might need to give one individual a sweet-natured soul of middling capabilities and another a soul of towering genius or discouraging limitations. The angels expected Albert to show good judgement in what kind of soul he provided. It must support the predestined course of the individual in question, but it must also allow that individual to enact his or her life in a manner that was unique and meaningful for all concerned. If Albert's boss hadn't been such a superb instructor, Albert might well have collapsed under the burden of so much responsibility. But she continued to coach him, patiently and persistently, until he finally felt up to the job.

She left him to it then—not as some kind of abandonment, but merely by turning her attention to another trainee. Albert knew that, if he needed her, he had simply to call, and in any case, he was surrounded by other angels-in-training who were engaged in the same work. He assumed that he could call upon them for advice as well. Thereafter, Albert reported to his job "as regular as clockwork" and carried out his duties with growing skill.

Once Albert got past his initial nervousness, he came to love his new job more than any other he'd ever held. If he'd once felt fondness for the microbiota he'd infused, now he felt intense interest in, and empathy for, the people he awakened. In his off periods, he'd frequently visit his mother so that he could follow their fortunes. Albert's sister was still watching condors and other birds of prey, a job for which she apparently had a special affinity. But Albert's mother had graduated to watching ever-more-complex beings, and she was currently watching a small cohort of European colonists who were invading the New World.

Albert had learned that watchers were granted a certain amount of latitude because they needed to stay attentive to perform their duties. This latitude included permission to "take a break" and go watch some other being or beings for a while to get a fresh perspective. So if Albert had a particular yen to know how someone on Earth was doing, he could ask his mother to turn her attention to that person for a spell, and Albert could share her insights. He always found the experience immensely fulfilling, plus a strong motivation to continue improving his performance.

Albert was painfully aware at times that he needed more practice, particularly in handling the soul portal. From the first, back when he'd worked with one-celled organisms, he'd seen how reluctant nascent souls were to leave Heaven and enter the flesh. The soul-smidgens he'd dealt with then had been too small and weak to put up much of a fight, and he'd never failed to close the portal before one could slip back out of its body. But as Albert had progressed to higher and higher life forms, he'd faced increasing difficulty doing this part of his job.

By the time he was dealing with great apes, he often had to slam the door shut rather than close it gently. If he didn't, the soul would dive back through the portal, shoulder past him, and flee into the distance, often trying to conceal itself behind an angel or another disembodied soul. On such occasions, Albert would have to chase after it, shamefaced, and try to reason with it until it would grudgingly consent to be born.

Sometimes, even his best powers of persuasion would fail, and he'd have to engage in a lively game of chase, hide, and seek, eventually tackling the errant soul and dragging it kicking and screaming, figuratively speaking, back to his work station. Then, keeping a firm grip on it, he'd open the portal, thrust it in, and use his foot to shove it into its new home so that it remained off-balance while he locked the exit. Such events always left him tousled and disheveled, and he'd cringe as his fellow workers laughed merrily at his predicament.

From the outset, Albert had assumed that, if ape souls were difficult, human souls would be more so, and his expectations were often met. He never had trouble when he was given the job of re-introducing an old soul. An old soul was an old hand and had volunteered for, or acquiesced to, rebirth. But new souls could be as slippery as eels, and Albert needed to master the exactly right timing of soul-selection, portal access, soul-download, and portal closure. His fellow workers showed a facility that amounted almost to a graceful dance. But Albert was still awkward. Each download involved entirely too much clumsy improvisation.

Then came the day when Albert met Janie. Albert had seen Janie from a distance before. He'd catch sight of her on his way to or from work now and then—a bright, inquisitive, inventive little spirit with a warm, friendly demeanor... happily at play among the seraphim and cherubim.

He could tell at a glance that she was a new soul, as new as they come—as lovely and unspoiled by care as a just-formed star. He knew that her destiny would be to become incarnate some day. He prayed for her sake that the day would not come soon. And had he thought about it, he would have prayed that it wouldn't be his job to send her into the world. But he didn't think about it because there were so many spirits working in his team. Odds were that someone else would have that responsibility.

However, the job did fall to him. One shift, Albert checked his list and found Janie on it. He took the trouble to do a little research and learned that, although she wouldn't be a planned child, she'd at least be a wanted child. Moreover, she'd be born into comparatively easy circumstances. When he examined her life's milestones, he found that she'd face no famines, wars, or plagues, just the usual troubles to which flesh is typically heir. So, armed with the knowledge he'd need if her download turned into a negotiation, Albert summoned Janie and opened the portal leading to her body.

Janie took one look at that seemingly dark corridor and pulled back in fear. She grasped Albert around the waist, clutching at his cassock, and begged not to be thrown into that place of shadow. Albert sighed sadly and plucked her little spirit-hands from his garment. He explained that the darkness would last only an instant, and after that, she'd begin a kind of adventure—an important life ordained by God—an opportunity not to be missed.

But Janie had no basis for understanding what he said. As a new soul, she had no concept of what an Earthly life could be like. She escaped his grasp and grabbed the rope encircling his waist. Albert suddenly regretted the choice he'd made regarding his personal presentation. He had to peel her tiny spirit-fingers from the cord, all the while repeating his reassurances.

He picked her up as tenderly as he could and placed her in the portal. She immediately thrust her spirit-legs against the body waiting for her and tried to climb back out into the light. Albert tried to close and lock the portal door. Because he sympathized with her terror, he tried to do so gently, but the edge of his cassock got wedged in the door jam, and he had yank it out and then hastily slam the door before she could escape.

At that point, something went wrong. Perhaps she pushed from the other side just as the door closed. Perhaps he applied uneven pressure to the door as he closed it. Albert never learned exactly what happened. All he knew was that the portal broke. It was almost completely shut. The remaining gap was too small for Janie to use as an exit route. However, he could see and hear her through the gap, and more to the point, she could still see and hear him.

Janie began to cry for help. Heartbroken on her behalf, Albert felt more like crying than he had since his death. He sat down so that he could peer into the gap and see her more clearly. Casting about for some way to calm her, he began singing a lullaby that his mother had sung to him when he was a baby. Slowly, the simple peasant tune seemed to take effect. Janie fell quiet and simply stared up at him through the gap. She curled her spirit-fingers around the edge of the portal door, and he stroked them softly with his own.

Janie sniffled and said, "What shall I do? I can't get out."

Albert said, "It's true that you can't come back here now. But if you go forward, at the end of your Earthly life, you will return, and you'll have, oh so many splendid stories to tell... all about what you've seen, and heard, and felt, and done... just like me... just like all the souls who've lived a life inside a body."

"You got put inside a body?"

"Yes, and although there were sometimes hardships, I don't regret a minute of the experience."

"Would you go again if you had the chance?"

"No, Sweetheart, I wouldn't. I like the life I'm living now too much. But my baby sister chose to go again, and she's having a wonderful time."

Janie seemed to sit and consider. "Will you forget me once I go?"

"Never, Sweetheart. In fact, I promise... I'll ask if my mother can become your spirit-guide, and my whole family will watch over you your entire life."

Janie seemed to consider further. "All right. How do I get into the body?"

This question Albert definitely knew how to answer. "You just let go, little one, and when next you awaken, you'll be inside, experiencing everything your body encounters."

There was a moment of silence and then, "OK."

Albert heard the sound of her soul entering the body. As soon as he did, he stood up and looked around to see if any of his fellow workers had witnessed his *faux pas*, but they all seemed oblivious. He wondered if he should go and confess his error to the boss, but he felt too embarrassed, and in any case, he reasoned, what was there to confess? Janie's soul was safe inside her body where it belonged, and what harm could a broken portal possibly do? He would just go and warn his father that Janie's soul-extraction might prove complicated. With any luck, he and his father would figure out how to repair Janie's portal before the time came for her death.

So it was that Jane Marie Hanson (spelled with an "o," not an "e") entered the world, yet unbeknown to the angelic hosts, she would remain in contact with Heaven throughout her entire Earthly life.

2: The Curtain Rises on Janie...

Janie's future parents were highly-successful, upper-middle-class, professional people. They'd met as undergraduates at Stanford and managed to sustain their personal relationship through her three years of law school at Hastings and his medical school, internship, and residency (UCSD and UCLA).

After passing the Bar, she chose corporate law as her field and swiftly climbed the ladder of success in her firm. Due to long hours, rapacious billing practices, and a razor-sharp legal mind, she'd made partner by the age of thirty-five when our story begins. She was impressive in every respect. When she entered a conference room or court-room, her opponents quailed.

She stood almost six feet tall in her stocking feet and had the blond, blue-eyed, fair-skinned looks of a Valkyrie. Her facial features were chiseled, her body was hyper-fit and super-model-thin, and her expression was habitually that of a goddess who was judging those present and finding them sorely lacking. Outwardly cold, she reserved her carefully hidden warmth for her husband, who might never equal her in earning power, but who, thanks to his intellect, could at least engage her mind.

Her husband had entered the field of oncology, specializing in cancers of the gastrointestinal tract. Before long, he'd become disenchanted with surgery, chemotherapy, and radiation treatment protocols, and he'd begun researching immunotherapy alternatives. This led to a career as head of research at one of the most prestigious cancer treatment facilities in the Los Angeles Basin, a large complex near Pasadena.

His career was also his life's passion, and he seldom left his lab for any length of time. Physically, he was completely his wife's opposite: five-foot-six; compact in frame; with a tan complexion, dark wavy hair, and brown eyes. His journal articles were always meticulously prepared—well-substantiated, crisply written, and utterly clear. In person though, he came off as a bit of a class clown—enthusiastic, jolly, and even a little insouciant.

To facilitate his commute, he and his wife bought a 1930's Spanish Revival mansion in San Marino. They paid to have it restored to its former glory, and they sacrificed part of the rose garden to extend the garage to three bays. One bay held the Mercedes Benz sports car that he drove at break-neck speed down the freeway to work every day. One held the sturdy old Volvo reserved for the hired help, and the last bay held a Rolls Royce.

No one in the family actually drove the Rolls. The only one who drove it was the chauffeur. His job was to take Mrs. Hanson to the office, to depositions, to court... anywhere and everywhere that she wished to go, day or night. Most of the time, she sat in the back seat dictating legal briefs. But occasionally, she would treat herself to a shopping trip on Rodeo Drive. On those days, she'd sit surrounded by upscale shopping bags and clouds of acid-free tissue paper admiring her most recent purchases. Meanwhile, the chauffeur would fix his attention on the road, trying to ignore the conspicuous consumption going on in the back seat and longing for the moment when he could return to his rooms over the garage and put Mrs. Hanson out of his mind.

Dr. and Mrs. Hanson conceived their daughter while attending a medical conference in Maui. It was something of a junket, and normally, Dr. Hanson would have given it a pass, but he was seeking funding for a new lab, and he wanted to go schmooze the room and find potential charitable donors. Also, knowing that the hotel would be one of the finest in the islands and eager to enjoy some rare "together time," he prevailed upon his wife to take some of her accumulated Personal Time Off and go with him.

After each day's activities, they went for a long walk on the beach, retired to their room, consumed champagne and strawberries, and generally enjoyed more intimacy than they had in years. The night before they planned to return home, the rubber broke. Because that kind of thing had happened many times before, always without issue, they thought nothing of it at the time. They flew back to LA considerably more relaxed than when they left and completely unaware that they were now expecting.

They didn't tumble to the truth until six weeks later. When Mrs. Hanson finally had to admit that she was late, she took a pregnancy test, phlegmatically shared the result with her husband, and began planning for the disruption that pregnancy and childbirth would cause to her career and their carefully arranged domestic routine.

First on the agenda was an amniocentesis. Mrs. Hanson's OB-GYN informed her that, because the child she was carrying would be a "late-maternal-age baby," it would be at much greater risk of having physical and/or mental birth defects. Mrs. Hanson might have a miscarriage, a stillbirth, or worst of all, a child who was viable, but who might never be able to attain an independent, successful adulthood. Dr. and Mrs. Hanson weren't interested in investing time and resources in anything but a perfect baby, so as soon as amniocentesis became feasible, they paid to have the fluid sampled, and when the test revealed that the embryo was genetically normal and healthy, they allowed the pregnancy to proceed.

Having received that reassurance, Mrs. Hanson turned her attention to more everyday matters. Dealing with the household would not be a problem. Mrs. Hanson had long-since hired a reputable cleaning service for inside the house and an equally well-recommended gardening service for outside. The entire property was maintained so impeccably that it could have been photographed for *Architectural Digest* without a moment's warning. No, what Mrs. Hanson needed was help with all things "baby-related." She did as she'd always done. She contacted the top home-care agency in the region and contracted for 24-7 in-home help.

The agency sent her Gisela Rosa Rodriguez, a woman they billed as "a treasure." The agency didn't exaggerate. Mrs. Rodriguez, whom Dr. and Mrs. Hanson decided to call "Rosa," was a trained Certified Nursing Aide. She helped care for Mrs. Hanson during her first trimester when nausea and water retention threatened her professional effectiveness. During the second trimester, Rosa ensured that Mrs. Hanson took her vitamins and ate a good diet. (The cook had quit in disgust, and Rosa had taken over the kitchen. Fortunately, she was a far better cook than the departed woman could ever have claimed to be.) And in the third trimester, when Mrs. Hanson could no longer see her own feet, Rosa helped with bathing, dressing, and fetching things, so that Mrs. Hanson could continue to show up at the office looking like a fashion plate, despite having had to exchange her usual four-inch spike heels for pumps.

Dr. and Mrs. Hanson were not the kind of people who'd leave anything to chance. No natural childbirth for them... Instead, they arranged for their obstetrician to perform a scheduled C-section a few days before the baby's due date. Thereafter, they planned to have Rosa tend Mrs. Hanson through her recovery, care for the baby as its live-in nurse, and possibly stay on board permanently as the infant's nanny. This arrangement was completely acceptable to Rosa, especially when the Hansons bought out her contract with the agency and installed her in the mansion's maid's quarters with a raise in pay to boot.

The maid's quarters were comfortable and well-appointed. They featured a private entrance off of the driveway, a large bed-sitting room with a view of the rose garden, a private bath, and an "airlock" hallway to the kitchen, the butler's pantry, and the rest of the house. Rosa gave up her studio apartment, moved her few possessions into her new digs, and notified her family of her good fortune. Her family members were thrilled.

Over time, the Hansons came to realize just how lucky they truly were to have found Rosa. She was not only a CNA and great cook, she was also efficient at running the household, deeply caring toward their daughter Janie, and best of all, legal. Thanks to her early marriage to an American-born auto mechanic and her own studies, she was now a U.S. citizen, as were her two children. The mechanic was unfortunately dead (car crash), but Rosa's son and daughter were alive and doing well.

Rosa's son was sole proprietor of a gardening business. He'd started with one truck and the labor of numerous "cousins" (some of them picked up at dawn outside the local convenience store). The cousins did most of the ditch-digging and heavy labor, and for their troubles, they were fed two large burritos for breakfast and lunch and paid in cash before they left in the evening. Rosa's son would visit his mother on Saturday mornings, and some neighbors, mistaking his truck for that of the regular gardening service, walked across the street and engaged his help for their own yard.

He did a good job for them, and in time, this led to other referrals in the neighborhood, more trucks, some actual employees, and increased business success. Rosa's son was the type of man who recognized where his good fortune had come from, and he was careful to thank Rosa for it whenever he got the chance.

Rosa's daughter also visited her mother, usually on Sunday evenings, and whenever she did, she always brought her own little son and daughter with her. These children would play quietly under Rosa's watchful eye while Rosa did the mending and her daughter prepared her second grade lesson plan for the following week at school.

Dr. and Mrs. Hanson almost never ventured into the kitchen of their own home, and Rosa's family always came and went through the servant's entrance that led to Rosa's rooms, so the Hansons weren't the least bit put out by the frequency and duration of Rosa's family visits. As for

Janie, these visits would be the closest thing to family that she'd know growing up, so in her world, they would count as quite a blessing.

Now I don't want you to get the impression that Janie's parents didn't love her. They took great pains to give her the best of everything. For example, while Janie was still gestating in her mother's womb, her mother made sure that she played music by Bach and Mozart every chance she got. Mrs. Hanson had read that Bach promoted excellence in math, and Mozart fostered general brain development, so if she had any say in the matter, the baby would hear a steady diet of the classics, even if it drove the cook and chauffeur mad.

Of course, Mrs. Hanson also did other, more conventional things to prepare her baby for the world. She did gentle exercise every day as soon as her morning sickness abated. She got far more sleep than she'd been accustomed to getting, and with Rosa's help, she ate a good diet and took all the pills the OB-GYN prescribed.

Inside the womb, Janie appreciated all that her mother was trying to do for her. She soon came to enjoy the classical music. Certainly she liked it far more than the muttered arguments she heard while her mother was at work. Janie came to recognize a variety of voices—her mother and father of course, her mother's law partners, Rosa's son and daughter... but the voice with which she truly bonded was Rosa's. It was a warm, rich contralto— softly loving and infused with gentle laughter. Janie could hardly wait to meet the origin of that kind, reassuring voice. When Albert had a free moment one day, Janie reached out of her body and told him so. In return, she heard him say that he'd add Rosa to the people his mother was watching on Janie's behalf.

Classical music wasn't the only music that Janie enjoyed prior to her birth. Sometimes, in the quiet of the night, she would replay in memory the simple peasant tune that Albert had sung to her on her Entry Day. At other times, she would extend herself into the portal and put her spiritual ear to the gap. Almost always, she was rewarded with angelic choir music—so much more glorious than any Earthly composition, however beautiful—in truth, the inspiration that all composers leveraged as they strove to complete their own works.

Janie waited patiently in the womb for her emergence into the world, noting each improvement as her body developed toward completion. Her notochord grew into her spinal column and brain. She grew a heart, and that heart began to beat. Her circulatory system became more complex, supporting her developing lungs, liver, kidneys, and digestive tract. The tiny flippers at the ends of her limbs manifested hands and feet, fingers and toes. Her face began to look increasingly human, and one day, her mouth and right hand found each other, and she began sucking her thumb.

There came a day when Dr. and Mrs. Hanson went to an OB-GYN appointment for an ultrasound. Inside the womb, Janie wriggled a bit because the sound waves tickled. She could hear the doctor's voice fairly clearly as he announced that Janie was a girl. Of course, Janie didn't speak any English yet, but she didn't really need to do so to understand. At the beginning of the appointment, Janie had felt her watcher arrive at her side, and the watcher (whom Janie called "Nana") told her what the doctor had said. Janie was pleased. Janie's mother had been a girl. Rosa and Nana had both been girls. Being a girl was apparently a good thing, and Janie looked forward to being one too.

On the day of Janie's birth, Dr. and Mrs. Hanson drove to the hospital for the planned C-section. At first, Janie was a little bit apprehensive, but then Nana came and joined her again. Nana explained that Janie might experience some difficulties because her parents had arranged for her to be born before her time. But Nana promised to buffer Janie against any trauma and help her deal with the insults of the birth process.

Mrs. Hanson's doctor met with her briefly in pre-op to explain the procedure. Then nurses prepped Mrs. Hanson for surgery. They helped her change into a sterile gown and lie down on a gurney. They inserted an I.V. line, hung a bag of normal saline, administered a sedative, and wheeled her into the operating theater. There the anesthesiologist put a mask over her face and had her count backwards from ten. At "seven," Mrs. Hanson succumbed, a surgical nurse swabbed her belly with disinfectant, and her OB-GYN made his first incision.

Inside the womb, Janie suddenly felt sick and disoriented as some of the anesthesia crossed the placental barrier into her system. But she didn't have to deal with the feeling for very long. Suddenly, a bright light invaded the warm, dark space she'd been inhabiting. Gloved hands cut open her amniotic sack and pulled her little body out into the cold air of the operating theater. For a moment, the umbilical cord continued to pulse, but then, someone clamped it off and cut it, and Janie's circulatory system was on its own.

Nana's spirit enfolded her and said, "Almost there, little one. Be brave."

Someone put a tube into Janie's mouth and suctioned fluid out of her mouth and nose. Then that same someone held her upside down by her feet and spanked her smartly on her backside. Blinded by the light, bitterly cold, and now stinging from that gratuitous slap, Janie inhaled deeply and shrieked in displeasure.

"Welcome to the world," Nana told her. "Things will get better from here."

A nurse took Janie from the doctor's hands, cleaned her little body briskly and thoroughly, affixed an I.D. band around her leg, took a foot print for her medical record, and wrapped her in a soft, warm blanket and knit cap.

While these activities were going on, the doctor turned his attention back to Mrs. Hanson. He delivered the afterbirth, cleansed her womb, and closed her incision. He used sutures on her womb and the layers of muscle that overlay it, and he finished the outer layer of skin using staples and a sterile bandage.

As soon as he did so, the anesthesiologist revived Mrs. Hanson. The reversing agent worked fairly quickly. The nurses barely had time to remove the surgical drapes and cover Mrs. Hanson with a warm sterile blanket before she began to rouse. As soon as the nurses were sure that Mrs. Hanson would be able to appreciate the experience, they placed Janie wrapped in swaddling clothes on Mrs. Hanson's chest and draped Mrs. Hanson's right hand over her newborn child. Then they raised the sides of the gurney to prevent falls and wheeled Mrs. Hanson into the recovery room.

In Recovery, the nurses elevated the back of the gurney slightly so that Mrs. Hanson could get a better look at her tiny daughter. Mrs. Hanson spent a few minutes examining Janie's face dispassionately. Then she asked, "Ten fingers, ten toes?"

A nurse replied, "Absolutely perfect."

"Good." Mrs. Hanson sighed deeply. "I'm awfully tired, and I could use some pain medication. Could you take the baby and give her to her father or something? I need to rest."

"Of course you do. I'll take her down the hall to the Neonatal ward, and you can see her again soon."

The nurse took Janie from her mother's arms and walked away, down the hall, and into the ward where rows of cribs awaited, many of them already occupied by squalling infants. She placed Janie in a crib. Then she posted Janie's identity information on the foot of the crib to make sure there would be no mix-ups. Because Janie's parents hadn't picked a name yet, the placard read "Baby Girl Hanson," but the medical record number was unique and would ensure that Janie was later paired up with the right people. The nurse paused to stroke Janie's head softly. Then she left to go find Janie's father.

Janie rested quietly and relatively comfortably in her crib. She heard Nana say, "This is where I leave you, little one. You're going to be OK, and remember, I'll always be watching over you, so you'll never be alone." Then Janie felt Nana's spirit withdraw. She barely had time to process this change when she heard a tapping on the ward's hallway window. Janie heard the rustle of scrubs as a nurse went to answer the summons.

There was a murmured conversation. "Hi, I'm Dr. Hanson. Can you tell me how my wife is doing?"

"She's doing great. She's in Recovery and will probably be there for another hour at least. Because you're a doctor, I may be able to get you in to see her, or you could wait in the Waiting Room, and I'll come get you when we move her to her room."

"I'll wait. I don't want to disrupt your routine. But could you point out my baby? This gentleman is my father, and he's flown all the way from Minnesota to see his granddaughter."

"That's great! Congratulations, sir. I'll push her crib up against the window so you can get a good look at her, and of course, once your wife has a room, I'll bring the baby to you."

Janie felt her crib jostle slightly as the nurse pushed it across the ward. Reflexively, she curled her fists tighter and yawned. Then she heard a man's voice that she didn't recognize.

"Just look at her! What a beauty."

"I don't know that I'd call her a beauty, Dad. With that complexion and those features, she looks more like me than Miranda."

"And what's wrong with that? I always found a cute little brunette irresistible. That's why I fell in love with your mother. Just look at that sweet little shock of brown curls on her head... Who wouldn't find that adorable."

"Most babies lose any hair they have at birth, Dad. She'll probably be bald as an egg in a couple of weeks."

"No matter. She'll grow it all back. What a charmer! Our little angel... I wish your mother was still alive to see her."

Ridiculous, Janie thought, reacting more to his spiritual energy than to his spoken words. She knew perfectly well that she was nothing like an angel. She remembered hearing and seeing angels in Heaven, and body-bound like she was, she couldn't imagine anyone mistaking her for one of them. Janie yawned again and decided that this would be a good time for a nap. She turned her face to one side, and tired out by her ordeal, she fell into a deep sleep.

* * * * *

Later that day, the hospital staff assigned Mrs. Hanson a private room on the OB-GYN Surgical Floor. Dr. Hanson and his father joined her there, and true to her word, the nurse brought Janie in her crib. The nurse asked Mrs. Hanson if she would like some privacy to try and nurse Janie, but Mrs. Hanson poo-poo'ed the idea. After all, Dr. Hanson was a doctor, and his father could simply turn his back. So the nurse helped Mrs. Hanson sit up, take Janie into her arms, and try to get Janie to latch onto the nipple and suck.

Half an hour later, the nurse suggested that she go fetch a staff member who coached new mothers on lactation and nursing. For a moment, Mrs. Hanson looked as if she'd like to tell off the nurse for suggesting that there was anything Mrs. Hanson couldn't do if she put her mind to it (especially something as natural and brainless as feeding a baby). But she evidently overcame her resentment and said that she'd be glad to meet with the coach.

The nurse left, and minutes later, she returned with a pleasant-looking woman and a bottle of baby formula. "Now, we don't want to make a habit of this... It would defeat the whole purpose. But your baby hasn't had anything to eat today, and she may be too weak to attach to the breast, so we'll give her a little something to start with... priming the pump, if you like. Here, you take your baby, hold her like I showed you how to do earlier, and give her the bottle."

Mrs. Hanson took Janie into her arms and gently pressed the bottle's nipple to Janie's lips. Janie opened her mouth, accepted the nipple, and began to suck down formula with a reassuring vigor. While Janie fed, the coach continued the lesson.

"The principal reason we advise new mothers to feed their babies breast milk is that the colostrum contains immune agents from the mother. These agents protect the baby during its first few months of life. That's how long it takes the baby's own immune system to mature and begin functioning. Also, even the best baby formulas fail to give the baby the perfect nutritional profile that breast milk provides."

Mrs. Hanson nodded a bit absently. "I know. I read up on all of this on the internet."

"Good. Then you have an advantage over many mothers I see. OK, let's try to withdraw the bottle now and reintroduce the breast."

Mrs. Hanson did so, but again, Janie failed to attach. Mrs. Hanson grimaced in frustration. "Is she having trouble because I'm so flat-chested?"

"We find that the size of the mother's breasts has no impact on her success as a wet nurse, as long as the breasts are natural and not surgically altered or enhanced. Sometimes, though, the mother's milk doesn't come in until she hears her baby cry. Has your baby cried yet?" Mrs. Hanson shook her head.

Janie lay comfortably in her mother's arms and wrinkled her nose. Why would she want to cry? she wondered. She was warm and securely held, her diaper was dry, and her tummy was full. So far, life on Earth was pretty good. She did agree with the coach on one point though. Her mother's breasts were bone dry. There was no point in attaching to the nipple when there was nothing to be gained.

The coach approached the bedside. "May I?" she inquired. Mrs. Hanson repositioned Janie, and the coach tested one of Mrs. Hanson's breasts. "Oh dear, as I feared, your milk hasn't come in yet. I can't express any colostrum. Until your milk does come in, we have a couple of options. First, we can give you breast milk donated by other lactating mothers. We always keep some on hand for situations such as this. Second, we could continue with the formula, but as I've said, that choice could impact your baby's health."

At that point, Dr. Hanson intervened. "I understand, but I'm not really comfortable with donated breast milk. I mean, what do we really know about the health of the donors? They may appear to be healthy, but some illnesses have long gestation periods. I think we should go with the formula. We'll give our daughter the best one on the market and simply keep her in quarantine until her immune system develops. A new baby should be kept away from strangers for the first three months of life in any case."

Mrs. Hanson nodded her agreement. The coach frowned a bit and handed back the bottle. And Janie accepted the nipple gladly and resumed feeding.

At that point, Janie's grandfather judged that the time was right for him to turn around again and face the proceedings. As soon as he caught sight of Janie's performance, he grinned and exclaimed, "Look at her go!" He didn't realize that what he said simply served to increase Mrs. Hanson's stress.

Mrs. Hanson grimaced and handed Janie to her husband. "Here. If she's drinking from a bottle, there's no reason why you can't hold her." Her husband obliged.

The coach sighed. "OK, we can try again this evening. If all goes well, you'll be discharged from the hospital tomorrow. Patients are usually discharged at about 2:00 in the afternoon, so we may be able to get in a morning coaching session as well. Hopefully by then, your baby will cry, and your milk will come in." The coach shook hands with Mrs. Hanson, Dr. Hanson, and Grandfather Hanson in turn. "Congratulations on your beautiful baby girl. I'll see you again soon." And with that remark, she left the room.

Dr. Hanson sat down in the room's arm chair and continued feeding Janie. Grandfather Hanson perched on the foot of the bed and watched, his face radiating satisfaction. Mrs. Hanson also watched for a while, but then she turned her face to the wall and dozed off. The coach did return that evening and the next morning as planned, but Mrs. Hanson's milk never came in, and Janie ended up being a "bottle baby," an outcome that didn't faze her in the least.

*　*　*　*　*

After the hospital discharged Mrs. Hanson, the chauffeur drove her and her baby home. Janie rode in an infant car seat the chauffeur had installed in the Rolls that morning. Dr. Hanson and his father followed in Dr. Hanson's two-seater sports car. As the cars pulled into the garage, Rosa came out to greet her employers. The chauffeur killed the engine and stepped out to open the Rolls's rear door. Rosa leaned in, extracted Janie from her car seat, and carried her into the house. Dr. Hanson helped his wife out of the back seat. Her progress was slow and awkward because she still had pain from her incision.

Grandfather Hanson followed Rosa into the house and watched as Rosa installed Janie in a crib in the living room. He tried to help Rosa settle Janie—spreading a blanket over Janie's feet, smoothing Janie's clothes, and trying to tuck a stuffed animal in beside Janie's head. However, all this unwarranted attention began to get on Janie's nerves and she started to fuss.

Rosa sighed deeply and gently pushed Grandfather Hanson's hand away. "Please, Mr. Hanson. The baby is tired. Let's let her take her nap now. When she wakes up, you can hold her and play with her as much as you like."

Grandfather Hanson saw the wisdom of this advice and backed away. Just then, Dr. Hanson entered supporting Mrs. Hanson. Dr. Hanson walked his wife over to the couch and helped her sit down. "Dad, could you pour us all some champagne? I'd like to toast Miranda and the new baby." Here was something that Grandfather Hanson could do, and he was quick to comply. He even poured a glass for Rosa, who accepted it only to be polite, for she didn't believe in drinking on the job.

They all held their glasses aloft, facing Mrs. Hanson on the couch, and Dr. Hanson exclaimed, "To my lovely and brilliant wife, in thanks for one of the greatest gifts a wife can give her husband."

Grandfather Hanson added, "Here, here!" and drank a long draught from his glass.

Rosa said, "Congratulations!" and pretended to take a sip.

Grandfather Hanson took a seat in an arm chair and asked, "So, have you two come up with a name for the baby yet?"

Dr. and Mrs. Hanson shook their heads. Mrs. Hanson murmured, "It's so confusing. There are so many names to chose from. I suppose we should consult one of those baby-naming web sites. One of them might help."

Mildly exasperated, Rosa cleared her throat to get their attention. When they turned to face her, she shrugged in a deprecating way and said, "Maybe you could name her after her grandmothers. As I recall, they've both passed away, and it would be a lovely way to honor them."

Grandfather Hanson slapped his knee enthusiastically. "That's a wonderful idea, Miranda—Marie after *your* mother and Jane after my wife."

Dr. Hanson shook his head. "Oh no, Dad, 'Marie Jane Hanson?' That's a terrible name. It just doesn't flow at all."

But Mrs. Hanson was looking thoughtful. "What about 'Jane Marie Hanson?' That flows quite nicely."

Grandfather Hanson stood up. "Perfect! Jane Marie Hanson... We should go update her birth certificate immediately."

"Coming, Dad. Just let me get Miranda upstairs and tucked into bed. She's had quite an ordeal and needs her rest." He helped his wife rise from the couch and shuffle off in the direction of the stairs. Grandfather Hanson left to go tell the chauffeur to ready the Rolls. And Rosa found herself alone in the room with Janie.

Rosa walked to Janie's crib and gazed down at her sleepy baby face. While Rosa watched, Janie stirred and opened her eyes. As an experienced mother, Rosa knew that, at such a young age, Janie wouldn't really be able to see much more than a blur of light and shadow. Her eyes wouldn't focus, and when they opened, it would be purely due to reflex. However, Rosa believed the saying that the eyes were the windows of the soul. So she continued to gaze down at her young charge, and as she did so, she noticed something odd.

As a CNA, she'd cared for more infants than she could count—children with blue eyes, green eyes, brown eyes, and eyes so dark that they looked almost black. But never had she seen eyes like Janie's. The child seemed to gaze back at her with eyes that were infinitely deep, like pools of water or some kind of long tunnel, and at the bottom, a bright, shining, spiritual light. Shaken, Rosa reached out impulsively and smoothed the brown curls from Janie's forehead. "*Bienvenido, Juanita*," she whispered. "I can tell you're going to be someone very special."

*   *   *   *   *

From that day forward, Rosa became Janie's principal caregiver. Relieved of any responsibility for her daughter, Mrs. Hanson recovered quickly and was able to return to work after only four weeks. Dr. and Mrs. Hanson provided electronic baby monitors so that Rosa could still carry out her household duties while listening for Janie's cries. But Rosa was a very hands-on kind of person. She preferred instead to carry the baby in a sling against her side while she did the cooking and her other tasks. That way, she could check on Janie immediately whenever Janie stirred.

Wet diaper? Changed before Janie could feel any real discomfort... Hungry? The bottle appeared as if by magic. So attentive was Rosa to Janie's needs that Janie virtually never cried. Even if Rosa hadn't been so attentive, Janie probably wouldn't have cried much anyway, attuned as she was to the Infinite. Whenever she got bored, Janie had only to extend a portion of herself into the portal, and there, at the gap in the door, she could converse with her Uncle Albert, visit with her watcher Nana, or even catch a glimpse of angels as they passed by.

Meanwhile, back on Earth, Grandfather Hanson decided that he'd had enough of Minnesota winters, so he moved to a 1920's Craftsman Era cottage not too far from the Caltech campus. He enjoyed the cultural events and scientific lectures that the Institute made available, and he loved being within easy driving distance of his son and granddaughter.

Dr. Hanson's research career continued on an upward trajectory with increasingly important discoveries being made and increasingly large grants being received.

As for Mrs. Hanson, her career flourished as well. She was still secretly smarting over her failure to nurse her infant, but she soon found a way to compensate for this inadequacy by building her daughter an exquisite and expensive nursery suite. Mrs. Hanson hired one of the finest interior designers in the county and gave him *carte blanche* to knock out walls and install new windows and doors, assuming of course that he respected the architectural purity of the house.

Soon, Janie had a sunny, airy bedroom, playroom, and bathroom all her own. The bathroom was liberally decorated with authentic Spanish tile. The playroom was well-stocked with books and toys calculated to expand her skills and stimulate her mind. And both bedroom and playroom were furnished with rare, collectable Monterey painted antiques. The effect was utterly charming. Sadly, Janie was almost never in her suite to enjoy it. She was either riding on Rosa's hip in the sling or taking a nap on Rosa's bed, protected from falling by a circle of rolled-up blankets.

As for mental stimulation, Janie got to listen to Rosa singing while she worked, Rosa conversing in rapid Spanish with her children, and Rosa telling Janie the English names of things whenever Rosa took her out in the garden for a walk. After a few months when Rosa felt confident that Janie would stay healthy, even if exposed to a little dirt, Rosa began letting Janie play on the kitchen floor with wooden spoons, pots and pans, and even the occasional root vegetable. Likewise, when Rosa moved her base of operations out into the back yard, she let Janie crawl around on the grass, finding and examining fallen leaves, geranium flowers, and bugs. Rosa watched to make sure Janie wouldn't ingest any of these treasures, but Janie was allowed to stroke wooly caterpillars and pluck snails off of the shrubbery to her heart's content, much to the amusement of the gardener.

Janie proved to be a precocious little tot. She stood up for the first time at a far younger age than Rosa's own children had done. Not long after, Janie took her first steps. She somehow divined that, if she leaned on a tree or a piece of lawn furniture, she could pull herself up and then stagger along for a yard or two before she lost her balance and landed plop on her well-padded, diapered derrière. Whenever this happened, she would giggle, immediately pull herself upright again, and go charging off in another direction. Rosa would watch this performance shaking her head gently and smiling indulgently.

When Janie displayed her new abilities in front of her parents, they began talking about enrolling Janie in an exclusive, elite preschool so that Janie could get a head start on reading, dancing, playing piano, and other accomplishments. Rosa would listen to these discussions and privately roll her eyes to the ceiling. "*Dios mio!*" she would mutter. "The child can't even speak yet." Fortunately, the Hansons' plans for Janie's education remained more theoretical than practical, so the discussions continued, but nothing came of them, and by and by, Janie reached the age of two.

By two years of age, most kids have acquired a rudimentary vocabulary—mama, dada, wawa, and the most important word of all, no! The child is growing tired of being under the parents' care and control, and he or she is trying to assert his or her independence. But Janie felt no such need. Spiritually, she was able to engage in quite sophisticated conversations with Nana and Uncle Albert anytime she wished, and from the moment Rosa had looked into Janie's eyes, Rosa had treated Janie with an unusual degree of respect.

Rosa knew well that most children Janie's age were a real handful, but Janie had continued to be quiet and well-behaved in all circumstances, so much so in fact that Rosa had asked the Hansons for permission to take Janie to church on Sundays, and not having strong feelings either way, they'd agreed.

So every Sunday morning thereafter, Rosa dressed herself and Janie in their Sunday best, and Rosa drove with Janie in the Volvo to the nearest Roman Catholic Church. The liturgy had changed a lot since Albert had attended Mass. It was no longer sung in plainsong, it was no longer in Latin, and even minor points of doctrine differed, but in essentials, the faith had remained the same, so sometimes, Albert and Nana would join Janie on these excursions, just for old-times' sake.

Rosa would enter the church's dark, quiet nave, bless herself with holy water, and genuflect before the cross. Then she'd lead Janie by the hand to a pew and help her to take a seat. The pews were all designed for the frames of full-grown adults, so Janie's tiny legs would stick straight out in front of her, and her head would barely reach the top of the pew's back. She would listen to the organ music play, take in the bright colors of the stained glass windows, inhale the musty scent of the incense, and watch in awe as the priests, altar boys, and choir marched solemnly down the center aisle and took their seats in the sanctuary.

On these occasions, Rosa always came prepared. She wore a mantle of white lace over her head and always carried a prayer book, a small hymnal, and a rosary. She'd told Janie that the rosary had been a wedding present from her husband, and it was quite beautiful—rose quartz and silver beads on a silver chain with a sterling silver crucifix. Even on days that weren't a Sunday, Janie would sometimes see Rosa take out the rosary, finger its beads, and repeat her prayers.

Finally, after the senior priest, Father Timothy, had seen Rosa and Janie in the congregation for the entire Trinity season, he stopped them on the porch one day and introduced himself. Rosa introduced herself in turn and explained that Janie was her charge, not her grand-daughter. Father Timothy bent down, welcomed Janie, and offered to shake her hand. Feeling a bit shy, she took refuge behind Rosa's skirt, but she did extend her tiny hand and briefly take hold of Father Timothy's weathered fingertips. As she did so, he felt a surprising little jolt of energy. Bewildered but intrigued, he asked, "Has the child been baptized?"

Rosa shook her head sorrowfully. "No, Father. I don't think her parents are Catholic. In fact, I'm not sure they're even Christian. They're good people, but..." She let her voice trail off.

Father Timothy sighed. "Would you be willing to ask them if the child could be baptized? Please don't take the risk if you're afraid of offending them. I just hope..."

Rosa nodded. "I'll ask, Father. We'll see what they say." She smiled wryly up at Father Timothy. Janie peeped out from behind Rosa's skirt and smiled up at him too.

That evening, Grandfather Hanson happened to join his son and daughter-in-law for dinner. Rosa made their favorite meal, a savory pot roast with lots of onions and a huge summer salad. After she'd cleared the dishes and washed up, she sought out Dr. Hanson and found him sharing a brandy with his father in the den. She rapped timidly on the door jam to announce her presence and then entered the room.

"Dr. Hanson, you know I've been taking Janie to church with me on Sundays. She's always a very good girl and never gives anyone any trouble. Well, today, the priest introduced himself and asked if she'd been baptized, and I said, 'No.' Would it be OK with you, sir... I mean, would you mind very much if..."

"You had her baptized..." Dr. Hanson finished. "I don't see why you would. No disrespect to you, Rosa, but we're not Catholic, so I really don't see the point."

Grandfather Hanson intervened. "Now, son, what harm could a little oil and water on the forehead possibly do? Rosa is a good woman, she's doing a great job of helping to raise Janie, and if it makes her feel good to have my granddaughter baptized, I have no objection, and I don't see why you would either."

Dr. Hanson took a swig of his brandy. "Oh, very well. Just don't get her mixed up in Confession, the Mass, and all that, OK?"

"Yes, sir. I understand." Rosa turned to leave the room but stopped herself and returned. "Do you and your wife want to attend the ceremony?"

Dr. Hanson waved his snifter dismissively. "Heavens, no. In fact, I see no point in even telling Miranda about it. Baptize Janie if it pleases you, but leave us out of it."

"Yes, sir." Rosa turned on her heel and left. When she reached her room, she said a prayer of thanksgiving for Janie's sake and three prayers for the souls of Janie's immediate family. As she'd told Father Timothy, they were good people, but apostates in the eyes of the Church.

The following Sunday, Rosa and Janie stayed after Mass so that Father Timothy could baptize Janie. Father Timothy had his housekeeper, the choir master, and Rosa herself serve as godparents, and after explaining to Janie as well as he could what was about to happen, he anointed her forehead with oil and water and committed her soul to God.

As so often happened, Janie gleaned more from his spiritual energy than from his actual words, but she had no qualms about having this nice man mark her face with a damp cross. Uncle Albert and Nana had already explained what the cross meant, and Janie felt a sense of exaltation, knowing that, by accepting it, she was declaring her love for the Almighty Creator of all things.

3: Janie Works Miracles...

When Janie was three and a half, Rosa's daughter came for a Sunday afternoon visit with her two children and their brand new puppy. The puppy was a scruffy mutt, a rescue adopted from the local shelter. But Janie found it delightful as it frolicked around the back yard, wagging its tail enthusiastically and licking any face it could reach.

Curious to know more about it, Janie extended a little piece of her soul until it touched the dog's soul. Immediately, she learned that the dog was a boy dog, and he was overwhelmingly grateful to have been taken into a forever-home. Janie was able to get a quick glimpse through the dog's eyes, and everything he saw was worth exploring. Everything he heard was exciting and new. Everyone around him inspired his love and loyalty. He was no longer lonely and scared. His belly was full of good food. He felt trust that he'd be treated kindly. And he was filled with joy whenever he saw Rosa's grandchildren, the wonderful beings who petted him and played with him every day.

Janie withdrew her bit of soul back into her own body. As she played with Rosa's grandchildren and their pet, she conceived a new notion. It would be splendid to help some other animal to have a good and happy life, and it would be better still to have that animal's companionship.

After Rosa's daughter took her brood home, Janie approached Rosa with a question. By that time, Rosa was in the kitchen, cooking dinner. Janie toddled up to Rosa and gently tugged on the edge of her apron to get her attention. Rosa paused and looked down at Janie. "What is it, Juanita? I know you want something. Your eyes are big as saucers."

"Rosa?" Janie pursed her lips an instant. "Is it hard to get a dog?"

Rosa sighed and resumed chopping vegetables. "Not hard, little one. There are far too many dogs who need homes. But a dog is a big responsibility. You'd need to feed him every day and give him clean water... and take him for walks and clean up his poo and pee... It's almost as much work as having a baby. And like a baby, you'd have to teach him how to behave. If you don't teach a dog, he'll make messes in the house, chew up the furniture, and even bite people. I'm not sure you're old enough to have a dog yet, and in any case, you'd have to ask your parents."

"Oh." Janie looked down and studied the toe of her shoe. "Are all animals that hard to take care of?"

"Not all. My son has a cat, and he only changes the cat box every other day or so. He set up a kibble feeder too, so he only has to give the cat food once a week, plus wet-food treats sometimes when he comes home at night. Cats are easier."

"Do you think Mother and Father would let me have a cat?"

Rosa shook her head sadly. "I think I remember your mother saying that she's allergic to cats. If she is, the dander would make her sneeze. Her eyes would swell up, itch, and turn red, and her nose would run. You wouldn't want your mother to feel like that, would you?"

Janie shook her head. "No... I guess I'll ask if I can have a dog."

"Well don't be discouraged if they say no, little one. Like I said, you may be too young now, but you're growing up, and someday soon you might be ready." Janie nodded and walked out of the kitchen.

Dr. and Mrs. Hanson had a family tradition that they'd eat dinner together in the dining room every night. As soon as Janie had become old enough to sit still in a chair and feed herself, she'd been allowed to join them, and that night at dinner, she sprang the dog question on her parents, much to their surprise.

"Why in God's name would you want a dog?" her mother demanded.

Her father put down his fork and said, "I'll bet this comes from all of those Animal Planet shows she's been watching in the afternoon."

"Dogs are warm and soft and fun to play with," Janie explained.

"Why not something less burdensome, like a house rabbit, a guinea pig, a hamster, or a cute white mouse?" Her mother had entered "negotiating mode."

"Not a rodent!" her father protested. "Rodents breed like, well, rodents. We'd start out with one or two pets and end up with God alone knows how many."

Janie thought back to her days in Heaven before she'd entered her body. As she recalled, rats were quite intelligent and made good playmates. But they'd gotten a bad reputation due to the plague and all. So she thought she could understand some of her father's reaction.

"Parrots!" Her mother exclaimed, "or cockateels or cockatoos—even parakeets, canaries, or finches... Parrots can be taught to talk, they live a hundred years, and they're very elegant. And canaries can be quite pleasant to have around the house because they sing so beautifully."

"Why not macaws while we're at it? They'll shriek the house down. Or mynah birds... I've heard that they learn to talk too, repeating your most intimate bedroom moments whenever you invite guests into the house. Be reasonable, Miranda. Birds are messy. They shed feathers and bird droppings constantly."

"But in a cage, Darling. They'll be confined to a cage."

"If we're going in that direction, I'd rather get fish. I can just imagine saddling poor Rosa with the job of changing the cage liners several times a week so the cages don't stink. At least with fish, you can hire a service to clean and maintain the tanks."

Janie tried to imagine cuddling a bird or, worse yet, a fish. As she recalled, the bird spirits that she'd met were proud, independent beings who wanted to be free to fly. Even the flightless birds like barnyard fowls, ostriches, and their kin had preferred a "free-range" lifestyle. No, this conversation was not going to result in the kind of pet she wanted, and she saw no point in continuing it. She waited for a lull in her parents' give-and-take and then said, "Never mind. I don't want to cause any trouble. I just thought I'd ask."

Her mother looked mollified and her father, relieved. "Well that's all right then, sweetie," he said, reaching over to pat her hand.

Janie finished her dinner in silence while her parents discussed their work days. Then she went upstairs to bed. She felt a little bit sad and discouraged, but she promised herself that someday, maybe when she was grown up, she would get a dog or a cat—maybe both.

This conversation left her parents feeling a bit sad too. After all, weren't they denying their daughter an important part of childhood if they didn't allow her to have a pet? Suddenly, they were painfully aware of all the children they saw in the neighborhood... the boy next door with his Golden Retriever... the girl across the street with her two Siamese cats... To assuage their guilt, Janie's mother had the chauffeur drive her to Beverly Hills that Saturday. She went to the most upscale toy store in town and bought a magnificent teddy bear. It was truly a work of art.

Unlike the tawdry bears manufactured by the millions overseas, this bear was painstakingly crafted of the finest materials. Its fur was a dense, silky-soft, golden-brown plush with belly fur of a slightly lighter shade. All of its limbs were jointed so that it could be posed, and its head could be turned somewhat from side to side. The pads of its feet and toes were all covered in dark-brown velvet, and its nose and mouth were embroidered on in tough, black thread. Velvet lined its ears, framing a handsome, symmetrical, well-designed face, and its glass eyes glinted in the light as if they belonged to something genuinely alive.

Mrs. Hanson was quite pleased with her purchase and couldn't wait to get home and present it to her daughter. She made sure her husband was in the room when she did, and she told Janie, "This is from both of us. We wanted you to have something warm and soft that you could play with whenever you wanted."

Janie reached out and took the bear into a tight embrace. "Thank you," she murmured. She buried her face in its soft fur, concealing the tears that had started to leak from her eyes.

Mistaking Janie's reaction, Dr. and Mrs. Hanson were happy with the success of their gift. "What will you name it?" Dr. Hanson asked.

"T-bear," Janie replied, being careful not to let her voice waver because that would have betrayed the fact that she was crying.

"That's a great name. You go ahead and have fun playing with T-bear, Sweetheart. Your mother and I have to go now... Things to do..." They left the room, and as they walked away down the hall, Janie heard her father say, "Well done, Miranda."

Janie continued to cry silently into T-bear's fur for several minutes. But then she sniffed a few times, dried her eyes, and went to find Rosa. Rosa never failed to help her feel better, and although she wasn't sure why she did it, Janie took T-bear along with her. She found Rosa sitting on the back porch shelling peas into a bowl. Janie sat down beside Rosa and held T-bear in her arms beneath her chin.

"What do you have there, *chica?*"

"Mother and Father just gave me this teddy bear."

"It's a very nice bear. Do you like it?"

Janie was fundamentally an honest child, so she thought a minute before speaking. "It's the most beautiful teddy bear I've ever seen, maybe the most beautiful one in the whole world. But I wanted a pet, something alive who could not only play with me but also be my friend. I wish this bear was alive."

For a moment, Rosa looked startled. Then she said, "Oh no, don't wish for that, Juanita. See how the eyes are only glass? Your bear would be blind. And see how the ears are only flaps of cloth? He'd be deaf too. What a sad life he would lead. He couldn't walk or talk or smell or taste or feel anything around him. No, only God can make living things, Juanita. We should leave that job to God."

Janie felt these words strike into her very core. She couldn't deny their wisdom, but still, she yearned to have the companionship of a real, living being—a being with a soul like her.

"You understand what I'm saying, don't you, little one?"

Janie nodded. "Yes, Rosa, I understand."

"Good girl. Now go and wash your hands. Dinner will be served in just fifteen minutes, and I'm sure your parents will expect you to be ready and at the table."

After dinner that night, when Rosa helped Janie get ready for bed, Janie insisted that T-bear be tucked in beside her. Rosa pulled the covers up to Janie's and T-bear's chins. Then she kissed Janie on the forehead, turned out the lights, and left the room.

After she'd gone, Janie lay in the dark reviewing all that Rosa had told her that day. Janie didn't want to be selfish. She didn't want to condemn T-bear to an unbearable life, but neither did she want to be so lonely anymore. Then, inspiration struck. She examined the idea that had come to her from all angles, and no matter how she looked at it, she couldn't see any pitfalls or drawbacks, so she decided to give it a try.

Janie remembered clearly how Uncle Albert had opened her portal and put her soul into her body. Now she extended a piece of her soul into her portal and up to the gap in the door. She waited patiently until a small soul wandered by. It was a very tiny soul, so tiny that Janie suspected no one would miss it for a very long time. She whispered to it, coaxing it to come closer and closer to the gap, until out of curiosity, it poked its head inside, and she grabbed it.

It struggled a moment in her grasp, but she sang Uncle Albert's lullaby to it until it calmed down. Then, she turned and opened up a portal into T-bear and pushed the little soul inside. Perhaps because the soul was astonished to find itself inside a body not created by God, it didn't try to jump back out. Instead, it looked around itself in frank bewilderment.

"Don't be afraid," Janie told it. "You and I are going to be best friends, and I will leave my soul connected to yours so you can share everything that happens in my life. You'll see using my eyes, hear using my ears, and feel and smell and taste, just like I do. Best of all, we'll be able to talk soul-to-soul with each other, so we'll never need to feel alone. Is this OK with you? Because if it's not, I can take you out again and put you back in Heaven."

The tiny soul considered what she'd said. It knew that it was a very small soul indeed and probably intended for a quite elementary body with a short, limited existence. Here it was being offered the chance to experience life, albeit secondhand, from the viewpoint of a human being. Moreover, that human being was offering to take good care of it for as long as it lived. The tiny soul had liked the lullaby that Janie sang to it. In truth, the soul was beginning to just plain like Janie. So it let her know that it wanted to take her up on her offer and continue to live inside of T-bear.

Delighted, Janie gave T-bear a long, loving hug. She withdrew her soul back out of her own portal and simply left a piece connected through T-bear's portal to what was now T-bear's soul.

So began one of the most unusual "imaginary friend" relationships in the history of children on Earth. In the

days, weeks, and months that followed, Janie and T-bear
were truly inseparable. She would talk to T-bear and pause
as if to listen to his answer. She would play with T-bear
and take him with her everywhere she went, including
church. She even waited until no one was looking and then
made the sign of the cross on his forehead using holy
water from the font. Just as she had declared her undying
love for God, she wanted T-bear to be able to do the same.
And of course, they slept together every night, tucked up
warm and snug in Janie's bed—a little girl who was lonely
no more and the miracle that she'd created.

*   *   *   *   *

To live in a body is to dwell in a vast causality web in
which every event spawns at least one, and usually more,
subsequent events. The difference between an ordinary
event and a miracle is that the ordinary event only impacts
beings in space-time while a miracle also impacts beings in
Paradise. As soon as Janie worked her miracle with T-bear,
a sequence of Heavenly events was spawned that would
continue throughout her entire Earthly life.

The first thing to happen was that a soul-manager in
charge of animating worms looked around for the soul
she'd planned to download into a nematode and couldn't
find it. She was normally as conscientious as Albert, but
she too hated the thought of suffering embarrassment in
front of the boss, so she "borrowed" a soul intended for
the next nematode in line and used that one instead. This
act created a ripple effect at her work station—an "off by
one error" that propagated through every being she
awakened thereafter.

Now that's not as serious an error as you might think.
God creates an infinite number of bodies and an infinite
number of souls to go with them, but as any
mathematician can tell you, infinities can be of different
orders, and if you don't match up the elements in two
infinite sets correctly, the discrepancy can be identified if
the audit is careful enough.

For quite a while, there was no audit. All beings slated to receive a soul actually got one, so no alarm was raised, and no inquiry was made. But then the boss, who was also a very conscientious soul, decided to do a spot check. She counted the souls under her team's purview who were still awaiting download and—she came up one short. Impatient with what she assumed was her own carelessness, she counted again—same result. Now she was both annoyed and concerned. She began an audit of her subordinates' work stations and quickly identified the missing soul as a worm soul. She questioned the angel in charge, and shame-faced, that angel admitted what she'd done.

The boss was compassionate. She reassured the junior angel, saying that she wasn't angry, just intent on fixing the mistake. Then she visited the Watchers and asked the head watcher to locate the missing soul.

The head watcher took on the assignment believing that the little soul would be trivially easy to find. But such was not the case. The watcher was able to determine that the missing soul was not yet in a God-created body, but neither was the soul to be found anywhere in Heaven. This result flummoxed both the head watcher and the head of soul management. They decided that they had no choice but to report the situation to the council of archangels.

The two angels approach the council and requested an audience. The council agreed to see them immediately as the council had no major interventions on its agenda for that day. The two angels presented their conundrum and awaited the archangels' judgement. They had to wait for quite a while as the archangels, bored by the lack of any current assignment, spun out their discussion into a lengthy if desultory debate.

To conserve time for those readers still encased in flesh, I'll summarize that debate here. Michael—Warrior against Satan and Guardian of the Orthodox Faith—asserted that the issue didn't concern him as, apparently, no heresy had been committed. Gabriel—Might of God and Herald of

God's hidden mysteries, including God's own Incarnation—said he'd be interested to hear how the matter was
resolved because it did concern the incarnation of a spirit
as ordained by God's Wisdom. Raphael—God's healer—
cautioned the angels that, when the tiny soul was found, it
might be traumatized by having been a lost soul for so
long. He warned that they might need to bring the soul to
him for healing before they sent it to fulfill its destiny. And
not to be outdone, Uriel—Light of God—shook his head
sorrowfully over the plight of that lost little soul and
wished the angels good luck and God-speed in finding it.

The two angels stood waiting in vain for some kind of
instruction or direction as to what they should do. The
debate wound on with evidently no end in sight. Finally,
one of the three lesser archangels approached them and
whispered, "We'll take the situation under advisement.
Keep us informed of your progress. Thanks for your
report."

Realizing that they'd just been dismissed, the two
angels glanced at each other in exasperation and dismay,
departed to their respective work stations, and set the
matter aside for later consideration. Thus it remained
unresolved, something like the angelic equivalent of a
pebble in a shoe—an irritant that they couldn't address,
yet one they couldn't ignore either.

*   *   *   *   *

Back on Earth, Janie and T-bear were completely happy
together. T-bear was amazed at the richness of human
existence, and Janie was delighted to have so engaged and
grateful a confidant. For a year and a half, she continued to
take T-bear everywhere with her, and her constant loving
embrace gradually took its toll on his artificial body.

He got jam stains on his fur, so Rosa showed Janie how
to clean him by rubbing his fur with corn meal and then
vacuuming the powder away. When Janie took him for a
walk, holding him only by his paw, he suffered a small tear
in the stitching of his shoulder, so Rosa got out her sewing

kit and mended the rent with matching brown thread. And gradually, his once sleek, dense fur became matted from Janie's hugs and kisses, so Rosa gave Janie a soft brush and showed her how to groom T-bear until he was silky and fluffy once more.

With Rosa's coaching, Janie was able to take excellent care of T-bear, and he held up far better than the toys of most children her age. Nevertheless, T-bear was man-made, not God-made, and his fur began to wear a bit thin in spots. Janie was concerned that T-bear would feel cold if this trend continued, and she cast about in her mind for some way to help him. After all, she'd been able to address all his other ills. Then, one brisk autumn day, Rosa dressed Janie to go outside in a pair of corduroy pants and a brightly-colored wool pullover sweater. That's when Janie got her second inspiration.

"Rosa," she asked, "is it hard to make a sweater?"

"Not for people who know how to knit. But knitting takes a lot of training and practice."

Rosa knelt down to help Janie put on her shoes, so she didn't see the look of concentration that came over Janie's face. "Do you think I could learn to knit?"

Rosa tied the second shoe and stood up. "I don't see why not. Your Grandma Hanson could knit. See the afghan on the foot of your bed? Your father told me that she made it, and as you can see, it's very nice."

Janie glanced at the afghan. She'd always liked it, and now she knew exactly what to do. She picked up T-bear and followed Rosa out of the bedroom, down the stairs, and out into the back yard. But instead of going to play in the piles of wind-blown leaves, she sat down on a lawn chair with T-bear in her arms and told him what she planned to make for him. T-bear was pleased. He thought it would be fun to wear clothes like Janie, and he said so.

So Janie extended a bit of her soul into her portal and called to her Uncle Albert. He was always glad when Janie visited him, so he paused in his work to speak with her.

"Uncle Albert, do you know my Grandma Hanson?"

"No, Janie, I don't, but I'm sure she's here with us. Would you like me to ask your Nana to check on her?"

"Please, and if it wouldn't be too much trouble, I'd like to meet her. I'd like to ask her to do me a favor."

Albert frowned and pursed his lips. "I'm not sure that's such a good idea. After all, she's dead and you're still alive. I don't think the living and the dead are supposed to have conversations with one another."

"You're dead, and I talk to you."

Albert couldn't refute this truth, nor would he willingly forego conversations with Janie going forward. As he thought about her request, he realized that he honestly couldn't see how a meeting between Janie and Grandma Hanson could hurt. After all, they'd be reunited in Heaven after Janie died, and it wasn't as if Janie was unaware of the Afterlife now. "OK, I'll ask my mother to locate Grandma Hanson and see if she'd like to meet with you. I'll let you know what I learn, but for now, Janie, perhaps you should go and play as Rosa intended."

Janie was an obliging child, so she withdrew her soul into her body and did as he asked. And that night, as Janie and T-bear lay in bed, snuggled under Grandma Hanson's afghan, Grandma Hanson came to Janie's portal and knocked politely on the door.

Janie extended a piece of her soul to go meet Grandma Hanson. "Oh, Grandma, I'm so glad you've come!"

"How could I not? You're my granddaughter and my namesake. I may be in Heaven, but I still love you with all my heart, and I'm amazed and thrilled that we can meet like this."

"I'd like to meet with you often, Grandma. I want to get to know you, and I want you teach me something. This afghan is so beautiful. Can you teach me how to knit? I want to make a sweater for T-bear."

Grandma Hanson smiled at Janie through the portal gap. "I'd love to teach you to knit. Few activities gave me as much pleasure toward the end of my life. I'm so glad that you're interested and that, despite all that separates us, we still have something in common that we can share."'

So it was that Grandma Hanson began Janie's instruction, and that instruction progressed with astonishing speed and ease because, as a disembodied spirit, Grandma Hanson was able to pour her own skill, knowledge, and memories directly into Janie's soul, rather than having to explain things in the conventional mortal way.

The next evening at dinner, Janie asked her parents to buy her a big skein of yarn, some #2 circular knitting needles, a set of crochet hooks, a tape measure, and a good pair of scissors (not the kind with dull, rounded tips like the pair they'd given her for paper crafts).

Janie's mother was bewildered by this request, and she was about to refuse, but Rosa happened to enter the room then to clear the table, and she exclaimed, "What a good little girl and so talented! Why I was more than a year older when I knit my first potholder. You must be so proud." Rosa exited with her arms full of plates and flatware, and Janie's mother, bridling at this praise, promised Janie that she'd receive the supplies and tools she needed.

Janie's mother was as good as her word, and soon, Janie was staying up late every night, communing with Grandma Hanson and learning knitting basics. Before long, Janie could cast on, knit, purl, make ribbing, knit stockinette stitch, increase, decrease, and cast off. Armed with these skills, she embarked on T-bear's sweater. Soon she'd made all the pieces, and she'd done a very creditable job too—no dropped stitches, all rows neat and even, work that would have made Grandma Hanson proud even if she'd done it all herself at the height of her Earthly skills.

A day later, Janie had crocheted all the sweater pieces together and gently pulled the finished garment over T-bear's head and forelimbs. He looked terribly handsome in it, and Janie glowed with happiness, knowing that he would never be cold now, no matter how gray or damp a day might be.

Of course, Janie's parents couldn't help but notice when T-bear showed up sporting his new apparel. Her mother's eyebrows would have risen up to her hairline if she hadn't just completed Botox treatment that day. Her father exclaimed in surprise and then got ahold of himself. "Janie, can you hand T-bear to me?" She did, and he studied the sweater carefully, looking for flaws or any sign of amateur work. "This is beautiful, Honey. Did you make it all by yourself?" Janie nodded, and he handed T-bear back to her, subdued by his sudden realization that his daughter might possibly be a genius.

After Janie and T-bear went to bed that night, Janie's parents renewed the conversation about sending Janie to an elite private school. Janie was now five, old enough to enter Kindergarten. But most private schools in the area were booked solid. To get a spot for their child, most families had to make a reservation while the child was still in the womb, and even then, admission wasn't assured. The child still had to pass a rigorous I.Q. test.

Fortunately or unfortunately depending on your perspective, Janie's mother was an alumnus of Westwood School for Girls, and as a "legacy," Janie would be guaranteed acceptance there. So the next morning before breakfast, Janie's mother placed a phone call, and at breakfast, she informed Janie and Janie's father that Janie would join the Kindergarten class for Spring Term, and she'd start first grade in the fall.

At first, Janie was sanguine enough about this development. She announced that she and T-bear would enjoy making new friends. But then Janie's mother explained that T-bear couldn't go. Janie would attend class each day without him.

Janie was appalled. Her immediate fear was that, if she and T-bear were separated by too great a distance or for too long a time, the connection between them would be severed, and T-bear would be left blind, deaf, and helpless for the entire duration of her school day. She wondered briefly if T-bear could simply go to sleep and await her return, but that approach scarcely seemed fair. Then she questioned whether the time had finally come for her to return T-bear to Heaven rather than put him through such an ordeal. But the mere thought practically broke her heart. T-bear wasn't just her dearest friend, he was almost her only friend, and she'd promised to love and care for him always.

No, given that stand, Janie could see only one way forward. As she sat at the table, ostensibly focused on eating her mashed potatoes, she conveyed her plan to T-bear's spirit, and he conveyed his approval to hers. She put her plan into action the very next day.

For some time, Rosa and Janie had taken a walk together every day, often in the late morning or early afternoon. Usually, they simply strolled around and around the garden, but sometimes, they'd venture out into the neighborhood and circumnavigate the block. T-bear had always accompanied them on these excursions, but now Janie took to leaving him on her bed up in her room.

At first, she had to stretch the connection between them simply to make it downstairs and remain in touch. But soon, she could walk to the far end of the garden and preserve the link between them. So Janie began a gradual process of escalation, asking Rosa to take her farther and farther out into the neighborhood, until one day when they walked all the way to Huntington Gardens, and Janie's soul continued to touch T-bear's for the entire trip there and back again.

That night, Janie asked her mother how far away the Westwood School for Girls was from their home. Her mother picked up her cell phone, punched some buttons, and quoted Janie the mileage. "But don't worry, Darling.

The chauffeur will drive you. You won't have to take a bus."

Janie smiled politely, for how she'd get to school was irrelevant. What she needed to know was how much farther from home she'd need to travel to practice maintaining the spiritual link.

Janie began leaving T-bear at home when she and Rosa went to church in the Volvo. By this time, Janie's parents had noticed that Janie and T-bear were apparently no longer inseparable. They congratulated themselves on their daughter's growing maturity. If she outgrew T-bear, then he could be consigned to the hope chest at the foot of her bed and serve thereafter merely as some kind of childhood keepsake. Little did they imagine that, rather that leaving T-bear behind, Janie was actually working assiduously to form an ever-stronger bond with him.

In the final phase of Janie's plan, she asked Rosa to take her on sight-seeing tours of the Los Angeles Basin. They would take the Volvo to the Caltech campus, Old Town Pasadena, City of Charity where Janie's father worked, the Santa Fe Dam park, and her mother's favorite stomping grounds, Beverly Hills, Bel Air, and Santa Monica. Janie found that she could now maintain the connection with T-bear effortlessly, no matter how far away from him she traveled. So now she could look forward to going to school, confident that he'd be able to share every moment of the experience with her, and for his part, T-bear was overjoyed at the prospect of receiving an education, something that surely would have been denied him had he been put into a worm as planned.

*   *   *   *   *

Meanwhile, up in Paradise, Nana was beginning to experience some anomalies as she pursued her watcher job. Janie's parents and Rosa were no problem, and Grandfather Hanson was certain to be in one of two locations—either at the Hansons', visiting his kin and cadging some of Rosa's excellent cooking, or at home pursuing one of his many hobbies. But Janie herself had suddenly become quite difficult to track and oversee. Most of the time, she could be found in or around her home, most often in Rosa's company. But sometimes, Janie seemed to become delocalized like an electron, smearing out over great distances or even appearing to exist in two places at once. Baffled, Nana sought guidance from the head watcher, only to be rebuffed. The head watcher had been irritable ever since the tiny worm soul had gone missing, and he had no patience now for a watcher who couldn't keep track of one, simple, innocent little girl.

*   *   *   *   *

Spring came, and Janie entered Kindergarten. Fall came, and she entered first grade. She and T-bear encountered many new ideas and much to spark their curiosity. So when they found themselves alone in bed at the end of the day, Janie would often reach out to Grandma Hanson and ask her questions.

In life, Grandma Hanson had been a school teacher before she married Grandfather Hanson, so she was very good at answering questions while motivating Janie to delve even deeper. Before long however, Janie began asking the occasional question that Grandma Hanson couldn't answer. This sparked Grandma Hanson's curiosity in turn, and because she had all the resources of Heaven at her fingertips, she began consulting experts to get the information that she and her granddaughter craved.

Although neither Janie nor Grandma Hanson gave the matter any thought, this consultation led inevitably to further miracles, and it altered the course of Janie's life profoundly. For example, after Janie's first grade teacher passed out sheet music and led the class in a sing-along, Grandma Hanson taught Janie how to read more complex music and play the grand piano that stood in the corner of the Hansons' living room.

For a time, Janie was content to play two-handed song standards from the 1950's and 1960's—tunes that Grandma Hanson had enjoyed in her youth. But eventually, Janie and T-bear longed for something a little more challenging, so Grandma Hanson persuaded Johann Sebastian Bach to teach Janie about music theory, and she engaged Frédéric Chopin to teach Janie how to play nocturnes. Franz Liszt asked for the job, but in life, his extraordinary prowess had owed as much to his extremely long fingers as to practice and skill, so Chopin was deemed a better instructor for a pupil whose fingers were still less than two inches long.

After school, Janie would fetch T-bear from her bed upstairs and take a seat with him beside her on the piano bench. Janie's legs were too short for her feet to reach the piano's pedals, but she could still produce a very creditable rendition of whatever tune she chose to play, and before long, she and T-bear began collaborating on compositions of their own. Janie would painstakingly rule additional lines on the notebook paper provided for her school work, and she and T-bear would attempt to capture some of the magnificent harmonies that she could hear if she pressed her spiritual ear to the gap in her portal.

After transcribing a large number of these melodies, Janie and T-bear decided to organize them into a longer composition, a rhapsody featuring variations on the peasant lullaby that had meant so much to both of them. Once the work was finished, Janie began practicing it daily, committing it to memory, just as she would have had to do if she'd planned to perform it for an audience in a concert hall.

As luck would have it, she gained an audience far sooner than she'd anticipated. Janie was playing the rhapsody one day when Grandfather Hanson arrived at the house early. Usually, he timed his entry to coincide with that of his son and daughter-in-law. But that day, he'd spent several hours running errands, and he was eager to install himself in a comfortable arm chair and order one of Rosa's delicious snacks. He walked in on Janie, listened for a minute in growing amazement, and then ran to fetch Rosa so that there'd be a second witness to Janie's performance. Janie played on, oblivious to their presence. So when Dr. and Mrs. Hanson arrived home, Janie had no idea that Grandfather Hanson would immediately begin selling them on the idea that Janie was a piano prodigy who should have music lessons.

To Janie's annoyance, her mother engaged a piano teacher a week later. Initially, the piano teacher came to the house five days a week, taking up time that Janie wanted to spend with T-bear, composing and playing their own music. The piano teacher believed in starting each pupil at his or her current level, so she began the engagement by having Janie play exercises from an instruction book, the object being to gauge Janie's existing knowledge and skill.

Janie found the exercises boring, so after a week of this nonsense, she departed from the notes on the page one day, doing a complex jazz improvisation on the tune and then ségué-ing into a Bach toccata that she particularly liked. She finished the toccata and turned around on the bench in time to see the piano teacher staring at her with her mouth hanging open. Janie scooted herself off of the bench, picked up T-bear, executed a stiff little bow in the piano teacher's direction, and left the room to go find Rosa.

Rosa had obviously heard the music stop, and deducing that something had gone wrong, she dashed from the kitchen, past Janie and T-bear, and into the living room. There she found the piano teacher collapsed on the couch.

"*Ai! Dios mio!*" Rosa breathed. She hastened to the piano teacher's side, sat down, took her hand, and began patting it reassuringly. "*Señora,* if the lesson is over, would you like some tea? I made some cake this morning. It's very good. I can bring you a slice and a cup and teapot on a tray... Yes, why don't I do that. I'll only be a minute..."

Rosa left the room and returned with the promised snack as soon as she could. She found the woman packing her sheet music into her briefcase by handfuls, regardless of any pages that she might bend, crease, or tear. "Oh, no, no, no, *Señora!* Here, let me do that. You sit down again and eat some of this delicious cake."

As if in a daze, the piano teacher complied. Rosa alternately straightened out the woman's music, packing her bag for her, and plied the woman with more tea and cake. The woman seemed almost calm again when Mrs. Hanson arrived home early from the office. Catching sight of Mrs. Hanson, the piano teacher put down her teacup and fork, stood up, and walked over to Mrs. Hanson with shaky dignity.

"Oh good," Mrs. Hanson exclaimed. "You're still here. I..."

The piano teacher had drawn herself up to her full height, and now she interrupted in a trembling voice. "Mrs. Hanson, there is absolutely nothing I can teach your daughter. I suggest that when she's tall enough to reach the pedals on the piano, you consider having her audition for the Los Angeles Symphony Orchestra. I will send you an invoice for my time. Good evening." With that, the woman strode across the foyer and flung open the front door. She would have left without her briefcase, but Rosa dashed out the door and down the front walk after her. Rosa thrust the briefcase into the woman's hand, and after glancing down at it with an air of surprise, the woman proceeded on her way with the briefcase in hand.

In the kitchen, Janie and T-bear sensed the spiritual reverberations of this exchange. "Oh dear!" thought Janie. "Maybe we should do something else instead of music for a while." T-bear agreed, and the two of them went upstairs to go hide their compositions in the bottom of Janie's hope chest.

That night, Janie let Grandma Hanson know that she'd enjoyed learning to play the piano, but now she wanted to try something new. That morning, her teacher had assigned the class an art project. Janie and her fellow students were instructed to draw a picture of their parents using crayons and craft paper. Janie had been disappointed by the crude likeness she'd produced, and she asked if Grandma Hanson could teach her how to draw better.

Grandma Hanson obliged, and after Janie had absorbed lessons on one- and two-point perspective, use of light and shadow in rendering, and use of color to add highlights and dimension, Grandma Hanson found herself working once more beyond her depth. So, true to form, Grandma Hanson brought in some consultants to help Janie—Michelangelo to teach her anatomy, Da Vinci to teach her portraiture and composition, Caravaggio to teach her chiaroscuro technique, and Rubens to help her capture subtleties of light and surface textures.

Eventually, Janie asked her parents for canvas, stretcher bars, gesso, brushes, oil paints, linseed oil, and turpentine. Her mother started to remonstrate, but her father, who by now was beginning to harbor a secret dread, hushed his wife and assured his daughter that she'd receive everything she'd requested.

For a while, Janie feared that her mother would inflict a drawing instructor on her, a hapless successor to the piano teacher who'd run away. Fortunately, her mother seemed to have learned from that experience because no drawing instructor appeared. And when Janie subsequently produced a portrait of her mother and father that was worthy of display in the Louvre, her parents simply shivered, ordered Rosa to see to the framing, and left Janie and T-bear to their devices.

4: Janie Becomes a Healer...

Early on during Janie's art instruction, she'd discovered that she could communicate better with her teachers if she spoke with them in their own original language. So by the time she painted her parents' portrait, she'd acquired a pretty thorough knowledge of Italian—not modern idiomatic Italian of course... rather the Renaissance-era Italian used by Machiavelli in his seminal political work, *The Prince*. Sometimes in their spare moments, she and T-bear would amuse themselves by conversing with each other in Italian, and from her talks with Uncle Albert, Janie learned that Old Italian was in some ways quite similar to Latin, so she picked up Latin too.

Now Latin is the root of all the Romance Languages, so once you learn it, other such languages come fairly easily. After listening to Rosa talk with her children and grandchildren in Spanish, Janie decided that it would only be courteous to learn Rosa's first language so that Janie could speak it too.

Finding a Spanish instructor was simple. Janie asked Grandma Hanson to introduce her to Velázquez. Janie wanted him to educate her about the conventions of Spanish Court painting, and while he was at it, he could teach her Spanish at the same time. Imagine Rosa's surprise when Janie "spontaneously" began speaking Spanish, and not the Central American Spanish that Rosa herself spoke—the grammatically correct, elegant speech of kings and queens in a bygone era.

Rosa was pleased that Janie could now understand Rosa's native tongue. Rosa's command of American English was quite good, but no one is ever as comfortable with a second language as they are with their first. So the speed and quality of Rosa's communications with Janie improved, and Rosa was able to impart much more of her wit and wisdom to Janie thereafter.

Gratified by this outcome, Janie cast about for another language that might also prove useful in the future. She consulted Grandma Hanson on the subject, and Grandma Hanson suggested French. After all, French was "the language of love," and it was spoken still in the eastern provinces of Canada as well as portions of Louisiana and the Caribbean islands.

So Janie asked Grandma Hanson to introduce Janie to the painter Eugene Delacroix. Because Delacroix had lived through the French Revolution, both his painting style and manner of speaking were a bit overwrought from Janie's perspective. But she learned a lot about impasto brush work from their association, and she became fluent in modern French as well, so she deemed their interaction a success.

Janie didn't know anyone beside Delacroix who spoke French, so she asked Grandma Hanson for ideas on how she could keep her skills fresh. Grandma Hanson responded by referring Janie to a number of poets, playwrights, and novelists who'd written in French. By this time, Janie knew better than to ask her parents for aid in pursuing her interests. Fortunately, Janie always had a resource to whom she could turn. She asked Rosa to drive her to the local public library. There, with Rosa's help, Janie got a library card and checked out several of the books that Grandma Hanson had mentioned.

Unfortunately, reading French literature wouldn't help Janie maintain her French accent. Nearly half the letters in a French sentence are silent or part of a diphthong it seems. But reading would help Janie extend her vocabulary and master the finer points of French grammar, plus she genuinely enjoyed what she read, especially when she stumbled on the works of Colette—hardly age-appropriate content for a little girl of six, but then for so many reasons, Janie was astonishingly mature for her age.

So the local librarian got to wonder why a domestic servant like Rosa would be interested in classics of French, Spanish, and Italian literature, and Janie's parents got to ponder their daughter's prolific and impressive career as an illustrator and painter, but Janie herself had no worries at all. She simply went in whatever direction her intellectual curiosity led her, becoming a musician, a composer, an artist, a linguist, and before long, much, much more.

* * * * *

Christmas was coming. Everywhere that Janie went (home, school, church...), there were decorations in red, green, and gold and nonstop seasonal music. Dr. and Mrs. Hanson spent a lot of time at the dinner table comparing calendars to ensure that they'd make it to all the critical parties, and Mrs. Hanson gave Rosa daily updates on which events would take place at their house, requiring that Rosa act as *de facto* caterer. Consequently, Rosa did a lot of shopping during this period, stocking up the pantry and getting ready for the marathon rounds of roasting and baking that she knew were coming her way.

Mrs. Hanson also spent a lot of time shopping, much to the chauffeur's dismay. Most gifts she just ordered on line and had them shipped directly to their destinations. But some presents were so crucial socially that her personal intervention was required. Fortunately, Mrs. Hanson had most gifts that she bought wrapped by professionals. But she brought home the gifts for Janie and Dr. Hanson still in their original packaging.

The chauffeur staggered from the garage into the house burdened by armloads of shopping bags. Before Rosa could protest, he put them down on the kitchen table. Mrs. Hanson sailed in behind him, removing her scarf and gloves. "Rosa, be a dear, wrap these presents, and put them under the tree when it's ready. I think the wrapping paper is still in the closet under the stairs."

Rosa blinked. "Yes, *Señora*, and when *will* the tree be ready?"

Mrs. Hanson paused, opened her purse, fumbled for a minute inside, withdrew a business card, and handed it to

Rosa. "These people do the best holiday home decorating in the county. They routinely stage mansions in Beverly Hills for charity events. Give them a call and get on their schedule. Tell them money is no object. Dr. Hanson and I will be doing a lot of entertaining this year." With that remark, she left the room.

"Yes, *Señora*." Rosa frowned sadly down at the card and shook her head.

"Typical..." the chauffeur muttered, and he beat a hasty retreat out of the house and back to his comfortable rooms over the garage.

Upstairs in Janie's room, she and T-bear felt the spiritual reverberations of this exchange, and Janie also shook her head a bit sadly. Just two nights before, she and Uncle Albert had had a lovely chat about the true meaning of Christmas, and she was currently engaged in making gifts for Rosa's family and her own.

Because oil paints would take a month to dry, time she didn't have, Janie had decided to do a dry-brush watercolor picture for each person on her gift list. For Rosa's children and grandchildren, Janie was doing miniature portraits of Rosa, and for Rosa herself and Janie's parents, Janie was doing miniature portraits of herself with T-bear. She'd worked in watercolors before, but this was her first attempt at gouache and dry-brush techniques, so she'd consulted the previous evening with Andrew Wyeth, and she was finding his advice beneficial.

Janie's work was a far cry from the gifts her little school chums were assembling during that same period—gold spray-painted pine cones, macaroni necklaces, lopsided clay ash trays, and tissue paper collages that would have had no chance of pleasing parents as demanding as Dr. and Mrs. Hanson. But by the same token, Janie had no intention of letting those school chums know just what she was capable of producing. She was no fool. She'd come to understand human nature much better than most people surmised.

By this time, Janie had reached second grade. She was now well-versed in how to hide her many accomplishments from her teacher and her fellow students, so she was seldom teased and never bullied. She would simply look around her to gauge how others were responding in a situation, and then she'd ape their behavior—only she'd perform a little bit better than they did to guarantee that she received a top grade. Her teacher loved her and often glowed with pride at how well Janie absorbed her lessons. The teacher would have been astonished to learn that, actually, Janie was "coasting," and if she'd had the chance, she could have earned several college degrees from top universities already.

Be that as it may, throughout the run-up to the Christmas holiday, Janie and her classmates sang "Jingle Bells," cut out paper snow flakes, made chains out of strips of craft paper to decorate the classroom walls, and grew more and more restive despite the teacher's efforts to keep them focused and entertained.

At home in Janie's room, T-bear felt all a-flutter whenever he contemplated the coming celebration, and down in Rosa's rooms off the kitchen, Rosa had suddenly begun to behave in a very mysterious manner, whisking something out of sight whenever Janie and T-bear approached.

Each day when Janie came home from school, the chauffeur would open the back door to let her into the house, and delicious smells would waft out of the kitchen—gingerbread one day, cookies the next, and Rosa's own special tamales the next... Janie and T-bear were as excited over the coming feast as they were at the prospect of giving and receiving presents.

And presents there clearly were. Well before Janie's parents' first party, the decorators arrived, worked their magic, and left after erecting a glittering eight-foot-tall Douglas fir tree in the living room. It stood beside the grand piano, framed in the picture window, where in theory at least, guests would be able to see it as they strolled up the walkway to the front door. Beneath the tree was a pile of boxes wrapped in shining foil paper and adorned with bows of silver and gold. Rosa had done a very artistic job, and Mrs. Hanson made a private "note to self" to dispense with professional wrappers in the future, save herself the expense, and rely on Rosa for everything.

Meanwhile, as crazy-busy as Rosa was, she still made time for Janie. When Janie asked, Rosa drove Janie to the local art supply store so that Janie could buy frames for the watercolor miniatures. Janie wanted to do the framing and wrap her gifts herself, so Rosa gave her a few pointers and then turned her loose at the kitchen table with gift wrap, tape, scissors, and ribbon.

As with everything else that Janie attempted, she made a clean job of it, and Rosa smiled as she carried the finished packages to the living room and placed them under the tree. This left Janie with only one more gift on her list, and she felt confident that she'd be able to complete it in time for Christmas day if she put her mind to it.

Janie worked on that last gift every day after school until school let out for the holiday. Then she worked on it all day every day until it was finished. She glowed with happiness as she wrapped it, took it downstairs, and placed it under the tree. Then, having achieved all that she'd set out to do, she relaxed and began enjoying the season with T-bear.

Whenever there was some simple cooking task for which they wouldn't be in the way, Janie and T-bear would help Rosa in the kitchen. And when Rosa was too busy to include them, Janie and T-bear would sit at the piano and play Christmas carols to entertain Rosa and keep up her holiday spirits. Sometimes, when Janie's parents weren't around to be disturbed by her performance, Janie would even play devotional music such as Masses written by Bach and Beethoven, interpolating and transposing as necessary to fill in the parts for orchestra and voice. And of course, Janie would play her rhapsody, usually as the final piece she performed right before her parents were due to come home.

During the two weeks before Christmas, Dr. and Mrs. Hanson would leave the house almost every night right after dinner to attend a cocktail party or a reception. And each weekend, they'd host a gathering for several dozen of their closest friends and business associates. On these occasions, Rosa would serve a buffet lunch in the dining room, and the Hansons would allow Rosa to bring in her son and daughter to clear the dishes and tend bar.

Janie and T-bear thought this arrangement was somewhat disrespectful to Rosa and her family, but the extra money they were paid for their services came in handy, and Janie and T-bear understood that Dr. and Mrs. Hanson would rather have Rosa's family in their home than some strangers hired for the day.

At last Christmas came. On Christmas Eve, Rosa took Janie with her to Mass while Dr. and Mrs. Hanson attended one last party. That night, as Rosa tucked in Janie and T-bear, she sang them a song called "La Posada" about the Holy Family's search for room at an inn. The next morning, Rosa served a big traditional breakfast to Janie and her parents. Afterwards, Dr. Hanson called Rosa and the chauffeur into the living room and presented them with generous bonus checks. The chauffeur, gratified that he hadn't been putting up with Mrs. Hanson for nothing, touched his right hand to his forehead in a quick, respectful salute before leaving the room. Rosa clasped her check to her heart, teared up a bit, and smiled tremulously.

"OK then, presents!" exclaimed Dr. Hanson. "Miranda, you sit over there at the end of the couch."

Rosa started to leave the room, but Janie cried, "Can Rosa stay? I want Rosa and T-bear to watch me open my presents."

Just then, the front door opened, and Grandfather Hanson entered. "Sorry I'm late, son. It gets harder every year to get these old bones in motion. Could you help me carry in the presents from my car?"

Dr. Hanson walked outside with his father to fetch the presents. Janie dashed upstairs to fetch T-bear. Mrs. Hanson, bowing to the inevitable, graciously waved Rosa to an armchair at one side of the room. Soon, everyone was ensconced in their seat, and Dr. Hanson was playing Santa Claus, handing out gayly-wrapped packages.

Everyone exclaimed when they opened the portraits from Janie. Grandfather Hanson was particularly pleased and gave Janie a big, warm hug. "You're so talented!" he said, ruffling her dark brown curls. "I've always called you my little angel, and you certainly paint like one. I'll bet you'll be famous one day."

Not if I can help it, Janie thought. In her soul, she could hear T-bear laugh at her reaction.

An hour later, only a few gifts remained beneath the tree. Everyone except Rosa sat surrounded by piles of gift wrap, ribbons, and the presents they'd received. Everyone looked happy and content.

Janie had received many exquisite gifts from her parents and Grandfather Hanson—pretty dresses, Madame Alexander dolls garbed in exotic costumes from all over the world, Steiff stuffed animals, gloriously illustrated picture books... Janie was well aware that, if she'd let all this splendor go to her head, she could have ended up a very spoiled little girl indeed. But when you've conversed with some of the greatest minds ever to grace the planet, you are better able to keep your balance and view material blessings in their proper perspective. So Janie just pointed to one of the remaining bundles beneath the tree and said, "Can I open that one next, Daddy?"

Her father frowned, a bit perplexed, but he reached for it and handed it to her, reading the label as he did so. "Aha. I see this one's for T-bear."

Janie smiled proudly. "I made it for him myself." She pulled off the paper and held out the contents for all to see—a small but handsome Fair Isle sweater with a matching stocking cap and scarf. The stocking cap had holes for his ears and a pom-pom, and the scarf ends were adorned with fringe.

Janie heard T-bear's soul exclaim, "Oh, they're beautiful! Thank you!"

"You're welcome," she told him. "Now we can wash your other sweater, and you'll always be clean and warm."

At this point, to everyone's surprise, Rosa interrupted the proceedings by standing up and fetching the last package from beneath the tree. "If you'll permit me, Dr. Hanson," she said. She turned and handed the package to Janie. "This is from me and my family to you, Juanita, with all our love."

Wide-eyed, Janie took the package from Rosa's outstretched hand and pulled off the paper. She gasped when she saw what was inside. Suddenly, she understood why Rosa had spent so many hours sequestered in her room doing secret things. Rosa had made a rag doll, but it was far from ordinary. It was in fact a veritable princess of all rag dolls everywhere.

Rosa had stitched the head and body from the still-lovely remnants of a cream-colored linen table cloth that she'd found in the mending pile. On the face, she'd embroidered gently curving brows, brown eyes with a hint of light in them, a cute little nose, and rosy lips that curved into a smile. Then Rosa had covered the head with curly brown hair made of yarn that she'd knitted tightly and then unraveled again. The hair was drawn into two braids tied with blue satin ribbons, and a dress of blue cotton percale clothed the body. Janie checked. Yes, beneath the dress, Rosa had provided a muslin slip and ruffled muslin bloomers, and on the feet, she'd embroidered white socks and black shoes.

"Oh, Rosa, thank you! I love her!" Janie cried.

Rosa smiled, her eyes bright with unshed tears. "You're very welcome, Juanita. My mother made one for me when I was your age. Merry Christmas."

Grandfather Hanson stretched out his hand, and Janie handed him the doll so he could examine it. He turned it this way and that, taking in every detail. "Absolutely beautiful work, Rosa. Thank you for thinking of our Janie." He handed back the doll. "What will you name her?"

Janie didn't hesitate an instant. She and T-bear had already reached agreement on that point. "Her name is Susan."

"That's a lovely name, Honey." Grandfather Hanson stood up and stretched. "Well, this has been a great Christmas morning. Who's for some cocoa and cookies?" He headed toward the dining room as he spoke.

"Now, Dad, remember what too much sugar does to your health."

"Now, son, it's just one day, and a day to celebrate at that..."

Dr. and Mrs. Hanson rose and followed Grandfather Hanson out of the room. Rosa stood up, gave Janie a quick, furtive hug, and then hurried after them to go produce the expected snacks. Janie and T-bear remained behind. Janie changed T-bear into his new outfit. As she did so, she told him, "I've been thinking. How would you like a little sister?"

T-bear said, "I'd love a little sister. I assume you mean Susan?"

Janie confirmed that that was exactly what she had in mind. "I did it once. I think I can do it again. The only new task will be connecting both my soul and your soul to hers so that we can all live life together. I'll have to try it to know if I really can. For all I know, three souls may be much harder than two."

T-bear indicated that he thought the goal was well worth the risk. So that night, Janie extended a portion of her soul into her portal yet again. She enticed a tiny passing soul to approach her. Then she snagged it and inserted it through a portal into Susan. Next, Janie made sure that she was still connected to both T-bear and Susan. Finally, she asked T-bear to try to open a connection of his own directly to Susan. By that time, he had so much practice maintaining his connection with Janie that he found it relatively straightforward to do so. So there they were, three souls linked together with one providing access to Earthly experience.

Susan was astonished to awaken in her new body. Through the links, she gained immediate awareness of T-bear's and Janie's lives. Susan had been on her way to incarnation as a dragonfly when Janie kidnapped her. But now, there was no doubt in Susan's mind that this life would be far richer and more interesting than that of a bug, even a pretty one that flew. So unlike T-bear, Susan didn't need any consolation or reassurance after finding herself in a different situation than expected.

Up in Heaven, the angel currently in charge of insects looked around him for the soul he'd planned to download next and swore a mild oath when he couldn't find it. Having once been a general in the army of Caesar Augustus, he had a very different temperament than Albert, or the gentle lady in charge of worms for that matter. The insects soul-manager stormed over to the boss and demanded to know how he was supposed to do his job when somebody had misappropriated one of his souls.

Had the boss had a physical halo or feet for that matter, she would have snatched the halo off her head in frustration, thrown it on the ground, and stamped on it. Taking the insects-angel in tow, she charged over to the head watcher and asked, "By any chance, can you see a dragonfly soul running about loose?"

The head watcher looked around, then shook his head. "Not here," he said. "I suppose you want me to review all the incarnate souls too." She nodded. "That's going to take some time," he warned her. She shrugged. So he extended his gaze, but without result. He turned and addressed the insects-angel. "Not in a God-ordained body either, so it's not the case that some other angel took it, whatever you may think."

"Well I hope you don't think that I've been careless. I didn't just lose it, you know."

Not for the first time, the boss of soul-management wondered if a former general had the right temperament for their kind of work. Maybe she should try to get him transferred to Michael's squadron. She sighed. "This is the second time this kind of thing has happened. I hate to say it, but I fear we'll have to report this loss to the council of archangels, not that doing so will do much good."

The head watcher sighed in turn. "I'll go with you of course." He turned to the insects-angel. "You, go back to work, and try not to misplace any more souls while you're at it."

The former general bridled at the slight, but he turned and went back to his work station, and his two superiors left on their unpleasant errand.

Meanwhile, back on Earth, Janie, T-bear, and Susan were already practicing long-distance link maintenance, just as a precaution, and they were making good progress. When Rosa took Janie to Mass the Sunday after Christmas, Janie left Susan in Rosa's room and T-bear upstairs, yet all three remained in touch the whole time.

As luck would have it, Nana chose that point to look in on Janie, and she was bewildered to find the girl apparently in three places at the same time. Nana quickly withdrew her gaze and frowned in thought.

*   *   *   *   *

Spring had come. It was a crisp, blustery Sunday afternoon. Rosa was in the kitchen, visiting with her daughter and grandchildren. Normally, Janie, T-bear, and Susan would have joined them, but today, the three friends felt a strong need to be outside. Actually, they felt a strong need to be as distant from the dining room as possible, but the back yard was as far as they were able to go.

Janie's parents were in the dining room, talking with the guidance counselor from Westwood School for Girls. As soon as Janie had heard the opening salvo of their conversation, she'd immediately fetched T-bear and Susan from their room and fled. The counselor was trying to persuade Janie's parents that Janie needed a bigger academic challenge. The results of the second grade aptitude tests had come back, and despite the care that Janie had taken to rein herself in, her scores showed that she was already reading and performing math at the fourth grade level.

Janie's parents weren't the least bit surprised to hear these results, but they feared that their daughter—undeniably a peculiar child and one quite small for her age—wouldn't fare well if she skipped third grade and entered the higher level. They were arguing for more enrichment activities instead. They pointed out that their daughter had already shown an interest in music, art, and languages. Perhaps more instruction in those areas would keep her intellectually engaged.

The guidance counselor agreed that more outside tutelage in those areas would be a good idea, but she countered with a further proposal. Mindful of the world-wide need for more STEM workers, she suggested that the Hansons enter Janie into a program emphasizing Science, Technology, Engineering, and Math—this last at a much more advanced level than she'd studied thus far.

Out in the back yard, Janie couldn't actually hear what the grown-ups were saying, but she could feel the spiritual tension building between them, and she dreaded what might befall her as a result of whatever decision they might reach. So she picked up T-bear and Susan and walked to the very end of the rose garden—the farthest point from the house—and she sat down on a concrete bench in a paved alcove beneath some fruit trees.

She placed T-bear and Susan on the bench beside her. That morning, Janie had finished knitting a blue cable-knit cardigan sweater for Susan, and the doll was wrapped in its warm folds, so Janie had no fear that Susan would be uncomfortable despite the intermittent gusts of cold wind.

As Janie sat trying to shut out the reverberations of her parents' argument, a particularly sharp gust swayed the boughs above her head, and she saw something small fall to the ground at her feet. Being careful not to step on it, she stood up and then knelt down beside it. It was a baby bird. She glanced up, and there among the new green leaves, she could just make out a nest.

She turned her attention back to the bird, extending a bit of her soul until it touched the bird's soul. Immediately, she gasped. The little thing was terrified and in dreadful pain. He lay in a crumpled heap, his eyes still tight shut, his beak open, his tiny rib cage fluttering with the effort to draw breath, and his wings askew—one of them clearly badly broken.

The poor thing was so new to the world that he hadn't even grown a covering of down yet. His pale naked skin reminded Janie of the chickens that Rosa would roast in the oven for Sunday evening dinners. As Janie looked down at the bird, she wondered why his scrawny neck hadn't snapped when he hit the ground. Such a thin neck would barely have supported the bird's head, even when he was safe among his fellows.

Despite the pain and fear in the bird that Janie was feeling, she extended her soul farther and saw that the bird's portal was beginning to open. But the bird, sensing that she was with him, sent her a desperate appeal. He didn't want to die. He wanted to fly above the tree tops. He wanted to peck for delicious grubs on the lawn. He wanted to sun his feathers dry after a spring shower. He wanted to *live*.

Impulsively, Janie reached out and pulled the bird's portal door closed. Then, she reached in the opposite direction to her own portal door. She knew that Heaven was literally awash in healing energy. Her Uncle Albert had told her that newly deceased souls bathed in it to forget the pain of their Earthly lives. Now she drew some of that energy into her own soul and then passed it into the baby bird.

Ever so tenderly, she stroked the bird's back and chest with her fingertips—mending its damaged organs, stopping internal bleeding, coaxing its broken ribs to realign themselves and heal... As she did so, the fluttering of his chest settled down, and he began to breathe without pain. Then, very gently so as not to injure the delicate creature further, Janie stroked her finger along the bones of the broken wing, straightening them and causing them to knit together again. When she was finished, the bird gave a chirp of profound relief. But he was still in trouble. He was still lying naked and cold on the ground where any predator or just plain exposure might kill him.

Janie consulted T-bear and Susan as to what she should do next. Susan was too new to the world herself to have an opinion, but T-bear urged Janie to try to place the bird back in his nest. So Janie told the bird what she was about to do. Then she scooped up the baby bird in her hands, stepped up onto the bench, and tried to reach the nest. It was just out of reach.

T-bear said, "Go ask Rosa to come and help."

Janie thought that this was an excellent idea. With the baby bird still cupped in her hand, she dashed to the back door and into the kitchen. Rosa looked up startled as Janie burst in. "Rosa, please come quick. This bird fell out of his nest, and we have to put him back right away!"

Rosa glanced down at the bird cupped in Janie's hand. "Aye, Juanita, if he fell on the ground, he must be badly hurt, and he'll surely die. It will probably be best just to keep him here where he'll be warm and safe until he passes away."

"No, Rosa, he'll be fine. I know it."

Janie gazed up into Rosa's eyes, and for the second time, Rosa saw something in those eyes that gave her pause, a light of some kind that she couldn't ignore and couldn't explain away. She nodded and wiped her hands clean on her apron. "OK, little one, I'll come. Show me the nest."

Janie led the way to the bench and pointed with her free hand to the nest in the boughs overhead. Rosa stepped up onto the bench, Janie handed Rosa the bird, and Rosa placed him carefully beside his two siblings. Then she stepped down and walked away, back to the kitchen and her family.

Janie listened carefully, and she heard all three babies cheeping together. Because she was still connected to the bird she'd saved, she could tell that he was the only boy. His siblings were both sisters. Just then, the mother bird arrived home with a fat grub in her beak. "Give it to your son," Janie told her, and the mother bird did. The father bird followed with another grub in *his* beak. Confident that the baby bird would now be well-looked-after, Janie wished him a long and happy life, and then she withdrew her soul completely back into her own body.

The sun was beginning to set. Janie picked up T-bear and Susan and returned to the house. As she passed the dining room, her father called to her, "Janie, come say hello to Mrs. Compton. Out of consideration for our schedules, she came all the way from your school to see us on her Sunday off. Wasn't that nice of her?"

Janie heard T-bear snort in derision. He didn't like Mrs. Compton much, and he'd already expressed the view that nothing good would come of her visit. Janie reminded him that good manners were always important. With T-bear clasped under her right arm and Susan under her left, she didn't have a free hand to offer to Mrs. Compton, but she nodded her head in a polite way and said, "Thank you. That was very kind of you." Mrs. Compton beamed. Janie turned to her parents. "I've been playing in the garden, and if it's OK with you, I'll go upstairs and change into clean clothes for dinner." Her mother gestured that Janie could leave, and Janie beat a hasty retreat.

That evening, Janie's parents waited until Rosa served dessert before they broached the topic that was on their minds. They asked Janie if she would like to transfer to a science magnet school so that she could fulfill more of her intellectual potential. When Janie asked where the magnet school would be, her father told her that there was an elementary school affiliated with one of the universities in the area.

Janie spoke of losing the friends she'd made at the Westwood School. Her mother argued that she'd make new and better friends at her new school. So Janie realized that her parents had already made up their minds and asking her for her views was simply window dressing. She decided that she'd better put a good face on the matter so she exclaimed, "I've always wanted to know more about science. This should be fun!" Her mother smiled a tight smile of approval and gave her father a look that said as clear as day, "I told you so." And so the matter was settled.

The following fall, Janie entered the fourth grade at University Elementary School, skipping third, and a male mockingbird sang outside her bedroom window every night—a glorious serenade that he meant only for her.

Up in Heaven, an angel working in the Receiving Department had waited in vain for a bird soul to return. The soul had been slated to arrive in the spring. Summer passed, and then the fall, and still no bird. The angel was kept extremely busy by her other duties—a steady stream of returning souls, all of whom needed orientation and some of whom needed healing. So it was quite a while before she had the chance to give the issue much thought. But when she did, she decided to consult her supervisor, who just happened to be Albert's father.

Now Albert's father was already a little bit nervous because he and his son had conspired to keep Janie's broken portal a secret. So he wasn't too happy to hear that a bird soul was missing. "Don't worry about it," he told his subordinate. "All souls return to Heaven in the end. Leave it to me. I'll take care of it."

His subordinate went away satisfied, and Albert's father headed over to the Watchers to consult his wife. "I'm missing a bird," he told her. "Do you think you could spot it for me?"

"I don't see how I could tell which bird is overdue. There are so many."

"Well, keep your eyes open, and let me know if you see anything strange."

Nana winced, thinking of Janie showing up in three places at once—in her view, an embarrassing failure of her watcher skills. "OK, and Honey? I heard from the head watcher that two small souls have gone missing. They were slated to become a nematode and a dragonfly, so if you receive any surplus souls of that type, could you let us know?"

"Sure, Darling. Sure," and he left to return to his station.

*   *   *   *   *

At first, Janie struggled in her new school. The Westwood School for Girls had offered a curriculum emphasizing the liberal arts. Now she took class units in subjects such as Introductory Algebra, Physics, Inorganic Chemistry, and Biology. So Janie did what she'd always done. She appealed to Grandma Hanson for help, and Grandma Hanson connected her to consultants as needed.

Archimedes taught her basic math, physics, and engineering principles. Euclid schooled her in geometry. Leibniz gave her lessons in pre-calculus. Newton drilled her in Newtonian mechanics and calculus, and Einstein tutored her in special and general relativity. Just for the sake of completeness, Janie also took a seminar on astrophysics from Steven Hawking, and she counted herself lucky that he'd recently become available.

Two others who'd recently become available were Richard Feynman and his friend and sometime competitor, Murray Gell-Mann. They quarreled briefly over who should teach Janie about quantum mechanics, but in the end, they agreed to a team-teaching arrangement. Thus, Janie was able to learn about quarks, elementary particles, recent developments in string theory, and quantum electro-magneto dynamics.

These lessons stood her in good stead when she tackled chemistry. Knowing what she knew, she understood why the periodic table of elements was arranged the way it was, and she could visualize the electron clouds surrounding the atoms in a molecule, so she was able to deduce the molecule's shape and how it would interact with other molecules around it. When Janie's regular teacher finally assigned the class some simple laboratory exercises, Janie proved to be precise in her measurements and careful in her lab technique. Consequently, her yields were always extremely high and very pure, and her results were "spot-on."

Thus, all went well until Janie started the unit on biology. The science of biology had advanced rapidly in recent decades, and most of the experts who could have educated Janie were still alive. But Grandma Hanson did manage to find a few souls to help. Mendel himself got her started with Mendelian genetics. Darwin imparted his theory of evolution. And Watson and Crick told her about DNA, giving her a foundation for studies in genetic transcription. After that, Janie was pretty much on her own.

Fortunately, Janie was by nature a determined and resourceful child. Janie's parents gave her a generous allowance each week, and having no un-met needs and virtually no interest in material things, Janie had saved it all. Now she deduced that, if she was going to excel at biology, she would need to find a way to learn from those living experts, and she knew just how to go about it.

One afternoon after school, she went up to her room, opened her hope chest, and pulled out the clutch purse that her mother had bought for her from a boutique in Beverly Hills. She sat down in the middle of her bed with T-bear and Susan in attendance. Then she opened the purse and spilled its contents onto the counterpane—crisp bills and handfuls of shiny coins. Janie counted. She knew that what she planned to buy was probably quite expensive, but she found that she'd accumulated hundreds of dollars, so she had hope that she'd be able to afford at least some of what she sought.

Janie returned her money to her purse, went downstairs, and found Rosa. "Rosa, could you drive me to Caltech?"

Rosa put down the blouse she was mending and asked, "Why do you want to go there, little one?"

"Because the students have to have textbooks, so there must be a book store. I want to buy some books."

"I'm sure there are book stores nearby with much nicer books than you'll find there."

"But they won't be the kind of books I want. Please take me to Caltech, Rosa."

Rosa sighed, put down her mending, stood up, and went to fetch her purse. Janie followed her out to the garage and got into the Volvo. Half an hour later, with help from a passing student, Janie and Rosa had located the Caltech student book store and gone inside. Janie approached the student intern who was working the register and asked for directions to the biology section. The intern leaned over the counter, looked Janie in the eye, and asked, "Is this a joke?"

Janie drew herself up to her full height and said, "No. I want to buy some textbooks on biology, biochemistry, and genetics. I need them for school."

"Little girl, anything you can find here will be way over your head."

Janie stared back at him a moment. Then she said, "Did you know that sickle-cell anemia is due to a single A-T transposition in DNA? It could potentially be patched in a patient's marrow stem cells using CRISPR-Cas9 technology."

The intern blinked. Then he said, "Follow me. We only order enough new textbooks to meet the needs of students enrolled in current classes. But every year, at least some students sell their used textbooks back to us, and we resell them to students who are short on cash. I don't think anyone would mind if I sold you some used textbooks. I can tell you which ones are reasonably up-to-date."

He was as good as his word, and a few minutes later, Rosa staggered up to the register carrying four heavy textbooks, all versions published for the previous year. One was a comprehensive introduction to the biological sciences, one was the preeminent text on biochemistry, and one was a thorough exposition on genetics and the internal workings of prokaryotic and eukaryotic cells.

The fourth book had simply caught Janie's eye as they walked past the shelves. It was intended for students pursuing pre-medical studies, and it covered immunology, epidemiology, and oncology. Oncology was the word that had attracted her attention. Janie knew that her father worked in the field of oncology, and she thought that, by reading this book, she might get a better idea of what he did for a living.

The intern took the textbooks out of Rosa's hands and began ringing them up. When Rosa saw the total, she gasped, but Janie was unfazed. She opened her purse and began pulling out bills. Having nothing but small bills, she had to pull out quite a few, but by now, the intern had apparently made his peace with this unusual sale, and he didn't try to rush her, not even when some students lined up behind her, waiting to make their own purchases.

The other students stared openly at Janie and Rosa, and one of them seemed about to make some remark. But the intern caught the student's eye and shook his head, and the student held his peace. Rosa accepted a shopping bag containing the books. The intern accepted Janie's money and tucked it into the register drawer. Then Rosa and Janie left the store and trudged off to the visitor's lot where Rosa had parked the Volvo.

As soon as the book shop door closed behind them, the first student in line exclaimed, "OK, which one is the future Nobel Laureate, the housekeeper or the midget?"

The intern grimaced behind his counter. "The midget, but don't laugh. I'm betting she'll actually get a Nobel Prize, assuming she wants one."

*   *   *   *   *

Janie and Rosa took their purchases home, and for months thereafter, Janie studied late into the night each night, learning as much as she could about how God-created bodies really worked. Fall gave way to winter and winter to spring. Summer break came, but Janie, T-bear, and Susan hardly noticed. Yes, Janie received a glowing report card, and for a while at least, she could dispense with the daily car rides to and from her school. But the three friends were completely engrossed in reading about what could go wrong, leading to illness, and Janie came to know in her heart that preventing and healing illness was what she was meant to do on Earth.

Janie remembered well her experience saving the baby bird, and because T-bear and Susan were spiritually connected to her, they remembered the experience too, just as poignantly and painfully as if they had mended the bird themselves. In fact, many times during this period, T-bear and Susan thanked Janie, not only for giving them life, but for enabling them to live that life in bodies that were impervious to pain.

As their studies progressed, T-bear and Susan began to feel very protective of Janie, knowing that her body *could* get sick or injured, and if she did, then they would feel it too. Fortunately, Janie was blessed with a strong immune system, and her parents had made sure that she'd gotten all the appropriate childhood vaccines. So she enjoyed robust good health, and neither she nor her friends had to suffer much—that is until what T-bear came to call "the event."

It happened this way. The end of summer had come, and the days were growing shorter. Rosa, Janie, and her friends still chose to sit on the back porch whenever they could. Rosa would peel fruit for fruit salad, string beans, or shell peas while Janie read aloud—never from her textbooks... (Rosa found them deadly dull...) but from the picture books and young-adult novels that Janie's parents had supplied in such abundance.

One evening, Rosa finished her task and went inside to start dinner. Janie closed her book, set it aside, and simply enjoyed watching the sunset with T-bear and Susan. Suddenly, she heard a loud crash of breaking glass and Rosa's anguished scream.

"Aye, Janie! Help! Help me, please!"

Janie jumped up and ran into the kitchen. She found Rosa standing over the sink with her hand wrapped tightly in a dish towel. The towel was already soaked with blood and more was dripping into the sink.

"Watch out for the glass. Go call 911!"

Swiftly, Janie stepped over the shards littering the floor. She ripped Rosa's apron off of her body and tied it tightly as a make-shift tourniquet around Rosa's upper arm. Then she forced Rosa to let her take the towel-bandaged hand into her own two small ones. She knew that, at the rate Rosa was bleeding, a call to 911 might not yield results in time.

So Janie braced herself internally and extended a part of her soul to touch Rosa's. She reeled as the pain hit her. It was absolutely horrendous. Instinctively, she severed her ties to T-bear and Susan to protect them. Then she extended another part of her soul to syphon healing energy from Heaven. She began pouring the energy into Rosa's hand—closing the gushing artery, joining the ends of capillaries and veins, mending the severed tendons... knitting together layers of muscle, connective tissue, and skin... As she did so, she felt Rosa's agony melt away, and when it was safe, Janie re-established her connections to T-bear and Susan so that they'd be able to experience the world again.

Janie continued to hold Rosa's hand, applying finishing touches to the healing she'd wrought—preventing scar tissue and ensuring that all the nerves would be fully functional... She was about to drop the hand and remove the towel and tourniquet when she noticed something ominous, a blob of tissue in Rosa's right breast that didn't belong there. Janie focused her soul-energy, and as she did so, she recognized the tissue for what it was, a cancerous tumor.

Alarmed, Janie scanned the rest of Rosa's body. She found no other tumors, but she did detect uncounted millions of cancerous cells floating through Rosa's veins— metastatic tumors just waiting to happen. Janie grimaced in anger. She'd listened to her father's talk at the dinner table. She knew what this tumor might mean for Rosa— excruciating, disfiguring surgeries... radiation treatments that left first and second degree burns... chemotherapy that made Rosa so sick she couldn't eat... and even with the best outcome, a long, frightening recovery in which Rosa would have to fight continually for every moment of additional life on Earth.

Janie felt resolve crystalize within her. She didn't care if cancer was part of God's plan for Rosa. Rosa was a good woman, beloved by her own family and incalculably precious to Janie's. Janie would have none of it. She kept up the link she'd formed with Rosa's soul and poured in more spirit-force. She utterly destroyed the tumor. She tracked down each and every cancerous cell and obliterated it. Then, for good measure, she boosted Rosa's immune system so that, if the cancer ever returned (God forbid!), Rosa herself could identify it and fight it off.

When Janie finished, Rosa was not only no longer injured, she was in perfect health. Janie withdrew her soul back into her own body. She untied the make-shift tourniquet and gently unwound the bloody towel. Rosa stared down at her unblemished hand in awe. Then she began to tremble and weep violently. She cried tears of nervous reaction to all the fear and trauma that she'd suffered. She cried tears of joy at finding herself whole again against all odds. But most of all, she cried tears of shock at the completely impossible thing that Janie had just done.

Janie reached out her hand, meaning to comfort Rosa, but Rosa evaded her grasp, fell to her knees, and took Janie's hands in hers. Struggling to control her sobs, Rosa gasped, "Thank you! Oh thank you... Santa Juanita." Rosa bent and kissed Janie's hands and then let her tears flow once more. But now Rosa cried for Janie because Rosa knew that the lives of most saints were exceptionally hard, and more often than not, they ended in tragedy.

Out on the back porch, T-bear and Susan reacted to what Rosa said with sober approval. After all, to them, Janie was the creator who had worked miracles to give them life. In their view, calling Janie a saint was no more than she deserved.

Up in Heaven however, the moment that Rosa spoke the word "saint," a sound like a deep-throated bell reverberated through the firmament. Angels everywhere paused in their work, and even the archangels sat up and took notice. They all knew that, somewhere on Earth, a miracle had just occurred, and as none was slated to be worked there right at that moment, the situation demanded an immediate and thorough investigation.

5: Saint Janie...

Fortunately for Janie and her family, the word "immediate" has a different meaning in Paradise than it does on Earth. One must remember that, from the angelic perspective, God created the Heavens and the Earth in seven days, but on Earth, the process took roughly four-point-five billion years. So Janie had some time...

Rosa and Janie never reached an explicit agreement to keep "the event" a secret. They didn't need to... Janie kept it secret because she'd long-since decided that hiding her activities from her parents gave her and her friends greater security and her parents, greater peace of mind. As for Rosa, she believed that the longer it took the world at large to recognized Janie's true nature, the longer Janie would be able to enjoy a quiet, somewhat normal childhood. So neither one of them ever spoke a word about it, and the only other two beings who knew could only communicate via spirit-link with Janie herself.

Nevertheless, the event did bring about one dramatic change. About a week after Janie's brush with Rosa's undiagnosed cancer, Janie startled her father at the dinner table one evening by saying, "I've decided to fight cancer when I grow up."

Her father had been chewing a mouthful of steak, medium-rare, so he couldn't answer at first, but her mother spoke into the silence, saying, "That's wonderful, dear. I'm sure your father is very proud that you plan to follow in his footsteps."

Her father swallowed, took a sip from his water glass, and spoke in turn. "I am, but I should caution you that getting into my field isn't easy. You have to get good grades, earn a bachelor of science degree from a top university, graduate from medical school, serve as an intern and then a resident... It's a lot of work just to become a fully-qualified doctor, and then one must take additional courses and serve additional years in one's specialty to become an expert oncologist."

Janie was unconcerned. "I know. I have been studying hard, and I've been getting good grades. If I keep it up, I should be OK. Don't you agree?"

Her mother interrupted her father before he could reply. "Of course, dear. You're a very smart little girl, and a good student, and we'll help you all we can."

Her father frowned in concern. "Don't get her hopes up too high, Miranda. I knew a lot of brilliant guys during our school days who tried hard, but failed to go the distance in the medical field. And we should remember... She's still very young, and she may change her mind. If she does, no problem. There are scads of worthy careers out there, and because she's her mother's daughter, I have to believe she'll be a big success in the one she eventually chooses."

Janie smiled and took a sip from her own water glass. "Don't worry. I'll choose fighting cancer. So, what can I do to get started?"

Now it was her mother's turn to put on the brakes. "Unfortunately, you're still too young to be a candy-striper or some other kind of hospital volunteer. Maybe we can arrange an internship of some kind for you when you enter high school. College admissions committees love that kind of stuff. But for now, probably the only option is for your father to bring you to work with him some day. If you promise not to get in his way, you can shadow him and the nurses and learn something about what they do."

Janie's father glared across the table at his wife. "As you know, Miranda, I spend most of my time in the lab these days, and we have to take stringent precautions to keep our samples uncontaminated."

"But you still hold clinic every Monday." Janie's mother was now using the voice she employed in court for final arguments.

Janie's father winced. "I suppose I could show her Reception. She'd see all the patients waiting for chemo infusions and radiation treatments. She could get a sense of what state they're in and what the treatment environment is like..."

"Splendid idea!" Janie's mother smiled warmly at her husband. "I believe that a Monday school holiday is coming up. Are you planning to hold clinic that day?"

"I have to... huge patient backlog..."

"OK then. Janie will accompany you to the office that day. And be clear, young lady. Stay out from under foot. Take something to read so that, if you have time on your hands at some point, you aren't a bother. And when you've had enough, call Rosa and have her come and pick you up. I'd suggest the chauffeur, but I already know I'm going to need him myself that day."

Janie clasped her hands together in excitement, her eyes shining. Her father watched this reaction and didn't have the heart to object further. So a couple of Mondays thereafter, Janie got to go to City of Charity with her father. He made an effort. She had to give him that. He took her to see the infusion center, the pharmacy, one of the radiation treatment rooms that was down for maintenance, and a conference room where a group of new patients was taking a class on what to expect during treatment. From Janie's perspective, though, he saved the best for last because, as 9:00 AM approached, he said, "OK, Honey, time for us to go to Reception. I've got my first patient in only ten minutes."

Janie thought that the reception room was very-well-appointed. There was a coffee bar with urns of coffee, decaf, and hot water for tea. There were baskets of black teas, green teas, herbal teas, and dehydrated soups. A tray held boxes of different kinds of fruit juice and bins of individually-wrapped crackers. Obviously, the staff was doing everything they could think of to tempt their patients to eat something and hydrate.

Janie also saw attempts to distract the patients from their troubles—racks of magazines which, unfortunately, no one seemed inclined to read, and an overhead television that no one seemed to watch showing scenic vistas from various national parks.

Janie studied the people around her. They seemed to fall into small clusters with an obviously ill person at the center, surrounded by one or more care-givers. One group in particular caught her eye. The patient was a young woman, perhaps thirty, sitting in a wheelchair. Her skin was paper-thin and gray, and her bald head was covered with a skillfully-arranged bandana. Beside her sat her husband. He kept plaguing her to try a sip from the bottle of juice he held, but evidently, she couldn't stomach it. On her other side sat a woman who looked to be her mother. The mother was there as baby-sitter for the two small children at their feet—a boy of about six and a girl of about four. The children were clearly restless and bored, and the boy kept poking and tickling his sister, making her squeal and cry out.

Finally, the cancer-ridden woman could take no more. To her husband she said, "Frank, please, go get me some cold water. I think I might be able to get it down. And Mom, please take the children outside. Bringing them here was a mistake. I think I saw a patch of lawn outside where they could play."

Her husband rose and left in search of cold bottled water. Her mother stood up, grasped the two unruly children by the necks of their shirts, and propelled them from the room. Thus, the poor woman was left alone for the moment, but at least she was at peace.

Janie saw her chance. She remembered a refrigerated water fountain out in the hallway. Janie went to the coffee bar and got a clean paper cup. She went out to the fountain and filled the cup halfway with cool water. Then she returned to Reception and walked to the woman's side. "Ma'am, I heard you ask for water. Would you like to have this cup until your husband comes back?"

The woman nodded, extended an unsteady hand, took the cup, and drank from it until it was empty. Then she handed it back to Janie. Janie asked, "I'm waiting for my father. Would you mind if I sat beside you until he comes? I promise to be quiet." The woman shrugged, and Janie sat down.

As soon as she did so, she warned T-bear and Susan that she was about to perform a healing and they should prepare themselves. Then, she extended her soul to touch Heaven and the woman. What she saw in the woman appalled her. The woman had end-stage metastatic kidney cancer. Tumors had virtually destroyed one kidney, compromised another, and infiltrated her liver, her lungs, and her brain. For years, she'd been fighting to live for the sake of her husband and children, but all conventional treatments had failed her, and she was here today to see if an experimental immunotherapy might buy her some additional time—a "Hail Mary" if ever there was one.

Janie got to work. She let Heaven's healing energy gush into her like a torrent, flow through her like a river, and flood into the frail body of the woman beside her. Janie tracked down and eradicated tumors. She healed tissues, restoring function to severely damaged organs. She encouraged neural nets in the brain to reform, bridging gaps left by now-vanished metastases. And she identified and destroyed free-floating cancer cells throughout the woman's body. At last, the woman was cancer-free. As Janie had done for Rosa, she finished by enhancing the woman's own immune system so that it would be able to fight cancer successfully by itself going forward. Then, she withdrew her soul back into her own body and dared to take her first look at the exterior of her patient.

The transformation was amazing. The woman's skin had pinked up, and her eyes, formerly yellow from jaundice, were now clear. Also, she was sitting straighter in her chair and breathing comfortably. Janie cleared her throat softly to get the woman's attention. "Excuse me. If you want, I can go get you some more water."

The woman seemed to come out of a trance. "What? Oh, yes please..." Janie went and fetched more water. When the woman reached for the cup, her hand was rock steady if still thin. Clearly, she would still need to sleep, eat, and exercise for a long time before she'd completely regain her health. The woman drained the cup and then handed it back to Janie. "Thanks, Sweetheart. You're a saint."

Janie smiled a wistful little smile. Then a noise caused her to look up. The woman's husband was returning with a bottle of water in his hand. Janie stood up and walked to the front desk as if to make an appointment. Behind her, she heard the man utter a faint cry. She turned and saw him kneeling on the floor beside his wife. They were embracing, and even at that distance, she could see that they both had tears in their eyes.

Janie quietly left the room and went to find a place where she could read her book. Spiritually, she was immensely gratified to have helped the woman and her family, but physically and emotionally, Janie felt weary. After all, she'd had to endure contact with the woman's suffering, and so had T-bear and Susan. They all needed a break, a chance to recuperate.

Meanwhile, up in Heaven, as soon as the woman spoke the word "saint," the deep bell chimed for a second time, and more than one angel gasped at the implications.

*   *   *   *   *

Janie reached the lobby and found an unoccupied bench beside an artificial palm tree. She sat down, shrugged off her back pack, and took out her book. She found, though, that she didn't have the energy to read it yet, so she simply rested and communed with T-bear and Susan as they, too, came to terms with what she'd just done. They all would have been happy to sit like that for hours, but they weren't going to get the chance, for Janie heard a loud, rasping cough issue from somewhere above her, and she looked up to see a man staring down at her.

She recognized him as one of the patients who'd been waiting in Reception. He was exceptionally tall and thin as a rail. Like so many others she'd seen there, he had sallow skin stretched tightly over the bones of his face, giving the impression of a skull with living eyes. His crew-cut hair was gray and sparsely distributed on his pate, but two days' worth of stubble covered his cheeks and chin. His shirt was rumpled and thread-bare, his jeans were sweat-stained, and traces of dried mud caked his cowboy boots. Clearly, personal presentation wasn't a priority with him.

He tried once more to clear his throat, and Janie noticed that he had sores on his lips and a small, black, necrotic area on one side of his nose. He tried to smile at her ingratiatingly, and she caught a glimpse of nicotine-stained teeth. She glanced down and saw that the fingers of his right hand were stained yellow too. A heavy smoker then... so lung cancer, cancers of the throat and mouth, something like that...

"I seen what you done." His voice was raw and hoarse. "May I sit down?"

Janie returned her book to her back pack and scooted herself and the pack to the end of the bench. The man took a seat at the other end. At least he had the courtesy not to crowd her.

"That gal and her family... They looked like good people. I'm glad she's goin' to be OK. She *is* goin' to be OK now, ain't she?" Janie nodded. "Thought so..." He leaned forward and rested his elbows on his knees, letting his hands dangle limply from slack wrists. "I ain't like her. Never done one good thing in my whole life if you ask my ex-wives. Worked as a ranch hand 'til arthritis got me and I couldn't ride no more. Then I got my license and drove long-haul trucks. And every time I got a few bucks in my pocket, I went on a bum's holiday—smokin' and drinkin' and carryin' on... Sometimes I got me a new wife that way. Sometimes I lost me an old one. You get what I'm sayin', little girl?" Janie nodded again.

He struggled to draw in a slow, deep breath, and he let it out as a sigh. "I just want you to know who you're dealin' with before I go any further. I know I'm goin' to die soon, and I'm finally tryin' to clean up my act and be honest. Prob'ly too little too late... I'll find out soon enough. Never been a church-goin' man. Can't say I even believe in it despite what my old Ma tried to beat into me. If there's nothin' hereafter, I'm OK with that—just slip into darkness and know nothin' more. But what if I'm wrong and I end up burning in the flames of Hell like my old Ma used to talk about. I'll tell you true, little girl. That thought scares the sh... I mean, the stuffin's out of me."

He paused for a minute to catch his breath and turned his head to face her. "See, here's the thing. I got a son. I ain't hardly seen him since his ma walked out on me years ago. I hear he lives in this town with a wife and two kids. That's why I come here... to try and make things right before I die. But when I called him, he wouldn't talk to me. Can't say as I blame him. But I can't give up either. I need more time... just enough to do this one thing. 'Cuz I got to believe that somewhere, deep down, he's still hurtin' because I was such a selfish bas... uh, jerk. You get what I'm sayin'?"

Janie nodded and inched a little closer to him on the bench. "Do you want me to make you all well again like that woman?"

He grimaced and tears filled his eyes. "No, I don't think I deserve that after the way I've lived. If you can, could you make me just well enough so I get another year or two? If I can't reach my son by then, well, I just don't deserve to, and at least I'll know I tried my best."

Janie frowned introspectively and consulted T-bear and Susan. She wasn't sure she believed in half-measures, and they agreed that they didn't either. On the other hand, however, if this man learned that she had cured him completely, might he not backslide and resume his selfish ways?

T-bear was philosophical. In his view, the potential outcome wasn't their problem, and they shouldn't try to pre-judge. Yes, the man might backslide, but given his current frame of mind, maybe he'd take advantage of his unexpected good fortune to genuinely change for the better and do good works for others going forward. T-bear believed that Janie should stay open to the possibility of an epiphany... of enlightenment...

Susan seconded this view, so Janie told them to brace themselves as she reached out to the man and to Heaven. When she first touched his soul, the contact filled her with revulsion. He was absolutely right that he hadn't lived a good life, and all his misdeeds had sullied and corrupted his spirit until Janie shuddered at the filth. But then she delved a bit deeper and found much that was terribly sad—a father who took off before this man was even born... a mother who did her best but who had to scrape for a living and who resorted to a belt, a hairbrush, or a shoe when the kids wouldn't mind... an upbringing devoid of higher education or any cultural advantages... and of course, a lack of faith and the strength and hope that it could have conferred...

There was nothing Janie could do about the man's ignorance, his loneliness, or his lingering grief, but she could heal his body, so she gritted her teeth and began. She did as she'd done for the woman and for Rosa—destroying tumors, killing free-floating cancer cells, repairing organs and tissues, and boosting his immune system. But in his case, she did even more.

Janie made her way through his entire circulatory system, especially his heart, removing arterial plaques and restoring his hardened arteries to youthful resilience. She cleansed his lungs of decades-worth of soot deposits and scar tissue. She regenerated his liver until there wasn't a single trace of cirrhosis. And she finished by changing the enzymatic pathways of his metabolism so that even one drink would make him disagreeably ill and even the smell of second-hand smoke would be nauseating.

By the time Janie finished, she was exhausted. As she withdrew her soul back into herself, she heard Susan say, "Maybe one healing per day is all we can manage." T-bear agreed emphatically.

Janie glanced over at the man. He was staring down at his own hands in astonishment, turning them this way and that. He flexed his fingers. Janie knew that he'd feel no arthritic pain. He reached up and felt his lips, his face... Janie knew that the pain of his lesions would be gone. Certainly, all external evidence of cancer had vanished.

"Oh my god!" he exclaimed, and he turned to fix Janie with stare that was half awestruck and half fearful. Janie noted that his voice was now a rich, mellow baritone. The rough huskiness had disappeared.

Janie sighed. "Just so you know, Uncle Albert says that all souls go to Heaven. But some of them, the ones who regret how they lived, can come back and try to do better in another life. You should believe what Uncle Albert says. He knows what he's talking about."

The man chewed on his lower lip a moment. Then, as if gathering his courage he asked, "Who's Uncle Albert?"

"He's one of the angels in charge of incarnation. We've always been really good friends." The man blinked, then held terribly still. Janie continued. "You've been given a second chance. I think Uncle Albert would want me to tell you this. Go and sin no more."

The man made a strangled sound in his throat, closed his eyes for a moment, and nodded. "I hear you. I promise. I'll go make things right with my son, and I'll do good. I won't let you down."

Janie studied him, her eyes large and solemn. "I hope you mean it. I hope you don't forget..."

"Forget you? Never! It ain't every day a man meets a real, live, honest-to-god saint."

Janie shook her head. "Please, don't call me that. I don't think the Church would like it. My Sunday school teacher told us that there are strict requirements for sainthood." Janie began ticking them off on her fingers. "You have to be either a martyr or a confessor in life, then be dead for five years, work at least two miracles as intercessor for the faithful, be elevated to Venerable and then Blessed status, and finally be approved for sainthood by the Pope. None of that applies to me."

The man shook his head and smiled. "Little girl, you've changed my mind about angels and such, but you ain't changed it one whit about the Church as you call it. I don't hold with all that rigamarole. In my own way, I was prayin' for a miracle, I got one, and you gave it to me. So as I see it, you're a saint, and nothin' you can say will make me believe otherwise."

Janie shook her head again and sighed deeply. "I disagree, but I understand. And now, don't you think this would be a good time to try to talk with your son?"

"Yes... yes, now when I got somethin' real special to tell him. You're right, and no phone call this time. I'm gonna go stand on his doorstep until he lets me in!" With that, the man stood up and walked off down the hall—his back straight, his head held high, and his stride as vigorous as that of a much younger man.

Janie watched until she lost sight of the man in the distance. Then she stood up, shouldered her pack, and went to find her father. She wanted to tell him that she'd seen enough for one day. She wanted to call Rosa and go home.

In Paradise, the angels were already all a-flutter over the fact that someone on Earth, someone whom mortals believed to be a saint, was working unauthorized miracles. So they spooked like skittish colts when the deep bell tone rang out for the third time. The head watcher looked up and exclaimed, "An apostate has just found faith! This time, there's been a *comprehensive* healing—body, mind, and *spirit*. The archangels will have to act now!" And he went to round up the heads of Shipping and Receiving. Such a serious matter demanded that they approach the council of archangels as a united front, so they'd better compare notes and get their stories straight.

*   *   *   *   *

The first thing the three angels-in-charge did was interview their own staff. The soul-management angel in charge of Shipping already knew that two of her subordinates had misplaced souls, and no superfluous nematode or dragonfly had ever turned up. The Watchers had confirmed that fact. And Albert's father, the soul-management angel now in charge of Receiving, also knew that one of his subordinates had awaited the return of a bird soul in vain. His wife had tried her best to identify which bird was overdue. She'd even asked for the help of her daughter who excelled at "bird watching." But the two of them had ultimately given up the effort as a bad job, and the head watcher was aware of that fact as well.

The head watcher summed up their findings thus far: two new souls were missing, an incarnate soul was AWOL, and now three cancer patients had been given spontaneous remissions, two of them souls who'd been very close to death. The head watcher then asked if anyone else had something unusual to report... anything? anything at all... Albert's mother hesitantly raised her hand. The head watcher addressed her, giving her permission to speak. She hesitated, and her boss said, "Well? Don't keep us waiting."

"A little girl that I watch occasionally appears to be fuzzy somehow. At times, she even appears to be in two or more places at once."

If the head watcher had possessed eyebrows, they would have risen in surprise. "And you didn't report this because..."

"It was odd, but it didn't seem important. She's supposed to have a soul, and that's what she has—one soul..."

"Yes, but if that soul isn't secured entirely within her own body, then something has gone wrong. Who downloaded her?"

Albert's father and mother exchanged glances. Then Albert's father spoke. "Our son, Albert. He works in Shipping."

The head of Shipping sighed and shook her head. This meeting was not going well for her and her team.

"Albert, come here."

Albert pulled up his cowl, covering his head and part of his face. Then he shuffled forward until he stood directly in front of the head watcher. He could only assume that he was about to get a severe reprimand and possibly lose his job.

"Albert, look at me. Did anything go wrong when you downloaded... What's her name?"

"Janie... Not really... I mean, she did resist a bit. Human souls often do in my experience. But I talked to her and sang her a lullaby, and then she completely stopped struggling. And the damage to her portal door was negligible. When her time comes, we should have virtually no trouble extracting her."

"The damage to her..."

"...portal door..." The head of Shipping was doing the angelic equivalent of sitting slumped on the ground with her head in her hands.

The head watcher spoke very softly. "Albert, please show me Janie's portal door."

Albert turned in resignation and led the way. Every angel who'd attended the meeting followed. As these things are measured in Paradise, the angels were quite a distance away from Janie's portal. So on Earth, a great deal more time elapsed before the angels arrived at their destination, and Janie used that time productively.

Janie, T-bear, and Susan had developed a routine. Every morning, as soon as they awoke, Janie would bathe, dress, go downstairs, eat breakfast, and then climb into the Rolls for her commute to school. The drive from San Marino to West L.A. took over an hour even on the best of days, so Janie had plenty of time to pursue her vocation.

Coincident with her commute, cancer patients would start to arrive at City of Charity for their appointments. Janie would extend her soul out of the car, all the way to the hospital, and begin browsing for potential clients. She had her best luck with those who came for outpatient treatment at the Infusion and Radiation Oncology Centers. She'd gently touch each soul until she found the one she wanted to help that day. Then she'd access Heaven and effect a cure.

Some souls she touched didn't need her help. She could sense that their treatment protocol was working or that they were destined to heal on their own. Others weren't suitable because she could sense that God's plan required that they be "called home." But for some souls she touched, there was no compelling reason not to interfere, and the doctors' best efforts were failing. These patients were the ones that Janie would select—one per day, the maximum that she could safely address if she, T-bear, and Susan were to go on living their own lives successfully.

Sometimes, Janie would find more than one candidate at once. When that happened, she'd cure the sickest one first and make sure that she learned when the other candidates would return so she could help them later.

In this way, Janie kept a low profile. She didn't want a repeat of the man who saw what she was doing and followed her out to the lobby. And because none of those she helped ever saw her face, or even knew that she existed for that matter, no one ever embarrassed her again by calling her a saint. Consequently, the deep, reverberating bell stopped ringing in Heaven.

Only one person took note of her activities and then only indirectly. When analyzing the latest statistical reports, City of Charity's Head of Administration saw a sharp up-tick in the number of spontaneous remissions among their patients. But because improved outcome statistics could only help the center's ability to raise money and recruit top talent, he simply sent a congratulatory memo to the oncology team and then dropped the issue completely.

Thus, Janie, T-bear, and Susan had peace. For the entire rest of their time together, they could do good works, learn new things, express themselves through their art and music, enjoy life's simple pleasures, and spend time with loved ones, especially Rosa and her family. It was a very good life indeed.

However, there came a day when the Heavenly Hosts finally reached Janie's portal. Albert pointed it out with a trembling hand. The head watcher bent down, squinted into its minuscule gap, and said, "I'm sorry, but this won't do." Then he turned his gaze on Janie herself. She wasn't performing a healing right at that moment, but she was browsing for candidates, so he was able to see for himself that she knew how to extend her soul outside her body—well outside.

Just then, she chose her patient, extended herself to the very margin of Heaven, and began syphoning healing energy at a great rate. Several angels jumped back involuntarily as the energy swirled madly around their "feet" and down through the gap into Janie's soul. In less time than it takes to relate what happened, Janie completed the healing and withdrew into herself like always. But this time, the entire process had been "caught on camera" so to speak. The head watcher had seen it all.

He turned and scowled at Nana. "I take it you've never observed Janie doing this before?"

Nana drew herself up to her full height. "Never!"

The head watcher returned his gaze to the mortal girl. "What's this? Why is she still maintaining extensions of herself outside her body?" He lengthened his gaze and followed the soul-links Janie had created. "Oh-ho! I think we've found our two missing souls."

The head of Shipping exclaimed, "Really? Where?"

The head watcher shook his head in bemusement. "In two completely artificial bodies. That's why the Watchers couldn't find them. If I hadn't followed her soul-links, we never would have looked in the right place."

The head of Shipping suddenly felt a very non-angelic anger well up within her. "That's outrageous! How dare she steal two souls! We must make her give them back immediately!"

Albert cleared his throat. "Excuse me. I'm confused. Isn't it the case that all souls return to Heaven in the end?"

"Of course!" The head watcher impatiently dismissed Albert's question.

"Then she can't have stolen them, only borrowed them. Right?"

That remark brought the head of Shipping up short. "Yes, but... but... now they're ruined. If they've spent all this time linked to a human soul, we can't use either of them now for its originally intended purpose."

Nana spoke up. "It's true that they've grown far too much to fit into a nematode or a dragonfly, but wouldn't they now be suitable for use in two humans?"

"Yes, but we'll still be short..."

Albert's father stepped in. "True, but I get back souls all the time who've not only not grown as God intended, they've back-slid. Why, just the other day, I got back a pair of so-called human souls that would be perfectly suited for future use in a worm and a bug. I believe some folks in India even subscribe to the belief that such an outcome is appropriate."

The head watcher couldn't help himself. He burst out laughing, and an angel's laugh is irresistibly infectious. Soon, the entire angelic congregation was giggling... chortling... guffawing...

The head of Shipping paused as if to consider. "OK, you find me two souls, one for a worm and one for an insect, and we'll call it even. I guess that the purpose of life on Earth *is* to grow souls after all, and there's no denying that these two have been given an unparalleled growth opportunity. We'll use them in two humans as you suggest—neither new souls, nor old souls in the traditional sense, but old souls all the same. By this time, they've probably earned the right to experience God-created bodies of their very own."

Albert needed clarification. "So, if I understand you correctly, you want Janie to give them back right away."

His father answered him as gently as he could. "Well, we can't wait for them to die. Technically, their bodies aren't actually alive, and their portals connect directly to Janie, not to Heaven. So when she dies, if we haven't resolved this issue and retrieved them, they'll be stuck for who knows how long in an inanimate, insensate Limbo. I'm sure no one wants that to happen to them."

Albert shook his head. "No, of course not. I'm just thinking of Janie. She'll be so lonely without her friends. And if you mend her portal, she won't be able to talk to anyone here either."

The head watcher closed his eyes, seeking patience. "You say she's been talking to people here? Who?"

Albert realized that he'd just made a gaffe, but he couldn't refuse to answer now. "Well, to me... sometimes to my mother whom she calls Nana... to her Grandma Hanson... and she loves to listen to angel-song. It inspires her to write her best music."

If the head of Shipping had possessed a hand or a forehead, she would have pounded the heal of her hand against her forehead in vexation. "Albert, living souls are not supposed to talk with us. They're supposed to talk with others of their own kind. It's part of what causes them to grow, and as we've already discussed, causing a soul to grow is the whole point."

Albert frowned and looked down, studying his sandaled toes where they protruded from beneath his cassock. "With respect, I disagree. I'm willing to bet that Janie has grown far more than any other kid you can name. Just look at how she's chosen to use her gift. She willingly suffers every day to help others. Isn't that the essence of spiritual greatness?"

The conference of angels fell silent, contemplating what he'd said. No one had an answer.

At last, the head watcher spoke. "One thing is sure. We're going to have to tell the archangels about this, and they'll expect us to have come up with a proposed solution. I doubt that we can effect one without their help, but I doubt equally that they'll allow us just to throw the situation as is into their laps."

Albert's father stepped forward. "How about this... We forget about the missing bird. We've always known it will return to us at some point. As for the two 'borrowed' souls, we reach through Janie, retrieve them now, and incarnate them in two human bodies as soon as we can. Then we mend Janie's portal so that she leads a normal Earthly life hereafter. Can we all agree on this approach? Because if so, my wife can continue to be her watcher, I'll continue to await her arrival when her time comes, and no further unauthorized miracles will occur."

There was a loud chorus of, "Here! Here!" and the conference of angels disbanded. Even Nana departed. Only the three head angels remained, plus Albert. The three head angels glanced nervously at each other and then invoked the archangels.

Michael appeared first. When Michael was annoyed, the light of his manifestation tended to take on a ruddy glow, and he'd draw himself upright until he resembled nothing so much as a pillar of fire. "You dared to call me?" Nervously, the head watcher outlined the situation for Michael, along with the proposed solution. Michael sighed impatiently. "I approve your proposal with only one possible caveat. Did the little girl ever claim to be a saint?"

Albert astonished them all by answering. "No, in fact when someone else called her one, she asked him to stop and explained why the term didn't apply to her."

"Good, then no heresy has occurred, and the matter doesn't concern me. The mortals were simply mistaken, and we all know how frequently that happens." Michael vanished.

Gabriel and Raphael arrived at that moment. Gabriel looked around him and said, "I take it Michael's come and gone already? Typical. So, I hear you need help with a problem of incarnation." The head watcher explained. "Alright, I can extract the borrowed souls, and Raphael here can heal them, but someone should prepare the girl. After all, an encounter with one of us can shake a mortal down to the very foundation of his or her being."

Albert surprised everyone again. "OK, I'll do it." Raphael stepped aside and gestured graciously to Janie's portal. Albert leaned down and called into the gap. "Janie, Janie, please come. I need to talk with you."

A moment later, they all heard Janie's spirit voice reply. "I'm here, Uncle Albert. What's happened? What do you need to tell me?"

Uncle Albert spent a long time sitting beside the gap in Janie's portal door, explaining to her all that had happened—how her miracles had had unintended consequences, and how the Heavenly Hosts now needed to put things right again.

Everyone heard Janie begin to cry softly as she realized the implications of what he said. "So you need T-bear and Susan to go back to Heaven."

"Yes, Sweetheart, I'm afraid we do."

"But they'll get to live new lives in human bodies all their own?"

"Yes, I promise they will."

"I don't want to be selfish. This is a very good opportunity for them, isn't it?"

"The best they could possibly hope for, and you can be proud that you helped make it happen... Sweetheart, are they here with you now?"

"Yes."

"And do they understand what we propose to do for them?"

Janie sobbed and then said, "Yes, they understand, and I'm telling them that I agree it's a good thing... that they shouldn't worry about me because I'll be fine. I mean, I'll miss them of course, but I'll be happy knowing that they're happy."

"Good girl, Janie. Do you or T-bear or Susan have any more questions?"

"Susan wants to know if they'll have to die to come to you."

"No, Janie, they won't have to die because, technically, they never got to live. You've heard about the archangel Gabriel, haven't you?"

"Yes, Father Timothy talked about him in church."

"Well, Gabriel is going to reach through you now, through the soul-links that you created, and he'll take T-bear and Susan out of their bodies and back into Heaven. Then he'll close off the links so that you'll be whole and complete in your own body. Do you all understand?"

"Yes."

"And are you all ready?"

"Ye-yes..."

Gabriel reached forward, opened Janie's portal, and extracted T-bear's and Susan's souls. Then, in the same moment, he mended Janie's portal door and closed it all the way.

Raphael reached out and enfolded T-bear and Susan, healing the inevitable grief they felt at being separated for the first time from their creator and beloved friend. Then he bore them away, for such a profound healing is not the work of an instant, and they must be made completely whole before they could be reincarnated.

Once Gabriel and Raphael had gone, the three lesser archangels saw no reason to hang around, so they departed too.

Only Uriel remained. He regarded the head watcher, the chief of Shipping, and Albert's father for a moment. Then he bathed them in loving light and unbounded approval. "Well done, and now that the crisis has been addressed, I'm sure that all of you are eager to return to your stations." Taking the hint, they all dispersed. That left Uriel alone with Albert. Again Albert began to fear that he was in for a tongue-lashing, but to his surprise, Uriel said, "Walk with me."

They set off across the Heavenly Realm, going nowhere in particular. After a while, Uriel began to talk, and he spoke desultorily. "Your name is Albert, isn't it?" Albert nodded. "I thought so. You know what I like about dealing with mortals, Albert?" Albert shook his head. "The uncertainty. Yes, we set them a predestined overall course, but how they traverse that course, exercising Free Will, can be utterly surprising. You create a little girl, and against all odds, she transforms herself, if not into a Saint, at least into a Venerable or Blessed being.

"Oh, I know, I know..." Uriel made a deprecating gesture. "She had lots of help, but for what do we exist if not to help them? After all, this whole 'growing souls' thing was our idea. And who's to say that her becoming a Saint wasn't part of God's plan to begin with? Can anything happen without God's consent? Does anything exist that God doesn't create? These other angels, I ask you..." and Uriel shook his head indulgently. "So, Albert, I just wanted to say, 'Thank you for treating Janie with so much love, understanding, and kindness.' I'll be keeping my eye on you. I think you have what it takes to be a tremendous force for good." And with that, Uriel disappeared.

Albert blinked and looked around him. To his surprise, he found that he was standing beside the doorway to Janie's portal again. Albert stood a moment, stroking his chin thoughtfully. He couldn't be sure what Uriel had meant by all he'd said, but Albert did know what his own inclination was.

He looked around him carefully once more to make sure that no one would see... that no one was paying any attention. While he checked that his act would go unnoticed, he tore off the hem of his robe and knotted it into a wad. Then, he unsealed the door to Janie's portal and wedged it open a crack with the ball of spirit-matter that he'd produced.

It wasn't fair, he thought, that such a good little girl should lose all her friends at once. Albert was determined that she'd still have at least Grandma Hanson, Nana, and him in her life. And if she occasionally used some spirit-energy to heal the suffering of others on Earth, well, Heaven had an infinite supply, so what harm could she possibly do?

Soul Survivor

1: Susan's Story Begins (Again)...

Prologue

Jane Marie Hanson was born with the spiritual equivalent of a birth defect. The angel-in-training who put her soul into her body accidentally broke the portal that connected her to Heaven, and he was too embarrassed to admit his mistake and get help fixing it. Thus, she remained in contact with Heaven for her entire life on Earth. She could hear angel-song. She could converse with departed spirits—her Grandma Hanson for example, but also with such luminaries as Newton, Einstein, Da Vinci, and Johann Sebastian Bach. This ability gave her the interests and the performance of a towering genius—a math and science prodigy certainly, but also a polyglot linguist, a world-class artist, and a concert-level pianist and composer.

These abilities frightened and confused most of the adults around her, including her parents. She had the good sense not to reveal her true abilities to her school classmates, but that magnitude of deception inherently leads to distancing, and therefore, she had no true friends her own age. Janie, as she was called, was growing up a very lonely little girl until the day when she asked her parents for a pet and they gave her a teddy bear instead.

After consulting with her only real friend, her nanny Rosa, and giving the matter careful thought, Janie decided to create a friend. So she "borrowed" a tiny soul from Heaven, opened a portal from her own soul into the teddy bear, and downloaded the soul. To give "T-bear" the ability to experience the world despite the fact that his body was simply a toy, Janie maintained the link between their souls 24-7.

T-bear was able to see through her eyes, hear through her ears, and smell and taste and feel and learn from everything that Janie encountered. Before long, his tiny soul, which had been intended for a nematode, grew to be surprisingly sophisticated, almost like a fully-fledged human soul. And like many human children, he and Janie began to crave another companion, a little sister, so Janie made one out of a beautiful rag doll that Rosa had given her for Christmas.

Janie and T-bear named their new sister Susan, and to give Susan the same good quality of life that T-bear enjoyed, Janie and T-bear cross-linked their souls with hers on a permanent basis. Susan's soul had been designed to occupy a dragonfly, but just as T-bear had grown prodigiously due to his life experience, so too did Susan, and for a couple of years, the three friends were very happy together.

Unfortunately, all Earthly experiences are fleeting, and before long, the miracles that Janie had worked came to the attention of the Heavenly Hosts. To put it mildly, they were *not* pleased. For one thing, they wanted to get back their two missing souls so they could meet their worm and insect quotas. For another, they were alarmed that a little girl was working unauthorized miracles that impacted them.

The angels held an intervention of sorts, discovered Janie's portal defect, and located the missing souls. The archangel Gabriel personally stepped in to retrieve T-bear and Susan. Then he sealed Janie's portal properly. Next, the archangel Raphael took T-bear and Susan into his custody so they could be healed before being infused into real bodies as God had intended. But all the angels agreed that those bodies could no longer be the simple, transient forms of a worm and bug. T-bear and Susan were now more suited to incarnation as human beings. To balance the supply of souls with the supply of bodies, two more tiny souls would have to be found elsewhere.

That's when an angel who retrieved the souls of the dead came up with a brilliant idea. He'd just received two returning human souls—souls who'd failed abysmally in their first shot at life. He proposed that they be infused into the worm and insect bodies—a fitting outcome given their shriveled, stunted natures. The conference of angels burst out laughing at this notion and agreed that it would solve their problem nicely. So two wicked, selfish beings met with justice, and T-bear and Susan were given a chance at life that might never have come their way if Janie hadn't intervened.

One final note... After the angels disbanded and returned to their duties, the archangel Uriel remained to talk with the angel-in-training who'd accidentally started it all. Uriel told Albert, for that was his name, that Albert had huge potential to do good. Then Uriel vanished, and Albert inexplicably found himself standing beside Janie's now-sealed portal. After contemplating Uriel's message, Albert decided that Janie had work to do. Besides, he couldn't bear to see Janie so cruelly deprived of all her friends, including those "on the other side." So he used a wad of spirit-matter to prop open her portal door a crack, giving her back her access to Heaven, and to the infinite quantities of healing energy that Heaven contains.

As Albert returned to his own work station, much was still in doubt. Would Janie discover that her portal had re-opened? If so, would she continue to converse with spirits and heal the sick as she had before? Had she learned not to "borrow" souls? If she did choose to work miracles, would the Heavenly Hosts notice, and if they did notice, would they attribute those miracles to her given that they now assumed that her portal had been sealed? As a comparatively new angel, Albert hadn't yet acquired the power of foresight. However, he reasoned that, whatever Janie did, because her heart was kind, she couldn't possibly do any real harm.

*   *   *   *   *

As it happened, Albert was right to have faith in Janie. Naturally, she was grief-stricken at the loss of T-bear and Susan. Where for years she'd known a warm, reassuring pair of spiritual connections, now there was emptiness, a blank. She was glad that T-bear and Susan would now have the chance to lead human lives of their own, but she couldn't imagine how she'd survive, cut off from almost every loving contact. (Her parents were, after all, professionals.) She spent the rest of that day alone in her room crying, clutching the empty shells of her former friends. Then, when Rosa called her to come to dinner, she dried her eyes and carefully arranged the teddy bear and doll against her bed pillow before she went downstairs.

At the dinner table, Janie's parents noticed how dis-spirited she seemed. Her father, a doctor, thought to ask her what was wrong, but then he saw her reddened eyes and nose and heard her frequent sniffles, and he judged (wrongly) that she'd come down with a cold. He ordered Rosa to bring Janie a mug of hot chicken broth and to rub Janie's chest with aromatic balm before she went to bed.

Janie made no attempt to set her father straight. She just did her best to finish her supper despite having almost no appetite. Then she used the supposed cold as an excuse to go to bed early without finishing her homework. She put up with Rosa's ministrations as the good woman rubbed Janie's chest with an oily salve and pulled two successive old T-shirts over her head to soak it up. Janie snuggled down under the covers smelling strongly like a eucalyptus tree, and from long habit, Rosa tucked the teddy bear and the rag doll in beside her. Then Rosa left the room and turned out the lights.

As soon as Rosa was out of earshot, Janie gave in to tears again, finally crying herself to sleep. But in the middle of the night, Janie awoke from a beautiful dream. She'd been hearing angel-song, just as she had before Gabriel fixed her portal door. For a minute, she lay in the dark, smelling the balm and feeling the presence of the stuffed toys beside her. Then she realized that she was still hearing it. As she'd long been wont to do, she extended a piece of her soul into her portal, expecting to bump hard up against a tightly-shut door. But instead, she felt the door give slightly, and when it did, she saw a sliver of brilliant light and heard the angel-song grow louder.

Janie's heart leapt within her. "Uncle Albert, Uncle Albert," she called.

Through the crack in her portal door, Janie glimpsed one of Uncle Albert's eyes peering in at her. "Shh, Janie! Not so loud! We have to be careful, or they'll find out and seal the door again, maybe this time for good."

"Oh, Uncle Albert!" Janie was crying softly, but this time from relief. "I'm so glad to see you. Does this mean I can still visit with you and Nana and Grandma Hanson?"

"And others too, little one. We'll just have to be secretive and not get caught. Now go to sleep. You've had a trying day, and you need your rest if you're going to keep your health."

Janie sniffled and did as he'd instructed. She withdrew her soul back into her body and sank into slumber. The next morning in the car on the way to school, she did as she'd been doing for months. She extended her soul to the cancer center where her father worked, picked one of the patients there, extended her soul again to access Heaven's healing energy, and gave the patient an unexpected and total cure. As always, the healing process left Janie drained physically and emotionally, but never had she felt such profound soul-satisfaction, knowing that she'd still be able to relieve people's suffering.

*   *   *   *   *

Meanwhile, in Paradise, Raphael worked on healing T-bear and Susan. Of the two, T-bear had been on Earth longer, and his attachment to Janie was more profound, so Raphael judged that Susan would likely be ready for reincarnation sooner. Part of the healing process was about reviewing ones past life and learning from that life's experiences. Of course, all of T-bear's and Susan's experiences had been vicarious, but that didn't change how vivid the two souls had found them. Susan had been particularly moved by all she'd learned about art and languages. As someone who'd lived in constant communication with two "soul-mates," she'd found the nuances of human speech and iconography important and compelling.

Another part of the healing process was about the spiritual equivalent of house-cleaning. Raphael explained to Susan that all she'd known and experienced during her first life would remain a part of her for all eternity. But although her soul would be able to access those memories again after she died, during her next Earthly life, all she'd be able to recall would be a general sense of her own identity, skills and preferences that would guide her course, and a few key recollections that would manifest as dreams or *déjà vu*. Her job was to select which of her most treasured memories she'd take with her and the form in which they'd appear.

For Susan, there was no question. Against Raphael's recommendations, she chose to keep her art and language skills, retain a belief that she'd once had soul-mates, recall that a teddy bear and someone named Janie were somehow important to her, and remember that her own name was Susan Hanson. Raphael was gravely concerned that these memories were far too specific to her old life and might limit her ability to commit to her new one. But he'd given her the option of choosing what to take, and he decided that he shouldn't go back on his word.

So Susan entered the final phase of her spiritual healing. Raphael led her in meditation and prayer, strengthening her for the ordeal ahead. Entry into a body could be daunting, the birth process was never easy, and Susan's soul must be made ready to accept without question whatever form she was given—male or female, healthy or impaired, in any race, culture, or region of the world.

Raphael was still preparing Susan for her transition when Gabriel stopped by to see how things were going. Gabriel was surprised to see that Susan hadn't yet returned to the land of the living. At the risk of giving Susan a set-back, he demanded to know what was taking so long and when she'd be turned over to the angel in charge of soul-download. Raphael cringed at the unfortunate interruption and tried to hush his colleague, but Gabriel would not be hushed.

"Don't presume to silence me. I'm in charge of incarnation, not you, and she looks ready to me. More to the point, don't you have a second soul to begin healing?—another child's toy as I recall?"

Raphael glanced at Susan and sighed. At Gabriel's words, she'd snapped out of her meditative state and was now listening to the two archangels with obvious concern. "Yes, but you have no reason to worry. I've been working with T-bear too, and he's making great progress. He just needs a little more preparation because he was on Earth a few years longer."

Gabriel gave the angelic equivalent of a suspicious snort. "Well, in my view, you should be focusing on him now so that we can resolve this situation as soon as possible and get things back on track. I'm going to go summon the head of the Shipping department. Make Susan ready to accompany her when she arrives." And Gabriel vanished.

Frightened by the precipitate pace of events, Susan tried to cling to Raphael's robe for comfort, but of course, one can't cling to a garment composed entirely of light. Raphael glanced down at her and then to one side as something caught his eye. His brother Uriel was approaching.

Uriel was strolling insouciantly in their direction, humming a hymn of praise to God as he came. As soon as Uriel reached them, he casually bathed Susan's soul in loving radiance. Then he turned to Raphael. "Dare I ask what has Gabriel so het-up?"

Raphael grimaced in frustration. "He wants to reincarnate Susan immediately. I think she needs a bit more time. But you know Gabriel... 'I'm in charge of incarnation, not you...' He takes this distributed delegation of responsibilities very seriously, and when he thinks he's right, there's no reasoning with him."

Uriel clasped his hands in front of him and looked thoughtful. "Perhaps I can help."

"I wish you would." Raphael glanced down at Susan again and saw that she was much calmer thanks to the light in which Uriel had enfolded her. Just then, Gabriel reappeared with the head of Shipping in tow.

Gabriel gestured down at Susan. "Here she is. I'd appreciate it if you'd infuse her into a body straight away."

"No problem. We have a long queue of human bodies awaiting souls right now. Something about everyone on Earth sheltering at home due to a pandemic... lots of bored prospective parents engaging in sexual congress..." The head of Shipping turned to the other two archangels. "This should interest you, Raphael. Whether they know it or not, by doing so, they're essentially self-medicating for their anxiety. The endorphins released by orgasm..."

Raphael cut her off. "Yes, yes, who do you think designed things that way? Until the advent of pharmaceuticals and talk therapy, sex, booze, and religious faith were just about the only psychotherapeutic agents that humans had. Now tell us what you plan to do with Susan."

The head of Shipping bridled at this rebuke, but she did as instructed. Consulting her list, she said, "Well, first in line is a boy in Andra Pradesh who..."

Uriel interrupted her with the angelic equivalent of a cough and frowned in disapproval.

She caught his expression and consulted her list again. "A family in Beijing is expecting fraternal twins..."

Uriel was already shaking his head. "Next..."

The head of Shipping pursed her lips and closed her eyes. "You have to understand. Statistically speaking, the majority of the candidates are going to be in mainland China and the subcontinent of India. I hope..."

"...that we can provide a body more in line with the needs of this particular soul. She's a special case..."

Gabriel couldn't resist stepping in. "...but we can't afford to give her any more special consideration than she's already received." He turned to his subordinate. "Please continue."

The head of Shipping glared at the archangels, shook out her list to its full length, and read the next entry. "In sub-Saharan Africa, there's a..."

Uriel cleared his throat again and addressed the head of Shipping. "Say, I have an idea. Didn't an angel-in-training named Albert cause this whole problem in the first place? Why don't we assign the job of finding Susan a new body to him? Think about it. We'll be holding Albert accountable for his mistake—teaching him to be more careful in the future—and you'll be able to return to your duties without this issue hanging over your head. From all you've said, I'm sure you must be extremely busy right now."

"I am." The head of Shipping considered Uriel's proposal. She had to admit that she was more than a little miffed at Albert, the black sheep of her organization. It would do him good to take a remedial assignment, and it would serve as a cautionary tale to the rest of the team. She sighed. "OK, we'll give the job to Albert."

Uriel beamed at her and saturated everyone present with glowing approval. "Wonderful. If you like, I can take Susan to Albert's work station. I'm sure I remember the way. Will that satisfy you?... Gabriel?... Raphael?..."

The two other archangels were perfectly aware of the way that Uriel was manipulating all of them, but they were no more proof against the Light of God than anyone else was, so they smiled and nodded their agreement.

"Great! Susan, let's go see your Uncle Albert. I'm sure he'll find a lovely new home for you." With that, Uriel took

Susan's soul into his angelic arms and vanished. As soon as he did so, those he'd left behind shook themselves as if to wake up and blinked their eyes a bit stupidly. Whenever Uriel departed, whoever remained inevitably experienced withdrawal symptoms...

Uriel and Susan materialized beside Albert, causing him to start violently in surprise. "So sorry," Uriel exclaimed. "I should have announced my impending arrival."

Recovering his composure, Albert hastened to reassure his august visitor. "No need to apologize. I'm delighted to see you. And Susan! You're looking well. I see that Raphael has been very kind to you." Susan smiled up at him. Albert turned his attention back to Uriel. "I assume that this isn't just a social visit. How can I help you today?"

Uriel dropped his voice a bit and spoke in confidential tones. "I've convinced the Powers That Be that you're the right person to find Susan her new body. Your boss was inclined to give her the first available opening, but I'd like to see her get a good fit if possible. Do you think you could do that for me?"

Albert was nodding enthusiastically. "Sure. I'll keep her here with me until I find something truly nice. I can continue my other duties while I do the search."

Uriel smiled. "I knew I could count on you. Susan, this is where we say good-bye for now. Enjoy your next Earthly sojourn. I look forward to hearing all about it when you return." And he was gone.

Susan gazed up at Albert happily, and he smiled down at her. "Why don't you get some rest, little one. I've got some work to do, but don't worry. As soon as I find your new home, I'll let you know." Susan yawned a big, contented yawn, settled herself against Albert's "leg" on the margin of his robe, and sank into slumber. For his part, Albert resumed instilling souls into bodies. However, now he did so with closer attention because he was on a dual mission—to bring those beings to life, of course, but also to find Susan the best possible future.

* * * * *

"Hmmm..." Albert examined the prospect in front of him and stroked his chin thoughtfully. "I wonder what Nana would say about these people?" Albert left Susan asleep beside his work station and went to visit the watcher who had once been his mother on Earth. As always, Nana was glad to see him.

"Albert! To what do I owe the pleasure?"

"I'm trying to find a good placement for Susan Hanson. I think I've found the right couple to be her parents, but I want to ask your advice."

Nana refocused her gaze on the couple he indicated and then nodded in approval. "Excellent choice... He's a linguist. She's an artist. I don't think you could find a better fit anywhere else in the world."

"Will Susan know much hardship if I place her with them?"

Nana sighed. "Into every life a little rain must fall, Albert. But by in large, Susan will have a good life, far better than she could possibly have elsewhere. She'll lose her mother to breast cancer at an early age. Thirteen percent of the population now gets it. And as a bonus baby, Susan will grow up in a family where her brother is old enough to be her father and her father is old enough to be her grandfather. But she'll be loved and cherished by everyone around her. Isn't that what's most important?"

"Yes. Yes it is. Thank you." Albert started to turn away, but he paused as another thought struck him. "Nana, could you watch over Susan in her new life the way you've been watching over Janie?"

"Of course—Janie, Rosa, Dr. and Mrs. Hanson, Susan, her new family, and for that matter, T-bear when his time comes. I haven't forgotten my promise, you know..."

Albert smiled. "Thanks, Mom. I love you." Nana returned her gaze to the souls she'd been watching when he arrived, and Albert went back to his work station.

As soon as he arrived, he gently shook Susan awake and said, "Good news, little one. I've found them."

Susan looked up at him with shining eyes. "Are they truly good people?"

"The best!" Albert picked up her soul tenderly, opened a portal into the minuscule blob of protoplasm that would become Susan's body, placed her inside, and closed the door. "Good luck, little darling," he murmured. Then he went back to his work.

*   *   *   *   *

Dr. Mason wasn't a medical doctor like Janie's father. He was a tenured professor at the University of the Cascades, Eugene. He'd gotten two PhDs, one in linguistics and one in Eastern European languages. Every day, he left the small farm on the city outskirts where he and his family lived and drove to campus to teach classes and supervise the work of his graduate students.

In fact, he'd met his wife on campus. He and another professor had asked Administration to supply an intern who could type up and submit their journal articles, and Administration had sent a young art student who needed to work part-time to cover her tuition, room, and board. She was not only a good typist, she was also a tall statuesque beauty with a fresh, ivory complexion and waist-length Titian-red hair. Fortunately, the other professor was gay, or a bitter battle might have broken out over who would court and marry her.

Allison (for that was her name) graduated with a Bachelor's in Fine Arts three days after her twenty-first birthday. That afternoon, Dr. Mason asked her to dine with him that night. She said yes. She also said yes when he proposed a month later, and by Christmas time, they were married and already expecting their first child, a son.

Daniel David Mason was born a couple of weeks after Labor Day, just as the new school term was getting underway, and as per the cliché, he was the apple of his parents' eye.

Despite their married happiness, Dr. and Mrs. Mason weren't without their worries. Even a full professor makes a modest salary. A stay-at-home housewife makes none. And a baby, even one as healthy as Danny, imposes an unending round of expenses. So Dr. and Mrs. Mason soon looked for some way to save money while still giving their son a good life. They didn't have to look far.

Mrs. Mason had grown up on a small farm just outside of Eugene. Many of the surrounding properties had been sold off to developers, but Allison's father genuinely loved the farming life and had refused to surrender his land. The frequent, heavy Oregon rains made for a short growing season, but with careful attention to drainage and selection of crops, he was able to produce bountiful harvests of fruit and vegetables each year.

So Allison asked her father and mother for permission to come live on the farm, and being doting parents who genuinely liked her husband, they agreed. Allison's mother was secretly glad to have her daughter back in the house again. Arthritis was making the household chores increasingly difficult, and getting up at dawn to feed the chickens and milk two nanny goats had lost its allure.

In time, Allison took over most of the cleaning, cooking, and baking, and as soon as little Danny could be trained to perform the tasks successfully, he got to feed the chickens, collect their eggs, and milk the two recalcitrant goats. These were not thankless jobs. Allison's mom was more than happy to baby-sit her grandson, giving Allison time to draw and paint, and the rambling old farm house was so big that Allison, her husband, and her son were able to have an entire wing of the place all to themselves.

Dr. Mason found the peace of the country very conducive to his studies. Before long, he was able to publish a textbook based on the content of the classes he taught. It found favor in the academic community and provided a small but steady stream of additional income for several years. It also led to occasional side jobs doing translation on a consulting basis. Thus, Dr. Mason found increased notoriety and success, and he was completely content to be living permanently under his in-laws' roof.

The Masons' life went smoothly for nearly two decades. Danny turned out to be academically gifted. He made it clear to his parents and grandparents that, when he grew up, he planned to leave the farm for good. One too many head-butts from the goats probably factored into this decision. But so too did his growing prowess as a computer programmer. It became clear that he was destined for a career as a software engineer—another language-based profession that clearly built upon the many long talks he'd had with his dad. Danny was accepted at Purdue with a full scholarship, and he left home at seventeen to find his own path in the world.

By this time, Allison Mason was thirty-nine, and she and her husband had long-since given up on the prospect of a second child. But to quote the title of Dr. Mason's favorite Bond film, "Never Say Never Again." The evening after their son Danny left home, Dr. and Mrs. Mason celebrated with a bottle of champagne, one thing led to another, and three weeks later, Allison Mason bought a pregnancy test kit and learned that she'd be bearing a second child after all.

By this time, Allison's mother was walking with a cane, and Allison's father had hired a couple of farm hands to do the planting, harvesting, and daily chores. But they were still game to help raise another grandchild and said so. Allison's mother began rubbing her hands with anti-inflammatory cream so that she could painfully and laboriously knit another baby afghan, and Allison's father went out to the woodshed and built a beautiful rocking baby cradle. Everyone looked forward to the new arrival and hoped that the baby would be sound and whole.

*   *   *   *   *

Susan's new parents were very different from Janie's. Not for them an amniocentesis and thoughts of terminating the pregnancy if the fetus had abnormalities... They understood as well as anyone the dangers of a late-maternal-age baby, but they were determined to see the pregnancy through, no matter what. They were also very much church-going folk, attending Methodist services every Sunday and sometimes twice on holidays. So what they did with their fears for their baby was pray. They prayed constantly. Up in Heaven, Nana sometimes had to figuratively cover her ears to shut out the din, they prayed so much. Oh how she wished she could communicate with them directly and tell them, "Enough already! My son Albert has checked out your situation thoroughly, and I can assure you: your baby will be born healthy!"

In the womb, Susan was already campaigning regarding the outcome of her birth. Like Janie before her, she took great pleasure in experiencing the development of her body and brain, but she was fundamentally unwilling to wait for that development to complete before she began making her wishes known. So she too prayed after a fashion. She would lie within her mother thinking, "My name is Susan Hanson! Name me 'Susan Hanson!' I want to be known as Susan Hanson!" She knew that, by doing so, she was fulfilling Raphael's misgivings regarding what she'd taken with her from her previous life, but she couldn't help herself. She had a very strong sense of identity, and that identity was tied inextricably to her previous incarnation as the soul-mate of Janie Hanson and Janie's other friend, T-bear.

At last, Susan's Birth Day came. Allison had had some complications during her pregnancy, so she'd had to spend the last four weeks in bed, but she managed to carry Susan to full term and deliver her via natural childbirth. As Nana had done for Janie, Nana attended Susan's delivery, but given that Susan entered the world in the way and on the day that God had intended, Susan had a slightly easier time of things. Allison's contractions forced Susan out into the light, the doctor cleared Susan's airway and slapped her backside, and a nurse cleaned Susan, wrapped her in a blanket and placed her in Allison's arms.

Allison looked down on her baby girl in a kind of awe. "Here she is!" she exclaimed to her husband. "Little Suzanne..."

Dr. Mason caressed Allison's face, brushing the sweat-soaked hair away from her eyes. "She's beautiful, Darling... absolutely perfect. Suzanne Allison Mason..."

Susan lay in her mother's loving embrace and thought, "Close enough. I can live with that." Then she gave a great gaping yawn and fell asleep.

* * * * *

The Masons took their baby girl home the next day and introduced her to her grandparents. They were as delighted to meet Suzanne as her parents had been. Allison's dad brought the cradle up to the Masons' bedroom so that Allison could have her baby within easy reach while she recuperated. Allison's mom defied everyone's expectations, dragged a rocking chair into the corner of the bedroom, and sat with her daughter, ready to run errands and provide care on a moment's notice.

As for Dr. Mason, he rearranged his class schedule so that he could still carry a full teaching load yet have more time at home. He spent many happy afternoons and evenings working in his study, taking frequent breaks to gaze down adoringly at his wife and child.

When Suzanne reached three months of age, old enough to have developed a more robust immune system, her brother flew home from Indiana for a two-week vacation before the start of fall term. Excited about having a baby sister at last, he stopped off in the airport gift shop to buy her a small teddy bear. Danny's grandfather had driven his old, slightly-rusted pickup truck all the way from the farm to the airport. He met Danny in Baggage

Claim and laughed when he saw his tall, gangly grandson toting a duffle bag and a stuffed animal. Danny grinned and said, "Cut me some slack, Granddad. I want to make a good first impression."

Danny and his grandfather made their way out to the parking lot, climbed into the truck, and headed up the highway toward the farm. They'd barely traveled a mile before the sky opened up, and they got caught in one of Oregon's typical downpours. Warm and snug in the cab, grandfather and grandson chatted desultorily as the windshield wipers swept back and forth at top speed. When they reached the farm, they turned off the road and lurched down the asphalt driveway to the house. Danny's grandfather let him out at the path leading to the front porch, then drove off to park the truck in the barn.

Danny dashed through the rain, up the front steps, and banged on the front door. His grandmother opened it and cried, "Get in here, Darlin', before you get completely water-logged." Danny dropped his duffle bag and the teddy bear in the entry way and gave her a hug despite his damp shirt and jacket. "Yes, yes, you're a good boy. Now go upstairs and get out of those wet things before you catch cold. You know you have to be healthy if you're going to hold the baby. Just hang up your clothes to dry on the shower bar over the bathtub."

Danny picked up his duffle bag and the bear and did as she'd told him. Not fifteen minutes later, he came down to the kitchen and cadged a cookie from the cookie jar on the counter. His grandmother was standing at the sink washing dishes, her cane leaning against a cabinet. "Not too many cookies now, Danny. We've been eating supper early because of Suzanne's schedule. If your mom can get to bed by 8:00, she can get some sleep before the baby cries and wakes her up in the middle of the night."

"OK, Grandma. I've just missed your baked goods. That's all."

His grandmother smiled. "Those aren't my baked goods you're eating. Oh, sure, they're from my recipes, but your mom made those cookies yesterday. She's already back on her feet and feeling fine."

Danny's mouth was full, and he was now holding a cookie in each hand, but he managed to smile and nod to show he was pleased by the news. His grandmother finished drying the last dish and put it up in the cabinet. "Danny, make yourself useful and go ask your dad if he's at a good break point. If you make the salad, and your father peels and microwaves the potatoes, we could have supper ready in an hour."

Danny swallowed the bite of cookie in his mouth and said, "Sure, Grandma." He left the kitchen and went upstairs, expecting to find his father in the study, but the room was empty. Danny headed down the hall, munching his final cookie, and peeked into the master bedroom. It was also vacant, so he walked to the end of the hall and stopped on the threshold of what had once been his room. It was completely transformed.

Suzanne's cradle stood in one corner next to the rocking chair. A changing table and a small bookcase stood against one wall, and Danny's father was wrestling with a crib that stood against the other. The crib's side was down, and no matter how hard he pulled and tugged, he couldn't seem to get it to latch in the upright position. Danny walked to his father's side. "Here, Dad. Let me do that."

His father stepped back and gestured at the offending piece of furniture. "If you can get that stupid thing to work right, then you're a genius."

Danny raised the side gate and supported it with his knee while he operated the catches at both ends. The side stayed up. Danny shook it and leaned on it a bit to make sure it would continue to meet the test. It did. "There you go." He looked around him at the pale pink floral wall paper and the lacy curtains at the windows. "Wow, Dad. Lots of changes..."

"I know. For you we did cowboys on horses. For her, well..."

"Dare I ask where I'm going to sleep tonight?"

"What? You don't want to crash on a bedroll in the barn?"

Danny laughed. "Granddad's last letter said the hired hands were living in the loft bedrooms." Decades earlier, Danny's great grandfather had partitioned off part of the barn's second story to provide lodging for a groom and a stable boy. The draft horses that had once worked on the farm were now a distant memory, but the loft apartments remained and had been put back into service.

"They are. Have no fear. Your granddad and grandma have fixed up their spare bedroom for you. If you can stand to look at Great Grandma's garish crazy quilt for two weeks, you'll be fine."

"I think I'll survive. I'll go fetch my duffle bag from the bathroom and take it to my room. By the way, where are Mom and the baby? I haven't seen them yet, and I'd like to say hello."

For a moment, his father looked perplexed. Then a light dawned. "I'll bet your mother took Suzy out to the barn to look at the chickens. That baby girl just loves our livestock."

Danny grimaced. "She's welcome to them. Growing up, I found the chickens completely boring, and if I never get bashed in the butt again by a pair of goat horns, it will be too soon."

His father laughed sympathetically and shook his head. "Sorry, son, but you know how it is. Everyone on a farm has to carry his own weight somehow, and those were the chores you could do."

Danny smiled wryly. "I know, Dad. I'm just glad I'm going to do something else for a living. Farming is hard work."

"And software engineering isn't?"

Danny's eyes lit up with mischievous glee. "Software engineering is *fun!*"

Just then, a call came from downstairs. "Yoo-hoo! Where's my Danny Boy? Come and see your brand-new sister!"

Danny and his father grinned at each other, left the room, and dashed downstairs. Danny's mother was standing in the entry hall shedding a wet yellow rain slicker. Her infant daughter rested against her body in a sling. Danny walked to his mother's side and kissed her on the cheek. "Mom, you look beautiful!" And she did— still tall and statuesque, her pale face still smooth and firm, and her hair still the glowing auburn of an autumn sunset.

Danny turned his attention to the round baby face peeking out at him from within her mother's encircling left arm. Little Suzy was comically her mother's miniature— lovely large hazel eyes, skin as fresh as dew-kissed flower petals, and a wisp of red-gold hair that promised to develop into Titian tresses in time. Danny bent down to get a closer look and said, Hello, Suzy. I'm your big brother Danny."

Suzy pulled her thumb out of her moist, rosy bud of a mouth and regarded him with a serious gaze. Then she thrust her thumb back into her mouth and shyly turned her face against her mother's side.

"Can I hold her, Mom?"

"Of course. Just let me get her changed into a clean diaper and her pajamas, and I'll bring her down to you. Go sit over there on the couch and put a pillow in your lap. I'll have her back in a jiffy, and you two can get acquainted."

Danny went and fetched a bed pillow and the teddy bear and made himself ready for this introductory visit. His mother was as good as her word and returned shortly with Suzy clad in a pink jump suit with feet, her diapered bottom disproportionately large and round. Allison lowered Suzy onto the pillow, being careful to support Suzy's head, and before Danny knew it, he was staring down into Suzy's eyes as she stared earnestly back into his. "Hello again, Cutie-pie. How come you look exactly like

Mom while I look exactly like Dad?—not that that's a bad thing... I just could have used some help attracting girls at school, and you look like you're going to turn out to be a real stunner."

Allison smiled at her two offspring. "She *is* awfully pretty, but then I'm biased. Don't sell yourself short though. Remember, I fell in love with your father because he was brilliant, but also because I thought he was really handsome."

"And I'm glad she did." Danny's dad entered the living room and sat down opposite the couch in an armchair. "What's that you've got there, son?"

"Oh! I almost forgot. I brought Suzy a small present." Danny reached out, picked up the teddy bear, and showed it to his father.

"Well that was nice of you."

Allison urged, "Well, go ahead... give it to her..."

Danny turned to look down at Suzy and showed her the bear. Suzy took one look at it, her eyes wide with alarm, and she shrieked in distress. Then she began crying with her eyes tight-shut and her balled fists waving in the air.

Astonished, Danny impulsively threw the bear across the room as far from his sister as he could get it. "I'm sorry. I'm sorry! Hush, Suzy!. It's all gone. See? It's all gone," he babbled, trying desperately to sooth her.

Allison intervened. "Here, give her to me." She picked up her daughter and began walking about the room, hugging Suzy to her with the child's face resting in the crook of her neck. "Shh-shh-shh, baby... Shh-shh-shh..."

Danny's dad stood up and went to fetch the bear. He picked it up and studied it, a look of bewilderment on his face. "This makes no sense. She loves the chickens. She adores the goats, and god knows they're not very prepossessing with those bar pupils and bad tempers. But she's terrified of a stuffed animal? Why?"

"I have no idea. But you have to believe me—I'm so sorry..."

Allison's efforts were taking effect. Suzy had stopped crying except for a few sniffles and a hiccup or two. "Sweetie, we know that, and it's not your fault. There's no telling how a baby will react to something new. Why I remember you were so upset by your first taste of oatmeal that you shoved the bowl violently onto the floor. Grandma had to mop the whole kitchen."

Danny's grandma poked her head in from the dining room. "I certainly did, and I'll remember that day for the rest of my life if I live to be a hundred. As you'll recall, Allison, it didn't just hit the floor. It spattered on the walls and cabinets too!"

Danny felt himself go red-faced. "Sorry, Grandma."

She limped over to the couch, drying her hands on her apron as she came. "Think nothing of it, Sweetie. It's all part of raising a family," and she kissed him on the top of his head. "Now, would you people do me a favor and come help me get supper on the table?"

Everyone walked out to the kitchen to do as she asked—all but Dr. Mason that is. He walked upstairs, taking the teddy bear with him, a look of thoughtful bemusement still on his face.

2: Suzanne Grows Up...

Suzy's early life on the farm was almost idyllic. Whenever Nana looked in on Suzy, she was pleased by what she saw. Suzy was surrounded by attentive family members—her grandparents, her mother and father, her brother whenever he came home from college, and even the farm hands when they could spare time from their duties. They all cherished her, protected her, and taught her a surprisingly wide range of skills—practical skills outdoors and in the farm house and academic skills including languages and art.

Knowing that Suzy was doing well went a long way toward reconciling Nana to her own situation. She'd become accustomed to speaking directly with Janie, and although she couldn't communicate with Rosa and the other members of Janie's family, she could hear about them second hand through the stories Janie told her. So watching Janie and her family was a very rich and rewarding experience.

Nana couldn't interact directly with Suzy however. Suzy's portal door was shut tight, and for all Nana knew, Suzy might not even remember that she had a portal. So all Nana could do whenever she watched Suzy was to give the child a warm feeling of perfect security and love, and if Suzy noticed—if Suzy somehow divined what that feeling meant—well, Nana might never know until Suzy returned to Heaven and Nana could finally ask Suzy what she recalled.

For Suzy's part, she spent so much time feeling perfectly secure and loved that she seldom noticed when Nana visited her. Oh, once in a while, Suzy would be playing in her room alone or out toddling about in the garden. Then, in the absence of any family members, she'd perceive the warmth that Nana conferred as something different, something special. But by in large, Suzy went about her day-to-day existence so contented that she was oblivious to Nana's influence, and Nana watched her, glad that all was going well yet feeling personally unfulfilled.

*   *   *   *   *

Suzy loved living on the farm. From the first, just as her father had observed, she'd absolutely adored the livestock. As a toddler, she'd pull herself upright by clinging to the heavy wire fence that surrounded the poultry yard. Then she'd watch the chickens for hours—their feathers gleaming each time the sunlight broke through the clouds. She'd gaze at them wide-eyed as they pecked and scratched, looking for insects, and she'd giggle happily at the sounds they made—cluck-clucking as they strutted about, their combs and wattles wobbling on their heads, and their bright little eyes peering this way and that. Suzy even liked their scaly, gray legs and feet and the way they'd sometimes pause in mid-stride with one foot held high.

Suzy wanted nothing more than to enter the yard and play with her feathered friends, so she was beside herself with joy when her mother took her into the pen one day, handed her a tiny tin pail of chicken feed, and showed her how to cast handfuls of grain around her, summoning the flock. Sometimes, a few grains of feed would fall on Suzy's shoes, and the chickens would lunge forward to peck up these stragglers, but Suzy was never startled or frightened. She might squeal in delight, scaring away a timid bird, but after a while, most of the flock came to accept her as a standard part of their environment, and some became so bold that they'd press against her legs, trying to knock the bucket of feed from her hand.

From feeding the chickens, Suzy graduated to hunting for eggs. After the grain was gone and the chickens had dispersed, Suzy would enter the chicken coop carrying a basket lined with an old dish towel. At first, her mother Allison would watch and give her pointers, but soon Suzy became quite clever at finding, not only those eggs deposited in the nests, but also the ones canny hens had hidden elsewhere around the yard and even in the barn.

Suzy's grandfather kept no roosters, so there was no need to candle the eggs after they were collected. Suzy would simply carry the basket into the kitchen and proudly present it to her grandmother. Neither Allison nor Grandma felt that Suzy had the fine touch required to polish the eggs, so Allison would usually perform that duty. But afterward, the two ladies were happy to give Suzy a treat and let her help them use the eggs that she'd just harvested.

Allison would place the family's unabridged dictionary on a chair and boost her daughter onto this high seat at the kitchen table. Then she'd tie another old dish towel around Suzy's waist like an apron. By this time, Grandma would have measured out all the ingredients for brownies, cookies, or some other batch of baked goods, and Allison would bring the mixing bowl to the table and hand her daughter a big spoon.

Suzy took her duty as cook's assistant very seriously. She would stir and stir until she felt like her arm was about to fall off and all the ingredients were mixed into a completely homogeneous batter or paste. Then she'd cry, "I'm done!" She'd watch attentively as her mother scooped the batter into buttered, floured baking pans or spooned little mounds of dough onto cookie sheets. The best part of the whole process came when the kitchen timer rang, and Allison would pull the finished baking out of the oven. The whole house would smell wonderful, and as soon as the pans cooled sufficiently, Suzy's grandmother would hand her a warm cookie or a brownie square to eat.

As Suzy grew older, her mother and grandmother gave her ever-more-challenging cooking tasks to do. When Christmas came, Allison mixed up a batch of molasses cookie dough and coached Suzy through the process of making gingerbread men. Suzy not only got to mix the dough, she got to roll it out on a floured cutting board and apply cookie cutters to make the different shapes—the little men, of course, but also gingerbread women, santas, reindeer, sleighs, Christmas trees, bells, and stars.

After the cookies came out of the oven and cooled, Allison helped Suzy mix butter and powdered sugar into a frosting and apply it to the cookies using a pastry gun. Suzy made faces and buttons on the gingerbread people, piping around the edges of the sleighs, and decorative squiggles on the bells and stars. She even used some of the frosting to glue raisin ornaments onto the Christmas trees. When she was done, the entire family gathered in the kitchen for cookies and hot cocoa, and Suzy received the grateful praise of her grandfather, father, and brother. It was a proud moment.

The following spring, Suzy made some progress out in the barnyard too. By this time, she'd learned a new trick with the chickens. They'd come to trust her so completely that she could quietly walk up to a hen and pick it up with her thumbs holding its wings to its sides and its legs dangling down between her fingers. Then she'd walk to a hay bale in the barn and sit down, placing the chicken on her lap.

The bird might cluck a few times in surprise, but not once did one try to escape. Instead, after a moment or two, the hen would relax, settling down onto her lap as into a nest. Then Suzy would begin to stroke it ever-so-softly between the wings with her fingertips. The bird would begin making faint little clucking sounds, its eyes would slowly close, and after a minute or two, it would go to sleep. Thereafter, Suzy could sit, gently petting the hen for as long as she liked, enjoying the silky-soft texture of its feathers and the warmth of its body against her legs.

One afternoon, Suzy was thus engaged in petting a chicken, when her grandfather caught sight of her. He walked to her side and spoke quietly. "That's quite a talent you've got there. Do you suppose you could hypnotize the goats too?"

Suzy lifted the hen out of her lap and carefully placed it on the ground. "I don't know, Granddad. Would you like me to try?"

"I sure would, Darlin'. We need the goats for milk and cheese, but I can't say as anybody on the farm has ever really warmed up to them. They're cussed creatures—stubborn and headstrong—and they made your brother's childhood a trial to him."

Suzy smiled. "I know. He's told me. Would you like me to try and make friends with them now?"

"Now or whenever you feel up to it. I've got to go see the hands about planting the vegetable garden. But the goats are out in their paddock, and if you're brave enough to go tackle them, I don't see how you could get hurt too badly. Mostly they'll just butt you with their heads. Their horns will leave bruises, but bruises heal." Suzy nodded to show she understood, and her grandfather left to go about his business.

Suzy stood a moment in thought, then headed out of the barn and down to the paddock gate. She peered through the rails at the two goats and considered the task she'd just taken on. She'd seen the goats before of course. In fact, she'd watched many times from across the yard as the hired hands tried to herd them out of their field and back into their stalls at sunset. Sheltering the goats in the barn was for their own safety, but the way they evaded the two men and fought back, you'd think the farm hands were trying to slaughter them.

The goats would dodge and weave until the two men lost their patience and used sheets of plywood to corner the beasts. Then each man would grab a goat by its horns and drag it—still bucking, kicking, and digging in its hooves—across the turf, into the barn, and finally, into its pen. Once there, the goats would suddenly discover the water and fodder provided for them and seemingly forget the whole ordeal. So by the time Allison came out to give them their evening milking, they always seemed to have gotten over all their objections. It was a nightly ritual that made no sense and gave everyone involved a royal pain, and Suzy hoped that, somehow, she'd find a way to put an end to it.

Suzy climbed up onto the gate and studied the goats. Both were large, brown and white, slightly-shaggy nannies—a young mother and her recently matured daughter. Together, they made a tight little herd of two, and so far they'd rejected every attempt to introduce a third beast, a stranger. The two goats were munching the grass that grew abundantly in their field, thanks to Oregon's even more abundant rain. They'd recently cropped one end of their pasture down to bare dirt, but Suzy knew that the grass would grow back in time. There was lots of land but only two grazers.

As she watched, one of the goats looked up from its feeding and caught sight of her. Immediately, its bar pupils contracted, and it bleated. The other goat promptly raised its head and fixed her with a stare that, even at that distance, looked hostile. The first goat charged with the second one following hard on its heels. The first goat slammed its head into the boards of the gate, and Suzy was hard-pressed to hold on, but she did. A second later, the second goat also butted the gate, even harder.

Suzy asked herself how the two beasts could run full-tilt into the gate and not damage themselves. After all, the boards were heavy and reinforced with two-by-fours. But the goats didn't even stop to shake their heads. They circled away and then charged again. Wham! This time, when they moved away, Suzy could see dents in the wood below her. Wham! She began to wonder how long they'd keep up this behavior before they realized how futile it was. The gate might be marred, but it was clearly going to hold up under the assault, and Suzy herself was in no danger of falling off her perch.

The goats charged her position two more times before they gave up and trotted off to a position about ten yards away. Then they turned and eyed her with distrust. Suzy called to them. "You know, you're just being foolish. I'm not going to hurt you, and if you keep this up, you'll get a splitting headache." One of the goats snorted, and the other shifted nervously on its feet. "We might as well be friends. After all, you need us to milk you and protect you, and we treat you pretty well given how you treat us." The goats bleated and shook their heads. "Oh, don't be silly!" Suzy threw her leg over the gate and dropped to the ground inside the paddock.

The goats backed away in alarm. For a moment, they both looked as if they'd like to bolt to the other end of the paddock, but Suzy stood calm and still, and after a minute or two, the beasts went back to staring at her. Suzy glanced at her feet and spotted a dandelion. Like everything else that grew in the paddock, it grew lush and green with plenty of tender leaves and golden flowers. Making sure to move slowly, she bent down, tugged it out of the ground, and held it out to the goats as a peace offering. The goats took one look at the plant in her hand, snorted, and backed away another few feet. Suzy simply stood her ground with the dandelion dangling from her outstretched hand.

She stood that way for at least two minutes, long enough that her arm began to ache. Then, just as she'd hoped, one of the goats, the smaller and possibly younger one, edged forward a step at a time toward the prize. When it finally reached Suzy, it reached out with its lips withdrawn, exposing yellow teeth, snatched the flower out of Suzy's grasp, and trotted briskly away.

Suzy watched as the goat devoured the dandelion, interposing its body between its prize and its companion. Suzy cast about her, spotted another dandelion, picked it, held it out, and made a soft, kissing noise with her lips. The second goat looked around, saw Suzy's offering, and trotted over to claim it. This time, Suzy held on, forcing the goat to snatch leaves and flowers off of the clump of foliage with its teeth. Only when it had almost denuded the plant did Suzy let go. By this time, the first goat had returned, hoping to get another treat.

Suzy began criss-crossing the field, avoiding piles of "goat patties," picking dandelions, and feeding the flowers to the goats. Before long, the beasts were quite happy to eat out of Suzy's hand, and she was able to get close enough that she could gently rub her thumb on their foreheads, making little circles right between their eyes. From there, she progressed to scratching them behind their ears and gently patting their flanks. And when sunset came, before the farm hands could arrive and ruin all her hard work, she made kissing sounds to the goats and led them, now docile and willing, back across the pasture, through the gate, and into the barn to their stalls.

As she closed the stall door behind the second goat, she looked up to see her grandfather smiling down at her. "Well done, Darlin'. Well done indeed! I'll go get your mother and tell her it's high time she teaches you how to do the milking. I'm thinking that the goats are going to be yours to care for from now on."

*   *   *   *   *

This event set a pattern. Curious to know what Suzy would prove able to do, all of Suzy's family members began setting challenges for her and then seeing how she would handle them.

Suzy's grandfather taught her to plant, tend, and harvest vegetables in the garden. When she mastered these tasks, he taught her how to climb a ladder safely, and under the supervision of the farm hands, she harvested fruit and nuts from the trees in the little orchard behind the house.

At this point, her grandmother stepped in. First, Grandma taught her to hull nuts. Next came instruction on how dry fruit, tomatoes, and peppers. Following that, Suzy learned how to make plum jam, peach preserves, and apple butter, as well as how to sterilize the jars in boiling water and cover the contents with a layer of molten wax to prevent spoiling.

Once Suzy was comfortable working with pressure cookers and double boilers, Grandma introduced Suzy to home-canning. Suzy learned how to pickle cucumbers, beets, onions, and other vegetables. That fall, she put up rows and rows of mason jars on shelves down in the cellar.

Finally, Suzy finished off her informal cooking course by learning how to make simple meals—breakfast fare such as hot cereal, pancakes, eggs and bacon, and hash-browns... lunches including all manner of sandwiches and casseroles... and suppers including hamburgers, sausages, roasts of all kinds, salads, and cooked vegetables. As part of this effort, Grandma insisted that Suzy learn how to bake for real, including making bread.

By this time, Suzy's parents had long-since contacted the local school district and registered Suzy as a home-schooled child. To follow recipes, especially for baked goods, Suzy would have to learn how to measure accurately and manage fractions. To understand fractions, Suzy would need a grounding in basic arithmetic. So at this point, her brother made his contribution. He wrote an application that would run on their father's home computer. It drilled Suzy on simple addition and subtraction, addition and subtraction with columns of numbers, the basic multiplication tables, multiplication of long numbers, short division, long division, and finally... fractions.

But because Danny was who he was (a software engineer), he wasn't willing to stop there. So the app. had user preferences that Suzy could set. The default base of the exercises might be base ten, but by changing those preferences, Suzy could also review the materials in base two, base eight, and base sixteen. She could even select a custom base such as seven, although that would be much less useful than the bases employed so extensively in computer science.

Suzy regarded the app. as a fun game to play, so she rapidly became proficient in simple math. She begged her brother to send her more such amusements, so he sent her textbooks on introductory algebra and geometry. Suzy seldom got stuck on the problems the books contained. But when she did, she found that her father was always able to help her find her way to the solution, and for his part, he enjoyed applying his teaching skills to help his daughter. Thus Suzy's education progressed well.

Dr. Mason had a sizable home library, and the whole family took turns teaching Suzy to read and write. Grandma proved to be especially patient and effective at these tasks. She started Suzy with her alphabet, progressed to spelling drills, and then introduced sentence diagrams as a way to instill proper grammar and punctuation.

Every step of the way, Suzy's family helped her to "walk before she could run." Once Grandma had taught her how to write good sentences, Allison taught her to create well-structured paragraphs. Once Suzy could write good paragraphs, her father taught her to craft rhetorically sound essays. And once she could express herself effectively in English, her native language, Dr. Mason helped her select classics of literature, read them, and write analytical critiques about them.

A day came when Suzy's professor father realized that, going forward, he would be hard-pressed to find enough new challenges for his daughter. He was reading a paper penned by his elementary-school-aged child, and it rivaled the work of some of his best college-aged students. Dr. Mason stayed up late that night talking with his wife about what they could do. The next morning, Dr. Mason and Allison embarked on a two-pronged approach. He began teaching Suzy to read and write German, and she began instructing Suzy in the topic nearest and dearest to her heart—fine art.

Suzy quickly proved to be a talented linguist with an unquenchable thirst for knowledge. To Dr. Mason's surprise, she also proved to be one of those unique people who can study multiple languages at the same time without getting them confused. Trying to fully engage Suzy's interests, Dr. Mason soon added Russian and

Romanian to the mix. Suzy seemed to pick up the Romance language as if she'd somehow heard it all before somewhere, and as for Russian, despite the different alphabet, before long she began reading works by Tolstoy and Turgenev that she found in her father's book case. Given how young she was, Dr. Mason judged at first that she might not understand all the nuances of their plots, but then she gave him critiques on what she'd read, and he had to give up that delusion.

During this period, Suzy enjoyed conversing with her father in her three new languages. She was polite enough not to do so in front of the rest of her family, for she knew that they wouldn't be able to understand. But she begged her father to put her in touch with other people who could, and Dr. Mason began taking her to the university from time to time so she could practice her conversational skills. At first, his other students treated Suzy indulgently as if she were some kind of class mascot. But when she whipped their behinds in the recitation sessions she attended, they had to abandon that stand and show her more respect.

Thereafter, if they wanted to talk privately among themselves in her presence, they would often resort to other languages that she didn't know yet. This practice irritated her, so she asked her father to teach her the rest of the languages in his repertoire. Presently, although English, German, Russian, and Romanian would always be her strong suits, she gained reading and writing proficiency in Polish, Czech, Slovak, and Hungarian as well.

The speed at which she absorbed these languages flummoxed her father and appalled his students. Unaware that she was acquiring these additional tongues, they'd continued speaking them in front of her until the day came when she decided to put them in their places by answering them in kind. After that, if students wanted to have a private conversation when Dr. Mason's kid was around, they'd leave the room altogether and check carefully to make sure the kid hadn't followed.

* * * * *

By the time Suzy reached the age of ten, she'd passed all her elementary school requirements, and her parents were debating whether or not they should send her to middle school. After all, she was living a somewhat unnatural life, surrounded entirely by adults of fairly advanced age. Her grandfather and grandmother were seventy-three and seventy-two respectively. Her mother was fifty, and her father was sixty-eight years old, a fact that ultimately made their decision for them.

For three years, the university administrative staff had been hinting gently that, in light of his advancing years, Dr. Mason might like to scale back the number of classes he taught, reduce the number of graduate students he supervised, and move gracefully toward the day when he'd become semi-retired as a professor emeritus. Whenever they raised the subject, Dr. Mason would hint somewhat less gently that age discrimination was against published university policy as well as state and federal law.

Dr. Mason was still in full possession of his mental faculties, and he still enjoyed teaching. The drive down to campus from the farm had become somewhat onerous, but he'd solved that problem by conscripting one of the farm hands to drop him off in the morning and pick him up at night. The drive-time cut into the farm hand's work day, but Allison was so committed to her husband's happiness and success that she agreed to step in and do some of the farm hand's chores.

So the stand-off between Dr. Mason and his employers continued unresolved until he came up with a brilliant idea. Throughout his career, he'd supplemented his income and kept his skills fresh by taking short-term consulting jobs on the side, especially translations of academic books and periodicals. Now he reasoned that he could boost his visibility in the academic community at large, and make himself indispensable to his immediate colleagues, if he increased the number of translations he completed. The question was how to do so given that he was already fully booked with classes, recitation sessions, and the translation commitments he'd already made.

The answer came to him in a flash one evening as he sat at the supper table across from his daughter. By that time, she was nearly as facile as he was with the languages he spoke. So during dessert, he asked her how she's like to make a little money for her college fund and help out her dad. She was naturally curious to learn how these goals could be achieved, and when he told her, she literally squealed with delight.

"Really, Dad? Translate real honest-to-goodness books and publish them? Will I get credit?"

Her father smiled. "Yes, we both will. You'll get credit for the initial translation, and I'll get credit for editing and quality-assuring your work. That way, you won't need to worry about making a mistake or mis-construing a passage of text. I'll be your safety net. What do you say? Are you game?"

Suzy exclaimed, "I'm in!" so he began to explain some of the realities of translation work. For one thing, knowing the language wasn't enough. One had to be able to understand colloquial as well as formal speech. For another thing, one had to become an expert on the subject matter of the work in question. For example, if one was translating a book on protein chemistry, one would have to make an in-depth study of that branch of chemistry to be qualified for the job.

Dr. Mason warned Suzy that, in the past, he'd translated works on world geography, the history of many ages and nations, every conceivable branch of science, classical and modern philosophy, great literature, and the arts. He pulled no punches and made clear just how much supplemental reading was required to do justice to the books he was addressing. Far from dissuading his daughter, however, this news seemed to excite her even more. She was eager to learn about the fields that he'd listed and quickly grasped that her work might open up even more fields to her view.

So the matter was decided. Suzy's parents notified the school district that she'd be home-schooled through middle school as well, and Dr. Mason put out feelers through his many contacts to attract more book translation business. Given his solid reputation as a linguist, the contracts rolled in, and before long, Suzy was in hog-heaven, delving into all manner of scientific and liberal arts topics.

That's not to say that her life was all work and no play. True, she still had no contact with people her own age. The youngest people she ever saw were her father's students (most of them in their early twenties), the farm hands (early thirties), and her brother (twenty-seven). Had she had less imagination, she might have concluded that she was simply the shortest person on the planet, like some kind of midget or dwarf. But Suzy read widely, including works by authors such as L. M. Montgomery and Louisa May Alcott, so she was familiar with the concept of childhood, and her mother Allison worked especially hard to ensure that Suzy would get to experience at least some of what childhood meant.

* 　 * 　 * 　 * 　 *

Early on, when Suzy was still a toddler, Allison would sometimes push the kitchen table against the wall, lay down an old plastic shower curtain as a drop cloth on the floor, and give Suzy sheets of butcher paper and bowls of tempera colors to use as finger paints. Suzy would play happily with these materials for hours at a time, producing paintings that surprised her mother with their composition and color balance. Suzy might end up wearing almost as much paint as she applied to the sheets of paper around her, and Allison might need to bathe her daughter thoroughly after every art session. But at night when the paintings had dried, Allison would carefully preserve them in plastic portfolio sleeves rather than taping them to the refrigerator door.

When her husband asked her why, she showed him Suzy's growing body of work, and he was just as surprised as she had been. Naturally, all the work was non-representational, but he saw similarities to the works of Picasso, Gauguin, Monet, Matisse, Mondrian, and Jackson Pollock. He knew these "influences" must be purely accidental, but nevertheless, they gave him pause—and Suzy never produced a single painting that was muddy, boring, or childish.

When Suzy's brother heard about her interest in art, he sent her a birthday present, a big box of seventy-two Crayola crayons and a dozen adult-level coloring books. At first, Allison put these gifts away. She believed that, at three years of age, Suzy was still too young for them and would simply scribble on the pages, ignoring the lines. But shortly after Suzy turned four, she spotted the box on the top shelf of her closet and asked about it. Allison didn't have the heart to lie about the box or withhold it, so she pulled it down off of the shelf, placed it in the middle of Suzy's bedroom floor, and let her open it.

Suzy loved Danny's gift. She spent the better part of an afternoon arranging the crayons in chromatic order in their box. The next day, she tackled the first picture in the first book. A couple of hours later, she brought the book to her mother and asked, "Can you help me take out this page and send it to Danny? I want him to know I like the books he sent."

Allison took the book from Suzy's hand and opened the cover. Suzy's execution of the design was flawless. Not once had she colored outside the lines, and more to the point, her choice of colors was subtle, inspired, and harmonious. Allison swallowed against a sudden lump in her throat. "Of course, Darling. I'll be happy to send this picture to Danny. If you like, I can add a 'thank you' note so he knows it's from you."

Suzy smiled, reached up, and hugged her mother around the waist. "Oh, yes, Mama. I'd like that a lot."

Over the next few years, Suzy gradually worked her way through all the books her brother had sent, and as she finished each book, her mother would add it to the growing body of work in Suzy's portfolio. In time, Suzy wore the crayons down to stubs, but their loss didn't trouble her because, in parallel, her mother was introducing new and even more wonderful art supplies.

As a professional fine artist, Allison had a vast array of media and materials in her studio. Right about the time when Dr. Mason decided to teach his daughter German, Allison began coaching her on how to use colored pencils, watercolors, and colored ink pens on acid-free drawing paper and illustration board. Almost immediately, Suzy began pushing the limits of these materials with the subjects and compositions that she chose. So Allison introduced Suzy to India ink, lettering pens, gouache paint, and dry-brush techniques.

These materials satisfied Suzy for quite a while, but eventually, she began to crave something more. She'd been browsing her mother's old art textbooks in the family library and wanted to be able to capture color in layers and show textures like the ones in the photographs. So Allison trotted out acrylic paints, prepared canvas boards, a palette and palette knives, and a selection of specialized brushes. Suzy was content with acrylic paint for a few months, but eventually, she became frustrated with how stark the colors were and how quickly they dried. Even when mixed with a medium to retard drying, they still resisted the kind of blending and layering that Suzy wanted to do.

Allison began to wonder if Suzy would ever be satisfied with any of the materials that fine artists typically used. She offered Suzy chalk, charcoal, and pastels, but Suzy rejected them all because they smeared. In desperation, Allison offered Suzy oil paints. She expected the experiment to lead to disaster. Oil paints could take weeks or even months to dry completely, many of the pigments were toxic heavy metals, and the turpentine and linseed oil needed to mix the paint frankly stank. But Suzy took to oil paints like a duck to water. She instinctively knew that she had to use them outside, or at the very least, in a well-ventilated room far away from any open flame.

With oil paints, Suzy seemed to find happiness at last. She salvaged many of the tools she'd used with acrylic paints, but she returned the remaining prepared canvas boards to her mother. To Allison's surprise, Suzy insisted on using actual canvas on stretcher bars, and she seemed perfectly willing to do the extra work of applying gesso to the canvases and letting it dry.

Suzy's first oil paintings were small studies of familiar scenes around the farm. To Allison's amusement, Suzy began with several portraits of the chickens in their yard. She did a good job of capturing the texture of their feet and wattles, the light glinting off of their feathers, and their bright little eyes. Next, Suzy took on the goats. She portrayed them grazing in their paddock, resting side by side on the grass in a splash of afternoon sunlight, and sheltering miserably beneath a tree in pouring rain. From the goats, Suzy moved on to even more challenging subjects—the farm hands working in the orchards and the vegetable gardens. She captured these scenes from a distance, so she didn't have to tackle human faces, only their forms, but she did a good job with their general anatomy, and the resulting pictures put Allison in mind of pastoral and agrarian scenes from the time of Constable.

After that, Suzy went farther afield, literally. She set up her easel on the drive leading to the farm house and portrayed her home, its Craftsman-era silhouette contrasting with the flowering fruit trees in the orchard behind it and the billowing clouds overhead. Next, she lugged her easel and paint box out beyond the paddock and portrayed the barn, its weathered red boards stark against the intense greens of the forest that bordered the farm.

Clearly, Suzy was searching for new subjects for her art, so the Masons began taking occasional road trips. In spring, they drove out to the coast and down to North Bend and Coos Bay. Along their route, Suzy got to marvel at the way the Coast Range was punctuated by waterfalls as Oregon's many rivers and streams spilled down the face of the mountains in their quest to reach the sea. Once on the coast, Suzy and her family climbed steep dunes of cream-colored sand; investigated coves filled with drift-wood, moonstones, and fossils; and strolled along the surf-line, listening to the boom and sigh of the waves. After that trip, Suzy returned home with enough photographs and memories to keep her busy for months.

Next, in fall, the Masons headed inland. Dr. Mason borrowed a tent and other gear from a colleague and took his family car-camping in the Coast Range and the Cascades. Suzy got the chance to explore the rain forest, picking and eating wild berries with her mother, finding exquisite white Trilliums on the mossy forest floor, and carefully stepping over black-and-yellow banana slugs so she wouldn't make a horrendous mess on her boots.

That trip was a great success right up to the last night. The Masons pitched their tent on a slight slope and carefully trenched around the uphill side, creating a channel to draw off any rain that might fall in the night. But even the best-laid plans can be thwarted if Mother Nature is sufficiently determined. The Masons were pan-frying hamburgers over an open fire when the skies opened up and drenched them in a torrential downpour.

Allison struggled to finish cooking their dinner while her husband stood over her holding an umbrella, but shifting winds kept blowing water into the frying pan, floating the meat patties off of its surface, and eventually, the rain simply put out the campfire altogether. At that point, the Masons retreated to their sturdy canvas tent and ate their cold burgers medium-rare. Then they shucked off their damp clothes, climbed into their sleeping bags and tried to get some sleep.

In the middle of the night, first Dr. Mason and then his wife awoke, ice-cold and shivering. The rain had continued unabated for hours, and water had streamed down the hill in sheets, overwhelming the water-break they'd built and saturating the walls and floor of the tent. Suzy, lying between her parents, was protected from the damp a little longer, but soon she awoke too, and with one accord, the Masons abandoned their sleeping bags, left the tent, and fled back to the car. There they sheltered until daybreak when the rain finally deigned to stop. Then, before the clouds could open up again, the Masons dashed out, struck camp, wrung out the sleeping bags as well as they could, loaded the car, and headed back toward civilization.

Along the way, they found a rustic roadside diner. Dr. Mason parked in its gravel lot, and the cold wet family went inside to have breakfast. That breakfast turned out to be worth the whole miserable experience—hot chocolate... large glasses of fresh-squeezed orange juice... eggs sunny-side up with ham, bacon, sausage, and hash-browns... waffles buried in strawberries and powdered sugar... and if the customers wanted, hot coffee or tea and a selection of muffins that one could take on the road.

The Masons sat in a booth by a window, feasting gratefully as their clothes and hair dried out. By the time they returned to their car, their good humor had been fully restored, and Suzy was already planning a painting in her head—not the towering pine and fir trees of their campsite, but a still life of the bountiful plates of food on their table.

For a time, Suzy feared that this grueling experience would convince her parents to give up on family excursions, but fortunately, Dr. and Mrs. Mason were able to put the memory behind them. Thereafter, Dr. Mason would rent a small trailer and tow it behind their SUV. Never again was he willing to risk camping out in the rain. But once he could assure his family of mobile shelter, he was ready to get back on the road.

The Mason's made their next trip the following summer. They drove through McKenzie Bridge, past the Three Sisters, to Bend. That trip was the first time that

Suzy had ever seen high desert, and she was astonished by the arid terrain and the huge, uninterrupted vault of azure sky overhead. Fortunately, she'd brought her sketch pad and some colored pencils. While her mother and father reclined in lawn chairs, soaking up the scenery, Suzy made nearly a dozen thumbnail sketches, plus photos, to remind her of what she'd seen.

Their next journey offered even greater novelties. They drove to Mount Hood, climbed the trail that led to the caldera, and marveled at its bleak, almost lunar landscape. After descending from the peak, they hiked up caves that had been formed by volcanic vents and spent hours afterward brushing the fine dust of volcanic ash from their shoes and pants legs. Suzy and her family found the volcanic desolation sobering. The Mount St. Helens disaster was fresh in their minds as it must be for all citizens of Oregon. So to counteract the vague depression that had come over them on the mountain, they drove back through Portland and stayed for a few days.

Portland proved to be an ideal antidote. Suzy and her parents found and photographed the city's three enormous city-block-sized fountains. They visited the science museum, the zoo, and the public rose garden at the city outskirts. Finally, they finished up with a day of window shopping. They found Portland to be eminently walkable and the people there very friendly. Admittedly, Suzy also found the city a bit overwhelming due to its size. It was the only true metropolis she'd ever seen, putting even Eugene to shame. But since it presented neither the concrete canyons of New York City nor the claustrophobia-inducing sprawl of Los Angeles, Suzy was able to bear up and enjoy the experience on the whole.

After returning from their Portland vacation, Dr. Mason and his daughter resumed their translation work, and in spare time between other tasks, Allison and Suzy began work on the paintings their trips had inspired. For a time, Suzy continued to produce mainly landscapes and still-lifes. But by the time she reached the age of twelve, she felt confident enough in her skills that she was ready to attempt some portraits.

She began with her grandparents. She painted each of them as they'd appeared in their youth, basing her work on faded color photographs from the family photo album. Then she painted them as they appeared in the present—a dual portrait in which her grandfather sat with his arm around his wife's shoulder. By that time, Suzy knew how to mix pigments in linseed oil to produce subtle color glazes. So in these portraits, light appeared to glint off her grandparents' eyes, her grandfather's cheeks showed a faint shadow of a beard, and a rosy blush touched her grandmother's lips and cheeks. It was the first time that Suzy had tried to do a life study, and she found the experience much more interesting than simply copying an image that someone else had produced.

The effects Suzy achieved were stunningly realistic, and Allison found herself comparing her daughter's work to that of European masters such as Rubens and Gainsborough. Allison toyed with consulting a gallery owner she knew about the portraits, but then she considered Suzy's age and sheltered upbringing, and she contented herself with getting the portraits framed and hanging them in the living room. There would be time enough in Suzy's life for the fame and acclaim that potentially awaited her.

Suzy's grandparents were pleased with their portraits to say the least. So Suzy decided to paint her parents as well. Again, thanks to old photographs, she was able to portray them as they'd appeared when young, and she did a joint portrait of them as they currently appeared. Given how busy her father was, she relied on a current photo for that effort, but her mother Allison agreed to sit for her portion of the portrait.

Suzy enjoyed painting her mother's portrait so much that she wrote to her brother asking when he planned to visit them again. She explained that she wanted him to sit for her, and to her delight, he replied that he hoped to spend two weeks with them at Christmas. Moreover, he hinted none too subtly that he might be bringing someone with him, and that he hoped Suzy would be willing to paint her likeness too.

This news sent the Masons into transports of joy. At twenty-nine, Danny had enjoyed gobs of professional success—a Bachelor's, Master's, and PhD in computer science and software engineering, all from prestigious universities, and a high-paying, influential job in California's Silicon Valley. But possibly because he'd always been so focused on his career, he'd never seemed to enjoy much success with the ladies. Now, he was holding out hope to his family that he might have found "the one" at last, and they were more than ready to welcome her into the family and celebrate the good news.

Suzy wrote back that she'd be glad to paint him and his friend. Then she turned her attention to painting a self-portrait using a mirror. The effort greatly increased her respect for Rembrandt and all the other artists who'd done the same, but in the end, she achieved a result that satisfied her. At that point, she decided to put aside her paints and brushes for a while and wait for Danny's visit, but evidently, the Universe had other ideas.

The very night that Suzy began what she'd intended to be a hiatus, she dreamed a vivid dream. In it, she saw herself in a mirror, not as she currently was, but as she might appear when all grown up. She had her mother's long, flowing Titian-red tresses and her father's straight, fairly pointed nose. Her hazel eyes were wide and intelligent, and her skin was a luminous ivory overspread by a faint, shell-pink blush. She heard a melodious voice say, "You must paint yourself like this someday..."

Enchanted by the image before her, Suzy reached out her hand to touch the glass, but as her fingertips brushed it, it rippled like the surface of a pond, and when the ripples cleared, the image in the glass was completely different. It showed a slightly built girl in her late teens or early twenties with curly brunette hair and a rosy, tanned complexion. For a moment, her brown eyes regarded Suzy with a wistful expression. Then she bent down, picked up a worn teddy bear and an old rag doll, turned, and walked away into the distance.

The next morning when Suzy awoke, the dream was still completely clear and fresh in her mind. When Suzy came down to breakfast, she asked her parents, "By any chance, did I ever have a teddy bear or a rag doll when I was little?"

To her surprise, her father frowned and then stood up and left the table. He returned a few minutes later holding a small teddy bear. It was in such good condition that it might have been new. He handed it to her. "When you were just three months old, Danny gave that bear to you as a gift, but it seemed to frighten you somehow, so I put it away until you were older, and I just never got around to giving it to you until now. I hope you'll forgive me for the oversight."

Suzy examined the bear. It was nothing like the larger, more sophisticated stuffed bear in her dream. But Suzy was a polite child. "Thanks, Dad—for keeping it for me and for giving it to me now."

"You're welcome."

Suzy set the bear aside until after she'd finished breakfast. Then she took it upstairs, and when her father went to call her to come start their work day, he found her roughing in the outlines of yet another portrait, but one unlike any painting of hers that he'd seen yet. Even at that stage, he could tell that Suzy was painting a young girl sitting with a teddy bear and a rag doll. Obviously, Suzy couldn't possibly be portraying such subjects from memory, so he concluded that she'd finally branched out and was now painting scenes from her imagination. From one perspective, he was right of course, but from another, he couldn't have been more wrong.

3: Suzy Saves Her Family...

Albert was beside himself. "Janie, Janie! I need to speak to you. Please come right away."

"I'm here, Uncle Albert. What's wrong? Why do you need to talk with me so urgently?"

"You spoke to her... to Suzanne, I mean. You can't do that! You'll get us all into terrible trouble!"

"Oh, Uncle Albert, it's no big deal. First of all, I spoke to her while she was asleep and dreaming. I'm certain that she construed what I said as something produced by her own subconscious mind. Second, you've told me that, despite Raphael's guidance, she chose to remember T-bear and me. She chose to remember that she'd had soul-mates. So we're embedded deep in her mind and spirit, and given that we're already in there somewhere, one brief contact doesn't really change anything. Third, how do you know that anyone saw or heard what I did? I was very careful and very quick. It's like you told me at the outset. We have to be secretive, but if we are, we can still get away with me keeping in touch."

Albert passed his hand over his face and prayed for patience. "Nana saw you, and Nana instructed me to warn you not to do the same thing again. She can't be sure that her boss won't be checking up on her, on you, on the whole situation..."

This view gave Janie pause. "The head Watcher is still watching?"

"From time to time... He does quality assurance checks. You can count on it, especially since you worked all those miracles and came to his notice."

"I'm still working miracles, Uncle Albert. You know I am. I do a healing every day. Are you telling me that I need to stop?"

Albert sighed. "No, Sweetheart, don't stop. I can't be sure, but I think Uriel wanted the healings to continue, and in any case, spontaneous remissions were happening even before you intervened."

"But not as many."

"No, not as many, but that's a risk that Nana and I still believe is worth taking."

Janie pursed her lips in thought before speaking. "I'm sorry I upset you and Nana. I just wanted to see how Suzanne was doing. After all, it's been more than twelve years, and she was my dear friend... in some ways like a daughter to me."

Albert nodded sympathetically. "I know, Sweetheart, but you have to trust Nana and me. We'll let you know if she's in trouble in any way, and until she is, we all need to back off and let her live her own life, her new life. That was the agreement we all made the day when Gabriel reclaimed Susan's and T-bear's souls."

Janie began to cry softly at the memory of that loss. "I know, Uncle Albert... OK, I won't talk to her again, but can I just reach out and touch her soul from time to time? I'll be so quick. She won't even notice it."

"Now, Janie, you know that's not true. She will feel it, and because she took the memory of soul-mates with her, she may eventually realize what she's experiencing, abandon her current life course, and go off in a futile search for you and T-bear, ultimately ruining her life. That isn't what you want for her, is it? It can't be."

Janie was crying now in earnest. "All right. I'll let her be. But please, I'm counting on you and Nana. Watch over her, protect her, and guide her. Make sure that if she is suffering for any reason, you let me know right away."

"I will, Janie. I promise. Now go tuck your soul back into your body, little one, and try to have a good rest of the day."

*   *   *   *   *

Suzy worked on the portrait of her dream visitors for nearly a month before it satisfied her. The painting was the most difficult one she'd ever attempted. The dream was still surprisingly clear in her mind, but she had no photograph, no physical model, no point of solid reference that she could consult. She could only record as faithfully as possible what she remembered and then live with the result for a day or two, evaluating how the content of her canvas still fell short of the image she was trying to capture.

She never achieved perfection, but after approaching it asymptotically, she did reach a point of diminishing returns. There came a day when she woke up in the morning, took a long look at what she'd produced, and exclaimed, "Close enough!" That day, she set it aside to dry, and once it did, she asked her mother to help her get it framed so she could hang it on her bedroom wall.

By this time, Allison and Suzy had become very close through their shared passion for fine art, and Allison was happy to help her daughter get the framing done. She was extremely impressed with Suzy's first "fantasy" composition. The painting included many quite challenging features—the silky ringlets surrounding the girl's head, the plush fur on the body of the teddy bear, and the lace adornments on the dress of the rag doll.

Allison also noted that Suzy had used several techniques from eighteenth and nineteenth century portraiture. For example, Suzy had placed a tiny crimson dot at the corner of each eye to make them look brighter, and she'd used a pale blue wash over most of the whites of the eyes so that the stark, white highlights would stand out better, making the eyes look as if light was reflecting from their moist surfaces.

Allison liked the painting so much that she bypassed the simple, modern wood frames she normally favored and went for a wide antique frame of gilt and carved wood. When she saw the painting surrounded by all that splendor, she was glad that she'd gone to the extra expense. The painting was obviously important to Suzy. Her daughter had invested heavily in producing it, and the result was worthy of an old master. It deserved a regal setting.

When Allison got the framed painting back from the shop, she carried the heavy package from her car in the barn, into the house, and up the stairs to Suzy's room. Then she fetched a hammer, a level, screw eyes, picture wire, and a heavy-test picture hook. She used the screw eyes to affix the wire to the back of the frame. Then she measured where she wanted the picture to hang and drove a nail into the wall, securing the picture hook. Next, Allison hefted the heavy frame and held it slightly above her head, maneuvering until the wire caught on the hook. Once it did, she slowly lowered the frame until it rested flat against the wall, and she used the level to make sure the frame was hanging straight.

Allison stepped back and sat down on Suzy's bed to examine the result. She was pleased with the painting's position, but suddenly, she felt rather tired. Perhaps she should have waited and asked one of the farm hands to help her carry the heavy package into the house. She'd meant to return the tools to their tool box right away and go back to doing her chores. But the longer she sat, the more she feared that she'd pulled a muscle in her arm or chest when she lifted the frame onto the hook because she was beginning to feel sore.

Allison began rubbing her shoulder and pectoral muscles, hoping to relieve the soreness. Suddenly, she stopped and gently ran her fingers over her chest wall. There was a lump—not a big one or a hard one, but a lump all the same. She felt a chill go down her spine. She probed around the edges of the lump and tried to tell herself that it could be anything. It could be a lipoma or some other kind of benign cyst. But what if it wasn't?

As a farmer's daughter, Allison had always been a tough realist who believed that it was better to know the truth rather than to live with self-delusion. Marshaling her energy, she stood up, gathered up her tools, went downstairs, and put them away. Then she climbed the stairs again and went to her husband's study. There she found him poring over a passage of text with Suzy. "Darling, I need to talk with you." Suzy stood up to leave the room and give them their privacy, but Allison waved her back into her seat. "You need to hear this too, Sweetie. I'm afraid I've found a lump in my breast. I need to go see the doctor right away."

Suzy watched as her father's face went gray. "Suzy, go find one of the hired hands and tell him to bring the car around. Then go ask your grandma to call the doctor and make an emergency appointment. Fortunately, it's still before noon. He should be able to work us in before the end of the day."

Suzy did as she'd been told. She moved and spoke as if trapped in some kind of nightmare. Her secure and happy world had just shattered, and nothing seemed real anymore. When she told the farm hand to bring the car, he dropped his tools where he stood and ran to comply. And when she passed the message to her grandma, she watched for the second time as an adult, one of her caregivers, reeled from shock and struggled to rise to the demands of the moment.

Suzy left the kitchen as her grandmother dialed the phone. She reached the front door just as the farm hand roared up in their SUV. She held the door open as her father walked toward her, his arm around his wife's waist, and in the absence of any direction to the contrary, Suzy slid into the back seat of the car beside her mother before her father closed the car door.

Their trip into Eugene didn't even register in Suzy's memory. She was too frightened by the thought that her mother might be deathly ill. Their family doctor ushered them into his exam room minutes after they arrived. Clearly, he was as alarmed as they were and had postponed at least two other appointments to make time for them. He thought to ask if Suzy should go out and wait in the waiting room, but Allison said no, that she needed her whole family around her. So the doctor did a preliminary exam and then told her with a grave face that he thought the lump might well be cancer.

While they sat there, stunned and grieving, he went to order a CT scan with contrast and a biopsy for her at the local hospital. For several minutes, they could hear his voice rising and falling in his office down the hall. When he returned, he said, "Well I do have *some* good news. The oncology surgeon has had a cancellation and is willing to see you in two hours. He can do a needle biopsy and get it to Pathology right away. As for the CT, Radiology has agreed to work you in at the end of the day. The scan is scheduled for 8:00 PM. I know that's late, but because the lump is big enough to be palpable, we don't want to take the chance that it will undergo metastasis if we wait. So let's move fast and get this thing taken care of."

Allison nodded with tears streaming down her cheeks. Her husband wrapped his arms around her and held her head to his chest. Suzy suddenly felt as if she was somehow superfluous or in the way. Never before had she experienced so acutely how strong the bond was between her parents. She couldn't imagine how her father would carry on if her mother died. The realization could have been devastating, but Suzy was her mother's daughter. She drew herself up to her full height and swore a private oath—that she would be there for her parents no matter what happened. She would support them as they had always supported her, no matter what that might take.

Suzy watched as the doctor reached out and shook her mother's and father's hands. Then he placed a hand on each of their shoulders and said, "The hospital will notify me of the results as soon as they come in. Remember, I'll be here for you every step of the way. Good luck."

Suzy and her parents left his office and walked out to the car. The farm hand had been taking a nap in his seat behind the steering wheel. He awoke with a start when they opened the car doors and climbed inside. "Where to now?" he asked.

Suzy's parents were dumb with grief, so Suzy answered. "The hospital. I think we're going to be there until at least 9:00. Maybe you can go get some dinner and then come back."

"Do you want me to get something for you guys too?"

Suzy shook her head. "I don't think we're going to have much of an appetite, and Mom can't eat before her CT." The man pursed his mouth in grim resolve and started the car.

The drive to the hospital seemed to take almost no time at all, and because they had an appointment, they were able to get directions to the correct floor and fill out the intake paperwork fairly quickly too. More than once during that process, Dr. Mason thanked his lucky stars that he was still a full professor at the university. By that time, he was covered by Medicare of course, but he'd retained medical insurance through his job for both of his dependents, and now Allison was really going to need that coverage.

The needle biopsy and blood draw went smoothly and caused her little pain. The CT scan was relatively painless too and didn't upset her given that she didn't suffer from claustrophobia. To be on the safe side, her doctor had ordered a full scan from the crown of her head all the way down to her mid-thigh. If she'd already undergone metastasis, he definitely wanted to catch it now.

As Allison was leaving Radiology, she asked one of the technicians how soon the results would come back. He told her, "We typically post them in twenty-four hours, but if there's a significant finding, we'll inform your doctor immediately, and he'll call you to discuss the results."

Allison nodded in dumb misery, and her husband encircled her shoulders with his arm. Together, Suzy and her parents made their way back out of the hospital to the parking lot. There in the distance they spotted the farm hand waiting in their SUV. Suzy told her parents, "Wait here. I'll go get him." She jogged across the lot to the car, knocked on the driver-side window to get the man's attention, and when he let her into the back seat, she instructed him to drive to the row where her parents stood, saving them the long walk.

Before long, they were speeding up the highway on their way home. As they pulled into the yard in front of the house, Suzy thought she'd never been so glad to see it despite the fact that, in one dreadful afternoon, nearly everything in her life had changed. The hired hand dropped them off at the front porch and then drove away to park the car in the barn. Suzy and her parents climbed the steps to the front door, and as her father fumbled with his keys, her grandma opened the door to them and ushered them inside. "I've left a pot of hot soup cooking on the range. Suzy, be a good girl and dish up bowls-ful for your mom and dad. I've got to go to bed."

Suzy did as her grandma had asked, and before long, she and her parents had filled their stomachs, and her parents had gone off to bed. Suzy stayed up to put the pot of soup away in the refrigerator and wash the dishes. Then she went up to bed too. As she changed into her nightgown and pulled the covers up to her chin, she said the most heartfelt prayer of her life. "Dear God, please help my mama get well, and please help my whole family to stay strong. I promise to help all I can. Just please let me know what I need to do. Amen."

*   *   *   *   *

The next twenty-four hours were beyond hard. Suzy's whole family held their breath, waiting for the doctor to call. Finally, the phone rang, and Suzy's father answered it, putting it in speaker mode so that everyone could hear.

The doctor got right to the point. "Allison, I'm afraid you do have cancer. The pathology report shows a stage 2 carcinoma of the right breast. The cancer hasn't spread to any lymph nodes yet, but the tumor is just large enough to qualify for stage 2 status."

Allison started crying, so her husband spoke for her. "Why didn't anyone catch it earlier? She had a mammogram just six months ago, and the results were negative."

"Carcinomas of the breast are fairly rare and hard to diagnose because, initially at least, they're soft. Usually, mammogram technicians are seeing sarcomas, which are hard and show up better on a scan. The important thing is that we've caught it now, and we should begin treatment right away.

"Now you do have some options. The safest course is to get a full mastectomy. Later on, once you've recovered fully, you can see a plastic surgeon to get the breast reconstructed. However, you need to know that a mastectomy is pretty invasive, has a long recovery period, and can lead to complications like post-surgical infection and skin death due to reduced blood supply.

"The second option is a lumpectomy followed by radiation therapy. I've consulted the hospital's oncologist, and for this type of cancer, he recommends targeted radiation treatments five days a week for six weeks. These treatments are done on an outpatient basis, so you'll need someone to drive you to Radiology every day and take you home again. Treatment time is usually about half an hour, but you may need to sit in a waiting room if the treatment facility gets backed up. And be clear... Radiation treatments will take their toll over time—first- and possibly second-degree burns on your skin and a sense of muscular weakness or exhaustion that will grow until you may need help to stand and walk.

"The recovery time for radiation therapy is usually two to three months after cessation of treatment, and depending on how much radiation your oncologist prescribes, you may have as much as a two percent chance of getting some other cancer later due to your radiation exposure. On the plus side, however, radiation therapy continues to work for as long as six months after treatment ends. So even if micro-tumors still remain *in situ* afterwards, they can succumb and disappear as the body's immune system does clean-up in the area during the healing process.

"In any case, regardless of which surgical option you select, you may need to undergo chemotherapy to kill any cancer cells that are floating free in your body. If so, your oncologist will select the best chemotherapy agents for your particular type of cancer and the frequency at which they must be infused. You'll need a caregiver to accompany you to the Infusion Center too, and although your oncologist will try to adjust the dose to match your tolerance level, you're almost certain to experience nausea and vomiting down the road, so anything you can do now to gain weight will be good."

At this point, Suzy's grandparents were crying too. Her father managed to choke out a question. "How soon does Allison need to have the surgery?"

"The hospital can schedule her appointment as soon as she tells them which option she prefers. I'd recommend getting the surgery done within the next few days. We don't want to give the cancer a chance to spread to her lymph nodes, or worse yet, her liver, lungs, or brain."

Allison's tears were streaming down her face, but she clutched her husband's hand for strength and managed to blurt out, "I want the lumpectomy."

"OK then, I'll call the hospital and let them know. You should hear from Scheduling by the end of the day. In the meantime, try to get some rest, hydrate, and eat a good diet. I know it's hard, but every little bit you can do to improve your health now is valuable.

"By the way, regarding diet, there aren't many scientific studies to back up what I'm about to say, but anecdotal evidence shows that cancer cells live almost entirely on carbohydrates, especially sugars, so if you can stand it, switch to a diet high in protein, fat, and cruciferous vegetables. Patients who do this seem to have a better long-term outcome. On the other hand, during the worst of your chemo treatments, eat anything that will go down and stay down. I knew one patient who survived for four weeks on ice cream and pretzels. I told her, if that's all you can eat, then eat as much of it as you can, and she pulled through.

"Oh, one more thing... About vitamins, antioxidants are normally quite good for the human body, but your radiation oncologist may tell you to stop taking them during treatment because they interfere with its effectiveness. If so, do what he says. And I can't believe I'm going to say this, but try to avoid stress."

Startled, Allison burst into satirical laughter. When she could catch her breath, she asked, "What relaxes me most, Doctor, is doing my art projects. What do you think? Can I continue my work?"

"Yes, as long as you stay away from toxins and carcinogens. Your liver and kidneys are going to be struggling to deal with the chemo drugs and the by-products of your other treatments. Don't over-tax your body's clean-up crew."

"So no paints, but some nice pencil sketches should be OK."

"Precisely. So... any other questions? Because I've given you a lot to think about, and I'd really like to go call the hospital and get things rolling. If you come up with other questions later, we can always talk again. Like I said, I'll be here for you."

Allison sniffled and said, "That's fine, Doctor. Go make the call, and thanks for giving us so much information. We're grateful for your help." They all heard the doctor hang up, and Suzy's father pushed the button on their phone to end the call.

Allison, her parents, and her husband continued to sit around the kitchen table, probably lost in gloomy thoughts. But Suzy excused herself and went upstairs. The first thing she did was to pack her paints and other supplies back into the case where she usually stored them. Then she pushed the case to the back of her closet. Next, she went to her mother's studio and gave it a thorough cleaning, packing up most of Allison's supplies too. Before Suzy left the studio, she placed a pad of illustration paper on the drafting table that served as her mother's work surface, and she laid out pencils, pens, and drafting tools as a kind of gentle encouragement. Finally, she returned to the kitchen, and striving to sound helpful and calm, she said, "Hi, Grandma. It's almost time to start supper. What can I do to help?"

Allison started to rise from her chair. Fixing supper had become her nightly responsibility, but her husband put a gentle restraining hand on her shoulder, and Grandma rose from the table instead. "I'll get a chicken ready for roasting. If you like, you can peel some carrots and chop some onions to go in the pan. Then you can make a tossed green salad. Wash and shred the lettuce, cut the tomatoes, and slice up a lot of that purple cabbage to go on top. Next, cut up some apples and cheese for dessert..."

In less time than it takes to relate, Allison's mother and daughter were working side-by-side to get the evening meal on the table. Allison and her husband left the kitchen to get out of the way, and Allison's father saw the wisdom of their actions and followed. So Suzy, young and spry, and Grandma, hobbling painfully due to her arthritis, finished the job, and once supper was served, the whole family sat down and forced themselves to eat a hearty meal. After all, hard days were coming, and they needed to fortify themselves for what lay ahead.

*   *   *   *   *

Five days later, Allison had her surgery. The surgeon got good margins on the tumor, and the hospital discharged her to go home the next day. Her oncologist told her that she'd be given four weeks to recover before she started radiation therapy. Initially, she had a drain, but her surgeon removed it by the end of the week, leaving her with nothing but some bruising and some pain. Her doctors offered her prescription pain medication, but she opted for Tylenol instead. She didn't want to risk an opioid addiction, and she was mindful of what her family doctor had told her about protecting her liver.

Tylenol was only able to reduce Allison's pain, not eliminate it completely, so raising her arms to pull garments over her head became impossible. Her mother came to the rescue. Grandma approached Suzy one afternoon and said, "Sweetie, I need your help to bring something down from the attic." Curious, Suzy followed her grandmother up the narrow stairs that led to the top of the house. Her grandmother stumped about in the near darkness for a while, carrying a flashlight and her cane. Then she exclaimed, "Ah-ha! There it is. Suzy, come and fetch that case there on the end table. Be careful. It's heavy."

Suzy hefted the case and followed her grandmother out of the attic and down the stairs. When they reached Grandma and Granddad's spare room, Grandma gestured that Suzy should put the case down on the desk beneath the window. Then Grandma hobbled over, unfastened the latches at the sides of the case, and said, "Boy, I hope this thing still works. It's been up there rusting and gathering dust for who knows how long. Take the cover off, Darlin', and let's see what we've got."

Suzy grasped the handle and lifted, and an old Singer Featherweight sewing machine came into view. Her grandmother bent over it and examined it in the sunlight streaming through the window. "Looks OK..., and the cord's in pretty good shape all things considered. Go ahead and plug it in, Sweetie. It's time I taught you how to sew."

Suzy's grandmother was as good as her word. Suzy pulled up a second chair so that Grandma could sit beside her and coach her through what she had to do. Under her tutelage, Suzy learned how to clean and lubricate the machine, thread it, replenish and replace the bobbin, and sew straight lines on a sample piece of fabric. As soon as Suzy could do that much, Grandma bade her stand up, go upstairs, and fetch a few of her mother's flannel night-gowns. When Suzy returned, Grandma led her to the kitchen, cleaned off the kitchen table, and showed her how to lay out and mark the gowns with a narrow scrap of soap.

Grandma marked the first gown straight down the middle of its front. Then she took a pair of sheers and carefully cut along the line she'd made, opening the gown like a coat. "OK, Darlin'. Now we go do a quick machine hem on both sides, and I'll teach you how to sew on snaps."

Suzy cried, "Oh, I get it. Mama won't have to raise her arms any more because we can help her put on the gown like a blouse and then use the snaps to close it."

Her grandmother beamed and patted her approvingly on the shoulder. "I'm sorry to put so much of the work on you, Sweetie, but with the arthritis in my hands, I can't even hold a needle anymore, and your mother needs these garments altered right away."

"No problem. I'm happy to help." And she was. Every day seemed to bring some new task that Grandma devised for Allison's comfort and care, and Suzy became Grandma's other pair of hands, enabling those tasks to be accomplished. Suzy had always been eager and quick to learn, and she was now more glad than ever that it was so, for she'd had no idea just how many skills her grandmother had yet to impart. Now they must transfer that knowledge under great time pressure because the four weeks flew by, and Allison would soon begin her radiation treatments.

*   *   *   *   *

Albert and Nana stood at Nana's work station, watching as Suzy made lunch for her family all by herself. Albert remarked, "She's taken over almost all of her mother's work and a lot of her grandmother's too. How is this impacting her father and grandfather?"

Nana looked pensive. "Well, the family has lost a little income because Suzy no longer has time to help her father with his translation work. But so far, he's been able to compensate and honor all his contracts. All he does these days is teach class, supervise his students, and translate books at home. He no longer has time to help his father-in-law with the farm at all, and it's sad, but he scarcely has time for his wife or daughter either. He's desperate to keep his job and his clients. His family needs the money and health insurance to cover Allison's bills."

Albert's brow wrinkled with worry. "So who's nursing Allison?"

"Her mother and Suzy. Suzy's grandfather is supervising the farm hands full-time, and he's had to resume doing some of the chores himself. They're putting quite a strain on his heart. He's almost seventy-six years old, you know. I'm worried about how vulnerable this family is becoming. If either Allison's mother or her father dies, I fear that the other will follow soon after. And we already know that Allison won't beat this cancer. So when she goes, her parents may go too due to their grief.

"I haven't looked into the terms of the parents' will. I assume it provides for their son-in-law and granddaughter in the event that they alone survive, but frankly, I can't see how Dr. Mason could run the farm himself. He's a professor, not an experienced farmer, and Suzy is far too young to take on that kind of responsibility. They'd probably have to sell or lease the land and move somewhere else. I think that so many losses in such rapid succession could be a terrible blow to Suzy's soul. I'd hate to see such a sweet girl become embittered or depressed."

Albert nodded sadly. "Loss of faith..." he murmured. "Despair is a pitfall that few humans can avoid completely." Nana sighed, and the two angels stood silent for a moment. Then Albert asked, "What's happened as a result of Suzy's prayer?"

"It's been answered, and much sooner and more positively than a lot of prayers I hear. She prayed that her family would be strengthened, and they have all found ways to rise to the challenge. In fact, they're all growing spiritually by leaps and bounds. By the time Allison dies, they'll all be absolutely formidable. Suzy also prayed that she be shown what she needed to do to help, and that is exactly what her family members are doing. Even her mother's doctors are instructing her in what she needs to learn."

"But what about the third part of her prayer? She prayed that her mother would be healed."

"I know, but that isn't according to God's plan, and as a result, I'm afraid we're really in for it. Suzy and her entire family have been praying for a cure non-stop, and now they've referred the matter to the minister of their church."

Albert shrugged. "So? What do we usually get from such referrals? 'We pray that so-and-so be healed... Lord, hear our prayer...' It happens only once a week and lasts seconds—hardly what I'd call an onslaught."

Nana fixed him with a reproving stare. "Not this time, son. This morning, the minister turned around and referred the matter to the entire congregation and their extended families. He's created a vast prayer circle, and many members have already started praying for Allison several times a day. You and I both know that one can't petition the Lord with prayer, but these people sure are trying. Their incessant demands are going to drive me crazy, yet for their prayers to be answered, we'd need a miracle."

Nana had been gazing off into the middle distance as she spoke those words, so she missed the expression that passed over her son's face. "Yes, we'd need a miracle..." he murmured. He stood a moment in thought. Then he said, "Thanks for talking, Nana, and thanks for watching Suzy and her family. I've got to go back to work, but I hope to visit again soon." Nana turned and smiled as he left. Then she turned her gaze back to the girl on the farm.

*   *   *   *   *

Allison's doctors were worried. Her cancer treatment wasn't going as smoothly as they'd hoped. Her surgical incision healed on schedule, but she continued to experience pain in the area. Her surgeon checked, but she didn't seem to have any infection or underlying necrosis. He could only assume that he'd inadvertently cut some nerves while excising the tumor, and if so, the pain would continue until the nerves knit together, a process that could take six months to a year, assuming it ever happened at all.

Next, Allison completed the planned course of radiation. Fortunately for her, the hospital had recently acquired a new treatment machine. Essentially a computer with a sophisticated positioning system, it did a far better job than the old machine of controlling the radiation dose. It even used baffles to confine the beam to the exact region that needed to be targeted as the machine rotated around the patient.

Nevertheless, Allison did suffer burns. Her skin proved to be far more sensitive than most patients', and after a couple of weeks, it began peeling off in sheets, leaving her with open lesions that had to be covered with burn ointment. And because of the progressive weakness, she had to be supported whenever she got out of bed to use the facilities.

Needless to say, except for trips to the hospital and the bathroom, Allison was essentially bed-ridden. Down in her study, the sketch pad and colored pencils waited in vain, for she simply didn't have the energy to draw anything. To distract her daughter from all the pain and embarrassment, her mother sat and read to her by the hour, and whenever Suzy could spare time from all her new responsibilities, she'd come upstairs and visit too.

Suzy was the one who laundered sheets and remade the bed. Suzy was the one who made sure the vase in the corner was always filled with fresh flowers and foliage from the garden. Suzy was the one who made up the trays of food and carried them upstairs. But it was Grandma

178 G. C. Ellis

who sat and endlessly coaxed her daughter, for it was the chemo that took the greatest toll. "Here, just one bite. No, no, now swallow! Good. See? All done. You don't have to take another bite for five whole minutes!"

Suzy became adept at blending up high-calorie, nutrient-rich milk shakes. At night after her father had gone to bed, she'd use his computer to scour the internet, looking for suitable recipes. Because Allison was slowly starving to death... If she tried to swallow more than a scant mouthful at a time, not only would she lose what she'd just swallowed, she'd lose everything she'd eaten in the past hour or two. Her liver and kidney numbers were getting worse by the week as her body began consuming itself to make up the nutritional deficit, and Allison's once statuesque frame was turning into a living skeleton—a skeleton from which strands of red hair fell away whenever Allison shifted position on her pillow.

Sometimes, Suzy would enter the kitchen late at night and find Grandma crying over the sink. At others, she'd go out to the barn to feed the chickens and fetch the eggs, and she'd find Granddad sitting gray-faced on a hay bale, his hands clenched in front of him in an attitude of prayer. And always, when Suzy saw her father, his face bore the haunted look of a man in torment, and he walked with the unconscious shamble of a zombie. Never had Suzy prayed so often or so fervently. She prayed for her entire family... her mother most of all of course. But the pain in her household was an almost palpable thing, and she longed with all her heart to see it evaporate and give way to the kind of happiness they'd once known.

During this period, Suzy really had only two consolations. She knew that the people at church were all praying for her family too, and better still, her brother took to calling every evening—sometimes for a few minutes... sometimes for an hour—just to cheer up whoever was free to pick up the phone and talk with him. One of the farm hands even rigged up a sling to hold the phone receiver next to Allison's ear so that she could talk with her son without having to support any weight.

Suzy was amazed at how good a job Danny did of focusing their chats on uplifting and light-hearted topics. Only once, when he knew that Suzy was the only one on the line, did he drop pretense and ask her how she thought their mother was doing. Suzy told him the doctors' latest assessment, and she heard him choke back a sob. She guessed that, could she have seen his face during those calls, she would have seen him struggling to put aside his own grief and fear to be there for those he loved. "Do you think she's going to make it?" he asked.

"I don't know, Danny. We're all praying, but she's not doing well."

"And she's suffering. I can hear it in her voice." He paused. "Is there anything she needs? Anything at all... I can send money. I've made lots of money, and I don't really have any way to spend it."

"I can't think of anything—except prayers... more prayers. We need a miracle, Danny."

Danny was silent for a minute. Then he spoke more forcefully, as if he'd just come to a decision. "I'm going to take a leave of absence from work and come home. I can help out on the farm... take some of the burden off your shoulders and Dad's. I wouldn't have waited this long except that I was finishing up a delivery for a major customer, and if I'd walked out before completing their release, I wouldn't have had a job to come back to..."

"I understand, and I'm sure Mom and Dad do too, but come home soon, Danny. I'm afraid, and I don't want you to get here too late."

Danny choked back another sob and said, "Me neither. I'd never forgive myself. That's why I've decided not to wait for Christmas vacation as planned. Look for me tomorrow or the next day at the latest. Tell everybody that I'm coming, especially Mom, and promise Grandma that I'll come alone so I won't be any trouble. I can bring a bedroll and doss on the couch if I have to... Be brave, little sister. Your big brother will be there soon."

"I'm so glad, Danny. Good night."

"Good night," and he hung up.

*　　*　　*　　*　　*

Albert stood by the door of Janie's portal filled with misgivings. Again and again, he knelt down, meaning to call her, but he'd always hesitate and stand up again. "What's the risk?" he asked himself under his breath. "She'd do two things, either or both of which might attract the Watchers' attention. If they did see her, they'd probably cut her off for the rest of her life, and I'd find myself infusing souls into microbes for all of eternity." Albert shuddered.

"But what if they didn't see her, or more to the point, isn't that a risk worth taking?" (Albert found that he was reduced to arguing with himself...) "I promised Janie that I'd let her know if Suzy was ever in trouble, and in such circumstances, could either one of us live with ourselves if we didn't do what we could to help out? For that matter, isn't spiritual growth in part about being willing to sacrifice oneself for others, and who's to say that someone in my position can't continue to grow spiritually?"

Having bolstered his courage, Albert knelt down and called, "Janie, please come quick! I need you!"

Janie didn't answer immediately, and it took Albert a moment to figure out why. It was after midnight her time, and she was sound asleep. He called again, a little louder this time, but still softly enough that he hoped he wouldn't jolt her awake. "Janie! Come quick! Suzy's in trouble!"

Albert heard a rustling as Janie turned over in bed. Then he saw a piece of her soul appear at the gap in her portal door. "What was that, Uncle Albert? Did you say Suzy's in trouble?"

"Yes, her mother's dying of cancer, and I need you to... I need a special miracle."

"How special?"

"I think the only way you can find her mother in time is to go through Suzy herself, so forget what I said about not touching Suzy's soul. I need you to touch her, to instruct her in fact, so that she leads you to her mother and you can do one of your healings for Allison."

"And if we get caught?"

"My whole family will defend you, but I was telling you the truth. The consequences could be dire. The archangels might seal your portal for the rest of your Earthly life."

"But if we don't do this..."

"Suzy could lose almost everyone and everything she loves."

"It's a no-brainer then. Wish me luck, Uncle Albert. I'm sure you'll know before I do what the outcome is."

* * * * *

Far across Heaven, the archangel Uriel had just called a meeting of the entire Watcher community. They all grumbled a bit at the inconvenience, but as Uriel began his opening remarks, he absolutely saturated them in his radiance, and they soon forgot, not only their objections, but everything else, including their normal duties. Uriel's remarks were lengthy and replete with abstruse details, so it was a good long time before the meeting broke up, and the Watchers were able to return to their stations...

* * * * *

"Suzy... Suzy, wake up and go to your mother. Go to your mother and take hold of her hand. Do it now!"

Suzy awoke from a dream in which she'd been hearing a beautiful voice. She sat up crying tears of joy, but she also felt a driving sense of urgency. She must go to her mother. She must take her mother's hand. She must do this immediately!

Suzy threw back the covers and swung her feet out of bed. As she was padding down the hall to her parents' room, she was suddenly gripped by a fear that the dream was some kind of premonition, and the reason she had to rush to see her mother was that her mother was about to die. Suzy opened her parents' bedroom door and tiptoed to her mother's side. Her father lay in the dark on his back, breathing softly. By the moonlight streaming through a gap in the curtains, Suzy saw that her mother was sitting up in bed awake.

"Suzy, what are you doing here?" her mother whispered.

"I had a dream. Can I sit with you for a while? Can I hold your hand until I feel better?"

Allison sighed. "Sure, Sweetie. Try not to wake up your father though. He was exhausted when he came to bed. Just sit here beside me on the coverlet, and I can hold your hand if you like."

Suzy sat down and took hold of her mother's hand. Immediately, she felt a jolt like some kind of energy pass through her, and then something powerful and completely unexpected took place. It was if Suzy could see herself from outside... her mother, herself, and the girl from her painting, all bonded inextricably together, surrounded and permeated by an intense golden light. The light flowed through Suzy's dream girl into Suzy, and from Suzy into Allison, and something about it seemed strangely familiar.

Allison sat with her eyes wide, unable to let go of her daughter's hand... scarcely able to breathe. Suzy felt her mother's pain and her fear of impending death. Suzy sensed every broken element in her mother's body. She sat and witnessed as the light seemed to knit up Allison's tissues. She served as a channel until her mother was strengthened and healed. Then the flow of light abruptly ceased, the girl of her dreams disappeared, and Allison dropped her hand with a gasp, leaving Suzy spiritually elated but physically and emotionally exhausted.

Shakily, Suzy stood up, bent, and kissed her mother on the forehead. "Thanks, Mom. I feel better now, and I hope you do too. Rest well. I'll see you in the morning."

Suzy returned to her room and climbed into bed. That night, she got the first truly restful sleep that she'd had since her mother's diagnosis. Something told her that her prayers had just been answered at last. Somehow she knew that her mom would now be OK.

4: Suzy Deals With the Aftermath...

Up in Heaven, Albert and his family were holding a family meeting, and for the first time, Albert had called it, not Nana or his dad. Albert's sister was also present. A child-angel, she normally watched birds, and frankly, she wasn't paying much attention to the proceedings. She'd been watching a nesting pair of bald eagles, and their chicks were about to hatch, so she was pretty distracted.

Albert was inexperienced at leading meetings, and it showed. He arrived at their rendezvous point with a topic, but no formal agenda. Then he greeted them nervously with one of the most lame openings that a meeting chairperson can possibly use. "You're probably wondering why I called you all here today."

Albert's father smiled and shook his head indulgently. "Just get to the point, son."

Albert cleared his throat in embarrassment. "Well, Dad, I wanted to let you know that... that..."

Nana tried to help Albert come to the point. "What have you done now, and how does it affect your father's work?" Albert's father had risen through the ranks to become head of Receiving, the cadre of angels who welcomed the souls of the dead into the afterlife, and Nana reasoned that, if Albert wanted to speak to both a watcher and a receiver, then he must have made another blunder of some kind.

"I, uh, I wanted you to know that Allison Mason won't be arriving here as planned. She's had a spontaneous remission and..."

"Her family has been saved!" Nana couldn't help herself. She burst into a spontaneous hymn of joyous praise to the Almighty, which caused Albert to experience a paroxysm of alarm.

"Shh... Mom, please! No one can know because..."

"You worked an unauthorized miracle," his dad finished.

"Well, not me exactly," Albert said, abashed. "I asked a friend to do it, and she obliged, even though she'd be running a great personal risk because..."

"She's still incarnate and not authorized to perform miracles either." Albert's dad closed his eyes, pinched the bridge of his nose, and sighed in resignation. "I don't suppose we know the name of this mortal miracle worker."

Nana was still so filled with joy that she could hardly contain herself, but at least she'd stopped singing. "I think I can guess, and I'm betting you asked to see both of us because, in addition to giving your father this news, you also want me to watch and make sure that there's no negative fallout, either for Allison and her family or for the miracle-working mortal in question."

"Who shall remain nameless..." Albert's sister had just joined the party for real, startling the rest of them with her unlooked-for interjection.

Albert nodded his vigorous assent. "Yes, who *must* remain nameless for her own protection. She only intervened because of, well, my angelic intercession, and I'd hate for her to suffer as a consequence."

Nana frowned in thought. "As I predicted, we've been receiving an absolute onslaught of prayer on this very subject. Literally hundreds of people have been praying that Allison be cured and her family be protected, uplifted, and supported. It seems to me that you had every reason to intercede. Just think what would have happened to that community's faith if you hadn't."

Her husband objected. "Albert may have helped preserve their faith, but at what cost? Suffering is allowed to exist in the world because it leads to spiritual growth. Allison and her family were fore-ordained to suffer, and those in their prayer circle were intended to learn an important lesson about prayer, namely that sometimes we don't get what we ask for because we're asking for the wrong thing."

Albert didn't want to disrespect his father, but he couldn't let these remarks pass without some attempt to refute them. "I see your point, but I can't agree that it's germane in this circumstance. Allison and her family *have* suffered—terribly!—and I'm certain that they've all grown spiritually as much or even more than our Lord intended. And as for the congregation of their church, what would you expect them to pray for? That Allison would die quickly and as painlessly as possible? That wouldn't be natural... That her family would recover from grief swiftly and move on as if they'd experienced no real loss? They're not that insensitive or self-involved. Allison is an unusually loving person, as are her family members, and they were looking at a tragedy that would have torn them apart."

Albert turned to Nana. "You said it, Mom. Allison's death would have destroyed them, causing her parents to die too, and maybe even her husband, leaving little Suzanne an orphan. How could I just stand by and let that happen?"

"You couldn't, son. I know what your father just said, but I'm sure he understands, and I definitely do."

"And so do I," his sister chimed in. Her hatchlings had shed their egg shells successfully, and she could now pay more attention to the proceedings before her.

Albert's father looked pensive. "OK then. Are we all in agreement on what must be done next?"

Albert took command of his meeting at last. "Here's what *I* want you all to do. Dad, I want you to simply omit any mention of Allison's recovery in your reports. To protect our mortal miracle worker, we need the miracle to go unnoticed for as long as possible. Mom..."

Nana's expression had suddenly gone blank as if she was focused inward, reliving some memory. "Uriel!" she exclaimed.

"What about Uriel?" her husband demanded.

Nana began laughing softly. "Son, I don't think there will be any long-term adverse consequences, even if this miracle does come to light. I think at least one archangel is backing your play, so to speak. So don't worry. I'll continue to watch everyone involved, and I'll let you know immediately if I see any reason for concern."

"And so will I." Albert's sister smiled at her family members' surprise. "What? My birds are all doing pretty well given the environmental crisis, so I'm sure I'll be able to work some humans into my schedule."

"Thanks. Thank you all." Albert felt a great sense of relief steal over him, knowing that he'd have his whole family's help. "Now, what's the appropriate way to end a meeting?"

"Well, Albert, you could do a lot worse than to follow Uriel's example of the other day. He just told us, 'God bless you and all your endeavors,' and then he disappeared." Nana chuckled again at the memory. Albert was still too awkward to have mastered the art of vanishing, but Nana was both proud and relieved to know that an archangel had his back.

*   *   *   *   *

The morning after Allison's midnight healing, she awakened famished for the first time since she'd started cancer treatments. Overjoyed by this change, her husband leaped out of bed and ran to find Grandma and Suzy. Grandma was so relieved that she collapsed on a kitchen chair and broke down crying. Suzy, who was understandably far less surprised, took over and swiftly whipped up a nutrient smoothy. While her father took the cup upstairs to his wife, Suzy kept on going, making up smoothies by the quart, knowing that her mother might need them soon.

Suzy was betting that her mother would be craving solid foods before too long, but from all that Suzy had read during her research, the human body couldn't digest solid food efficiently right after a long period of starvation. Some of the intestinal fauna and flora would have died and would have to be replaced. Also, the liver and kidneys would need a chance to regenerate and resume full function. So Allison would have to go through a carefully controlled bootstrapping process if she was to regain her health in an optimum fashion.

Upstairs, Allison took the cup from her husband's hand and sipped cautiously. Her nausea had completely vanished, and she no longer had to take a sip, suppress her gag reflex, wait for her stomach to settle, and then take another sip. She drained the cup in a series of quick gulps. As soon as she finished, she handed the empty cup back to him and said, "That was good. May I please have another?"

Astonished, he took the empty cup downstairs and into the kitchen. He was even more astonished when his daughter silently handed him a second cupful and took the empty cup to the kitchen sink to wash it.

Meanwhile, Grandma had pulled herself together. She was bustling around the kitchen, her arthritis forgotten, and she was talking to herself under her breath. "Bone broth... That will help, or better yet, chicken soup made with the whole chicken... and carrots and parsnips... or will that be too much fiber too soon?"

She pulled a big cast iron dutch oven out of a cabinet, set it on a back burner on the stove, poured in several cups of water, and started it heating. Next, she took a whole chicken out of the refrigerator, washed it, laid it on a cutting board, and chopped it up for soup meat. She put the bones in the water to boil and returned the meat to the refrigerator. Then she pulled out celery, carrots, parsnips, cabbage, and onions. These she chopped also, and to speed the cooking process, she put them in a glass casserole dish with a lid and steamed them in the microwave oven. Still on the fence about the fiber question, she took the soft-cooked vegetables and ran them through a blender before pouring the slurry into the soup pot. The kitchen was beginning to smell wonderful.

All that morning, Allison sat upstairs in bed consuming smoothies, while downstairs, Grandma boiled the chicken bones until nothing was left of them but calcium. Then she strained out the bones, fine-minced the chicken meat, and threw it into the pot. By that time, as Suzy and Grandma had predicted, Allison was asking for something more substantial to eat. However, although the soup was coming along, it still had a way to go before it would be ready to eat, so Suzy and Grandma went upstairs to help Allison get out of bed.

Suzy might be virtually certain that her mother had been cured, but that didn't change the fact that Allison had undergone severe muscular wasting. Suzy and Grandma had to brace Allison, one on each side, as she walked to the bathroom. There they helped her to bathe, wash her hair, and change into clean clothes— for the first time in weeks, something other than the nightgowns with snap closures that she'd worn for so long.

Once Allison was back in bed, comfortably attired in a soft flannel shirt and sweat pants, Suzy went to get her a bowl of hearty chicken soup on a tray. Allison took one bite and exclaimed, "Oh, Mom, this is the best soup I've ever had in my life!" At that, Grandma began crying again, and smiling with tremulous lips, she dabbed the tears from her eyes with the corner of her apron.

At that point, Suzy suddenly wondered what had become of her father, so she went in search of him. She found him standing beside her granddad under a big tree in the yard. The two men both had their hands folded before them, and their heads were bowed in silent prayer.

Suzy hated to interrupt them, but she'd already realized that something must be done if her mother was to stay on the road to recovery. Her surgery and radiation treatments were behind her, but her chemo treatments were on-going, and in Suzy's view, they needed to stop right away. But that would mean convincing Allison's doctors that a spontaneous remission *really had* taken place. The question was how to convince them, and whatever approach Allison and her family decided to take, they must buy into that approach unanimously. So Suzy approached her father and gently tugged on his sleeve.

Dr. Mason muttered, "Amen," and turned his attention to his daughter. "What is it, Suzy? Is Allison still doing better?"

"Better, Dad? She acts like she's feeling completely well. But we all know that won't last if she goes to her next appointment at the Infusion Center. We need to decide what to do because I'm afraid that, if she takes anymore chemo drugs, she'll simply get sick again, starve, and die."

Suzy's granddad clutched at his son-in-law's sleeve, his face the picture of anxiety. "But what if it's the chemo that's making her well?"

Suzy's dad shook his head. "I don't believe that, and I don't think you do either. But really, it doesn't matter what you or I believe, or what your wife thinks or Suzy either for that matter. The decision is really Allison's. Her doctors and her family have been trying to save her life, but instead, we've all been watching as she wastes away.

"Maybe she'd need the chemo to extend her days on Earth, but if so, we have to ask what her quality of life would be. Perhaps a better course would be to put her in hospice care and let her die with dignity. Yet after what I saw this morning, I can't help thinking that, maybe, just maybe, a miracle has occurred, and she really is suddenly better. If so, Suzy could be right. We need to talk. We need to ask Allison what she wants to do and agree on a plan. Ultimately, the potential risks and rewards are hers."

Granddad nodded, and the three of them walked back to the house. They reached it just as Allison finished her second big bowl of soup, this time with noodles. She wiped her lips on a napkin as her family entered the bedroom. "That was delicious, but I was wondering if I could have some scrambled eggs with dry toast next." She looked up, saw their expressions, and asked, "What? What is it?"

Suzy spoke first, surprising everyone. "Mom, I can't tell you how glad I am that you're feeling better. But we need to have a family meeting. For one thing, we need to know what you think about continuing cancer treatment. For another, we need to plan what we're going to do as a family going forward."

Without hesitation, Allison pushed the tray off of her lap and onto the other side of the bed. Then she threw back the covers and slowly swung her legs out of bed. "You're right, Sweetie, and you can't all stand around the edge of the room like witnesses at my wake. Help me downstairs to the dining room where we can sit together in relative comfort. Bring a pillow, put it behind my back, and I'll be fine."

Allison's husband stepped forward to help her stand up, and the rest of the family moved in a slow procession out of the bedroom, down the hall, down the stairs, and into the dining room as she'd suggested. Only Suzy ran on ahead to produce the requested eggs and toast.

Shortly after Allison took her seat, Suzy placed the plate, flatware, and a napkin in front of her. As the key decision maker for their discussion, Allison had taken the armchair at the head of the table. The rest of them arrayed themselves down both sides with Suzy in the other armchair at the foot. As Suzy's dad tucked the bed pillow behind Allison's back, she murmured, "I wish Danny could be here too."

"Don't worry," her husband told her. "He told Suzy that he'll arrive later today, and we won't do anything without discussing it with him first."

As soon as they were settled, Suzy surprised her family again by broaching the first discussion topic. She felt none of the insecurity that Albert had experienced... "Mom, I don't think you should have any more chemotherapy treatments. I don't think they're helping you. I'm certain that they're hurting you, and I believe there's a good chance you don't even need them anymore. The problem is, if you want to stop treatment, how do we convince your doctors that you're truly well? We don't want them to think that you're just giving up because then they might give up on you in turn."

"Good question, Sweetie. I don't want my doctors to give up on me. First, they warned me that, after all the radiation I've had, I've got a two percent chance of getting some other cancer in the future. If I do, I want them to be fully committed to helping me diagnose and beat it. Second, they also warned me that, even after five years when a breast cancer patient is theoretically in remission, breast cancer can return any time within ten years after the initial 'cure.'"

Dr. Mason spoke up. "I think the only way to convince them that you're truly well is to use the tools they'd choose to use themselves—PET scans and high-resolution CT scans. You could ask that, before you continue chemotherapy, you be scanned from head to toe. If there are any cancerous cells in your body, other than isolated individual cells I mean, they should light up on the PET like a Christmas tree, and the CT should show even tiny tumors."

Allison was looking thoughtful. "If my scans are clear, that should satisfy them about existing metastases, but one of the purposes of chemotherapy is to mop up free-floating cells that can lead to metastases later."

Grandma snorted in derision. "So their attitude is 'Better safe than sorry.' But we've been dealing with an entirely different kind of 'sorry.' For weeks, I've practically had to beg you to eat every bite of food you've consumed, despite all their talk about how well you've been tolerating your treatment protocol. I've had to sit at your bedside and watch as my daughter dies. Well, I think the 'cure' is worse than the disease. I'll tell you what. Let's stop the chemo, give you a chance to recover from all this 'medicine' they've been pumping into you, scan you regularly, and then, if more tumors crop up, we'll deal with that eventuality when we come to it."

She held up a restraining hand. "Yes, I get it... By the time the next scan happens and the tumors are found, we could be facing more surgery, radiation, and chemo—the works... But in the meantime, Allison will have had many more good days. She won't have been lying upstairs in her bed, or worse yet, a coffin." Grandma closed her mouth with a snap and folded her arms over her chest.

Granddad shifted uncomfortably in his chair. "Refresh my memory. How much do PET and CT scans cost?"

Suzy's dad shook his head. "A lot. Each one costs around ten thousand dollars. Her radiation treatments were nearly two thousand dollars apiece, and she had thirty of them. The only reason we're not bankrupt is that she still had health insurance through my job, so all we've had to pay this year is the 'maximum out of pocket charge,' seven thousand dollars."

Granddad's face went pale. "That's still a lot of money, son. I don't imagine that even a tenured professor makes much. How have you been able to afford it?"

Dr. Mason glanced at his daughter. "Some came from savings and some from consulting fees. For the savings, I have you to thank. We've lived with you for years, and you've never charged us a penny in rent. As for the consulting work, I wouldn't have been able to get or fulfill even a fraction of the contracts if I hadn't had Suzy's help."

Grandma spoke up. "Why on Earth would we ever charge you rent? You're family, and I can't tell you what a blessing it is to have your help and Allison's around the house and on the farm."

Suzy added, "And I'm happy to help too, Dad. Translation work can be a lot of fun."

"I'm glad you feel that way, Suzy, because you were right earlier when you said that we needed to come up with a plan for our future. Because I do have tenure, I can probably keep the university administrators at bay as long as I can think straight and carry out my teaching duties. But one of these days, I'll be too old, and they'll force me into retirement. Eighteen months later, Allison and Suzy will lose their university health insurance, even if they're still young enough to be eligible."

Dr. Mason turned to his in-laws. "And despite your decades-long generosity, Allison and I were never able to save much. I'll try to bring in more translation contracts for as long as possible, but old age and mental fog may thwart me there too. Frankly, until the recent scandals regarding Russia and the Ukraine, I was seeing my client list begin to thin out. But now, it's like it was back before the end of the Cold War. Anyone able to translate languages from former Eastern Block countries can get work and command a good salary."

Suzy tilted her head to one side. "So what do we need to do?"

"I could contact a gallery and sell my paintings," Allison offered. "That might help us rebuild our war chest."

Suzy seconded the notion. "I could sell some of my art too."

Dr. Mason smiled a bit sadly. "These are good ideas, and we can't afford to let any good idea go by. But we're going to have to make more changes still to make things work long-term." He turned to his father-in-law. "You're now seventy-five, and even with the two farm hands, running the farm is becoming a bit challenging. I think it's time we hire a farm manager who'll live on-site. If we're lucky, he'll have a wife who can help Allison and her mother with the housekeeping and chores."

Suzy protested, "I can help Mom and Grandma around the house."

Dr. Mason shook his head with regret. "You're going to be too busy, Darlin'. We'll come to your part in a minute."

Granddad was frowning. "Live on-site? Where?"

Allison suddenly sat up straighter and exclaimed, "Oh, I know. There's that old stone dairy down the hill. It hasn't been used since Grandfather got rid of all the dairy cows. We could renovate it... add a kitchen and a bathroom... There's plenty of space, even if we divide it up into several rooms."

Her mother was nodding her assent, but her father still looked unconvinced. "You have to spend money to make money in this world, and aren't we struggling with the fact that we don't have enough money as it is? Where are we going to get the cash to buy materials and pay for the construction? For that matter, how are we going to pay this farm manager and his wife, and don't say mortgage the farm! My father sold those dairy cows to pay off the mortgage once and for all. The best gift he thought he could give me was unencumbered land."

Suzy's dad hastened to reassure him. "We're not going to mortgage the farm. Put that notion right out of your head. We'll pay the man and his wife out of farm proceeds, but that should just motivate him to do his job right and make this place continue to show some kind of profit. What I was thinking was that Suzy and I could make the money to pay for the building materials, the farm hands could be pressed into service as construction labor, and you and I could act as supervisors and oversee their work."

Granddad stroked his chin thoughtfully. "We'd need plans... plans that would get the county's approval and pass inspection."

"Then Suzy and I will need to pay for an architect as well."

Allison pushed back her now-empty plate. "This plan is risky."

Her husband regarded her sadly. "Risky is all we've got. Your parents are in their mid-seventies, and thank god they're still in good health, but they won't last forever, and neither will I. I'm not much younger than they are. Any one of us could have a stroke or a heart attack at any moment, and we've already had cancer in the house. If we make sure the farm will continue, then whoever remains will still have food and a home no matter what happens.

"I pray that you really are well, Sweetheart, and if you are, you can help with household chores, make and sell art, do all the things you've offered to do today... But we've already discussed how uncertain your future will be, even if you have kicked your original cancer. You'll need those scans, so you'll need health insurance, and to secure that, we'll need a 'belt and suspenders' approach. We just can't rely safely on my job anymore. Danny has offered to help, but maybe that won't be enough. So that's where Suzy comes in."

Suzy started. She'd almost thought he'd forgotten her. "What must I do, Dad?"

"A lot of things... I know you're not yet thirteen years old, but I'd like you to try to pass your GED... test out of high school completely. You're a damn-smart kid, and we've been home-schooling you, not according to a standard school curriculum, but according to your interests and capabilities plus our areas of expertise. I'm betting you could get your diploma now, and if you do, I'm also betting that you could gain admission to the university in the fall."

"Go to college at thirteen? I'd be a little shrimp compared to the other students. They'd tease me unmercifully."

"If you went as an undergrad, that's true. But if you tested out of your undergraduate courses—lower division, major, and minor—I'm betting you could gain admission as a candidate for a Master's Degree."

"I'd be even younger compared to my peers, and besides, how would I test out of four years' worth of classes? That's unheard-of!"

"Not really. Some years back, the twelve-year-old son of two Princeton professors tested out of his Bachelor's of Science courses and entered Caltech as a PhD candidate in mathematics, so there are precedents. And in your case, you can point to a significant body of professional-quality work in the domain of linguistics and Eastern European languages. I won't be allowed to assess the qualifications of my own daughter, but I have colleagues in the field, both at the university here and elsewhere in the United States, and they can assess you fairly. If they recommend that you be granted a B.A. based on your test results and your work, then it will probably happen."

Grandma was looking confused. "What's the advantage of accelerating her education like that?"

Dr. Mason sighed. "If she has a Master's Degree, she can get a job as a teaching assistant. If she has a PhD, she can apply for a position as a full professor. Credentials are unfortunately important in this life. So far, she's been able to get consulting work because she had my backing and oversight. But what happens when I'm gone? She needs to launch her own independent career as soon as possible, and once she has, she can get her own health insurance through her job—and pay for her mother's insurance and healthcare too should that become necessary."

Everyone sat in silence for a moment, contemplating just how heavy a burden they were about to place on Suzy's young shoulders. Then Suzy spoke. "I'll bet I can pass any test that they throw at me."

"That's the spirit!" her grandma said.

Allison asked, "Can I get more of that delicious chicken soup?" Everyone laughed, and Suzy rose from the table to go fetch her mother another bowl-ful.

When Danny arrived that evening, he was astonished by how much his mother had changed for the better and amazed by the plan they'd devised. He promised to do all he could to help and said he was certain that his bride-to-be would too.

*   *   *   *   *

Up in Heaven, Nana turned to her daughter and asked, "Did you see what just happened there?"

"Yes. Suzy's dad passed her the baton, and she didn't fumble. She ran with it."

Nana nodded in satisfaction. "Yes, she did! 'Atta girl..." And it wasn't clear whether she meant Suzy or perhaps her own daughter.

*   *   *   *   *

The morning after Suzy's family held their strategy meeting, Allison called her oncologist's office and asked for an appointment. The clerk in charge of scheduling assured Allison that she already had an appointment for the day after her next infusion, but Allison insisted on one a week before the infusion date, something that seemed to knock the clerk for a loop. "You want to see him *before* your next treatment?"

"Yes. I want to receive a PET/CT before I have any further treatment."

"Oh, OK. Um... I'll have his nurse call you. There's no record of him scheduling you for a PET or a CT."

"I know there isn't. I want to see him and request that I have a PET/CT before I have any further treatment." Allison realized that she was already repeating herself and at higher volume, as if the clerk was possibly deaf or English-impaired.

"I'll have the nurse call you," the clerk said, as if she too was trying to make herself understood despite having little hope.

Allison gave up. "Good. I look forward to her call." She replaced the receiver in its cradle and sighed. She'd always found the clerk to be helpful before, but apparently the girl was only competent while following a pre-determined script, and Allison surmised that she'd just departed from that script when she asked for services that weren't yet authorized. God forbid that the patient should suddenly take the initiative...

Allison shuffled weakly back to the kitchen and sat down at the kitchen table. Her mother placed another full plate of food in front of her, and Allison began eating with good appetite. She'd already gained almost a pound and a half, although part of that weight was due to improved hydration, and her skin was beginning to lose the yellowish-gray tinge that it had had for the last month. Just then the phone rang, and her mother said, "Don't get up, Darlin'. I'll get it." Allison spooned another couple of mouthfuls into her mouth before her mother returned. "It's the nurse... Don't hurry! I told her you were eating breakfast and would come to the phone as soon as you could."

Allison stood up and returned to the phone. "Hello? Yes, this is she... Case number RL667259921... Yes, I called to ask for an appointment before my next infusion date. I want to receive a PET scan and a high-resolution CT scan before I proceed with any more chemo. Why? Because I want to see if I have any detectable tumors before I get another infusion... Yes, I understand, but I was sick as a dog—the chemo was killing me—and suddenly I feel great and I'm eating like a horse. So I want to know... Do I still have tumors or not, because if I don't, I want to propose that I forego further chemo for a while and give my body a chance to recover.

"What? Yes, I understand the risks. I also understand that my liver and kidney numbers were terrible. During my last visit, he was quite frank with me. He said I was in danger of suffering catastrophic multiple organ failure. And now I'm up, out of bed, and walking. So I want to know if I really need more chemo right now... Right... Well please ask if he can work me in because I can't get the scans unless he authorizes them. I won't know the answer to my question without the scans. And I really don't want any more chemo right now if I don't have to have it because I need the chance to recover from the treatment, if not from the cancer itself. OK, OK, yes, I can make 8:00 AM this Friday. Thank you. I'll see you then."

Allison hung up the phone with a mixed sense of triumph and exasperation. She'd achieved step one, but only with difficulty. Step two would be harder— convincing the doctor to order the scans. Then came step three, but she didn't want to think about that part yet. She felt too good to let herself worry about what the scans might show and what she might have to endure in consequence. She could smell the delightful scents of her mother's baking wafting from the kitchen. Far better just to enjoy the moment as much as possible... to make today as good as it could be.

*   *   *   *   *

By the time Allison saw her oncologist on Friday, she'd put on four more pounds, and the whites of her eyes were truly white again. Her husband accompanied her to the appointment, and he was proud of her when she managed to walk all the way from the car to the doctor's office on her own power. The doctor entered, and Allison was actually able to stand up and shake his hand, as tall and straight as she'd been before her cancer diagnosis had ever occurred.

Dr. Mason saw the doctor's astonished expression, and he smiled privately to himself as the doctor apparently abandoned his plan to talk his patient into showing some sense. Instead, the doctor did a full examination and ordered a blood draw for a STAT CBC and full metabolic panel. Then he asked Dr. and Mrs. Mason to go out to the waiting room to wait for the results.

Allison and her husband sat side-by-side in "chairs," holding hands and talking softly with one another. Allison ate one of the protein bars they'd brought and drank a bottle of juice. Finally, after an hour and a half, the nurse came out and summoned the Masons back into an exam room. There they found the doctor poring over the lab results and the rest of Allison's chart. Catching a glimpse of them out of the corner of his eye, he gestured at two visitor's chairs and said, "Take a seat."

Allison and her husband glanced at each other and then sat down. Finally, the doctor looked up and exclaimed, "I'm sorry to have kept you waiting, but at first I couldn't believe that I'd been given the results for the right patient. Your improvement is, uh, remarkable... liver function fully restored... kidney function completely normal... blood counts all within the normal range... If I didn't know better... If I'd never seen your chart or treated you, I'd have said that these results came from a totally healthy woman, perhaps even someone younger than you actually are."

Allison felt her husband's hand tighten on hers. "So perhaps a PET scan and a CT scan would be a good idea?"

"Yes, yes! If your other tests have turned around so dramatically, then we have to assume that the last scan report is now obsolete. We need new scan data, and you're correct. We need it before we proceed with any further treatment. Something has changed, and the currently prescribed treatment protocol may now be completely inappropriate."

"Thank you. How soon can I get the scans?"

"I want them as soon as possible. I'll have my nurse contact Radiology and set up the appointments. Radiology Scheduling will let you know when they are. I'll also have her schedule a follow-up appointment with me for a couple of days later so that I can interpret the results for you. Until then, keep up the good work. I'll make sure she includes the blood test results in your discharge instructions, so make sure you get them before you go."

With that, he stood up and left the room—a man perpetually in a hurry because there were too many cancer patients and too few oncologists—a group of professional people overwhelmed by the escalating demand for their services in what had become a ghastly kind of growth industry.

* * * * *

The next five years were eventful for the Mason family.

Allison's scans came back completely clear. Her doctor ordered that her chemotherapy be discontinued. Then he scheduled her for another pair of scans three months later. Those scans were clear too. Her doctor continued scanning her at three-month intervals for the rest of the year. Then he switched to a twice-a-year schedule. After two years, when those scans also proved to be clear, he switched her to once a year, and at the end of five years, he told her that she was at least in full remission if not completely cured.

Allison and her family were delighted by this feedback, but Allison wasn't willing to take any chances. Her new motto was "Fool me once—shame on you. Fool me twice—shame on me." So she asked her family doctor to continue giving her CT scans without contrast as part of her annual exam, and understanding her fears, he was happy to oblige.

In the meantime, while Allison was regaining her strength and returning to her former activities, Suzy was carrying out her part of her family's strategy, completing her education. She did indeed pass her GED exam and get her diploma. Then she entered into negotiations with the university.

Those negotiations proved lengthy and, at times, contentious. Her father's colleagues, both local and elsewhere, sent a flood of recommendation letters to the admissions committee. Suzy herself showed up at one of their review meetings with her existing body of work in tow—literally. She'd translated so many books and journal articles by that time that she needed a little red wagon to bring them from her father's car to the building where the meeting was taking place. At the meeting, she sat and watched as the committee chairman examined the collection, a look of growing consternation spreading over his face. In the end, Suzy triumphed. The university made her sit for a series of exams, but when she passed them all with flying colors, the academic standards committee decided to award her an honorary Bachelor's Degree with a minor in linguistics and a major in Eastern European languages, the exact outcome that her father had wanted for her.

Dr. Mason took all the substantiating paperwork for Suzy's degree, made a copy to keep in the house, and stored the originals in a safe deposit box at the bank. His wife took the rather handsome diploma and had it framed for display in their study at home. Suzy took a week off to savor her achievement before diving back into the fray. Then she tackled the next phase.

She hadn't forgotten her original goal, and now she applied for acceptance to the Master's Degree program. The only surprise to her parents was that she decided to apply for two degrees, one in languages as expected, but also a second in fine arts. Her mother almost burst with pride.

Suzy's studies kept her extremely busy—so busy in fact that she scarcely ever had time to observe the other changes going on around her. Her father and grandfather completed their plan to renovate the dairy and turn it into a livable house. After extensive interviews, they found and hired the farm manager, and as they'd hoped, he came with a very pleasant wife who was well able to function as an in-home aide and care-giver to Allison and her mother.

Suzy did all she could during this period to support her family's aims. She fulfilled translation contracts, brought in consulting fees, and did her utmost to earn her M.A. and M.F.A in record time. She hadn't forgotten that, ultimately, she must graduate with the credentials to begin an independent career of her own.

After five years, shortly after Allison was deemed "cured," Suzy emerged from her marathon academic effort with all the degrees she'd sought. She would have started applying for jobs immediately, but her parents had begun to notice ominous changes in their daughter, and they decided to intervene.

Suzy was now eighteen years old and a stunning beauty. She was tall and statuesque like her mother and sported the same lush mane of gleaming Titian-red hair. Her skin was pale, nearly translucent, and her hazel eyes looked almost dark gold in certain lights. With her father's straight, slightly sharp nose and her mother's naturally rosy cupid-bow mouth, she was exquisite enough to win pageants or go on the stage. But Suzy herself was oblivious to her own charms.

Now in her parents' view, she was fading slightly. The petal-pink blush that used to spread over her cheeks was gone, and her energy seemed to be flagging. She still did her work with determination and discipline, but she'd apparently lost her verve. At times, she seemed almost dis-spirited. So her parents stepped in and offered her the chance to go on the first long vacation of her entire life. They hoped that a good rest would put her back to rights and head off any stress-related illness that might be coming her way. Her mother secretly feared that, unless Suzy did take a break, she might get cancer too...

The timing was as close to perfect as it could possibly be. The farm manager was working out well, as was his wife. Suzy's grandparents were now eighty and seventy-nine respectively, but they and the farm would be fine given the new help available to them. So Suzy's father applied for permission to take a sabbatical.

At seventy-five, he was still holding his own at the university, but Administration still hoped to convince him to retire. They saw his request as a positive sign, possibly the overture to his gradual withdrawal from academic life. Perhaps, they reasoned, if he enjoyed a trip abroad, he might finally accept Emeritus status so that he could do more traveling before old age caught up with him. With this thought in mind, they granted his application with alacrity, and the Masons began making travel arrangements.

When Suzy packed her bags for their trip, she included a fresh sketch pad and an enormous new box of colored pencils. Her father planned to show her all the most scenic places in the countries they'd studied together, and she wanted to make sure she could capture her impressions as they went.

She had a camera of course. By that time, practically everybody did in their cell phones. But for her as for her mother, a drawing or a painting would always be superior to a photograph for the simple reason that it captured, not only what was in front of the artist's eyes, but also what was within the artist's mind.

And so, on one glorious late spring morning, they set out. After spending her whole life in a kind of academic cloister—a cozy yet constrained private paradise—Suzy was at last venturing forth into the wide world, and up in Heaven, angels cheered.

5: Suzy's World Is Transformed...

The Christmas after Allison's recovery, Danny married his fiancée in a small ceremony at the Methodist church near the farm. Everyone liked his new wife, Ellen. A fellow software engineer, she was pretty enough when she wore contact lenses instead of her usual coke-bottle glasses, and she was clearly very bright. In fact, unless she and Danny watched themselves, they tended to take conversational "deep dives" into the world of software development, losing everyone else around them. But although Ellen could be socially awkward at times like so many other engineers, she obviously had a kind heart and was as perfect a match for Danny as he was ever going to find.

The happy couple spent their honeymoon on the farm, allowing Ellen to get acquainted with Danny's family, and Danny himself took the opportunity to have long rambling talks with his mom and little sister especially—the first because he'd come painfully close to losing her, and the second because he needed to get to know her all over again given how much she'd grown up in just a few short years. During his conversations with Suzy, he shared some of his experiences circling the globe on various business trips, and the memories he'd imparted were very much on her mind as she boarded her very first airplane.

By the time Suzy and her parents completed the first leg of their journey, she'd come to regard plane travel as a necessary evil at best. Entrusting her luggage to the curb-side baggage handlers had made her feel insecure. Going through the pre-boarding TSA safety checks had left her feeling violated. The plane's take-off and subsequent maneuvers had outright alarmed her, and cruising at altitude made her at once claustrophobic because of the jammed coach compartment and motion sick due to air turbulence.

Thanks to Danny, the Masons had known how to book three seats together, and they also knew enough to get up periodically and walk up and down the center aisle a few times. Danny had explained about the danger of sitting for long periods during a trans-continental flight. One could develop blood clots in the legs that could break loose, causing a pulmonary embolism, a stroke, or a heart attack. The Masons were conscientious about getting up to exercise, and because they were seated together, they could do so without bothering any of the other passengers.

To help Suzy cope with the tight quarters and unfamiliar surroundings, Dr. Mason sprang for three headsets so that he and his family could watch in-flight movies together. They chose a high-quality, uplifting offering with no murders, car chases, or explosions, and Suzy was able to lose herself in the plot. Also, her parents took turns holding her hand, so by the time the air hostess began passing out drinks and refreshments, Suzy had calmed down and was beginning to enjoy the flight somewhat. Her mother exchanged places with her, giving her the window seat, and thereafter, Suzy amused herself by watching the billowing cumulus clouds pass beneath their wings and catching glimpses of landscapes below whenever there was a break in the overcast.

Roughly six hours after the Masons boarded their plane in Portland, they landed in New York, deplaned, and boarded their connecting flight. Suzy couldn't help but wonder if their luggage would miraculously accompany them or end up in some far-off place like Morocco. Their next flight lasted another several hours, and fortunately, it included meal service because, by that time, the Masons were famished. The Masons landed in Berlin, and after collecting their bags and passing through customs, they took a taxi to their hotel and collapsed gratefully into bed. They'd crossed eight time zones and were completely out-of-sync with the place in which they found themselves, but the body wants what it wants.

After a good, long sleep, the Masons got up, showered, dressed, and went downstairs to the hotel restaurant to eat. The American farm-style breakfast they craved was out of the question, but they were able to order a quite nice mid-afternoon lunch. While they ate, they reviewed their itinerary. First on their agenda was to rent a car and travel around Germany. They'd take in some of the museums and other attractions of Berlin and then head out into the countryside. Allison particularly wanted to see the fairy-tale castles built by Mad King Ludwig of Bavaria.

The Masons truly enjoyed Germany—the impressive public buildings and surviving churches in the cities, the towering forests, the quaint out-lying towns, and yes, the castles. Everywhere they went, Dr. Mason and Suzy practiced their German, and Allison and Suzy took photographs and made sketches.

From Germany, the Masons proceeded by train into Poland. They wanted to exercise their Polish, tour Warsaw, and see such historic sites as Nidzica Castle. Suzy and her mother loved Nidzica—its solid stone bulk perched on top of a forested hill beside a river, silhouetted against a turbulent cloudy sky—utterly different from King Ludwig's turreted confections. The two women took extensive photos and promised each other that they'd capture the landscape in oils as soon as they returned home.

From Poland, the Masons zig-zagged by train south into the Czech Republic, southeast into Slovakia, and then southwest into Austria, stopping in each country along the way. This path gave them the chance to speak Czech, Slovak, and then German again. They also got to tour the beautiful city of Prague, a number of walled towns dating back to Medieval times, and Vienna. In Vienna, they visited every museum and cathedral they could find, and because of Dr. Mason's academic reputation, they were able to gain admission to the famous Spanish Riding School and see the Lipizzan stallions dance.

For their final stop, the Masons had planned to travel to Romania, and if they'd simply consulted a map, their route would have taken them through Hungary. Hungary had its attractions, and both Dr. Mason and Suzy would have liked to exercise their Hungarian, but for over a decade, Hungary had been in the grip of political and social turmoil, so the Masons thought they'd better give it a wide berth and get to Romania by another route.

They ended up going back through Slovakia and briefly through a corner of the Ukraine. Neither Suzy nor her father spoke Ukrainian. But the Ukraine had been part of the Soviet Union for decades so the Masons were able to get by with Russian, and no one seemed to bear them any ill will for speaking it once they explained that they were American tourists.

Romania proved well worth the detour once they arrived. It too featured dramatic landscapes of tall snow-capped mountains, rocky escarpments, and towns dating back to the Middle Ages. Romania had been part of the Byzantine Empire and had later served as a battle ground for Ottoman Turks and Austro-Hungarians. In fact, the Masons discovered that Hungarian was still spoken in Romania's far northwestern province, so they got to speak some Hungarian after all.

But the highlight of their stay in that country was a tour visiting many of its Eastern Orthodox churches and monasteries. Their domes bore Byzantine-style mosaics, their sanctuaries were filled with triptychs and icons of the saints, and it seemed that every surface was carved, enameled, or gilded. Each church was a feast for the eyes and a balm to the soul. Photographs were forbidden, of course, but Allison and Suzy were undaunted by this restriction. They'd spend every evening in their hotel room sketching what they'd seen so they wouldn't forget a single exquisite detail.

All good things come to an end, and the Masons' European vacation was no exception. From Romania, they retraced their steps through a corner of the Ukraine, directly across Poland, and back into Germany. They caught a flight from Berlin to Maine which went better than Suzy expected. Then, after enjoying comparative freedom of movement throughout the European Union, they had to submit to a customs inspection in the U.S. that was extraordinarily thorough. America had cracked down to some degree on travel and immigration in recent years. So the customs inspectors took one look at the Eastern European stamps in the Masons' passports and added a lengthy set of questions to their interviews.

Eventually, Customs gave the Masons their luggage and let them go. They made their connecting flight by the skin of their teeth, and Suzy found that, on the last leg of their journey, she was simply too tired to worry about the odd noises and sudden bumps she experienced in the plane.

They touched down in Portland in late afternoon. The Masons deplaned, went to Baggage Claim, and discovered with gratitude that their suitcases had not been re-routed to some exotic foreign land. With their bags in tow, they walked out to the curb. There they were met by one of the farm hands who'd been circling in traffic, waiting to pick them up in the SUV. The long drive down to Eugene and out to the farm hardly registered in their minds.

That night, they consumed bowls of Grandma's delicious, hearty soup and then fell into bed. There, Dr. Mason dreamed of asking for directions in seven different languages, and Allison dreamed of castles silhouetted against steep tree-covered slopes. But Suzy dreamed of a young woman with dark curls who was walking along a bluff above the sea. As Suzy watched, the young woman turned and smiled at her with approval showing in her merry brown eyes. Then the woman turned away again and vanished.

*　*　*　*　*

For months after their return home, Allison and Suzy did as they'd promised themselves they would do. They turned the best of their photographs and sketches into paintings. Since her recovery from cancer, Allison preferred to work primarily in watercolors, but Suzy still favored oil paints. She painted her self-portrait with Nidzica Castle in the background. Taking artistic license, she changed the sky from the scudding gray clouds of early afternoon to the pinks and lavenders of impending sunset. Then she set the painting aside to dry and went on to other work. Only when she returned weeks later to varnish that painting did she realize what she'd done. The image of herself that she'd captured was an exact match for the image she'd seen in a dream long ago.

This realization upset her for several days. She didn't want to disturb her family, however, so she didn't share her observation with them, and when they all praised the painting highly, she just smiled politely and kept her silence.

She knew, though, that she'd have to find some way to regain a measure of equanimity. The longer she meditated on the subject, the more obvious it became to her that she'd really been privy to a whole series of inexplicable events. There was the first dream in which she'd seen her portrait, heard the melodious voice, and seen the young brunette. There was the second dream in which she'd been given urgent instructions to go to her mother's bedside and take her hand. Then there was the incredible experience of being a channel through which her mother was miraculously healed. And now there was the third dream in which she'd seen her "guardian angel" again, for that was how Suzy had begun to think of the mysterious young woman.

Although Suzy couldn't point to any logical reason for her belief, she did believe with all her heart that the young woman was real, and that she'd intervened to save Suzy's mother and indeed their whole family. Whenever Suzy was thinking deeply, she often drew what was on her mind to make it more focused and concrete for herself and others. Now, she did that in spades.

She prepared a canvas and roughed in a full-length portrait of the young woman on the bluff. Suzy painted the glowing vault of the sky overhead, the dramatic curve of the coastline in the background, the sunlight glinting off the ocean waves below, the verdant grasses in the foreground, and framed in this setting, the slender form of the woman as she recalled it—beginning to turn away, still glancing back over her shoulder, a faint enigmatic smile still gracing her lips.

After the painting dried and was varnished, Suzy had it framed in a manner similar to that of her original painting of the girl with the teddy bear and the rag doll. She hung the new painting beside the old one, and when Allison saw them together on the wall in Suzy's room, she reacted very strangely. She sat down abruptly on Suzy's bed, filled with a sense of overwhelming gratitude but also a vague unease, like she was seeing something not intended for mortal eyes... like she was seeing something forbidden from a dream. Suzy was present when this happened, and alarmed, she asked, "Mom, are you OK?"

Allison brushed tears from her eyes with her fingertips and said, "I'm fine, Sweetie, but I must admit that I'm glad these paintings hang in your room. I'm not sure why, but I don't think I'd like to encounter them every day elsewhere in the house." With that, she stood up and left.

After a while, Allison and Suzy had satisfied their need to translate images from their vacation into art. As their experiences passed deeper into memory, they continued to inform their work, but less explicitly. On Danny and Ellen's next visit home, they saw some of what Allison was creating, and Ellen in particular found it enchanting. So at her urging, Danny built a web site advertising Allison's latest works, and not only did she make sales as a result of her new marketing channel, she also gained illustration contracts with book publishers in the east. Most of her work went into picture books for children, and after one book won both the Newbury and Caldecott Awards, Allison became famous in book publishing circles. Critics often asked what inspired her gorgeous, golden, bejeweled images. Had they traveled to Eastern Europe and seen its cultural treasures, they would have known...

*   *   *   *   *

Meanwhile, Dr. Mason's business was also flourishing. Given the growing political tension in Hungary and its influence on the rest of Europe, the U.S. government found that it had an ever-increasing need for Hungarian translation support. One government agency in particular did its research and learned that Dr. Mason was widely regarded as an expert on the country and its language. So the agency offered a long-term contract to the university for translation services and specified that Dr. Mason must oversee the work.

At first, the university was very conflicted. Administration wanted to meet the need (and incidentally, earn the promised fees), but they were worried about entrusting so important an effort to a man now in his late seventies. When Dr. Mason heard about this concern, he pointed out, none too subtly, that his daughter could join him in the effort, and she was not yet twenty. Then ensued a lengthy negotiation in which Administration asserted that, if he was too old to ensure the security of the effort, she was far too young.

Hearing about this discussion, the agency sent a representative to Eugene to try and resolve the matter. The agent in question was himself an expert on Hungary, its language, and its inner workings. He met with Dr. Mason, quizzed him, and was impressed by Dr. Mason's expertise, his energy, and his clarity of thought. Then the agent interviewed Suzy.

Initially, he was taken aback when a girl in her teens entered the room. But she answered his questions just as well as her father had. So the agent recommended strongly that the Masons be given joint contract oversight, and both the agency and the university caved.

Seeing an opportunity, however, Administration imposed an additional requirement. Dr. Mason, they asserted, would now be too busy with translation work to continue teaching classes and supervising graduate students. If he was going to participate on this contract, then they insisted that he retire from teaching and accept Emeritus status at last.

Equally aware of the opportunities, Dr. Mason countered that, if he and his daughter agreed to participate on this contract, then the university needed to acknowledge the value of Suzy's expertise and skills by offering her a tenured position as his replacement.

Administration protested, "She'd be younger than her students!"

Dr. Mason would brook no refusal. "Take it or leave it," he told them.

Administration pointed out, "She has no PhD!"

Dr. Mason stood firm. "Her existing body of work already merits one, and you know it."

Administration whined, "You're being unreasonable, and you're jeopardizing the contract!"

Dr. Mason's retort was supremely unsympathetic. "Linking my retirement to the contract was your idea, not mine."

At this point, the agency stepped back into the discussion. Their representative sent a terse, harshly-worded memo that basically read, "Stop bickering, and give Dr. Mason what he wants. His demands are reasonable, yours are not, and if anyone is jeopardizing the contract it's you—something that your government will absolutely not tolerate given all that's at stake. So get in line or else—we will contract directly with Dr. Mason."

Thoroughly cowed, Administration agreed, and Suzy signed an employment contract with the university and the translation contract on the same day, in that order. Thus, she and her father achieved a long-held, financially-important goal. Going forward, Suzy would have employment with health insurance, and for the five years it would take Allison to qualify for Medicare, Suzy would be able to help Danny pay for private health insurance for her mother. Dr. Mason had succeeded in protecting the two women he loved most in life.

The next step was for Dr. Mason and Suzy to fill out the lengthy forms and go through the grueling process of gaining the necessary clearances. Having led extremely quiet and exemplary lives, they qualified easily—or as easily as that months-long process ever goes...

Before long, they were receiving a veritable flood of memos and other communications to translate. The assignments were always urgent, the deadlines were short, and Dr. Mason frequently thanked his lucky stars that he had his daughter to rely on. He would never have admitted it before his academic retirement, but he was beginning to notice a few signs of age-related frailty. He was beginning to slow down...

*   *   *   *   *

Dr. Mason wasn't the only one beginning to feel his age. Granddad and Grandma had finally reached the point where they could no longer participate in day-to-day tasks on the farm. Fortunately, they didn't need to do so. The farm manager and the farm hands were able to take care of everything outside the house, and Allison and the manager's wife took care of everything inside. Suzy would have like to help more, but her work had become quite time-consuming, and on those occasions when she had time off, her parents insisted that she use it to rest and work on her art.

Allison thanked God every day that she'd recovered from cancer. Her mother's arthritis now crippled her to the point where she needed help to get out of bed in the morning, bathe, dress, and walk long distances. Her husband was too feeble to lift her himself, so these tasks fell to Allison, sometimes aided by the manager's wife.

Allison asked herself what would have happened to her parents if she hadn't survived to care for them during these hard times. Fortunately, she had survived, so that question was mercifully moot.

For their parts, Granddad and Grandma did their best to enjoy what time they had left. On rainy days, they'd sit inside, cozy and warm beneath lap robes in their favorite armchairs. They'd read aloud to one another, listen to music, and watch movies on television. Danny had given them a DVD player one Christmas. He'd hooked it up before he returned home, and thereafter, he'd kept them well-supplied with classic movies like "You Can't Take It With You," and "Singing in the Rain."

Sunny days were better still. Granddad and Grandma would sit side by side in lawn chairs on the front porch, holding hands, talking, laughing, and sharing memories— still in love with one another after almost sixty-five years of marriage.

It was clear to everyone, including Danny, that Granddad and Grandma might not have much time left, so everybody did their best to make the remaining time good. Danny was now secure enough in his job that he could get away with taking time off, and he and Ellen had been with their company long enough that they each got five weeks of vacation, two weeks of holidays, and three weeks of sick leave per year.

Danny and Ellen still came to spend two weeks at the farm each Christmas, but now they developed the habit of dropping in for long weekend visits on Memorial Day, Fourth of July, Labor Day, and Thanksgiving. For Danny and Ellen, these visits were a welcome respite from the sixty-plus-hour weeks they worked in the Bay Area.

Ellen had come to love Danny's family as much as he did, and as it happened, she needed the breaks even more than he ever could. Regrettably, after spending her entire adult life dealing with workplace gender bias, the highly competitive behavior of her co-workers, and the unreasonably short deadlines of her assignments, she'd begun to suffer from a hormone imbalance which had led to uterine fibroids. Her OB-GYN had done a surgical procedure to remove them, but they quickly returned—giving her pain, leading to dangerous bouts of internal bleeding, and rendering her effectively barren.

Ellen's doctor warned her that the fibroids might cause her to hemorrhage heavily at any moment, and if they ever did, she would need an emergency hysterectomy. The prospect frightened Ellen, but she wasn't willing to give up her career to avoid it. As for Danny, he loved his wife and hoped she'd somehow escape that fate, but secretly, he was glad that they wouldn't be having any children.

Danny regretted that he and Ellen wouldn't be giving his parents the grandchildren they probably craved, but he knew in his heart that he and Ellen weren't cut out to be parents. They lived entirely for their work. It had brought them together in the first place, and it was holding them together still. Any children they'd produced would have ended up being raised by day-care centers, public schools, and baby-sitters, and Danny believed that children deserved better. So he and Ellen visited the farm whenever they could, and if the topic of children should chance to come up, Danny would simply deflect and change the subject.

Finally, there came the Christmas when Ellen's fibroid problem came home to roost, so to speak. Danny and Ellen flew to Oregon for their annual two-week visit, and Ellen, always at least a little anemic because of her fibroids, apparently caught a cold on the plane. By the time Danny and Ellen reached the farm, Ellen was running a fever.

Worried about bringing sickness into a house where frail, elderly people lived, Danny parked the rental car in the drive outside. He tried to use his cell phone to call his family and explain, but as usual in that location, his phone showed no bars. Giving up, Danny left his wife in the car and went inside to explain in person. While there, he used the living room phone to book a hotel room. Then he drove himself and his wife to the hotel via the local drug store.

Soon, he'd installed the two of them in their room, surrounded by cold remedies, hot chicken soup from room service, and a heating pad to ward off the chills that Ellen was beginning to suffer.

The next morning, Danny woke up with a fever of his own. He called his parents to let them know he couldn't come. But when his mother answered the phone, the first words out of her mouth were, "Oh, Danny, please stay at the hotel with Ellen. Granddad and Grandma both came down with pneumonia in the night, and your father and I are about to rush them to the hospital." Danny was devastated to learn that his precautions had been for nothing, but he assured her that he and Ellen would be fine on their own, and he promised to call later and find out how his grandparents were doing.

So Danny and Ellen survived for several days on a steady diet of room service food and old Christmas movies on TV. In response to Danny's calls, Allison gave news updates that were as encouraging as one could hope for... Grandma was on IV antibiotics and oxygen, but she seemed to be rallying, and her color was getting better. Granddad's case seemed to be milder. He was already sitting up in bed and demanding better food than the hospital kitchens could provide. Danny dared to hope that he and Ellen hadn't done irreparable damage after all, but then, abruptly, the good news came to an end.

His cell phone rang, and when he answered, he heard his mother's voice crying. "Mom, what is it?" His mother tried to tell him something, but he couldn't make it out. Then he heard his sister's voice, muffled, and Suzy came on the line.

"Danny, Grandma said she felt tired this afternoon, and she wanted to take a nap. She didn't wake up. She passed away in her sleep, and all the efforts to resuscitate her failed."

Danny felt himself choke up. "Does Granddad know?"

"Of course. We told him right away, and we were able to take him in a wheelchair to see her body. The nurses had made her look very peaceful. Dad is off making the arrangements for her now, and I'm looking after Mom and Granddad. We'll call again and let you know as soon as we've worked out the funeral details. I wish you and Ellen could be here with us now, but it's better that you stay where you are and get well. Please take good care of yourselves. I love you both. I've got to go. Good-bye."

Danny hung up the phone and gave Ellen the bad news. The two of them began to cry together, and presently, they each needed a big extra dose of decongestant to deal with the internal swelling caused by their tears. The decongestant contained both ethanol and a sleep medication, so despite their intentions, they both nodded off and slept for several hours, and they didn't wake up until Danny's phone rang again.

He answered and heard Suzy's voice. It held an edge that hadn't been there before despite her sorrow over Grandma's death. "Danny, brace yourself. I'm calling with more bad news. You know how patients in a hospital are put on all kinds of monitors? Well, about an hour after Granddad saw Grandma's body, his monitor showed that his heart was slowing down. The doctor came and gave him a stimulant, but it only worked for a few minutes. They gave him another dose, but that one didn't work for long either.

"It wasn't the pneumonia. His oxygen level was fine. The doctor said he might be developing an idiopathic cardiomyopathy, but that just means that something's wrong with the heart, and they don't know what it is. So they scheduled him for an emergency procedure to implant electrodes and give him a temporary pacemaker. But before they could get him into the operating room, his heart stopped altogether, and just as with Grandma, they couldn't get him back. Granddad has died too, and within hours of Grandma..." Suzy began to cry.

Danny was crying too, but as her much-older brother, he felt it was his duty to try and comfort her. "Suzy, we have to remember. They lived good long lives, and Grandma's arthritis had begun to give her frequent pain. You know what she used to tell us, that pneumonia can be an old person's friend. Her death may have saved her from far worse, far longer suffering. Ellen and I will always feel terrible that we brought this illness into their house. But at least they're still together. I don't think Granddad would have wanted to go on living without Grandma. Just think how lonely for her he would have been."

Suzy sniffled loudly. "I know. I've been telling myself the same things. Dad says we'll have one funeral for them and bury them side by side... One headstone with both their names and dates... That way they'll always be united."

Danny felt a lump rise in his throat. He swallowed against it and struggled to speak anyway. "I like that... together forever... just as they would have wanted to be... Suzy, I've got to go. I've got to wake up Ellen and tell her the news, and I don't think you want your big brother to embarrass himself by breaking down completely on the phone..."

"I understand. I'll be in touch," and she hung up.

The funeral took place three days later. The Masons buried their loved ones in the cemetery adjoining the Methodist churchyard. The grave site was next to the one where Granddad's parents lay. Danny and Ellen attended the funeral, all bundled up and still suffering from their colds. They also attended the reading of the will that followed.

The will held no surprises and struck everyone as completely fair. It put the farm into a trust for the benefit of Allison and all her descendants, with life interests for any widowed spouses who'd actually lived on the farm at some point. Of course, Danny and Ellen had no desire to live on the farm and work it. So really, the long-term beneficiaries were likely to be Suzy and any children that she might have. If she died without any heirs, then ultimately, the land would be sold, and the proceeds would be donated to a charity.

Afterwards, nobody had the heart to celebrate Christmas. Danny and Ellen flew home as soon as their colds resolved. Allison began the task of processing her parents' belongings, and Dr. Mason and Suzy returned to their work.

They continued translating documents to and from the Hungarian for a couple of years thereafter. Then on one late spring day, shortly after Dr. Mason turned eighty, Suzy left the study and went downstairs to fix a tea tray for her father and herself.

The day had been both beautiful and productive. They'd worked with the windows open—a soft fragrant breeze wafting in and the sound of birdsong in the distance. Dr. Mason had tackled a particularly difficult passage, and at first, he'd had a lot of fun with the challenge. But after a while, the strain of focusing so hard for so long had taken its toll. He'd felt a bad headache coming on, and he'd asked Suzy to go fetch refreshments while he took a brief rest in the corner armchair. She'd been happy to oblige.

Now she came back and set the tray on the desk. She turned, and at first, she thought her father had dozed off in his chair, but something about the angle of his head struck her as wrong. She stepped quietly to his side and pressed her fingertips against his neck. As she'd feared, he was dead, and given the headache, possibly from a hemorrhagic stroke.

Suzy felt her knees give way, and she sank down onto the carpet. She sat crying silently, feeling the tears flow down her cheeks. Then she rallied herself, got up, and went to tell her mother. Suzy spent the rest of the day alternately comforting Allison and placing phone calls. They buried him in the same cemetery beside his mother-and father-in-law. His wife planned to join him there someday. It was her wish that her family should all be together in the end.

After the funeral, Suzy continued to stand over the grave for a while. Danny and Ellen had led Allison away, and Suzy wanted a moment to herself. By that time, Suzy had learned that Danny and Ellen couldn't have children and they weren't the type to adopt. To Allison's great sadness, they were effectively dead ends on the family tree. The thought gave Suzy pause.

Suzy knew in general what she planned to do with her life. She'd stay on the farm, take care of her mother, and continue her translation work. In her spare time, she might even paint a little. These activities would all be good and meaningful things to do. But at some point, either Allison or she would die, and because Danny and Ellen didn't want the farm, their farming way of life would cease. If Suzy wanted it to continue, then she must somehow find a husband and have children. She suspected that Allison would probably be quite happy if she did.

The problem was that Suzy didn't want to marry just anyone. She wanted what her grandparents and parents had had. She wanted a soul-mate. If she survived her mother, she'd be very much alone most of the time without one.

She wasn't afraid of solitude per se. She knew that there was a big difference between simple solitude and the loneliness of being with someone with whom one didn't fit. *That* was what she truly feared. So given how secluded she was by her work and home circumstances... her interests and her abilities... her challenge was to find someone with whom she *did* fit and avoid ending up as her family's sole survivor.

Suzy stood a minute more over her father's grave, gathering her resolve. Then she spoke aloud to whatever angelic spirits might be listening. "I don't know how I'm going to find him, but somehow I will."

Up in Heaven, Nana smiled softly. "I certainly hope so, Susan."

Suddenly, Uriel appeared at her side. "Oh, I wouldn't worry about it. Somehow these things have a way of working themselves out. Now excuse me for not staying. I hear that her father and grandparents have arrived recently, and I'd like to go greet them." Then he vanished just as quickly as he'd come.

Midnight of the Soul

1: T-Bear Re-enters the World...

Prologue—The Story So Far...

Jane Marie Hanson was born with the spiritual equivalent of a birth defect. Albert (the angel-in-training who put her soul into her body) accidentally broke the portal that connected her to Heaven, and he was too embarrassed to admit his mistake and get help fixing it. Thus, she remained in contact with Heaven for her entire life on Earth. She could hear angel-song. She could converse with departed spirits and absorb their knowledge and skills. These abilities frightened and confused most of the people around her, so Janie was growing up a very lonely little girl until the day when she asked her parents for a pet and they gave her a teddy bear instead.

After consulting with her only real friend, her nanny Rosa, Janie decided to create a companion. So she "borrowed" a tiny soul from Heaven, opened a portal from her own soul into the teddy bear, and downloaded the soul. To give "T-bear" the ability to experience the world despite the fact that his body was simply a toy, Janie maintained the link between their souls 24-7. T-bear was able to see through her eyes, hear through her ears... in short, to experience and learn from everything that Janie encountered. Before long, his tiny soul, which had been intended for a nematode, grew to be surprisingly sophisticated, and when he and Janie began to crave another companion, Janie made one out of a beautiful rag doll that Rosa had given her for Christmas.

Janie and T-bear named their new sister Susan, and to give Susan the same good quality of life that T-bear enjoyed, Janie and T-bear cross-linked their souls with hers on a permanent basis. Susan's soul had been designed to occupy a dragonfly, but just as T-bear had grown prodigiously due to his life experience, so too did Susan, and for a couple of years, the three friends were very happy together.

Unfortunately, before long, the miracles that Janie had worked came to the attention of the Heavenly Hosts, and they were *not* pleased. First, they wanted to get back their two missing souls so they could meet their worm and insect quotas. Second, they were alarmed that a little girl was working unauthorized miracles that impacted them.

The angels held an intervention, discovered Janie's portal defect, and located the missing souls. The archangel Gabriel personally retrieved T-bear and Susan. Then he sealed Janie's portal properly. Next, the archangel Raphael took T-bear and Susan into his custody so they could be healed before being infused into real bodies as God had intended. But those bodies could no longer be the simple, transient forms of a worm and bug. T-bear and Susan were now more suited to incarnation as human beings. To balance the supply of souls with the supply of bodies, two more tiny souls would have to be found elsewhere.

That's when an angel who retrieved the souls of the dead came up with a brilliant proposal. He'd just received two returning human souls—souls who'd failed abysmally in their first shot at life. He proposed that they be infused into the worm and insect bodies—a fitting outcome given their shriveled, stunted natures. The angels burst out laughing at this idea and agreed that it would solve their problem nicely. So two wicked, selfish beings met with justice, and T-bear and Susan were given a chance at life that might never have come their way if Janie hadn't intervened.

After the angels disbanded and returned to their duties, the archangel Uriel remained to talk with Albert, the one who'd accidentally started it all. Uriel told Albert that he had huge potential to do good. Then Uriel vanished, and Albert inexplicably found himself standing beside Janie's now-sealed portal. After contemplating Uriel's message, Albert decided that he couldn't bear to see Janie so cruelly deprived of all her friends, including those "on the other side." So he used a wad of spirit-matter to prop open her portal door a crack, giving her back her access to Heaven, and to the infinite quantities of healing energy that Heaven contains. Within a day, Janie noticed that her portal had reopened, and thereafter, she continued to converse with spirits and heal the sick—cautiously so as not to get caught, but otherwise, just as she had before.

Meanwhile, elsewhere in Heaven, Raphael finished helping Susan to recover from her first life on Earth, and Gabriel insisted that she be reincarnated immediately. Uriel persuaded his brothers to assign that task to Albert, and Albert took special care to find Susan a good fit for her needs and interests. Raphael had allowed Susan to choose for herself what memories and skills she'd take from her former life into her new one. Against his recommendations, she'd chosen to take her previous name, her abilities as an artist and a linguist, and the memory that she'd once had two soul-mates.

Albert chose wisely when he selected Susan's new family. She grew up on a farm in Oregon surrounded by kind-hearted folks—her grandparents, her father and mother, and a much-older brother and his wife. There was a nearly twenty-year age difference between her parents, and Suzy (as they called her) was a "bonus baby" born when her mother was almost forty, so many of the people on whom she depended were nearing retirement age when she entered the world.

Suzy's childhood was idyllic. Oregon was beautiful, and she loved the farm, especially the livestock. Her father, a linguist, taught her Eastern European languages, and her mother, an artist, taught her to paint. Suzy's parents homeschooled her, and thanks to her innate talents, intelligence, and hard work, she earned her high school diploma in her early teens, followed rapidly by several college degrees. She joined her father in his profession, translating documents on a contract basis, and her life seemed like it would be quiet, but fulfilling, going forward.

However, every life includes its challenges and tragedies. Suzy's mother got cancer and would have died of it if not for Suzy's unique nature. Despite angelic warnings to stay away, Janie hadn't been able to resist looking in on Suzy from time to time. In Janie's view, Suzy was not just her former friend. She was almost like a daughter. And Suzy had become aware of these visits through vivid dreams that she'd had. When Suzy's mother was mere days from death, Janie answered the prayers of Suzy and her family by performing a miraculous healing. Suzy responded to this experience by painting portraits of her "guardian angel" as a child and as a young woman. In the child's portrait, Suzy included the images of a rag doll and a teddy bear.

Thereafter, for a while, life returned to normal for Suzy and her family. But the years were taking their inevitable toll. First, Suzy's grandparents passed away and then her father. As she stood over her father's grave, she resolved to continue his work, preserve the farm, and care for her mother in the future. But that was not all... She vowed that, somehow, she'd find her soul-mate, and up in Heaven, Uriel hinted that she might attain her goal.

*   *   *   *   *

If a non-corporeal being could be said to sit, then T-Bear was sitting. More to the point, he was watching and listening as several angels and archangels duked it out right in front of him. Now, being angels, they didn't speak in loud, harsh voices, nor did they use foul language, threats, or any kind of violence. They were intrinsically incapable of behaving so badly. However, they were indubitably angry, and that anger revealed itself in bursts of energy like the lightning and thunder that course through the sky during an Earthly storm... and T-Bear was enjoying the show.

Ever since Gabriel had extracted T-Bear from his stuffed-animal body, T-Bear had been in the care of Raphael, undergoing the spiritual healing required before

T-Bear could be reincarnated as a human being. From T-Bear's perspective, that process had been unnecessarily long and tedious—reviewing his past life... extracting lessons from his experiences... selecting memories and skills to take with him into his next life... meditating to achieve spiritual calm...

As a greatly-enhanced nematode soul, T-Bear had always been one to burrow straight to the heart of the matter. He was impatient with what he saw as Raphael's indirect methods. T-Bear asked himself why the archangel couldn't just ask him a few simple questions. "Remember anything upsetting?" No. "Do you think you've learned from your mistakes?" Yup. "Do you know what you want to take with you into your next life?" Yes, but I'd rather not tell *you* because I saw what happened when Susan revealed her list, and I want very similar things... my name, that I had two soul-mates, my understanding of music, and the entire, complete composition that Janie and I used to call the "Soul Rhapsody."

T-Bear was certain that Raphael would object, so he'd kept many things to himself. But his strategy had backfired because, when Raphael didn't get the clear and complete answers that he'd craved, he'd decided that T-Bear was still too traumatized to communicate effectively and that he needed further healing. Eventually, Gabriel had shown up and demanded to know what was taking so long. Raphael had explained. Gabriel had contradicted him. Raphael had bristled at this disrespect, and just when it looked like an angelic donnybrook was about to break out, the angel in charge of Watching had shown up to complain about another soul gone AWOL.

By this time, virtually none of the angelic hosts wanted to hear about missing souls. T-Bear and Susan had only come to angelic attention in the first place because the angel in charge of Shipping had inexplicably come up two souls short. But as Gabriel was quick to point out to the head watcher, he had personally sealed the portal door leading to the mortal known as Jane Marie Hanson, so it was inconceivable that she was "borrowing" souls or working miraculous healings anymore.

The head watcher waited for a gap in Gabriel's rantings. Then he interjected that he'd only brought up the matter because the missing soul belonged to the mother of the reincarnated being known as Suzanne Allison Mason, A.K.A. Susan Hanson. The Watching department thought that this was too much of coincidence, and as department head, he'd felt it was incumbent on him to report the issue.

Gabriel pulled up short. "Susan's mother?..." He frowned. Then he shook his head dismissively. "Raphael, did Susan possess any healing powers in her own right?"

"None. If she'd had any, they would have come to light during her healing process. I was very thorough."

Gabriel's frown darkened. "I remember... perhaps too thorough." He turned to the head watcher. "I appreciate your keeping us informed, but I don't see this issue as being worth pursuing. God's plan allows for the occasional spontaneous remission or an unforeseen recovery, and despite the appearance of a connection to recent events, that's all we're seeing here. We're all still just a bit hyper-vigilant... So, unless the head of Receiving also registers an exception, let's just let this one go."

The head watcher saluted and returned to his station. He was disappointed by the archangels' reception of his report, but there was nothing he could do about it. He simply resolved to keep a much closer eye on Suzy and her mother from then on.

T-Bear watched the head watcher's departure with relief. Although Gabriel felt certain that there'd been no miracle, T-Bear was just as certain that one had occurred. Not for nothing had he been in constant contact with Janie for all those years. He knew for a fact that Janie had loved him and Susan deeply. Janie would not have stood by and let Susan suffer. Susan's mother's recovery had Janie's fingerprints all over it. T-Bear wasn't sure how Janie had pulled off the cure given that her portal door was sealed, but he was sure that she'd found a way. "You go, girl," he thought.

Just then, T-Bear looked up and saw the archangel Uriel approaching. He'd seen Uriel before when the archangel came to fetch Susan's soul and take it to the Shipping angel named Albert. Now T-Bear felt a little jolt of excitement. Perhaps Uriel was coming to collect him too. Maybe, at long last, he was going to get his chance to inhabit a real, live human body.

Uriel drifted to a graceful stop in front of his two brothers. "Greetings, Gabriel... Raphael... How are things?"

Gabriel was still scowling. "*Things* would be a lot better if the soul you see before you had been reincarnated already..."

Raphael drew himself up to his full height, forming a shaft of light of apparently infinite length. "I've already explained. He's... not... ready!"

"So sad to hear that..." A look of benign regret spread over Uriel's face. "I happened to wander through Shipping on my way here, and they have an absolutely perfect match waiting for this soul. I'm not sure how much longer they can hold it open. After all, so many bodies... so little time..."

Raphael was apparently about to take a page from Michael's playbook. Whenever Michael was angry, he presented himself as a pillar of fire—very effective. Raphael's column of light was beginning to take on a distinctly ruddy glow. "I certainly hope you're not trying to tell me how to do my job, little brother."

"Oh, perish the thought! I just hoped that you were ready to transfer this soul, given the opportunity. The success of Susan's incarnation was certainly to your credit. You did a splendid job there." Uriel's presentation was bland and conciliatory. Gabriel repressed a very non-angelic snigger.

Raphael turned his wrath on his older brother. "And I suppose you think I should rush this soul into a body, ready or not?"

Uriel made a deprecating gesture. "Have we asked the soul in question what he thinks? What was his name again?... T-Bear?..."

Raphael snorted. "Yes, T-Bear." He turned and addressed the recalcitrant soul sitting behind him. "Here, you! Step forward." T-Bear scrambled to his feet and did as he'd been bidden. "Do you feel ready for reincarnation?"

T-Bear felt a surge of hope. Here at last was the direct question that he'd yearned to hear. "Yes. I may be only a 'bear of little brain,' but I'd sure like to begin my next adventure."

Uriel beamed at him. "That's the spirit. So, we're all in agreement? T-Bear feels ready. You, Raphael, have done your usual, excellent job of preparing him, and Gabriel agrees that it's time. Would you like me to take him to Shipping for you? I was planning to head back that way anyway, and I'd be glad to help."

Raphael grimaced and made a dismissive gesture. "Oh, OK, be my guest. But don't come complaining to me if something goes wrong because it turns out he wasn't ready after all."

Uriel assured him, "I'd never do such a thing, and I find a negative outcome inconceivable. The souls you prepare always do so well..." Before Raphael could say another word, Uriel picked up T-Bear and transported him across the firmament to Shipping, coming to rest beside Albert's station.

Evidently, Albert had been waiting for them. Uriel handed T-Bear's soul to Albert and said, "Tell T-Bear what you've found."

Albert smiled shyly. "It's not as perfect a match as I was able to find for Susan. You'll know early hardship—some family troubles and poverty. But given that you want to keep your music, you could do a lot worse. Your family will be musically gifted, and you'll have the chance to play music yourself from an early age. Later on, depending on how well you take advantage of some opportunities that will come your way, you may even be able to compose and publish music, as well as play at the concert level. Does this future sound appealing to you?"

T-Bear stared up at him with serious eyes. "Will I be able to find my soul-mates?"

Uriel answered him. "You'll be able to find true and lasting love. Of that I'm certain."

T-Bear sighed, thought a moment, and then nodded. "Yes, I'll take it, and thanks. I'm sure you had to work hard to find the right placements for Susan and me. I'm grateful, and I'm sure she is too."

Uriel stepped back to give Albert room to work. Albert bent down, opened the portal at his feet, placed T-Bear inside the body within, and sealed the door. "God speed, little bear," he said. Uriel smiled and bathed Albert in light.

* * * * *

In 1965, Maria Sanchez dropped out of high school at the age of seventeen to marry Roberto Gonzalez. Their fathers had been friends since childhood, so they'd known each other their whole lives, and Roberto was a very good catch. Maria had found school boring and irrelevant. Roberto and his father owned and operated a small business that did upholstery work of all kinds—for cars, commercial firms like hotels, and interior designers. Maria loved paging through the big books of fabrics, and she saw herself sitting at an industrial sewing machine or tacking down trim on beautiful pieces of antique furniture. So when Roberto asked her to marry him, she said yes without hesitation.

They were married two months later at the big Catholic church in the plaza near Maria's house. The wedding party was large because Maria was the youngest of eight children, seven of them boys, and Roberto had six sisters. Maria only had to add her mother's youngest sister to even out the wedding procession, and her mother and Roberto's sewed all of the bridesmaids' dresses themselves.

The reception took place in Maria's parents' back yard, and all of her female relatives brought food for the buffet. Colored paper cut-outs strung on wires fluttered in the breeze above the celebrants' heads, and Mariache music played on her father's old record player. Everybody ate, drank, sang, and danced late into the night, and when Maria and Roberto stole away, the party was still going strong.

Roberto took his bride to the little four-hundred-square-foot cottage that stood behind his parents' house. Once a two-car garage, it had belonged to his grandmother until she passed away the previous winter. Now it would serve as a starter house for the two of them. At first, Maria thought that the tiny dwelling was cute with its bedroom, bath, kitchenette, and main room. But soon she was beginning to experience cabin fever. There were no closets, no storage, and more to the point, no place where she and her husband could go to create "spaces in their togetherness."

If Maria stepped outside into the yard, she found herself immediately in her in-laws' domain. If she walked out into the neighborhood, she had to deal with the searing heat or freezing cold of Albuquerque, New Mexico's weather extremes. So Maria found herself taking refuge at the family's workshop. At least it was air-conditioned...

There she was never alone. Six days a week, Roberto and his father worked in the office or out back in the garage re-upholstering car seats. And in the main room, Maria's six sisters-in-law sat at a row of sewing machines running seams eight hours a day while a radio blared in the background. Maria herself eventually found her niche answering phones, meeting with customers, helping them select fabrics and trims, taking their orders, and collecting payments. The front counter and the sample room became her private domain, and there she finally found peace.

Three months after starting work at the upholstery business, Maria found herself pregnant. Roberto and his family were delighted, and Maria prayed that the child would be a boy, someone to carry on the family name and its business. As the months went by, Maria grew round and heavy with child. Her back and feet ached constantly, but mindful that she needed to keep her place if she was to retain her sanity, she kept on working at the shop right up to the day of her delivery. When her contractions started, she called to her husband, he drove her to the hospital, she delivered a baby girl, Juanita, and then went home. A week later, she placed her infant in the arms of her mother-in-law and returned to work, the only difference being that she now sat on a stool behind the counter instead of standing.

Over the next three years, Maria had two miscarriages. So she and her husband were relieved when she managed to carry another baby to term, and this time, the child was a boy (Eduardo). Maria and Roberto doted on their son. Maria set up a playpen in the back office so that she could bring the child to work with her every day and keep him close, both to her and to the scene of the action in what would one day, she hoped, be his source of income.

Meanwhile, her mother-in-law continued to baby-sit her daughter Juanita, and as no one seemed particularly interested in the girl, she was left very much to her own devices and practically had to raise herself. By the time the girl reached the age of ten, she'd figured out how to walk and take the bus to reach her mother's family. There she received a warmer welcome. Her Abuela Sanchez taught her how to make tamales, bake enchiladas, sew clothes, and play piano. These lessons would stand her in good stead for the rest of her life.

When Juanita turned eighteen, a young second cousin on the Sanchez side caught her eye at a family party. She'd just graduated from high school and was trying to figure out her next move. She didn't want to end up sitting at one of the sewing machines in her father's shop. Becoming a wife and mother sounded much more attractive, so she set her cap for the cousin, and she let him chase her until she caught him.

Her parents weren't pleased by the match. The boy had a mercurial temperament and no immediate prospects. Her father tried to start the boy in the family upholstery business, but he had no work ethic to speak of and little attention to quality in what work he did do. So, before long, Roberto had to fire him. This outcome didn't dim Juanita's ardor in the slightest. Having had inadequate fathering in her youth, she was desperate to secure attention from a man of her own, and attention her cousin lavished on her in spades. Before Juanita could "seal the deal" and get the boy to put a ring on her finger, she found herself in the family way.

The next thing she knew, she and her beloved were having a shot-gun wedding down at the county clerk's office with no guests in attendance except their respective parents. Immediately after the ceremony, the groom's father dragged his son down to the local Army recruiting office. There the irate dad told the boy that he'd either join up and prove he was capable of becoming a man, or he'd end up buried in a shallow grave somewhere out in the desert. Juanita's husband signed the papers, and the Army shipped him overseas. A week later, Juanita moved into Abuela Sanchez's back bedroom, and thereafter, she spent her days doing housework and sewing baby clothes.

Two weeks before the baby was due, Abuela Sanchez answered a knock on her front door one afternoon to find a man in an Army dress uniform standing on the stoop. Abuela Sanchez had never been all that fond of her wastrel great nephew, so she didn't feel any real shock or grief herself, but she did love her granddaughter, so she tried to break the news to the girl gently. "Juanita," she called. "There's a man here to see you."

Juanita emerged from the kitchen, drying her hands on a tea towel. She waddled across the living room until the man on the doorstep came into view. Then she stopped, her eyes growing wide as she realized the implications, and she fainted.

Fortunately, Abuela Sanchez had seen Juanita lose color and start to sway, so she was able to reach the girl's side in time to prevent her from hitting the floor. With help from the man from the Army, Abuela Sanchez half-dragged Juanita to the couch and made her sit down. Then Abuela Sanchez used cold compresses and rapid pats on the cheek and hand to bring her granddaughter around.

Once Juanita was clearly awake, the man delivered his news. Her husband had been driving a supply truck in Iraq when, due to his carelessness and excessive speed, the truck had overturned, and he was killed. Fortunately, no one else was in the truck at the time. Even more fortunately, Juanita would now be eligible for widow's benefits.

Unbeknown to Juanita, that would not have been true if her husband had lived a few more weeks. Due to his gross insubordination and incompetence, he'd been in line to receive a dishonorable discharge. But in view of his death, his commanding officer had decided not to file the papers. Despite all the C.O. had experienced in the Iraqi war zone, he could still feel compassion for a young woman about to deliver her first baby.

After the Army man left, Juanita sat on her grandmother's couch for several hours, crying. Very quickly, she stopped crying for her no-good husband and began crying for herself, her un-born child, and the predicament in which they'd now find themselves. Abuela Sanchez assured Juanita that she could continue to live in the back bedroom, and Juanita knew that, thanks to the Army's pension fund, she'd still have a little money coming in. But it wouldn't be enough to raise her child properly. She'd have to get some kind of job, and that might mean asking Abuela Sanchez to raise her child, just as Juanita's mother Maria had asked Abuela Gonzalez to raise hers.

Juanita didn't want that outcome for her baby no matter how much she loved her grandmother. So the next day, after strategizing with her grandmother over breakfast, Juanita bathed, crammed her girth into a clean dress, and took the bus to her father's upholstery business downtown.

When she entered the store, her mother stood up from behind the front counter in surprise. Juanita wasted no time on pleasantries. "Carlos was killed in Iraq. I heard the news yesterday. After the baby is born, I'm going to need some kind of job. Abuela Sanchez says I can use the sewing machine in her front room to do mending and alterations. You know I can sew. I'm really good at it. So I'm here to ask you. May I put up a card on your bulletin board, advertising for customers?"

Maria shocked Juanita by walking around the counter and giving her daughter the first hug she'd delivered in a long time. "Yes, of course you may, and I'll also advertise for you by word of mouth. Please don't take this the wrong way, but I'm proud of you. You've grown up, and I want you to know I'm sorry I didn't do more to help you when you were younger."

Juanita was astonished by this confession, but she managed to compose herself and return her mother's hug. "I forgive you, *Mamacita*. Let's not be strangers anymore. I'll let you know when the baby's Christening happens so that you and *Papa* can attend."

"I'd like that very much." Maria released her daughter and stepped back.

Juanita fished a hand-lettered flyer out of her purse and gave it to her mother. Maria walked to the bulletin board and pinned up the flyer with thumbtacks. Then she turned and smiled wistfully at Juanita. Juanita smiled back, turned, and left the store. An hour later, after a sweltering bus ride, she'd made her way back home and was cooling off with some of Abuela Sanchez's homemade lemonade.

That night, Juanita went into premature labor and had to be rushed by ambulance to the hospital. Shortly after midnight, she delivered a daughter, and in a fit of misplaced sentiment, she named the girl Carla after the girl's dead father. Then Juanita chose Maria as the baby's middle name in token of their reconciliation. Maria was touched when she heard the news, and she gave Juanita a beautiful hand-made Christening blanket to wrap the child in for the ceremony.

*   *   *   *   *

Juanita raised Carla as a single mom living in Abuela Sanchez's house. Juanita and Carla shared the back bedroom—a cramped space just big enough for two twin beds separated by a nightstand. The single closet didn't afford much room for their clothes, but Juanita made the most of what room there was. She found a little chest of drawers at a thrift store and crammed it into the bottom, leaving the bar for clothes that must be hung and the top shelf for shoes.

Carla didn't complain about the close quarters, mainly because she knew that complaining would do no good. Abuela Sanchez occupied the other bedroom, and Juanita worked hard all day, caring for her grandmother and her daughter, completing mending and alteration jobs for clients, and teaching piano to neighborhood children in the evenings and on weekends. Although still a young woman, Juanita had perpetual dark circles under her eyes and the exhausted gate of a woman who toiled without ceasing and never got any true rest.

Every time Carla proved herself capable of taking on a new chore, Abuela Sanchez or Juanita would teach her the necessary skills, and thereafter, they'd delegate the work permanently. So Carla quickly became a capable and reliable helpmate to them both. Add in Carla's school work, which she did on the kitchen table every afternoon when she came home, and the girl had very little free time either. She dreamed of a better life, but whenever she dared to share her dreams with either of the other women in the house, they would simply say, "Finish school, and get a good job. That's how to give yourself the best chance of making your life what you want it to be."

Carla heeded their advice about finishing school. She graduated with honors because she was fairly bright and willing to work hard. But then she seemed to lose her way, drifting all summer through a series of part-time, temporary jobs such as serving as a library page on the local college campus and picking up trash at the county fairgrounds.

In the fall when the weather cooled off, she finally parlayed the job at the fairgrounds into a full-time gig as a waitress at the various concession stands. Her customers were almost always in a party-mood and tipped well, so in her view, the money was good. Abuela Sanchez feared that the job wasn't suitable for a girl Carla's age, and Juanita worried that the job was a dead-end with no future. But Carla was happy, and for once, she decided to listen to her own heart, not the warnings of her family.

All went well enough until October when the fairgrounds hosted the annual two-week-long harvest festival complete with a rodeo competition. Carla loved the noise and excitement of the event. She'd leave home early in the morning to give herself time to watch the cattle-roping and trick-riding before her shift began. Then she'd stay late to walk through the Midway, admiring the crafts for sale in the booths, enjoying the carnival rides, and eating the dreadful food available from the stands where she normally worked.

One morning a few days after the festival began, she was sitting in the bleachers, waiting for a junior-level calf-roping presentation to start, when a shadow fell across her legs. She looked up and saw the most handsome man she'd ever seen. He was over six feet tall, lean, broad-shouldered, and deep-chested with chiseled features. He smiled down at her, and the corners of his blue eyes crinkled in his golden-tanned face. He swept his cowboy hat from his head, releasing a shock of thick blond hair. "Is that seat beside you taken, little lady?"

Carla giggled and moved over to make room. The man sat down beside her, close but not too close, and he extended a hand. "Name's Chet, short for Chester... Chester Ames. And your name is?..."

Carla shook the proffered hand and said, "Call me Carla." For some reason, she didn't feel quite comfortable revealing her last name.

"Carla... That's a pretty name. You like the rodeo, Carla?" He sat hunched forward slightly, his elbows resting on his knees, his eyes stealing glances in her direction between sweeps across the arena before them.

"I do. I've never come before, but I'm working the event, so I'd be silly not to see at least some of it."

Chet smiled. "I guess you could say I'm working the event too. I'm in the running for first place in bronco riding and bull riding too. If I win both events, I might just win the top prize this year."

Carla was impressed in spite of herself. "You're here with your own horse and everything?"

"Horse, tack, trailer, truck, the works... That's how life is for rodeo pros. You travel around the country from event to event, and if you can beat the competition, you can make a living at it and never once have to go herd cattle on someone else's ranch." Chet laughed, but the sound wasn't entirely a happy one.

Carla stared at him appraisingly. "Do you think you really can take the top prize?"

"This year? Yup... Wanna know why? Because last year, my big brother retired. He got himself a grub stake, bought that piece of land he's had his eye on, and now he's running cattle on it and teaching his sons every trick he knows. Now that he's cleared the way for me, I aim to follow in his footsteps. That's what my family does. We're rodeo royalty going back three generations."

"Wow." Carla was about to ask him another question when, abruptly, he stood up.

"That's my signal. Gotta go. Say, where can I find you if I want to see you again?"

"I wait tables at the beer gardens all afternoon—whichever one needs me, but usually the one right outside the arena."

Chet jumped to the ground and gave her a slightly mocking salute. "I'll come and find you then. Take care, little lady." And he ambled away, making it look casual even though, with his long legs, he was actually traveling at a fairly high rate of speed.

Chet was as good as his word. After the last rodeo competition of the day, he strolled into the beer garden, ordered a pint, and nursed it for an hour while making small talk every time that Carla passed by his table. When she got off work, he accompanied her around the fair, buying her hotdogs and winning a garishly colored stuffed teddy bear for her by pitching softballs at stacks of wooden milk bottles. They finished the evening with a ride on the ferris wheel, and while parked at the top, waiting for other patrons to board their seat below, he stole a kiss from her, and she found that she didn't mind one bit.

When their ride ended and they walked out onto the Midway again, Chet offered to see her home. But suddenly feeling shy, she told him that there was no need. She could find her own way safely.

"Over-protective father with a shotgun?" he asked.

Carla laughed. "Something like that..."

"Gonna be here again tomorrow?"

"Got to... I work here full-time. So if you like, you can look me up... same time, same place..."

"OK, I'll see you then. Take care of yourself." He turned and headed off into the crowd, and Carla threaded her way between the booths out to the front gate. When she arrived home, she changed out of her waitress's uniform and went straight to bed. All night long, she dreamed of the tall cowboy who'd given her her very first kiss.

*   *   *   *   *

Chet won the rodeo's grand prize. Through diligent courtship, he also won Carla. In his eyes, she was a prize worth winning—young, slender-waisted, shapely, and pretty, with golden skin, sparkling dark eyes, a mane of waving brown hair, rosy cheeks, and full lips that practically begged to be kissed. The two lovers never had to worry about where to meet for their trysts. Her house was off-limits for obvious reasons, but Chet had a fully-renovated Airstream trailer—a legacy from his father's own rodeo days. The Airstream had a comfortable double bed in the back, a miniature bathroom, and should the lovers crave something to eat besides Midway food, there was a fully-stocked kitchenette with a pantry.

Chet tried to behave responsibly. He used protection, but he hadn't counted on the incredible fertility of the Sanchez-Gonzalez line. When he had to leave town to attend the next rodeo event of the season, he begged Carla to go with him, but given what had happened between her mother and father long ago, she decided that she'd do well to stay behind, get her head clear, and then see if she and Chet still really wanted to be together. So Chet left town without her, but not until he'd promised to be faithful and extracted her promise to be faithful too.

Chet called Carla every evening from the road. His calls became the focus of her life, the bright spot to which she could look forward regardless of what else might be going on. By this time, Carla's mother and great grandmother had learned about the relationship, and to say the least, they disapproved. A rodeo cowboy had no fixed address... no prospects once the injuries began piling up... and he faced countless temptations at all of the fairgrounds he attended. Where would he raise any children that came along? How could he guarantee his wife a living? The litany was endless and tedious, and Carla did her best to ignore them and shut out their protests.

In fact, her family's harangues helped her make up her mind at last. She decided that she'd join Chet on the road as soon as possible, and she reached that decision *before* she knew she was expecting. As she stood in the bathroom staring down at the positive pregnancy test, she felt joy well up within her. She'd tell him the good news the minute he called that night. She'd ask him where he planned to go next, and she'd take a bus or train to meet him there. Carla went to the room she shared with her mother and packed her clothes into a suitcase, making ready to depart the very next day. Then she went to the living room to sit and wait for Chet's expected call. It never came.

Carla waited until 9:00 at night. Then she found the dog-eared card in her purse on which he'd written his cell phone number. She dialed the number and listened as the call rang endlessly and then went to voicemail. She hung up and sat on the couch, filled with misgivings. Had he forgotten his vow? Was he with some other woman? That would be too ironic given that she'd just learned she was carrying his child... given that she'd just resolved to join him after all...

She dialed the phone again and got the same response. What if he'd been injured that day? He'd been fine the night before, filled with light-hearted news... making jokes... calling her Honey and telling her how much he missed her... She tried to think back. What town had he said he'd go to next? Maybe she should call all the hospitals there. If he'd been in some kind of accident, she wanted to rush to his side right away. In desperation, she dialed the phone one last time. This time, it rang twice before a voice answered—a man's voice very like Chet's but not the same. "Hello?" the voice asked.

"Oh, thank God!" Carla exclaimed. "Please, don't hang up. I've been trying to reach Chet. Please tell me, is he all right?"

There was a moment of silence at the other end of the line. Then, in a sad tone, the voice asked, "Who is this please?"

"I'm... I'm Chet's fiancée. Please, tell me who you are."

"I'm his brother, James. I'm sorry, miss, but I don't know your name."

"It's Carla. I'm Carla."

She heard James sigh. "Carla, I'm so sorry to have to tell you this, but Chet was killed in a riding accident this morning. A horse he was breaking threw him, and he hit the ground at a bad angle. He broke his neck and died instantly."

"Oh, no! Oh, no!" Carla began to cry, but she tried not to make any sound because James was still talking.

"I flew in early this afternoon as soon as I got the news. I've directed the funeral home to send his body to my ranch. We'll bury him there, and if you want to come visit the grave site, I can give you directions on how to find us. I'm sorry I hadn't gotten around to notifying you yet. Chet told us that he'd met someone special and that he was in love, but he hadn't given us too many details—little things like your name, where you live, stuff like that... typical of him..." And Carla heard James begin to cry too. "I know you made him very happy, though, and I did plan to call you. I have your number after all. It must be in his phone about a thousand times, not to mention in his contact list under 'Sweetheart'..."

Carla was crying now in earnest. Still, she was able to choke out a few words. "He made me happy too. I don't know how I'll go on without him."

"Do you want our address and phone number?"

"Please." Carla grabbed a pen from the coffee table in front of her and prepared to add James's contact data to Chet's card. "Go ahead."

James spelled out his address and phone number for her and confirmed what she had when she read it back. Then he said, "I'd like to talk longer and hear about how you met Chet, but at this point, I'm exhausted. I'm sure you understand. It's been a really tough day."

"Yes, I understand. I have your number. I can call some other time." She felt her throat begin to close again. She managed to gasp, "I'm... so sorry for your loss."

"And I am for yours." And she heard the line go dead.

Carla ended her call and sat stunned... absolutely aching with grief. Unconsciously, she began rubbing her belly with one hand. When she caught herself at it, she realized that she'd forgotten to tell James the most important piece of news she could have relayed. Oh well, as she'd said, she had his number and could call some other time.

But somehow, she doubted that she would. Neither would she go to the trouble and expense of traveling to the ranch. Why should she when all she'd find there would be a recently-filled seven-foot-long hole in the ground, that and possibly a head stone? No, she needed to conserve her money and her energy. She had the baby to think of and plan for, and her focus must now be on breaking the news to her family and figuring out a way to make a better living.

The next morning at breakfast, when her mother asked her why she looked like she hadn't slept a wink, Carla broke down, and through renewed tears, she told Juanita and Abuela Sanchez the whole story. Her mother sat silent for an instant. Then she leaped to her feet and shouted, "How could you be so stupid? I've told you my story more times than I can count. How could you be so dumb as to repeat my mistakes?" Juanita left the kitchen, stomped off down the hall to the bedroom, and slammed the door, making the whole house shake with the force of her anger.

Abuela Sanchez sighed, rose to her feet as well, walked around the table, and embraced Carla's shaking shoulders. "Don't worry," she told her. "I've raised eight children of my own, your mother Juanita, and you. I may be in my late eighties, but my family is tough and long-lived. I think I have it in me to help raise one more generation. We'll get through this somehow."

Deeply moved, Carla placed her hand over one of Abuela Sanchez's withered, arthritic claws. "I know we will. We have to... for the baby..." The two women stood for a moment united in that resolve. Then they went their separate ways to begin their days.

*   *   *   *   *

Inside Carla's womb, T-bear did as his sister Susan had done. He lobbied ceaselessly to be given back at least some portion of his previous identity. "My name is T-Bear. Call me T-Bear. Please, let me be known as T-Bear..."

A little more than eight months after Carla got the news about Chet, she went into labor. She hadn't been able to afford much pre-natal medical care. Such care as she'd received had been through a neighborhood free clinic. So when she was certain that her baby was on the way, she had Juanita call Grandfather Roberto. He picked up Carla, drove her to the nearest Emergency Room, dropped her off at the front door, and then went to park the car. Carla struggled into the ER lobby and would have gone to the front desk to check in, but her water broke, and she collapsed on the linoleum floor.

Of course, as soon as she did so, she got the complete attention of the nurses on duty. They scooped her up and placed her in a wheelchair. They paged Obstetrics and got a doctor to come downstairs. They put Carla on a bed in one of the bays and pulled the curtains around her for privacy. And within half an hour, Carla had delivered her son and was holding him, wrapped in a blanket, on her chest.

A nurse asked Carla if she'd like her Grandfather Roberto to join her. Carla shrugged, smiled softly, and said, "Sure."

The nurse pulled a curtain aside and ushered Grandfather Roberto into the bay. He entered saying, "How much is the bill going to be? She has no insurance, so we'll have to figure out how we're going to pay for all this..."

"I understand, sir. Let's worry about that later. Right now, let's go meet your great-grandson." The nurse turned to Carla. "Do you know what you want to name him yet?"

Carla smiled down at her little boy. She already found him beautiful, and she couldn't help wondering if he'd inherited his father Chet's good looks. "Yes, I think I do. I think I'd like to name him Theodore... Theodore Bernardo Sanchez... Maybe Teddy for short..."

Roberto grimaced and said, "That's an idiotic name. The other kids at school will tease him terribly."

T-Bear thought, "A lot you know. That name is just about as perfect as I could have hoped for... I think I'm going to like having this woman as my mother. She listens well..." And he nestled down into her arms and went to sleep.

2: Teddy Meets His New Family...

Up in Heaven, the Receiving department was in an uproar. They'd recently collected the soul of a rodeo cowboy, and he was not adapting well to the change in his circumstances. Before long, the department head heard the ruckus and rushed over to try and calm things down. He arrived just in time to duck as the cowboy flung a double handful of spirit-matter at the department head's head.

"You've made a mistake! I can't be dead!" the cowboy bellowed. "I'm supposed to marry Carla! We're supposed to live together happily every after! We're supposed to buy some land, have children, and raise them on our ranch. This is just wrong!" He kicked violently at the insubstantial cloud-stuff beneath his feet and then stood with his fists clenched and a scowl on his face that would have frightened Lucifer.

The head of Receiving blanched. For a moment, he couldn't help but wonder if there had been some sort of error. No such mistake had ever happened on his watch, but perhaps one could have happened before his time. And if such an error did occur, it would be virtually impossible to reverse. By now, this man's body had undoubtedly been claimed and either interred or destroyed for both reverent and sanitary reasons.

The head of Receiving decided that he'd better check his records. "Please, sir?... sir?..." The cowboy continued to rant and rave at high volume, but the head of Receiving was both patient and persistent when he needed to get something done. "Sir?"

The cowboy paused in the middle of a highly creative string of cuss-words and turned to face the source of this interruption. "What?!"

"Sir? I'd like to help you if I can. But I'll need some information from you first, like your name..."

The cowboy drew himself up to his full height of over six feet. In life, the head of Receiving had been far shorter, so because he'd chosen to present himself very much as he'd appeared on Earth, the cowboy now seemed to tower over him. "Chester William Ames, and I'm supposed to be in Denver, Colorado, winning a rodeo competition, not cooling my heals here with you nitwits."

"Yes, sir. If you'll excuse me a moment, I'll go consult my records. Be right back..." The head of Receiving vanished briefly and then reappeared accompanied by the archangel Uriel.

Uriel looked the cowboy up and down. "This is the man?"

"Yes, and per my records, he's supposed to be here."

Chet opened his mouth to renew his protests, but Uriel deluged him preemptively in loving light. Chet's eyes went slightly out of focus for an instant. Then he shook his head and frowned. "Don't think you can get around me with your parlor tricks."

"Parlor tricks?" Uriel burst into delighted laughter, and because angelic laughter is contagious, everyone else began laughing too—everyone but Chet, that is...

"This isn't funny! Carla and I had found true love... the real deal. You can't take that away from me! It isn't fair!"

Uriel shook his head sadly. "No, it isn't fair if you look at Earthly life as a closed system. But it's not. Life is always and inevitably completed here. If you and Carla are meant to be together, then you will be, but after she too has passed away. From her perspective, the wait may be long, but then she'll join you here, and the two of you will know an eternity of greater bliss than you could ever have known on Earth. Just think of what life there is really like. There are blessings of course..."

"Eating a good meal together... Sitting on the front porch on a summer evening listening to the crickets... Sleeping beside each other warm and snug through a cold winter night..."

"Yes, all of that, and holding your new-born child in your arms... watching that baby grow up to adulthood... I agree that Earthly life can be wonderful. But there are also trials... finding the money to pay the bills during hard times... nursing a loved one through a long and painful illness... staying up nights sick with worry when a child has lost his way and is in trouble..."

Chet's expression was suddenly grave. "Was all that in store for me? Are you telling me that you've saved me from all that suffering?"

"No one can say for sure. Your path was only clearly defined up to the point when that bronco threw you. After that, there was an almost ninety-five percent probability that you'd end up here. But even if you hadn't, your life would never have been the same. In all of the other outcomes, you would have been at least paralyzed and possibly brain-damaged. Is that a life you would have wished on Carla?"

Chet grimaced. "Oh god, no!"

Uriel smiled softly, his eyes still sad. "Then are you willing to wait for her to join you here?... assuming that you're right and the two of you are destined to be together... If it's any consolation, to you, the wait will seem to take absolutely no time at all."

Chet's eyes were bright with unshed tears. "Yes, I guess I am willing to wait. After all, she's worth waiting for. I just wish we could have had children together. We talked about it, you know... how great it would be to make a baby..."

Uriel was still smiling, and the sadness had left his eyes. "Then I have a happy surprise for you. You did make a baby, a son. She's named him Theodore which means 'Gift of God'—an apt name given that he has an old soul and will be a musical prodigy. If all goes well, he'll be famous the world over. Would you like to watch him grow up?"

Chet's face filled with excitement. "Could I? That would be awesome!"

Uriel turned to the head of Receiving. "How delightful! Not only has Chet joined us, he's already proving to be perfect for one of our most important roles. If you like, I can introduce Chet to the Watchers and match him with a mentor so he can get started. Can you suggest anyone who might fill the bill?"

The head of Receiving was wearing a wide grin. "Perhaps my wife Nana would enjoy mentoring Chet."

"Splendid idea..." and Uriel swiftly departed with Chet in tow.

A moment later, they appeared at Nana's side. Uriel introduced the two of them and asked Nana if she'd like to train Chet. As Uriel explained more about who Chet was, Nana began nodding enthusiastically, her eyes twinkling mischievously and her smile broadening into a wide grin just like her husband's.

Chet watched as her expression changed. "Is there something going on here that I don't know?"

Nana hastened to reassure him. "Oh no, my dear. It's just that *I* was planning to watch over Theodore, but I'm watching so many souls already. I'll be very glad to have your help."

"OK then." Out of politeness, Chet behaved as if he accepted her explanation. But Chet was nobody's fool. Deep down, he remained convinced that, behind the scenes, many mysterious wheels were turning, and he privately resolved to explore the matter further when he had the chance.

*   *   *   *   *

Meanwhile, Abuela Sanchez and her immediate family were having to make a lot of adjustments. Carla came home from the hospital to find that, going forward, two bedrooms would simply not be enough. For one thing, the tiny room she'd been sharing with her mother Juanita didn't have space for a crib for Teddy, or for the bundles of clothes and bedding that Carla had sewn for him. For another thing, Juanita was too weary and work-worn to welcome having a squalling baby share her room at night.

So Carla took to sleeping on the living room couch, and she solved the crib problem by bedding down Teddy each night in a big laundry basket lined with blankets. She'd place the basket on the coffee table beside her. That way, if Teddy began to fuss, Carla would awaken immediately and feed him before his cries could disturb Juanita in the other room.

Carla was an attentive and loving mother to her infant son. She took him down to the free clinic for check-ups and vaccinations right on schedule, and at the point when she needed to resume work, she got the clinic to help her get a breast pump so that Teddy could continue to consume a healthy, natural diet rather than formula.

By this time, Teddy had won over his grandmother Juanita. She still chafed at the notion that Carla was an unwed mother and Teddy was illegitimate. But after consulting with the parish priest, Juanita decided that God would want her to forgive Carla and show compassion to an innocent baby. The latter was made all the easier because Teddy himself was so endearing. He had a sunny, placid disposition and almost never cried.

Also, although Juanita couldn't know it, except for Teddy's dark hair and brown eyes, he *had* inherited his father's good looks—looks derived from a combination of refined features and great bone structure. Juanita would stand over his basket, gently tickling him and crooning, "Who's a handsome boy? You're a handsome boy. Yes you are!" while Teddy giggled and waved his tiny fists in the air.

Juanita was usually too busy serving her various clients to do much baby-sitting. But sometimes, in between the clothing alterations, piano lessons, and housework that she did, she'd find time to hold Teddy on her lap and sing to him. She'd noticed that he seemed to really enjoy the times when she played music on the old upright piano in the corner. He'd fuss whenever her piano students played badly, so she'd sometimes have to put his basket in the back room and close the door before she started a lesson. But whenever she played or sang, Teddy would listen wide-eyed and make soft cooing noises.

Abuela Sanchez also sang to Teddy, but instead of the Spanish folk songs that Juanita favored, she chose songs that she'd heard on the radio in her youth. She'd bend over, cracking her back, and lift him out of his basket into her leathery, sun-burned arms. Then she'd shuffle around the living room singing, "Oh baby, won't you be, my lovin' teddy bear..."—changing Elvis Presley's lyrics to suit the situation and flavoring his hit with her strong Mexican accent. Teddy loved it. He'd laugh and squeal and nestle against her ample bosom in utter delight.

Abuela Sanchez did most of the baby-sitting, just as she'd promised Carla she would. All day long, while Carla was at work, Abuela Sanchez would fetch Teddy bottles of breast milk when he was hungry and play with him when he was bored. Then, when nap time came, Abuela Sanchez would carry him into her room and place him in a protective circle of folded blankets on her double bed. Often when Juanita looked for her grandmother in the afternoon, she'd find Abuela Sanchez and Teddy taking their naps side-by-side on the old quilted counterpane. Whenever that happened, Juanita would tip-toe out of the room and quietly close the door behind her so as not to interrupt their rest.

Meanwhile, Carla was struggling to earn enough money to support herself and her son. By the time she was fit to work again, the fairgrounds had long-since replaced her. So she had to go look for new jobs, and being an experienced waitress with a strong work ethic, she soon found some.

The first position she found was a part-time gig at a tourist-trap Mexican restaurant in Old Town. The female proprietor promised that, if a dinner slot opened up in the schedule, Carla would be first in line to take it. But at present, the only opening the boss had was a job handling the lunch-time trade. The tips weren't as big as dinner tips would be, but the restaurant did brisk business from when they opened at 11:00 until they closed at 3:00. So what Carla lost in tip size, she made up in quantity. Moreover, with her pretty face and shapely figure, she ultimately became almost as big a draw as the three-enchilada-plate special. The patrons loved her, and ultimately, so did her employer.

Her popularity worked in her favor. The man who ran a faux wild-west saloon down the street came in for a burrito one day, spotted her, and asked her if she'd like to work evening shifts at his place six days a week. The uniform wouldn't be as nice. Instead of the embroidered, all-cotton, full-skirted Mexican-style dress she wore at the restaurant, she'd have to wear a feather hair ornament, a satin bustier, a short velveteen skirt, black fishnet stockings, and lace-up black high-heeled boots. Carla knew from gossip on the street that the outfit was horribly uncomfortable, especially in the summertime. But she also knew that the costume was part of the ambiance, and the ambiance was what drew in the tourist clientele. Certainly, they didn't come for the watered drinks and industrial-grade margaritas dispensed from a carboy in the back room.

Carla knew that she'd soon tire of the bar's tape loop of tinkling piano music. She also knew that she'd have to become an acrobat to carry trays of drinks to tables while avoiding getting pinched on the derrière. But the pay the owner was offering was half-again as high as what she could pull down at the taco joint, so she squared things with her boss at the restaurant and then signed up for the additional shifts at the bar. The money from the bar job went a long way toward closing the gap between Carla's earnings and her expenses, but nevertheless, a small gap still remained. So Carla kept on looking for more work, and before long, a few more jobs came her way.

Albuquerque's Old Town was packed solid with shops selling rugs, baskets, pottery, and silver jewelry made by the nearby Native American tribes. Carla picked up a couple of hours each morning manning the cash register at a shop less than a block from the restaurant. If it had been one of the high-end shops, she would have been required to dress like an employee at an elite art gallery. But the shop was a low-end emporium catering to visitors who wanted to pick up a souvenir before they returned home. So Carla could get away with wearing her Mexican dress, and if she ran from one job to the next, she could make it to the restaurant in time to start her shift.

The shop was in a weathered wooden building that looked like it hailed from a ghost town. There was no air-conditioning, and inside, the wares were piled up in the glass cases like findings at a flea market. Carla thought it was sad that it was so. The individual pieces were beautifully crafted, and she wished that she could afford even one of the pendants or perhaps a simple ring. She loved the way the inlays contrasted with the sterling silver—turquoise and coral, carnelian and malachite, onyx and mother of pearl... so beautiful, and the metal-work designs were also splendid.

The shopkeeper caught her looking at a turquoise pendant one day, and he warned her that most modern turquoise was either artificially-colored, inferior-grade stone, or it might even be plastic. He advised her that, if she wanted real turquoise, she should walk down to the pawn shop at the edge of Old Town. There, Native Americans who were down on their luck would sometimes trade family heirlooms for cash. In the old silver pieces, the turquoise was real, and the designs weren't just pretty. To the tribal people, they still held spiritual significance.

Carla thanked the man for teaching her how to avoid being cheated, but in truth, she didn't expect to benefit from the knowledge anytime soon. After all, every penny she had was still going for food and other necessities. She didn't have money for frivolities like personal adornment. She tried to suppress her longing and just enjoy the wares that surrounded her two hours a day the way one would enjoy a field of flowers or the sky—something lovely, but not something that she could ever have for her own.

So Carla was occupied morning, noon, and night, six to seven days a week. In the winter, she picked up a one-day-a-week temp job selling Christmas ornaments at a boutique. In the spring and fall, she picked up temp jobs selling candy and ice cream. She couldn't go to church because all of her jobs required that she work Sundays. The Old Town shops closed on Mondays if they closed at all. Thus she almost never saw her son awake.

The good news was that she could take the bus between Abuela Sanchez's house and Old Town, but the bad news was that, after her shift at the bar, she wouldn't arrive home until after midnight. By that time, she barely had the energy to choke down whatever supper her mother had left for her in the refrigerator. Then she'd take a bath and collapse on the couch beside Teddy's basket, a basket that he would obviously soon outgrow.

Carla began to feel desperate. When the basket would no longer serve its purpose, she made a bed for Teddy out of folded blankets on the floor. Each day at 3:00 after her waitressing shift ended, she'd walk directly to the bar, let herself in through the back door using her key, and try to catch an hour and a half of sleep on a table in the back room before her next shift started at 5:00. Whenever she accidentally over-slept, one of the other barmaids would wake her. But sometimes they'd forget to do so until the bar was about to open. So more than once, Carla had to cram herself into her costume with only minutes to spare.

The life she was living was nerve-racking... too much to do... too few resources... absolutely no wiggle-room... Sleeping on the couch each night was giving her chronic neck and back pain, and working on her feet all day in bad shoes was giving her corns and bunions. Juanita was too busy with her own burdens to really notice Carla's coming crisis, but fortunately, Abuela Sanchez saw what was happening and stepped in. She invoked her authority as clan matriarch and summoned help in the form of her sons, grandsons, and great-grandsons. She had a plan, and she was going to need a lot of free labor to enact it.

Out in Abuela Sanchez's back yard, there stood an old one-car garage with an attached workshop. The building had been abandoned for years and it had begun to lean slightly to the left—its clap-board walls so weathered that one could no longer tell what color they'd been painted, and its asphalt-shingled roof so damaged by the harsh New Mexico sun that, during monsoon season, water poured through the ceiling as through a sieve.

Until Abuela Sanchez put out her call, everyone in the family had assumed that the building would simply continue to fall to wrack and ruin until it ultimately collapsed in a heap. After all, no one in Abuela Sanchez's house had owned a car for decades, and nobody had used the workshop since her husband died. However, she now put them all to work pulling down the old building, but carefully, so as to salvage as much of the lumber and the other materials as possible.

One of her grandsons was a general contractor, and he explained the importance of doing a one-wall remodel to avoid permitting problems. She heeded his advice and let him lead the project. She knew that he could keep them out of trouble, on this issue and on many others. Soon when she looked out of her kitchen window, she saw a tall stack of old boards on the far side of her back yard, and where the garage had stood, there was a bare concrete slab surrounded on three and a half sides by cinder block footings. One of the footings still supported a wooden wall, but it was propped up by two-by-fours and would clearly tumble down the instant they were removed.

Abuela Sanchez decided that it was time for phase two of her plan. She called her contractor-grandson, and throughout a long afternoon during which she plied him with all of his favorite foods, she outlined what she had in mind. He agreed that what she wanted was feasible, and the next morning, he and his relatives set to work.

What Abuela Sanchez wanted was a tiny cottage for Carla and Teddy—something similar to the starter house that her daughter Maria had lived in for so long. It didn't have to be fancy—just a small sitting room with two curtained alcoves for single beds... a kitchenette with a sink, a hot plate, a microwave oven, and a small fridge... and a little bathroom with a toilet and a shower.

The garage and workshop had been wired for power tools, so electricity would be no problem. The hard part would be connecting the cottage to the main house's water and sewer lines. The men would have to trench before they could start raising the walls. The contractor-grandson said he knew where they could get second-hand plumbing fixtures for not much money. He also knew an electrician who owed him a favor and would probably be willing to do the re-wiring for free. For the rest, they'd have to work mostly with supplies on hand. Abuela Sanchez kissed her grandson on his forehead and told him that he was a good boy. Pleased, he replied that she might have a completed cottage in her backyard in just a month or two.

Abuela Sanchez's male descendants got to work making authentic adobe bricks. The soil in the back yard was sandy down to a depth of a foot or so, but deeper still, it was all clay with embedded pudding stones—possibly the remnant of an ancient, long-gone river or an inland sea. The men shoveled the sand aside. In parallel, they made forms out of the worst of the lumber. Then they dug up the clay, extracted the pudding stones, and piled them in a heap beside the lumber.

True adobe is a mix of clay and straw. Abuela Sanchez wondered where the straw was going to come from until the evening when a great-grandson who worked at the fairgrounds came roaring up the street in his pickup truck. He screeched to a halt in front of her house. Then he backed expertly into her driveway and pulled to a stop. His brothers piled out of the truck's cab and began unloading its contents—a dozen bales of straw like the ones the fairground usually used to provide informal seating for visitors. Abuela Sanchez shook her head over this likely theft, but she knew that a few missing bales would never be noticed, not given the thousands the fairgrounds probably had, and one could argue that the straw had been appropriated for a very good cause.

The next time Abuela Sanchez looked out of her kitchen window, two great-grandsons were standing shirtless over a pit, mixing straw, clay, and water together with shovels. The contractor-grandson was barking orders, and his younger brothers were packing wooden forms with adobe and smoothing off the tops. Rank upon rank of bricks began to fill up Abuela Sanchez's back yard, and the drying bricks all looked handsome and well-made. The following day, when the first of the bricks were completely dry, the contractor-grandson supervised as his cousins strung twine on stakes to ensure that their work would be level. Then they began laying brick on the building's footings.

Given that they were working with adobe bricks held together with adobe mortar, they couldn't raise the wall by too many courses before they had to take a break and let things dry further. But still, the walls seemed to go up swiftly, and before long, the men began framing in windows using the lumber they'd saved.

At last, the walls reached their full height. Abuela Sanchez watched as the men applied a thick coat of protective plaster to the walls' interior and an even thicker coat of water-proof stucco to the outside. Then they framed-in partition walls, counters, and cabinets inside the cottage using the reclaimed lumber.

The most difficult part of the framing job entailed building the supports for the roof. The cottage would have a "floating roof" that rested its weight on pylons rather than on the adobe walls. The contractor had designed a simple solution in which insulation was stapled directly to the plywood between the rafters, the joists were all exposed, and the whole underside was spray-painted flat-black to make the "ceiling" disappear visually. On the outside, the plywood roof was covered with water-proofing and thin sheets of interlocking steel. It was a roof to last until the next millennium—monsoon-proof, virtually fire-proof, and likely to stand up to the searing New Mexico sun as well. Plus the wide eaves would give further protection to the adobe walls below.

Finally, the cottage was almost finished. The men spent a frustrating couple of days doing wiring and plumbing, but finally the cottage was ready for occupants—all but for one small detail that is. As his last act, the contractor-grandson took down the one remaining original wall that had justified the building permit. In its place, he erected a solid door with glass brick side-lights. Then he went to summon a more exacting inspector than the one the city had sent—his abuela.

She shuffled out of her kitchen door and up the driveway to the tiny house. She walked slowly around its perimeter, examining every detail of the outside. Then she asked to see the inside. When she saw what they'd been able to produce with the reclaimed lumber they'd used, she was impressed. The cabinet-work was neat and craftsman-like. The paint-work was clean and fresh. Curtain bars hung at the windows and in the alcoves, ready to receive curtains whenever they could be completed, and the concrete floor had been stained and water-proofed to look like natural stone. Even the cracks had been incorporated, resembling fissures in the native rock.

Abuela Sanchez turned to her grandson with tears in her eyes. "It's beautiful. Thank you."

The man pursed his lips. "There are a couple of things still to be done in my view."

"What more could any of you possibly do? This is already all that I'd hoped for and more..."

"I'm going to clean up your back yard, Abuela. We can use the pudding stone with cement to build you some decorative planters. We can bring in some top soil, mix it with the sand, and smooth it over so your yard is safe to walk in. I don't want any of you to trip in the dark. The way we've left things after all this construction, the whole yard is full of potential pitfalls."

Abuela Sanchez nodded. She saw the wisdom in what he proposed. But he wasn't done speaking.

"I'm also going to hit up the family for some additional help. You'll need at least a few pieces of furniture for the cottage—a couple of narrow beds, a small kitchen table, two chairs, and maybe a love seat or a little couch. An area rug might not be amiss either."

"You don't have to do that. We can get by somehow."

"Nonsense. We wouldn't even exist without you. We love you, Abuela, and Juanita and Carla have struggled long enough. We're proud of you all that you've done so well on your own, but now it's time for family to help family. All these weeks while we've been doing this construction job for you, I've watched what's been going on inside your house. You called us because Carla is in desperate straits, and her mother is just shy of forty, but she looks like she's fifty at least.

"Surely one of my brothers, nephews, or sons can find Carla a job that she can do—something that pays better and has better hours than the insane schedule that she's been keeping. As for Juanita, we should be using our connections to find her more profitable sewing jobs. There are interior design firms all over town now—serving the needs of the 'snow birds' who retire here from the northeast or vacation here during the winter. They want drapes and pillows and all kinds of froufrou stuff. Why shouldn't Juanita be the one to supply it?"

Abuela Sanchez smiled. "OK, you've convinced me. Go ahead. Find a new job for Carla and better customers for Juanita. I love them dearly and wish with all my heart that they could be happier." Her grandson bent and kissed her on the cheek. She patted his shoulder approvingly, and the two of them returned to the house.

*   *   *   *   *

When Carla finally saw the finished cottage, she cried. By the time Abuela Sanchez and Juanita took her to see it and gave her the keys, the rest of the family had come through and furnished the place completely. Nothing was new of course. One household contributed the still-functional fridge that had stood in their garage. Another donated the microwave oven their son had used while at college. Still another delivered towels and bed linens that they'd bought for their daughter's trousseau. When the girl's fiancé broke off the engagement, she'd demanded that the goods be removed from her sight. That was when her parents found that they'd lost the receipt, ruining any chance they'd had of returning the wares to the store.

Carla didn't care. She was delighted to have her own home with her own things—a place where she could raise her son the way she'd always dreamed of doing. For the family had found her a new job too. So now she worked a mere forty-five hours a week, doing simple book-keeping and reception work for her great uncle's construction business. She was so grateful not to be working multiple part-time and temporary jobs anymore that she did everything she could to help him and his employees, and before long, he was wondering how he'd ever gotten along without her.

For his part, Teddy was much happier too. He liked the new house as much as she did. More to the point, he loved his mother and was delighted that he now got to eat breakfast and dinner with her everyday, not to mention spending each weekend in her company. And during the week while his mother was at work, he still got to visit with Grandma Juanita and Abuela Sanchez. At ninety-three, Abuela Sanchez was noticeably beginning to slow down, but she was still a very happy, wise, and warm-hearted person.

As for Teddy's Grandma Juanita, she was now making enough money from her home-decor sewing clients that she decided she could finally afford to drop her piano students. The only child she continued to teach was Teddy. Time and again, she'd seen him climb laboriously up onto the piano bench and begin to finger the keys, so clearly he had the interest. Even though his little legs were so short that they stuck straight out in front of him when he sat at the keyboard, she began teaching him simple tunes from the introductory piano primer she'd always used.

Then he surprised her one day. He completed a tune that they'd been practicing. (So far, so good...) However, next he turned the page to a tune they'd never covered, and he played it note-perfect. At that moment, Juanita realized that her grandson could already read music.

As an experiment, she handed him the next practice book in the series and then listened, astounded, as he played his way through it over the following couple of days. Although she'd never used that book with any of her students, it was like he'd somehow heard all the tunes before. From then on, he continued to play as if he was simply remembering something that he'd learned quite thoroughly somewhere else a very long time ago. Juanita began pondering whether or not her grandson might be a piano prodigy, and if he was, how she would get him the proper instruction to help him capitalize on his talents.

For his part, Teddy wasn't worried. He was simply enjoying the process of getting reacquainted with his favorite instrument. He was a bit frustrated by having such short fingers, but he knew that, given time, they'd grow, and he remembered well how he'd once had a friend who'd faced the same issue... faced it and overcome it... a sweet-natured child with whom he'd written a gloriously beautiful piece of music. He hoped to be able to play that music again soon. He resolved to practice assiduously until he could.

*   *   *   *   *

When Teddy turned six, his mother Carla enrolled him in first grade at the local elementary school. The other kids in the class had already spent a year in kindergarten together, so they'd already formed their friendships and cliques. But Carla hadn't seen any use in the kindergarten curriculum, so she'd skipped it, and Teddy would be joining the first grade social *milieu* as if he was a new kid in town.

On his first day of class, Juanita fed him breakfast, made sure he was dressed properly for school, and then walked with him to the corner where the school bus would pick him up. As the bus approached, she bent down, handed him a brown-bag lunch, kissed him on the cheek, and promised to meet him there when the bus dropped him off in the afternoon.

The bus pulled up, its door opened, and Teddy climbed inside, not sure at all what to expect from the school experience. Two days earlier, he'd heard Carla complain to Abuela Sanchez that reading, writing, and arithmetic all had value, but in her view, building blocks, finger paints, clay ashtrays, and shoe-box dioramas did not.

The bus took Teddy and its other rowdy passengers to the parking lot adjoining the school's playground. There it shuddered to a halt, the doors opened, and the driver bellowed, "OK, kids, everybody out..." Teddy kept his seat until the initial stampede abated. Then he stood up, made his way up the center aisle, down the steps, and out into sunlight so hot and blinding that it felt like a hammer-blow. He turned to ask the driver a question, but the man slammed the door shut and drove away.

Teddy looked around for some other adult who could help him and spotted a well-dressed man standing underneath the portico, apparently supervising the stream of children heading toward the classrooms. Teddy approached him. "Excuse me, sir. Can you tell me how to get to the right room for first grade?"

"I have no idea, kid. I'm just waiting for my wife to return. She's dropping off our daughter."

Teddy was abashed. He looked around and spotted a young woman wearing a gingham shirtwaist dress and carrying a clipboard. He walked up to her. "Excuse me, ma'am. I'm trying to find the first grade classroom."

The woman scarcely looked up. She made a quick notation on her clipboard and then pointed toward one of the corridors. "That way, and hurry. The tardy bell is about to ring."

"Thanks!" Teddy dashed off in the direction she'd indicated. He heard her cry, "No running on school grounds!" He slowed to a walk and continued past a series of open doors. He peered into each one as he passed it, looking for a room full of children his own age. At last he found one. He went inside and tried to get the attention of the teacher. "Excuse me."

She continued writing on the blackboard, but at least she answered. "Yes, can I help you?"

"Is this the right room for first grade?"

"Yes. Take any seat. I'll get you all sorted out when I do roll call."

Teddy did as she'd bidden. He approached an empty chair, but the girl at the neighboring desk saw him coming and threw her sweater over the chair seat. "This one's taken."

Teddy turned and headed for another chair. The boys on either side of it began shaking their heads at him, warning him away. Depressed by this reception, Teddy walked to the back of the room and took a seat there. From that position, he had a clear view of all the other students, and he couldn't help but compare them to himself.

He saw that he was the only one carrying a brown-bag lunch. All the other children had brightly-colored tin lunch pails or no lunches at all, just money. Also, his clothes were considerably more faded and his shoes, a lot more worn and down at the heel. None of the other kids looked rich exactly, but Teddy saw clearly that their parents must be better off than the women in his family. Teddy grimaced and told himself that he should keep this a secret from Abuela Sanchez. She and Grandma Juanita had worked hard to make sure he'd have everything he needed. He didn't want to hurt their feelings by letting them know that they'd fallen short.

Just then, a bell rang loudly out in the hall. The teacher stopped writing on the blackboard, turned around, and said, "OK, class, come to order. First, we're going to say the pledge of allegiance. So stand up, put your right hand over your heart, face the flag, and repeat after me..." Teddy did as instructed. He found the words the teacher spoke to be a bit confusing, but also inspiring. Then the teacher told the class to take their seats.

"Next, I'm going to call roll. When I say your name, I want you to raise your hand in the air and say, 'Here...' Then walk *quietly* to the front of the room and line up beside the person I called before you. Once all of you are lined up at the front, I'll assign you your seats for the rest of the year. Does anyone have any questions? No? OK, here we go. Pablo Alvarez..."

"Here."

"Catherine Bailey..."

Teddy quickly deduced that his name wouldn't be called for some time and he could afford to look around the classroom at the bulletin boards. He liked the bold colors of the maps and posters displayed there, but although they featured lots of words and numbers, he looked in vain for any musical notes or symbols. He didn't see anything related to what had come to interest him most.

"Theodore Sanchez... Theodore?"

Teddy started, then raised his hand. "Here!" He heard his classmates snigger, and one boy muttered under his breath, "Oh, *Theodore*... His mommy must *really* love him!"

Teddy felt his face grow hot, but he scrambled to his feet, walked to the front of the room, and took his place in line.

"Estaban Zuniga..." One of the boys who'd waved Teddy away earlier now held up his hand and sauntered to the front.

The teacher closed her notebook and exclaimed. "Well done so far. Next, I want you to take your seats as follows. Pablo, you're in the front row all the way to my left." She pointed, and he took the seat she indicated. "Catherine, you're next to Pablo. The rest of you, continue taking seats in the front row until it's filled. Great. Now fill the second row starting with the seat behind Pablo."

Teddy watched as the rows filled, one after another. Finally, his turn came, and he took the first seat in the last row—as it happened, the seat closest to the classroom's back door. As he sat down, he placed his lunch under his chair on the floor. When a boy took the next seat in line, he pretended to stumble, kicking Teddy's lunch away toward the wall. Teddy got up to retrieve it.

"Alexander Turner, I saw that!" The teacher's voice cut like a whiplash. "One more trick like that and you'll go on report!"

Teddy wasn't sure what "going on report" meant, but he was sure it couldn't be anything good. He looked across the aisle and saw Alexander glaring at him. The boy mouthed, "I'll get you for this."

Teddy looked away and swallowed hard. In his whole life 'til then, he'd never known anything but kindness... hardship, certainly, but always kindness, and now he felt as if he was surrounded by a pack of hostile wild animals.

The teacher finished assigning seats and then swung into an introductory lesson on writing capital and lowercase letters. Teddy tried to pay attention, but his anxiety about his classmates kept distracting him. Finally, lunch time came. The teacher bade the class stand up and form two lines at the front of the room. Then she opened the front classroom door and followed her pupils out into the corridor. "Class, turn right," she commanded. Conducting the group from behind, she delivered them to the lunch grounds and let them choose their own seats at the picnic tables there. Then she left to return to her classroom.

Once again, Teddy found that he was unwelcome. He found a spot off by himself, sat down, opened his brown bag, and began to eat his lunch. He didn't get to make much progress. Alexander threaded his way though the crowd of children and made good on his threat. He swept Teddy's lunch from the table onto the ground and stamped on it. Then he pushed Teddy hard enough so that he fell off the bench, struck his cheek violently against the edge of a neighboring table, and hit the pavement, bruising both his knees.

"Here, you! Stop that immediately!" The male teacher assigned to watch the lunch area was running full tilt toward Teddy and his assailant. Alexander tried to flee, but as with all playground fights, as soon as the other kids caught sight of the attack, they clustered tightly around the two boys, hoping to witness what might happen next.

The teacher pushed his way through the crowd and grabbed Alexander by the back of his shirt. Alexander took a swing at the teacher, but his arms were too short to connect, and the man had too firm a grip on his garment. "Oh, going for a second charge of assault, are we? Hitting a fellow student would have gotten you detention. Trying to hit a teacher will get you expelled. Come on. It's the principal's office for you, and I wouldn't want to be you when your father gets the principal's phone call..." The man led Alexander away with the boy still struggling to get free.

"Oh, my dear!" Teddy was still sprawled on the asphalt. He looked up to see his own teacher standing over him. She bent down and helped him to rise. Teddy sucked air between his teeth as pain stabbed into his face and legs. "Come with me. We must get you to the school nurse right away!"

Teddy limped beside her up one hallway and down another. She stopped at a door, opened it for him, and urged him to go inside. A woman in a crisp, white uniform was sitting at a desk within. As soon as she caught sight of Teddy, she stood up exclaiming, "What in the world?!"

Teddy's teacher said, "Attacked by a fellow student, apparently for no reason. Quick, we need to see to that eye."

The nurse began to touch Teddy's face with gentle fingers. "I don't think the bones are broken, thank god. But we should get an X-ray just to be sure. In children this age, the orbit and cheekbone are really fragile. Let me go get an ice pack. I'd like to treat the swelling while I make the calls." Addressing Teddy she asked, "What's your name, Sweetheart?"

His teacher answered for him. "Theodore Sanchez."

"Where can we reach your parents, Theodore?"

"My mom's at work. I don't have a dad anymore. But I have a grandma. You could call her."

"Does she have a car?"

Teddy started to shake his head but thought better of it when the room began to spin. "No. We always take the bus. But Grandfather Roberto has a car."

"And do you know his last name?"

"Gonzalez. He's probably at work too. He makes new furniture covers."

"Gonzalez... upholstery... right!" Teddy's teacher was doing a search on the cell phone she'd taken from her pocket. She punched some buttons, and Teddy heard the phone begin to ring.

Meanwhile, the nurse had also placed a call. "911. What's your emergency?"

"I'm the school nurse at Canyon Elementary. We've got a student here with a facial injury. He needs an X-ray to rule out broken bones in his skull. Can we get him transported to the ER ASAP?"

"Where are his parents?"

"We're in the process of notifying his family. Apparently, the closest relative with a car is his grandfather. We're checking our records for the mother's contact number now."

"OK, we'll dispatch the EMTs and prepare for transport, just in case. Please stay on the line..."

"Oh my god!" Teddy looked up to see his teacher pointing with a trembling hand to his lower legs. He looked down and saw blood beginning to seep through the knees of his bluejeans.

Without missing a beat, the nurse put down her phone's handset on her desk, picked up Teddy, and sat him on her desk blotter. Then she grabbed a pair of scissors out of a mug full of pens and proceeded to cut the sides of his jeans legs all the way up to his mid-thighs. Carefully, so as not to cause more damage, she peeled the fabric away from Teddy's shins and knees. Teddy saw that his knees were skinned and bleeding, and that big, purple bruises were forming. He'd been shocked and more than a bit upset when the nurse began cutting away his clothing, but now he realized that, if she hadn't, given how fast the bruises were swelling up, in a few more minutes, he wouldn't have been able to remove his pants the normal way anyway.

"Quick! Go get me more ice packs," the nurse barked.

Teddy's teacher hastened to oblige, despite the fact that her ear was still glued to her cell phone. "Hello? Yes, I'm trying to reach a Roberto Gonzalez. Does he work there? Oh, he does. Good. Please get him immediately. I have his grandson here, and there's been a medical emergency."

Teddy began to lose track of all that was going on. He was holding an ice pack to his face, and it seemed to help ease the pain. He felt the nurse apply two more ice packs to his knees, and although he flinched at the additional cold, he was glad that she was trying to help him. Suddenly, Teddy heard his stomach growl, and he remembered that he'd hardly had anything to eat since breakfast. He looked up at his teacher and saw that she was still talking into her cell phone.

"Yes, Mr. Gonzalez. The school nurse says Theodore needs an X-ray to rule out broken bones in his face, and as we understand things, you're the only one in his family with a car. We also need to contact the boy's mother. Can you help us with that too?"

The nurse was also still talking on the phone. "Please have the EMTs pull into the faculty parking lot. It's at the closest point to my office."

Teddy's stomach growled again. He raised his free hand tentatively. "Excuse me, but may I please have something to eat?"

His teacher turned to him with a startled expression, but then she walked to the refrigerator that stood in the corner, opened the lower door, and pulled out a bottle with a brown and white label. "Are you allergic to chocolate?" Teddy shook his head. While still clutching her phone in one hand, she twisted off the bottle cap and handed the bottle to Teddy. "Drink this. You'll feel better."

Teddy took a sip. The liquid was delicious, and as he'd never had a milkshake before in his life, entirely unfamiliar. He drained the bottle dry and politely handed it back to her for disposal. She took it, frowning, and dropped it in the waste paper basket. "Thank you, Mr. Gonzalez. We'll hope to see you soon." She hung up, walked to the refrigerator, and returned with another bottle for Teddy.

Just then, the door to the nursing station opened, and two men entered. Both looked angry. "There! As you can see, Mr. Turner, your son has gravely injured this child, and he did so in front of hundreds of witnesses. If I were you, I'd be getting ready to pay this boy's medical bills and possibly punitive damages."

Mr. Turner took in Teddy's bruised face... the black eye forming beneath the ice pack... the cut-away pants legs... his bloody swollen knees... and the man exclaimed, "OK, I get it. Go ahead and expel Alex. I swear... after the way his mother has spoiled him, I don't see how anything short of a military boarding school is going to turn him around."

The school nurse was bristling. "Please, gentlemen, not in front of our student. Have the goodness to take this discussion back to the principal's office."

Just then, Teddy heard two new developments—the whoop of a siren as the EMT truck pulled into the parking lot outside, and a clamor of voices all speaking rapid-fire Spanish as his family arrived in force. The next few hours were chaotic, but fortunately, the outcome was good. The EMTs assured the family that Teddy didn't need ambulance transport. The ER doctors cleared Teddy—no broken bones, just a need for more ice packs and some analgesics so that he could get some sleep that night. And Mr. Turner and Grandfather Gonzalez had a frank talk, man-to-man, after which Mr. Turner wrote out a very big check for Teddy's benefit. Grandfather Gonzalez accepted the check as titular head of Teddy's family, and at that point, in the minds of most people present, the matter was put to bed.

But it was still a live issue in Teddy's mind. He accepted the need to go to school and get an education, but he had no desire to serve as some bully's punching bag again sometime in the future. As soon as he got the chance to talk with his teacher in private, he told her as much, and she could hardly find fault with his reasoning. So thereafter, Teddy ate his lunch in the classroom with his teacher, or if she couldn't be present, he'd visit the nurse's station or sit in a back room behind the school library.

He liked the library best. Some years before, the school district had lost funding for its music program. Most of the instruments were locked up in a storage room adjoining the also defunct gymnasium. But the upright piano had found its way into the room where books were catalogued and repaired. So whenever Teddy could arrange a visit, he would sit at the keyboard and while away his lunch hour playing snatches of his Rhapsody, getting ready for the day when he could finally do it justice.

3: Teddy Begins to Perform in Public...

"Did you see what that kid just did? Did you see?!" Outraged, Chet had leaped to his feet, snatched the cowboy hat from his head, and thrown it on what passed for the ground. "That little... That little... Why I'd like to... Well, somebody ought to *smite* that brat! That's what I think."

Nana looked up, her eyes filled with alarm. "Chet, calm down. You're now an angel-in-training, and angels are *not* in the smiting business."

"The hell they aren't. My granny used to read me stories from the Bible. Flaming swords, the seven plagues of Egypt... there's a whole lot of smiting in the Old Testament."

At the word 'hell,' Nana had actually flinched and looked around her to see if Chet had been overheard. "Please, Chet. We don't use that word here. If you must swear, use the word 'heck'."

"Or 'darn' for 'damn,' I suppose."

Nana frowned in thought. " 'Damn' isn't so bad, I guess. After all, we never actually damn souls..."

"Enough with the language lesson. What are we going to do about that pint-sized jerk who hurt my son?"

"*We* aren't going to do anything. *We* are in the Watching business. Corrective Action is another department altogether."

"Do you mean to tell me that that rotten... child... is going to get away with it? If so, maybe I should transfer to Corrective Action and do something to straighten him out."

Nana shook her head. "I don't think you'd like it— reporting to Corrective Action, I mean. That department is under Michael's purview, and he can be a very harsh task-master."

The way Chet was staring at her, it was clear that he was still fuming.

"OK, Chet, remember what Uriel told you about Earthly life not being a zero-sum game?... how life is *always* finished up here? Maybe that boy will get his comeuppance through a series of life lessons. Maybe he won't. If he doesn't, that's actually quite unfortunate for him because, when he arrives here, Raphael will make absolutely sure the kid sees the error of his ways and repents. The kid's soul may even get recycled as a punishment. Not too long ago, we sent two formerly-human souls back to Earth to live as a bug and a worm."

"Really?" Chet grinned and then began to shake with silent laughter.

Nana scowled at him. "It isn't funny, Chet. Humans have a lot of superstitions based on their concept of justice—Reincarnation... Limbo... Purgatory..." She glanced around her and lowered her voice. "Hell... But *our* concept of justice is based on helping souls to grow, and what happened to those two souls is undeniably the worst possible outcome. It's like we took two major-league baseball players and sent them down, not to the minors... but all the way back to Little League."

Chet sobered up, and he nodded to show that he understood. "But what about my son?" he asked plain-tively. "He's such a sweet little guy, and he's bruised. He's bleeding."

"Come here. Sit down again and watch what happens next."

Chet stooped, picked up his hat, perched it on his head, and resumed his seat beside her.

"You see?" Nana gestured at the events transpiring before them. "He's healing well, the bully's father has given him a big cash donation that's sure to be helpful in the future, and now he gets to spend more time playing piano. Don't you find that causality chain acceptable?"

"I guess so, but I'm betting he's going to think twice before he trusts anyone outside of his family again." Chet pondered the scene in front of him for a moment. "Say, maybe you could explain something to me. What I'm getting is that we just watch. We don't ever actually *do* anything. So what good is that?"

"Well, for one thing, they can sometimes sense that we're watching. That sensation can comfort the lonely and help deter those about to make serious mistakes. For another thing, who do you think is 'on the front lines' when it comes to hearing and answering prayers? We not only watch, we listen. Every living being that ever wishes for anything, utters a promise, or cries for help is under our protection. If the prayer is a worthy one... if it can somehow be made consistent with God's plan... then we refer the prayer to Uriel's team. They infuse the Light of God into the world via interventions that increase Faith. They're the ones who actually answer the prayers of incarnate souls."

Chet sat for a moment in silence. Then he simply said, "Wow."

" 'Wow' indeed! Your son's family is already strong in its faith, and not just because they attend Mass every Sunday. No matter what hardships they've faced so far, they've always addressed them with hard work, determination, and unstinting courage. When you chose to love Carla, you chose well. I'm not saying that she and her family are perfect. They stumble from time to time just like everyone else. But then they stand up, square their shoulders, and get back into the game."

Nana sighed. "I think it's high time that I tell you something important. I inherited the job of watching Teddy and his family because they're related spiritually to two other families I was already watching. Of course, I don't know what's in store long term for these families. But I suspect that Uriel has something up his sleeve where they're concerned—something wonderful. So watch and learn, Chet. It's not every day that we angels get to participate in a miracle, and I believe that one is coming."

*   *   *   *   *

When Teddy was seven years old, Abuela Sanchez reached her ninety-fifth birthday. For years, the Sanchez clan had been planning a fiesta just in case she reached the age of one hundred. But given that she now walked with a cane and sometimes needed three tries to get up off the couch, her granddaughter Juanita recommended that the family accelerate their time table.

Trying to make the party a surprise would have been pointless. There were far too many preparations entailing far too many people... The guest list alone would be huge. All eight of Abuela Sanchez's children were still alive—as were nearly all of their their nineteen children, thirty-six grandchildren, and twenty-five great-grandchildren. Add in spouses and fiancés, and the Sanchez party would need a banquet hall to accommodate everybody.

Unfortunately, they couldn't afford to rent a venue. They couldn't even afford a marquee with folding tables and chairs. So they did what they'd always done. They improvised. For days ahead of the event, pickup trucks pulled into Abuela Sanchez's driveway. Men-folk would unload card-tables, benches, lawn chairs, strings of Christmas lights—anything that could be pressed into service for the party.

Maria Sanchez-Gonzalez prevailed upon her husband to donate several bolts of no-longer fashionable fabric to the cause, and for days, the sewing machines at the upholstery shop whirred as his sisters made seat cushions and table cloths from the yardage. Maria then called upon her daughter Juanita to distribute these linens to best effect. Afterward, the back yard looked like a 1980s interpretation of the Arabian Nights, and the interior of the house did too.

All over town, refrigerators and freezers began to fill up as the female contingent of the family cooked and baked. They made platters full of chili rellenos, tamales, enchiladas, burritos, fajitas, ropas viejas, nopales, frijoles, and Spanish rice. Once they finished shopping, there was scarcely a tomato, an onion, an avocado, or a lime to be had in all of Albuquerque. The air around their houses filled with the scent of frying tortilla chips, salsa fresca, and guacamole. Their neighbors drooled and began angling for invitations to the affair. However, given that party real estate would be at a premium, the neighbors did so in vain.

Finally, the big day arrived. Juanita helped Abuela Sanchez to dress in a comfortable, but beautiful, traditional embroidered cotton dress. Then the two of them made their way carefully out into the back yard where an armchair had been set up to serve as Abuela Sanchez's throne for the day.

Guests arrived in droves. By 9:00 AM, there wasn't a parking place on the street for blocks. A tech-savvy great-granddaughter had set up a sound system, and her peers had spent a week recording song lists of Abuela Sanchez's favorite music—AM radio hits from the 1950s and 60s. At 9:30 precisely, the girl pressed "Play," and the party officially swung into action.

As each group of guests arrived, they came to hug Abuela Sanchez and kiss her cheeks. One of her grandsons who fancied himself a photographer would pose them with her and snap their picture using his digital camera before releasing them to go enjoy the buffet. Abuela Sanchez was in her element, exclaiming over each new arrival and clinging to their hands as she asked them how they'd been since she'd seen them last. This caused a line to form. It stretched from the front yard, down the driveway, and into the back yard, but no one felt impatient or offended. They were just happy to be there for her on her special day.

All morning long and into the afternoon, Juanita and Carla shuttled between the buffet in the back yard and the kitchen in the house. Carla leveraged her waitress skills to clear empty serving dishes and replace them with full ones. Juanita washed casseroles, baking pans, serving spoons, and glassware until she thought her hands would drop from her wrists. When Teddy saw how tired she looked, he quietly began approaching some of the other ladies and asking them to join her. Most of them looked down into his innocent big brown eyes and immediately went to help.

By late-afternoon, the family had consumed every gallon of Juanita's home-made lemonade plus the beer and margaritas. They switched to sodas just as the song playlists finally ended. This was the cue for many of the men-folk to go fetch their musical instruments from the living room where they'd left them. A cacophony of tuning ensued, but then the party entered its second phase as the sun began to set, the Christmas lights twinkled to life overhead, and the men started playing flamenco tunes and singing.

Teddy listened to the music enraptured. He'd heard some of the tunes before of course. But he never tired of the complex melodic lines, the many grace notes, and the exotic rhythms. In his head, he was recording all he heard and translating the arrangements for multiple instruments into a composition he could handle with two hands on the piano.

Darkness fell, and guests began to depart. In the kitchen, the women were claiming their now-clean dishes and wrapping left-over food for storage in Abuela Sanchez's freezer. Nobody in her household would have to cook for weeks to come. Meanwhile, a few die-hard relatives were moving the celebration inside. As men left toting their guitar cases, they freed up space in the living room, and other men carried in upholstered benches to create more seating.

At 8:30 PM, the sound of departing trucks abated outside. Abuela Sanchez still sat on her throne, but now it stood against the wall beside the hallway. As her children sat around her on the couch and benches, reminiscing, Juanita and Carla surprised them all with cups of flan. As everyone spooned the sweet custard into their mouths, Juanita turned to Teddy and said, "Play something for us, Sweetheart. Let them all hear how much you've learned."

His great-grandmother Maria exclaimed, "You've been teaching him piano? He's still so small!"

Juanita smiled. "That doesn't seem to matter... not with him. Show them what you can do, Teddy."

Teddy didn't need any more encouragement. He walked to the piano in the corner, pulled out the bench, and clambered on top of it. Then he uncovered the keyboard, flexed his fingers a couple of times, and started playing. At first he played the tune that Juanita had taught him most recently. He assumed that tune was the one she wanted to hear. But when it ended, he transitioned smoothly to the composition he'd been working on all afternoon—a medley of flamenco songs stitched together with airy improvisations. He was handicapped by the fact that his feet still couldn't reach the pedals, but he put his heart and soul into his playing and infused the music with far more drama and passion than a seven-year-old could be expected to produce.

When he finished, he fell silent and turned around, expecting comment. He found himself staring into a room full of shocked faces. Spoons hung suspended above bowls. Slack jaws hung open in astonishment. Eyes round with surprise stared back at him. So things remained for an instant. Then his mother Carla began to applaud, and the rest of his relatives followed suit.

Great-grandmother Maria cried, "Bravo! Bravo, Juanita. I had no idea that you were such a gifted teacher."

But Juanita was shaking her head. "It's not me, *Mamacita*. It's him. Teddy is extraordinarily gifted. I may have taught him the first tune, but I've never heard the second one in all my life. Where did you learn it, Teddy?"

Teddy colored a bit. "I listened to what our family played this afternoon."

His mother wasn't satisfied with this explanation. "But you added to it, didn't you?"

"Yes. I put it all together and made it work for just two hands."

Abuela Sanchez's eldest son rumbled, "A prodigy like Teddy will be a credit to our whole family. He deserves to have the best instruction that money can buy."

One of his younger brothers shook his head. "And where is that money going to come from? You know how we all live. We do all right, but nobody in the family has the kind of cash that you're talking about..."

Great-grandfather Roberto coughed to get everyone's attention. "You're wrong, you know. As it happens, Teddy has that kind of cash. When that rotten kid hurt him last year, the kid's father gave me a check for Teddy. I put that money in the bank, waiting until he needed it for some reason, and it's waiting there still. If Teddy needs instructors, we can get them for him."

Teddy's eyes glowed with excitement. "Really? I can have more piano lessons?"

Great-grandfather Roberto addressed him directly. "Really, son. After what I heard here tonight, I'm guessing you're going to be good enough to make a living with your music, plus reflect credit on our family as discussed. So work hard and make us proud, Teddy. A gift like yours is too valuable to throw away."

*   *   *   *   *

Three years passed, during which Teddy practiced four hours a day, seven days a week, with guidance from the best piano instructor in New Mexico. At that rate, Teddy would acquire the ten thousand hours of experience necessary to master his skills in another four years. But there was a hitch. Teddy was quite willing to play in front of his family, but he froze like a deer in on-coming headlights whenever the instructor asked him to play at a recital.

This, of course, would simply not do... To have a successful career as a musician, Teddy had to learn to perform in public. He needed to give concerts. He needed to record music in studios. He needed to share his gift with others, not only to contribute to society, but also for monetary gain. So Teddy's instructor began looking for venues in which Teddy could play, venues in which Teddy's exposure would be limited so that, if he did the musical equivalent of a prat-fall, his reputation wouldn't be too badly damaged, and his long-term success wouldn't be permanently compromised.

As it happened, Teddy himself ultimately solved the problem. He was sitting in the library anteroom at his school one day, eating his sandwich and playing the old upright Steinway, when the librarian happened to walk in carrying an armload of books. She had a light tread, and Teddy was playing a particularly loud passage, so he didn't hear her. She listened for a minute, truly impressed with his prowess. Then she put down her books and walked into his field of view. Naturally, he started as soon as he saw her and stopped playing. "Oh, please don't stop," she told him. "I was enjoying the music. You're very talented."

Teddy shrugged and deflected. "I have a good teacher."

He was hoping the woman would leave the room again, but instead, she leaned against the piano and said, "You know, PTA night is coming up—the big annual event in the auditorium. We always open the festivities with a few student presentations. Would you like to play something? I think the parents and teachers would all enjoy hearing you."

Teddy was about to refuse when his instructor loomed up in his mind. "Would it be just one tune?... something I select myself?..."

"If that's all you feel up to... But we could give you more time if you wanted it."

Teddy shook his head. "No, that's OK. I guess I can play one tune."

The librarian smiled. "That's great. I'll go tell the principal. And if you like the experience, we sometimes put on talent shows in front of the student body. The presenters sit on stage until their turn comes. We introduce them from the podium, and at the end of the show, the students vote on who should win a prize. I'll bet you could win if you wanted. Of course, you'd have to play something the kids understood—no classical stuff..."

Teddy felt like someone was pumping all the air out of the room, but he was too polite not to give her some kind of answer. "It's very nice of you to suggest it. I'll think about it and let you know."

The librarian left the room smiling, and Teddy tried to get back to the piece he'd been practicing. Unfortunately, he found that he was too agitated to concentrate, and before long, the warning bell rang, signaling that his lunch break was over and he needed to return to class.

Two weeks later, Teddy found himself standing in the wings on stage at his school. When he peered out at the audience from behind the curtain, he could see his mother, grandmother, and piano instructor seated in the middle of the front row. Teddy was feeling more than stage fright. He was also feeling intensely embarrassed. The other students standing with him were dressed to the nines in frilly dresses or miniature suits such as one might wear to church. Teddy on the other hand was dressed in clothes that were clean and neatly pressed, but in no way out of the ordinary—the same bluejeans, T-shirt, and plaid over-shirt that he typically wore to class.

The curtain rose, and the principal began to address the audience. Before Teddy could find any kind of composure, the principal began introducing Teddy's fellow students as they gave their presentations one-by-one. A boy from the sixth grade recited a lengthy poem and only flubbed a couple of his lines. A pair of identical twin girls with enormous bows in their hair did a tap-dance to recorded big-band music. A brother and sister put on a brief magic show, during which their pet rabbit escaped from his top hat, causing consternation throughout the auditorium. And so it went. After each act, the audience would applaud politely, and the student presenter would bow before walking off stage. Finally, Teddy's turn came.

The school's custodian rolled a baby-grand piano out onto the stage from the other wing, and Teddy's teacher placed a piano bench in front of it. Feeling like he was marching to his execution, Teddy forced himself to walk to the bench and take a seat. He purposely avoided looking out into the audience, dreading to see that sea of eyes. Teddy flexed his fingers, poised them above the keyboard, and began playing a Chopin nocturne that he'd mastered the week before. Soon, he was lost in the melody. He'd always liked Chopin's works, even during his first life.

Teddy finished playing, and as he'd been coached to do, he stood up from the piano bench, took a quick bow, and started to walk off stage. He was halfway to his destination when he was startled by a sudden roar of sound. He glanced at the audience and saw that they were all applauding loudly. Some parents had even risen to their feet shouting, "Bravo! Bravo! Encore!" Confused, Teddy glanced first at his family and then at the principal for guidance. The principal nodded to him in encouragement and gestured that Teddy should return to the piano. Teddy did as he was told.

He took a seat, thought an instant, and then rolled into Scott Joplin's "Maple Leaf Rag." He played it up-tempo and was gratified to see some people in the audience begin to move as if they longed to dance and could barely keep still in their seats. When he finished, he stood up again, took a second bow, and left the stage, doing his best to ignore the renewed pandemonium.

That evening, before Teddy and his family left the auditorium to go home, Teddy told his instructor about the talent shows, and with his instructor's blessing, Teddy approached the principal to sign up for the next one. That night was the last time Teddy ever suffered from stage fright. From that day forward, he was always perfectly able to perform.

*   *   *   *   *

The next time Teddy met with his instructor, he asked the man an important question. "Does it really matter where I practice as long as I put in my four hours per day?"

"I don't think it matters as long as the instrument is good. If the piano is out of tune or has choppy action, you'll develop bad habits as you try to compensate. Why do you ask?"

"Well, I think I told you that I've been playing an upright piano in a back room at school. It was out of tune at first, but I fixed it. It's a pretty good instrument overall."

The instructor's eyebrows had risen at this confession. "You fixed it?"

"Yes. The school's old music teacher is still there. He teaches fifth grade now, but he still has all his music stuff in his desk drawer. Early on, my teacher told him that I might be playing the piano at lunch time, so he loaned me some tools and showed me what to do."

"O-kay... But what does this have to do with your original question?"

"Well, before I gave him back his tools, I also fixed Abuela Sanchez's piano. It was in tune, but it's like you said. The action wasn't that great. I wanted something a little more crisp, so I repaired it, and now I'm thinking of fixing another piano still..."

"Um, where?"

"At the bar in Old Town where my mom used to work. She says they've always used canned music, but they have an upright piano against a wall in the front room. I thought if I fixed it, I could practice there and get some performance experience at the same time."

"Teddy, I don't think your plan is going to work. You're way too young to work in a bar—just a kid... It would be illegal."

"My mom worked there before she was twenty-one..."

"And I'm sure they fudged her employment records, something that could still come back to bite her in the future. What do you expect them to do about you—list you as a midget? The situation is impossible."

Teddy frowned thoughtfully. "But if I could work things out somehow, would it be OK to practice on their instrument?"

Exasperated, his instructor said, "Sure, but don't get your hopes up. Like I said, what you propose simply won't work."

Teddy's instructor failed to take into account his pupil's innate drive and cleverness. With his mom's blessing, Teddy took the bus to Old Town the next Saturday afternoon and marched into the bar. As the instructor had predicted, the owner quickly ushered him back outside, but Teddy took advantage of every second to argue in favor of what he wanted to do. By the time Teddy and the barman reached the front portico, the barman was already stroking his chin thoughtfully. "Live music, you say?"

"It draws people in. By now, everyone except first-time tourists have heard your piano tape-loop. If you want to pull in more customers, you should change the program, and a live performer can take requests. See what I mean?"

"Yeah, but who's going to play this live music—you? What are you, nine years old?"

"I'm ten. But I can play better than most adults you'll find. Why not give me a chance? There are practically no customers in there right now, so what could it hurt?"

"I could lose my license. That's what it could hurt."

Teddy pounced. "So push the piano out onto the porch. I'll play for you here."

"I can't obstruct traffic. It's against the municipal code."

Teddy turned and pointed. At the edge of the portico, the boardwalk ended in a faux hitching post. Any passers-by would have to step out into the paved street at that point anyway. Teddy looked back at the barman and raised his eyebrows inquiringly.

Knowing he was licked, the barman shrugged, turned, and yelled to one of his employees inside. "Hey, Sammy, roll that piano out here, please, and bring the stool with it."

A voice issued from within. "What?!"

"You heard me."

Teddy heard Sammy begin to swear under his breath as wheels badly in need of lubrication began to squeak and squeal. A moment later, the bulk of the upright piano slid through the door onto the portico floor. The barman gestured, and Sammy positioned the piano against the hitching post. Then he removed the stool from on top of the piano and placed it on the floor.

Teddy thanked Sammy politely and took a seat on the stool. It was too low... adjusted for an adult performer... so he got up, spun the seat around until it was at the right height, and then sat down again. He opened the keyboard and ran a few scales. The piano was badly out of tune, but the action was still pretty good. Teddy turned to the barman. "If you hire me, I can tune the piano for you for free... just part of the service I provide."

The barman looked flummoxed by this statement, so Teddy turned back around and began to play. Given that

Old Town was supposed to reflect the Wild West of the late 1800s, Teddy had decided on a short medley of rag-time tunes. He ran through his program, stopped, looked up, and discovered that, even in the few minutes he'd been playing, he'd gathered an audience.

The people applauded, and one woman stepped forward to ask, "Do you have a tip jar, Honey?" Teddy smiled at her and shook his head. "Well you should." She reached into her purse, pulled out a dollar bill, and handed it to him.

Teddy thrust it into his pocket and thanked her. Then he watched with a grin as she and her husband walked into the bar, followed by the rest of their party. Teddy fixed the barman with a meaningful look. "Well, what do you say?"

The barman let his pent-up breath out through his nose. "As a trial run for two weeks, three hours a day at minimum wage... You share your tips with the rest of the staff."

"Four hours a day, and I keep my tips."

"Done. You start tomorrow. I'll have Sammy wheel out the piano each day before you arrive. Make sure you keep your word about tuning it."

"I will." And he did.

From then on, except on rainy days that would damage the instrument, Teddy sat in the portico's shade every afternoon after school, playing rag-time and other popular tunes, pulling happy-hour and dinner customers into the bar. Before long, realizing what an asset Teddy was, the barman found a way to "mic" the piano and pipe the music inside too.

Teddy soon became a fixture on the street, for his music didn't just attract tourists who had a thirst. Customers would come from other streets to hear him play and then stay to shop for souvenirs or stroll down to the restaurant for a taco.

This pattern wasn't lost on the other store owners. The restaurant's proprietor took to bringing him a pitcher of iced lemonade and a clean glass at the start of his shift, and the man who owned the jewelry shop across the street came out to talk with him one day when he was on break.

"You know, son, you're missing a bet."

"I am?"

"Yes, you are. I see you've got yourself a tip jar, but you need to put in some seed money at the beginning of every shift. That way, the tourists will think you've already been working for a while, and if they see some dollar bills in the jar, they'll think that's the amount they're supposed to tip you. You'll get less pocket change and more real cash that way."

"OK, I'll try it. Thanks for the advice."

"And another thing, you need a placard with your name on it, telling people who you are. It would be better still if you had business cards, but they cost money, and I'm betting you're not exactly flush yet." He gestured to Teddy's clothes. Teddy looked down and grimaced. "Yeah, I though so. I was just thinking... If you had a placard or cards, other people might try to hire you for other gigs. You could parlay this job into a full-time career if you wanted to... By the way, you gotta name?"

"Teddy."

The man pursed his lips and shook his head. "Teddy's no kind of name for a musician like you. It's got no zing. What's your full name?"

Teddy hesitated, then took the plunge. "Theodore Bernardo Sanchez."

The man laughed. "Oh my god, what a mouthful, but when you think about it, it's absolutely perfect. You know what your name needs to be? T-Bear Sanchez... Not Bernie or Teddy Bear... They're both too cute, but T-Bear has a nice, almost jazz-musician sound to it. What do you think? Could you see printing that on a placard?"

Teddy was staring at him wide-eyed. "Yes, I believe I could."

"And Sanchez... Sanchez... Say, I don't suppose you're related to a gal named Carla Sanchez, are you?"

"She's my mother."

"For heaven's sake! What are the odds? Our Carla... We really miss her over at the shop. She was a great little worker, and so honest. We never came up short at the cash register or had any inventory at all go missing while she was there. It's so hard to find good help these days.

"Huh... I just had a thought. You stay right there a minute. I'd like to go get something for you to give to Carla. You know, our profits have gone way up since you started working here, and I'd like her to have a little something to remember us by... sort of a thank-you gift."

The man dashed back across the street and returned carrying a small, sealed ziplock bag. He handed it to Teddy. Inside was a silver pendant on a sturdy chain. The pendant was set with smooth, deep-red stones. "Carnelian... The gems are real. You can't cheat people with carnelian the way you can with turquoise these days. She *was* the genuine article, and now she'll *have* the genuine article too." He stopped speaking, momentarily abashed.

"Thanks," Teddy said. "I'm sure she'll love it."

The man shrugged. "Give her my regards, and thank you for all the good work you've been doing. Consider it a tip for you both." With that, he turned, crossed the street, went back inside his shop, and closed the door.

*   *   *   *   *

Teddy was right. Carla did love the gift. She put it on and went to show her mother and great-grandmother. After exclaiming over how pretty the necklace was, Juanita said, "You've got to go thank the man. That was a very thoughtful thing for him to do."

Abuela Sanchez nodded in agreement. "You could all go. Ask him out to lunch or something. He sounds like someone worth knowing better. After all, he's been kind to Teddy and Carla both—like he's trying to be a friend to us."

Carla was shaking her head shyly. "Oh I couldn't. He was my boss for over two years. Besides, I don't have the money."

Teddy put his hand on his mother's arm. "But I do. I've been getting a lot of big tips lately. We could go to that crêpes restaurant one block over from his shop. It's not very expensive, the patio is really nice, and I hear the food is good."

Juanita smiled. "I've always wanted to eat there. Let's invite him to go with us."

Carla smiled and shrugged. "OK, I'll do it. Let's ask him on Monday. That was always his light day for customer traffic. Maybe he'll feel he can spare an hour then."

And that's what they did. When the three of them entered the man's shop, he glanced up and started in surprise. Then he walked around the counter and extended his hand to welcome them. "Carla! How good to see you again, and our young musician, 'T-Bear' Sanchez..." Teddy grinned at the moniker. "And who is this lovely lady?" he asked, shaking Juanita's hand.

"I'm her mother, Juanita Sanchez."

"Tomas Hernandez... Very pleased to meet you. To what do I owe the pleasure?"

Carla blushed and said, "I came to thank you for this beautiful necklace. It was so kind of you to think of us. We'd like to treat you to lunch at the crêpes restaurant."

"Right now?" They all nodded. "OK, I think I can get away. He turned and called to his assistant. "Julio, watch the shop for me. I'm going to lunch. I should be back in...

what?... about an hour?" They all nodded again. "Yes, an hour."

Julio winked at him. "OK, *jefe grande!*"

Tomas ushered Teddy and his family out of the store. Once outside, Teddy led the way to the restaurant with Tomas, Carla, and Juanita following behind. Halfway there, Tomas offered his arm to Juanita, and perhaps tired from working all morning, she took it. In this fashion, he escorted her and her daughter the rest of the way.

When they reached the restaurant, Teddy approached the hostess and said, "Sanchez, party of four." The hostess dimpled at him, picked up four menus and led the way to the patio. When they reached the table, Teddy took the chair across from Tomas, and Carla and Juanita seated themselves on either side. For several minutes, Teddy and his party were engaged in studying the menu, but after they'd placed their orders, an awkward silence fell.

To break it, Carla asked, "So how have you been? How is your wife?" Tomas's face fell, and embarrassed, Carla said, "Oh! I didn't mean to pry. I hope I haven't brought up a painful subject."

Tomas shook his head. "No, no... It's OK. After all, you worked side-by-side with her for two years... more actually." He sighed. "I guess I don't mind you knowing. You remember how she used to flirt with all the male customers?"

Carla nodded. "She used to move a lot of jewelry that way."

"Well that's not all she used to move. Over the years, she had a couple of affairs, and I always took her back. I'm Catholic after all, and to me, marriage is a life-long sacred bond and forgiveness is essential. But one day, this guy came into the shop. She took one look at his Rolex and his custom-made boots, and she had to have him. A week later, with no warning at all, the two of them headed west to Los Angeles in his Ferrari, and I haven't seen her since. She sent me divorce papers through the mail."

"Oh, that's awful!" Carla's face showed her shock, and so did Juanita's. Juanita impulsively put a consoling hand on his sleeve.

Tomas shrugged. "I was pretty torn up about it. I wasn't looking forward to living the rest of my life alone. I went to talk with my parish priest, and that's when I got an even bigger surprise. He asked me a bunch of questions, and the story came out about all her affairs. He told me that I was entitled to an annulment because she'd never 'formed the requisite intent to commit to our marriage.' Of course, I asked about our kids. I didn't want to retroactively turn them into bastards. But he assured me that they'd remain legitimate in the eyes of the church. After all, I'd believed that we were married when we had them. So my children are OK, and I'm free as a bird." He shrugged again, tried to muster a smile, and gently patted Juanita's hand where it rested on his arm.

Juanita withdrew her hand and sat back. "Well I think she was a fool. He'll get tired of her, dump her for a new model, and then where will she be?... stranded in that dreadful city without a friend in the world." Juanita snorted in disapproval.

Tomas couldn't help but smile at this reaction. Just then, their food arrived, and everyone began eating.

Teddy found the crêpes to be just as delicious as advertised. He'd ordered the beef burgundy crêpe, the ratatouille crêpe, and a dessert crêpe stuffed with strawberries and drizzled with chocolate. The rest of his party faced plates that were just as wonderful.

As Teddy ate, he couldn't help but notice that his Grandma Juanita's attention was not entirely on her meal. She kept stealing glances at Tomas from time to time, and Teddy had to admit that Tomas was a man well-worth her regard. He appeared to be in his mid-to-late forties. His body was well-proportioned, his face was good-looking, and his black swept-back hair featured flags of silver at the temples. He smiled easily, and whenever he did, his eyes would light up and laugh-lines would crinkle at their corners. Teddy found himself wishing that Tomas *would* become a friend to their family. He seemed to be a very pleasant man indeed.

At last their luncheon came to an end. Teddy paid, left a tip, and stood up to leave the patio. Then Carla, Tomas, and Juanita followed him out into the street and back to the shop. They all paused on the front porch to say their good-byes, and Tomas shook hands all around, last of all with Juanita. Teddy couldn't help but notice that Tomas seemed reluctant to release Juanita's hand and let her go. Teddy exclaimed, "Well this was fun! Maybe we could do it again sometime."

Tomas's face immediately brightened. Looking into Juanita's eyes, he said, "I'd like that very much. Is there some way that I could get in touch with you to set up another date?" Teddy watched in delighted astonishment as his Grandma Juanita begin blushing like a school girl.

Evidently Carla saw the same thing that Teddy did, for she reached into her purse, pulled out a pen and a tiny note pad, scribbled their home phone number, and handed the note to Tomas. "Call us anytime, or you could send a message through Teddy. After all, he'll be right across the street almost every day."

Tomas looked at the slip of paper in his hand like he'd just been handed a check for a thousand dollars. "I will! Thanks!" He smiled at them all and then opened the door to his shop. "OK, Julio, I'm back!"

Out on the porch, Teddy smiled at his mother and grandmother. He was willing to bet real money that they'd be hearing from Tomas before the week was out, and as it happened, Teddy was right. Within a month, the Sanchez clan acknowledged that Tomas was Juanita's beau, and within six months, they realized that they'd better start planning a wedding.

The day that Tomas proposed and Juanita accepted, Tomas dashed across the street from his shop to the portico where Teddy sat playing for tourists. Tomas bounded up to Teddy with the energy of a much younger man. "She said yes! Your grandma agreed to marry me. I'm going to be your grandfather Hernandez!"

Teddy broke off playing with an abrupt discord. He stood up wearing an ear-to-ear grin and shook Tomas's hand enthusiastically. "What wonderful news!"

"And you made it all happen! My sons will be my groomsmen, but you have to be my best man!"

Teddy began to choke up a bit. "I'd be honored. Oh, Tomas, I'm so glad you'll be joining our family. I know that you and Grandma Juanita will be very happy together."

4: T-Bear Goes to Music School...

Tomas Hernandez married Juanita Sanchez on a lovely spring day the Saturday after Easter. Between the Sanchez clan, the Gonzalez clan, and the family Hernandez, the wedding guests pretty much filled up the church. The Altar Guild ladies had outdone themselves regarding bouquets in the sanctuary, and Juanita's mother Maria had pressured one of the Gonzalez family's suppliers into donating spools and spools of colored ribbons for bows and buntings on the pews.

Being the best seamstress in town, Juanita had decided to sew her wedding dress herself, and because she'd gotten married the first time down at the county clerk's office, she did it up right—yards and yards of ecru satin and a "candlelight" veil of tulle. Everyone present agreed that she looked lovely. As she walked down the aisle on the arm of her father, Roberto, her eyes sparkled, and her cheeks glowed pink. Gone were the dark circles under her eyes and the weary gate. Love had transformed her.

The reception started out in the church's parish hall. The venue was far from elegant—Navajo-white walls, vinyl flooring meant to look like tile, and exposed beams overhead. But the happy couple didn't care. Female relatives had set up a huge buffet on folding tables covered with colorful yardage from the upholstery shop, and anyone who could play an instrument pitched in to provide dance music. After Teddy had discharged his duties as best man (carrying the ring, standing at the groom's side, giving the first toast...), he was happy to take a seat at the hall's upright piano and join in the festivities.

At 5:00 in the afternoon, the Guild ladies politely reminded the bride's parents that they'd need the hall at 7:00 for a youth group meeting. This news didn't faze the celebrants one bit. They simply carried everything out to the waiting caravan of pickup trucks and moved the party to Abuela Sanchez's back yard as they'd done so many times in the past. Actually, Abuela Sanchez was pleased with the change because now she could sit in a comfortable arm chair while watching the party instead of the wheelchair that had been provided for the occasion.

The party continued until late into the night. At 11:00 PM, Carla found that Abuela Sanchez had dozed off, so she woke her and helped her to go inside and get into bed. At midnight, the bride and groom took their leave of their guests. Juanita threw the bouquet, and a young Gonzalez cousin caught it. Then Tomas and Juanita ran out to their truck through a hail of rice and drove away to his house where they planned to live together going forward.

For his part, Teddy kept on playing piano... his uncles and cousins kept on strumming their guitars... and the other guests kept on eating, drinking, singing, and dancing until the sky began to lighten in the east. Then all the female relatives began wrapping up their food dishes, and the men-folk began to fold the cloths and tables and load them into the pickup trucks.

When the last family had bundled their sleepy children into their truck cab and driven away, Teddy looked around him and sighed happily. His mother Carla was already asleep in the room she used to share with her mother Juanita. From then on, she would live in the main house and take care of Abuela Sanchez, and Teddy would have the adobe tiny-house all to himself. He locked up the main house, made his way across the back yard, entered his home, and fell onto his bed exhausted. As he drifted off to sleep, he felt grateful that he'd have the whole of Sunday in which to recuperate because, come Monday, he'd have to return to school and then go play piano outside the Old Town bar.

*   *   *   *   *

Having Carla take care of Abuela Sanchez had sounded good on paper, but quite soon, the Sanchez clan had to make adjustments to the plan. After all, Carla was still working full-time for her great-uncle's construction company, so the clan had to find someone to sit with Abuela Sanchez during the day. At first, they tried her eldest daughter-in-law, but Abuela Sanchez found the woman so annoying that the experiment ended almost before it began. Next, they tried her second daughter-in-law. That woman proved to be both cloying and controlling, treating Abuela Sanchez as if she was senile or childish when in fact she was still very sharp and completely capable of making decisions for herself.

The third time that her daughter-in-law crooned, "OK, Abuela, it's time for our afternoon nap," Abuela Sanchez astonished the woman by heaving herself out of her wheelchair, grasping a vase that had stood beside her on an end table, and flinging it in the general direction of the woman's head. Affronted and frightened, the woman grabbed her purse and charged out of the house. She didn't even bother to close the front door behind her. It stood open for the rest of the afternoon until Carla returned home. When Abuela Sanchez explained to Carla why the door was standing open, Carla laughed so hard that she thought she would burst. Then she phoned her mother Juanita and asked for her advice.

Juanita had spent almost all of her life with Abuela Sanchez—at first, receiving her care and then caring for her—so Juanita knew well what did and didn't work where Abuela Sanchez was concerned. Juanita promised Carla that she'd give the matter some thought and call back. Two hours later, Juanita phoned and told Carla, "It can't be anyone from our family, or the Gonzalez family either. None of them have the right temperament. But don't worry. I've thought of someone who might work. Tomas has a daughter-in-law, a sweet girl, and she's agreed to sit with Abuela nine hours a day, five days a week. All she asks in return is that she be allowed to bring her baby. I told her that we could set up a crib in the living room. She says the baby doesn't cry much, so I don't think Abuela will mind. Does this plan sound OK to you?"

Carla said yes, so the following morning, Juanita drove the girl to Abuela Sanchez's house, and after a pithy conversation in which Abuela Sanchez made it clear that she was *not* suffering from dementia, everyone reached agreement on the arrangements. Thereafter, Mrs. Hernandez took the day shift, Carla took nights and weekends, Abuela Sanchez had peace in her own house again, and Teddy heaved a great sigh of relief.

Until his grandmother had supplied Mrs. Hernandez, he'd been afraid that he'd have to give up his piano playing and rush home from school everyday to help out. He loved his great-great-grandmother deeply, but he also heeded what his instructor had told him, and his instructor had made it clear that, if Teddy didn't put in at least ten thousand hours of practice before he graduated from high school, he'd never be able to compete against other aspiring pianists out there in the wide world.

So things in the Sanchez household continued on an even keel. When Teddy was twelve, the Sanchez and Gonzalez families turned out in force to give Abuela Sanchez an enormous party for her hundredth birthday. By that time, she was a tiny bird of a woman, confined almost full-time to her wheelchair. Nevertheless, she managed to truly enjoy the event, and as usual with their parties, it lasted all day and into the night. By then, Abuela Sanchez had acquired something of a mythical stature among her relatives. Many of them secretly believed that she might never die, and for another few years, she seemed to justify that view.

Teddy graduated from middle school and entered high school. In seemingly no time at all, he entered his senior year and would soon graduate from high school as well. His grades were respectable. He'd worked hard and earned a place on the Honor Roll. But he wasn't so gifted academically that he'd be able to gain admission to a top college. Teddy and his family were essentially "betting the farm" on Teddy's abilities as a musician. His instructor handed him a list of colleges that offered degrees in music, and Teddy spent all of his spare time filling out application forms and writing college admission essays.

Teddy was nervous about what would happen if none of his applications was accepted. He wondered if he'd have to go to a junior college or a trade school to learn a trade. Worse still, what if he had to throw himself on the mercy of his Gonzalez grandparents and go to work in the upholstery shop? The work was honest and necessary in the community, and it provided a good living, but it didn't appeal to Teddy on any level. He understood that one had to find a way to pay the bills, and that one's work might not be all that spiritually satisfying, but he yearned to follow what he thought of as his destined course. He wanted to perform and compose, and he prayed that somehow an opportunity would present itself.

Then one morning, shortly after his eighteenth birthday, he woke up to hear his mother Carla crying. He got up and rushed into the main house to find her standing over the sink, weeping into a dish towel. Between her sobs, she managed to choke out an explanation. She'd gone into Abuela Sanchez's room to help her get up and get dressed, and she'd found Abuela Sanchez dead. She'd passed away some time in the night.

Teddy threw his arms around his mother and tried to comfort her. "Mom, she was a hundred and six years old. We're all going to miss her terribly, but you've got to admit—that's a pretty good run."

"I know," Carla sobbed. "I've got to call into work. I can't go today. I've got to call my mom and make funeral arrangements and..." She broke down again.

Teddy stood a moment in thought. Then he walked to the phone and dialed his mother's work number from memory. When his great-great-uncle answered, Teddy gave him the bad news and asked for a favor. Could his uncle please have his secretary call all the Sanchez relatives and let them know about Abuela Sanchez? Because Carla was really broken up and wouldn't be able to do anything more herself that day.

Teddy's great-great-uncle began to cry. After all, Abuela Sanchez was his mother and one of the few constants in his own long life. But he agreed to engage his secretary's help, and he told Teddy to assure Carla that she could take as much time off as she needed. She should not return to work until she was ready. Teddy thanked him and then hung up the phone.

Next Teddy called his grandfather Tomas. Tomas answered his shop's phone in the brisk voice he always used when conducting business. Teddy said, "Hello, Tomas, I have some bad news for Grandma Juanita, and I don't want to give it to her over the phone. I think someone she loves should be with her when she hears it, and as much as I hate to put this burden on you, I think that person should be you."

Teddy heard Tomas inhale deeply and then let out a long sigh. "It's Abuela Sanchez, isn't it? She's passed away."

"Yes, I'm afraid so. My mother found her this morning. I have no idea what to do about her body, or how to plan a funeral, and my mother is too overcome with grief to handle such things now. In any case, whatever we decide to do, we should consult Grandma Juanita about it first. After all, she was more like a daughter to Abuela Sanchez than a granddaughter."

"I agree. Listen, don't worry about any of this. I've dealt with deaths in the family before. I know a reputable funeral home. I'll call them to come and get her body, and they can keep her until we're ready to make final arrangements. Meanwhile, I'll go home and tell Juanita the news in person. Go take care of your mother and yourself. I've got this."

Teddy thanked him and hung up. Then he went back to the kitchen and sat with his mother until she could finally stop crying. Teddy made ice packs for her swollen eyes, and he fetched clean handkerchieves for her renewed bouts of tears. He listened to her reminiscences for hours, and not once did he worry about school. In his view, he could always square things with his teachers the next day. It wasn't every day that a family lost its matriarch.

By mid-afternoon, Carla was finally ready to get on with life. By that time, the mortuary staff had come and taken away Abuela Sanchez's body, reverently covered by a shroud on the gurney. Teddy offered to stay in the house with his mother for the rest of the day, but she shook her head. She wanted to be alone for a while, and suddenly, she remembered that her son had a gig playing piano in Old Town. She'd missed work that day, but she was afraid that, if he didn't go to his job, he might lose it, and lose the income they were relying on for his music education. So she exhorted him to go, and after a few protests, he did as she asked.

Once he reached the bar and sat down to play, he entered a strange, bifurcated state in which his mind was completely filled with thoughts of his family's loss, but his hands (so thoroughly trained) automatically played the cheerful tunes that passing tourists wanted to hear. Teddy was giving an expert rendition of a Scott Joplin standard when a shadow fell across the keyboard, and he looked up. Still playing, he saw a sober-looking gray-haired man standing over him. The man cleared his throat and asked, "Do you play requests?"

Teddy brought the Scott Joplin to a graceful close. "Yes, sir. What would you like to hear?"

"Do you know anything classical?"

Teddy didn't reply in words. He just played Chopin's "Minute Waltz," taking precisely one minute. In his view, it was a show-off's stunt, but it gave him the chance to warm up. From Chopin, he ségué-ed into a relatively brisk and self-contained passage from Beethoven's "Emperor Concerto." Then he switched to the overture from Mozart's "The Marriage of Figaro." All of the pieces he was playing were in some sense standards. He wasn't going to attempt anything really hard like Rachmaninov's third piano concerto for example. But classics the stranger had requested, and classics he would get.

Teddy had just begun a movement from one of Liszt's "Hungarian Rhapsodies" when the stranger put out his hand as if to signal that he'd heard enough. "Who taught you?" he asked.

"When I was a little kid, my grandmother Juanita, but since I turned ten, I've had a professional instructor." Teddy gave the stranger his teacher's name.

The man nodded as if the name was familiar to him. Then he did an extraordinary thing. He reached into his pocket, pulled out his wallet, and extracted a business card and a twenty-dollar bill. He wrapped the card in the bill and dropped them into Teddy's tip jar. Then he returned his wallet to his pocket. "I'm on the admissions committee at the Jacquard Institute of Music and the Performing Arts in New York. If you apply to our school, I'll make sure that you're accepted. I'm betting that you're going need a scholarship if you come. The cost of living in New York City is sky-high. I'm afraid you'll need to win the scholarship on your own. I can put in a good word for you, of course, but that's a different committee, and I'm not on it. Do you understand?"

Teddy nodded, so excited that his heart was racing fit to burst. The man nodded in return. "I hope that we'll hear from you soon. Thanks for playing for me. You've got a lot of talent, and I'd love to have the chance to help develop it." With that, the man turned and walked away.

Teddy reached into the tip jar, pulled out the twenty and the card it contained, and thrust them both deep into his pocket. Trying to control his breathing, he sat down again and forced himself to resume playing popular tunes. Later when Teddy looked back, he was never quite sure how he managed to finish out his shift that day, but he did. Then he took the bus home, swallowed some food that he scarcely tasted, left a note for his sleeping mother, and fell into bed.

The next day when he woke up, he pulled the card out of his pants pocket, called his instructor, and told him what had happened the day before. At first, his instructor could hardly believe what he was hearing. He kept demanding that Teddy repeat things he'd said. But when Teddy finally finished his account, the instructor exclaimed, "You've got to do it. You've got to apply. This is heaven-sent. We'll find the money somehow... I can't believe it! One of my students might go to Jacquard!"

*   *   *   *   *

"Is he really?" Chet was still sitting next to Nana and watching his son.

Nana stroked her cheek thoughtfully with a fingertip. "Nothing is guaranteed, but the probability is high. That's why my son Albert chose the Sanchez family for your son's soul. T-Bear... Teddy... was destined to be a highly-skilled musician, and they could help him achieve that goal."

Chet smiled in satisfaction. "So you angels were watching out for my boy from the start."

Nana smiled enigmatically. "From before the start, but you'll learn about that soon enough. Oh look! Here comes my husband, and from his expression, he's got some news to impart."

The head of Receiving took a seat beside his wife. "You're so right, my dear. Guess who came to us just now?"

Nana shot him a flirtatious glance. "You wouldn't happen to be talking about Abuela Sanchez, would you?"

Her husband gave a wry grimace. "Oh, you're no fun. You see everything before I can come and tell you. You being a watcher spoils the surprise."

She patted his shoulder fondly. "I couldn't help but notice. She's part of my assignment after all. But don't be peeved. I've only seen her as a very old woman. Tell me... How is she choosing to present herself now that she's here?"

Nana's husband cheered up. "As a teenaged girl, and she was quite a beauty in her day. She's so happy to be young again that Raphael's healers haven't been able to pin her down. She keeps telling them that she doesn't need their help. She had plenty of time on Earth to learn her lessons, and now all she wants to do is join the choir."

Nana laughed. "That's Abuela Sanchez—stubborn, opinionated, and very fond of music. Raphael's team doesn't stand a chance. They should just let her join and make her happy. I'm betting that she has a lovely voice, and as for hymns of praise, her whole life was one long aria."

*   *   *   *   *

Teddy applied to Jacquard and was accepted as planned. For weeks thereafter, he waited with bated breath to see if his scholarship application would be approved as well, for without financial aid, he knew he couldn't afford to go. Finally, a registered letter arrived, and he guessed before he even opened it what it would say. The envelope was fat. He reasoned that, if he'd been turned down, a single page would have sufficed. With Carla looking on, he tore open the envelope and pulled out a letter and a sheaf of forms and documents. Teddy could see immediately that the documents were complicated.

The first one he examined described the terms and conditions for a scholarship. The money would be paid quarterly directly to Jacquard as long as he maintained his enrollment there. That scholarship was only big enough to cover about half of his tuition fees, and it could not be applied to anything else. But at least it was a grant, free and clear.

The second document described a scholarship of another kind from a different source. That scholarship would cover the other half of Teddy's tuition. The money would be paid in a lump sum directly to Jacquard at the beginning of each academic year. However, if Teddy's grade point average dipped below a specified level at any time during that year, he and Jacquard must refund the balance of the money for that year, and he would not be eligible for more money until he raised his GPA back up to the acceptable level.

Teddy swallowed hard when he read that clause. Essentially it meant that, if he did poorly in even one class, he'd no longer be able to afford to continue his studies. He'd have to give up his dream, leave Jacquard, and go home.

After reading the second scholarship's terms, Teddy was almost discouraged enough to stop reading altogether, but Carla had already opened the third document and started to peruse it. "Teddy, look at this." She handed the document to him, pointing to a line in the first paragraph.

Teddy took the document from her hand and read the passage that she'd indicated. To his surprise, the document was an employment contract. It offered him a part-time job for the duration of his stay at school. He'd be called upon to play piano in practice sessions and recitals of all kinds. Teddy could imagine what that job might entail— Broadway show tunes for singers who needed to prepare for auditions... accompaniment for dancers in rehearsals... piano renditions for orchestras who were learning new musical scores... These potential duties didn't faze Teddy in the slightest. After all he'd already done in his brief career, he felt perfectly able to meet the demands of such employment.

The only challenge would be getting to the venues. Not all of them would be at Jacquard. Some of them would be at studios and theaters elsewhere in the city. Teddy wasn't looking forward to having to venture forth by subway, bus, or taxi. But the document promised him a salary that might be good enough to cover his food and rent if he practiced strict economies. Teddy was used to poverty. He felt confident that he could stretch the money to meet his needs. So without hesitation, Teddy found a pen and signed the contract. Then he signed the other two documents, accepting their terms as well. Teddy was determined to go to Jacquard, and obviously, Jacquard had worked hard to put together a financial support package that would enable him to do so.

His mother smiled, gathered up the documents, and went to photo-copy them at her office so that they'd have records of what he'd signed.

* * * * *

Teddy flew to New York with no more luggage than a carry-on duffle bag containing his clothes. To save money, he flew student stand-by, which meant that he got crammed into "coach" in a cut-rate cattle car of an airline. He arrived exhausted and hungry—a poor beginning to what would prove to be a grueling day.

Teddy found La Guardia completely overwhelming. He had to force himself to shoulder through the crowds of travelers to an information desk. There, a pretty girl in a uniform explained to him, none too patiently, how and where to get a cab. Teddy then made his way to the street and hailed one. Worried that he might not have enough cash to pay the fare, he asked the driver what a trip to Jacquard might cost. The driver quoted him an estimate that made Teddy feel faint, but he knew that he could cover it, so he tossed his duffle bag into the back seat and got in.

A long and confusing trip later, Teddy's taxi pulled up in front of the school. Teddy spent a minute counting bills out of his wallet and stuffing them through the slot in the plexiglass shield that separated the passenger compartment from the driver. When the driver was satisfied, Teddy opened the car door, hefted his bag onto his shoulder, and stepped out into a cacophony of noise—hooting car horns, sirens, and a babble of voices that filled him with longing for the peace and quiet of his home.

Trying desperately to shut out the din, Teddy pushed his way past pedestrians and entered the school lobby. As soon as the door closed behind him, the noise abated, and Teddy was able to think straight again and work out his next move. Naturally, he still carried the business card of the admissions committee member. Knowing no one else in that place, he decided that he'd try to see the man and get some guidance. So he asked around until he received directions to the administration office, and he made his way there, getting lost in the corridors only twice.

When Teddy reached the office, he learned that the man he sought was unavailable—scheduled to be in meetings for the rest of the day. Dis-spirited and bewildered, Teddy collapsed into a visitor's chair and put his head down in his hands. This gesture alarmed the secretary on duty. She was an efficient-looking gray-haired woman—not the least bit motherly or sympathetic in her demeanor. But beneath her no-nonsense tweedy exterior, she had a heart, and something in Teddy touched it.

It wasn't his delicately handsome face. She saw pretty boys every day of the week. She concluded that it must be his air of innocence. Clearly, he wasn't from the city. He was completely out of his element, and she'd always had a secret weakness for stray puppies. "What's the matter, Hon?" she asked him.

Teddy sighed and looked up. "I'm just tired and hungry, I guess. I don't know where to go to get food. I don't know where to go period. The school sent information on the dorms, but they're too expensive. I can't afford to live there. I just flew in from New Mexico. I'm supposed to start classes on Monday, and this place... New York City is just so..." At a loss for words, Teddy fell silent.

The secretary pursed her lips, opened a desk drawer, pulled out a small plastic bag containing energy bars, and handed it to him. Teddy accepted it gratefully. "Oh, thank you!"

She stood up, walked to a water cooler in the corner, dispensed some water into a clean coffee mug from the tray on top, and carried the mug back to him. By that time, Teddy had peeled the wrapper off of the first bar and consumed half of it. He accepted the mug from her hand and drained it dry. She took it and refilled it. By the time she returned, Teddy had finished the first bar and started on the second. "Slow down, Hon. You'll make yourself sick."

Teddy took her advice, but he didn't stop eating and drinking until the bars were gone. "Feel better now, Hon?" she asked.

"Yes, thank you so much. I didn't realize just how hungry I was. I mean, I had a headache, and I was feeling weak, but I've never had to go all day without food before, and I didn't know..." Teddy ran out of words and shrugged.

The secretary regarded him with a skeptical stare. "I don't know what these egg-heads were thinking, bringing a naive kid like you into this pressure-cooker and not even meeting you at the plane... You say you have no place to stay?" Teddy shook his head. "What's your name, Hon?"

"Teddy... My full name is Theodore Bernardo Sanchez, so my music customers used to call me T-Bear."

"Well, for god's sake, don't try going by 'Teddy' in this town. Folks'll chew you up and spit you out. Try 'Theo' or 'Bernie' or almost anything else. Come to think of it, 'T-Bear' isn't bad. If you need to pick up some extra money by playing music on the street, that moniker might help you."

"I play piano."

"Oh. Never mind... Kinda hard to carry one of them around, isn't it?" The secretary sat for a moment with a pensive look on her face. Then she stood up. "Come with me."

Teddy stood up and followed her—out of the office and down a hallway to where a huge bulletin board hung on a wall. The secretary examined the seemingly countless cards and notes thumb-tacked to its surface and then pounced. "Ah-ha! This one!" She pulled down one of the cards and handed it to him. He read it, and it was an advertisement for a roommate.

"As I recall, those guys have already stuffed seven students into a two-bedroom, one-bath joint. It's probably a complete dump, but the bathroom and kitchen facilities will work. The landlord would get run through the ringer if they didn't.

"What we typically see is that students spend almost no time at their apartment. It's just a place to crash at night. The rest of the time, they're in class here or out performing. So what they do to save money is, they build bunk beds in the bedrooms and sleep four or even more people to a room. This card means that one bunk bed is still free, and you might as well be the one to take it. That way, you'll be paying the lowest possible rent, and if this address is correct, you'll be able to walk to school—unless there's a full-on blizzard of course."

Teddy looked down at the card in his hand. Bunking with seven strangers in a dump wasn't a very appealing prospect, but the part about low rent and walking distance was. "I'll go call them right away."

"Let's go back to my office. You can use my phone." They did, and he did. Minutes later, he'd reserved an upper berth in a room that he'd share with an aspiring opera singer, a flautist, and a trombone player. His new roomies didn't want his signature on the lease. They didn't want the landlord to know just how many men they were housing under one barely-adequate roof. But they did want his share of the rent for the rest of the month, and in exchange for the cash, they'd give him the keys.

Teddy promised to meet and do the exchange that evening down in Jacquard's lobby, and he hung up the phone feeling greatly relieved because now he'd at least have somewhere to stay that night. He'd been afraid that he'd have to sleep on a bus stop bench or under a bush in Central Park.

He pulled out his wallet and began counting bills to make sure that he'd have enough money. He was dismayed to find that even a partial rent payment would take almost all of his remaining funds on hand—money that he'd been hard-pressed to accrue via months of tips at the Old Town bar. To be on the safe side, Teddy put his rent money in a different compartment in his wallet. Then he put his wallet away.

The secretary watched this performance and deduced what was on his mind. "You're already just about tapped out, aren't you, Hon?"

Teddy nodded sadly. "Jacquard has given me a job. I start work on Monday too, but I don't know when I'll get paid."

"You're a scholarship kid?" Teddy nodded. "Let me check." She turned to her computer and began mousing and typing. Presently she said, "You'll get paid every Friday. I'm guessing that you don't have a bank account here, so I've arranged for you to pick up your pay packet at the Accounting Office. Ask for a cash disbursement. You don't want to get stuck with a check. The check cashing agencies around here charge a pretty big percentage of the check's total for their service, and you can't afford to have them skim that much."

Teddy was nodding to show that he understood. "I don't know how to thank you. You've been so kind to me. Would you mind telling me your name?"

The secretary shook her head slightly and pointed to a brass name plate on her desk. "It's Doris... Doris Connover."

"Thank you, Doris."

Teddy turned as if he was about to leave her office, but she stopped him. "Hold your horses, cowboy. We still have to figure out the food angle. No way are you going to survive until you get paid on Friday unless you have something to eat."

Teddy's face fell. "But it's like you said. I'm almost tapped out."

"I know, but not for nothing have I watched our students in action all these years." She turned and called to someone unseen in the inner office. "Betty, be an angel and cover my desk for an hour. I've got a kid here who needs some help."

A short, overweight African American woman came trundling out of the back room and took a seat at Doris's desk. She made waving motions with her hands. "Go, go... Just don't be too long."

Doris pointed at Teddy's duffle bag. Taking the hint, he hoisted it onto his shoulder and once more followed her out of the office and down the hall. But this time, she led him completely out of the building, down the street, and into a delicatessen. "Best knockwurst in town," she told him as they entered the fragrant shop. Teddy couldn't help but wonder what knockwurst was.

Doris led Teddy through the narrow aisles giving instructions at high speed. "Always buy dense, hard-crusted breads, not those soft loaves you find in grocery stores. The tough breads keep better. Here!" She selected an unsliced loaf of pumpernickel and thrust it into his hands. "Remember, that's got to last you at least seven nights counting tonight and seven days until pay-day. So ration it carefully. Now, meat...

"Canned tuna and other canned meats can work well, but they're heavy to carry, and for a while, you're going to have to live like a nomad. So what you need is a preserved meat with no heavy container like dry salami." She pulled one off of a hanging rack and added it to his burdens. "Remember, seven days... Now, dairy... Are you lactose-intolerant?"

Teddy was juggling the duffle bag, bread, and sausage. "What's that?"

"Do you get sick when you eat milk products?"

"Never. Where I come from, we eat cheese or sour cream in almost every meal."

"Good to hear... Again, you want something that can last a long time without refrigeration, like individually packaged string cheese sticks." She picked up a package, scrutinized the label, and then picked up a second package. "Turns out two packages will cover the week—one stick at each meal." She placed the packages in Teddy's outstretched arms. "Now for the *pièce de résistance*—fruit...

"Most vegetables either require cooking or they spoil readily. Carrots are the exception, but I've never been too keen on raw carrots, myself. Also, if you eat too many raw carrots, you literally turn orange, which could work against you in an audition. So like I said, fruit...

"Bananas are a non-starter. To have them last a week, you'd have to buy them green, and by the end of the week, they'd be mostly brown mush anyway. Apples are better, but they bruise and get mealy as they dry out. I'm going to recommend oranges. You have to peel them, and they have bitter pips, but they're pretty resilient and very juicy. Given all the dry, preserved food you'll be eating—the meat and cheese—you'll probably welcome something tart and wet in your diet.

"One more thing... Canned and preserved meats are salty, and cheese is high in fat, so you'll need to hydrate to stay healthy on this kind of diet. Please, do yourself a favor. Don't waste your money on sodas or bottled water. The school has lots of drinking fountains. Get yourself a sealable cup or a sports bottle, and get your beverages for free. Pure water is better for you anyway." She thought a moment and then said, "Please tell me that you're not a Starbucks addict. Their coffees and teas are great, but expensive, and frankly, the caffeine will just make you jittery and hurt your performance."

Teddy shook his head. "I hate coffee, and I've never drunk tea."

"Good." They'd just come abreast of a stand covered by sacks of oranges. She selected a sack and added it to the pile of groceries that he was carrying. "OK, let's go to the register..." She led him, staggering a bit, back to the front of the store. The old man behind the register looked Teddy up and down with amusement showing on his face. "New student," she told him.

The man grinned and rang up Teddy's purchases. Teddy had just barely enough money left to cover the charges. He put his duffle bag down at his feet, pulled out his wallet, and counted out the remaining bills. When he finished paying for his groceries, he had only two dollars left. The old man stared as Teddy tucked the two bills back into his wallet and put it away. Then the man smiled, took a small bag of peppermint candies from beside the register, and handed it to Teddy. "Welcome to the neighborhood, son. I hope you'll be a big success."

Surprised, Teddy took the gift. "Thank you, sir!"

"Now put your food in that duffle bag I see at your feet, and make sure you eat as good as you can. None of that nonsense I see the other kids pulling—trying to live on peanut butter and breakfast cereal... Sheesh... Young bodies need good fuel."

"Yes, sir. Thank you." And Teddy and Doris left the store.

They walked together back to the school lobby. There, Doris turned to Teddy and said, "This is where I leave you. Stay here. Meet your new roommate. Pay the rent and get your keys. Then, come Monday, hit the ground running and show us all what you can do. OK?"

"OK!" Teddy watched as Doris walked away. Then he sat down on a bench to wait.

That evening, he traded rent money for keys as planned and followed his new roommate home to the apartment. It was just as Doris had predicted. The paint was peeling off of the walls. There were dark rust stains on all of the bathroom fixtures, and when Teddy and his roommate entered the front door, the other residents were engaged in stomping cockroaches in the kitchen.

But the linens on Teddy's bunk were clean, and as he'd reminded himself earlier, even these squalid conditions beat being homeless and living on the streets. So Teddy flung his duffle bag up onto the bed and climbed up after it. As he lay down, trying to get comfortable, he said several brief prayers—that the cockroaches wouldn't find his food before he could eat it... that he'd figure out how to survive in this crazy place... that he'd make good grades and be able to complete his studies... and that somehow he'd get over his terrible homesickness...

For Teddy was aching with longing for what he'd left behind—wide blue skies that he could see without craning back his head to catch a glimpse between concrete skyscrapers... the sigh of clean breezes across the desert, winds devoid of car exhaust and city noise... and most of all, his family. Teddy wished with all his heart that he could be with his family that very minute, instead of surrounded by millions of strangers, only two of whom had shown him real kindness that day.

*   *   *   *   *

Teddy did "hit the ground running" on Monday. He attended his classes and soon impressed his professors with his commitment to learning. For Teddy quickly deduced that there was an entire body of musical knowledge on which he'd completely missed out up to that point—composition theory for example... Teddy also started his part-time job, and before the week was up, rumors were spreading that, if you wanted the best possible musical accompaniment for your event, then T-Bear Sanchez was the pianist you should request.

Teddy rationed his food and made it through his first week without starving. On Friday, he collected his pay, tucked the cash in his wallet, and walked down the street to the deli to restock. By that time, some of his fellow students had coached him on the realities of life in the big city. He'd learned to guard his wallet carefully and never to flash a roll of cash in public. He continued to have friendly conversations with the store's proprietor, and the man seemed to enjoy having one customer at least that he could absolutely trust not to shop-lift.

In spare moments between classes, Teddy did further shopping and wrote letters. He bought the sports bottle that Doris had recommended, and given directions from a fellow student, he found a thrift store where he could purchase a used overcoat. One of his professors had mentioned that he'd need one, and Teddy didn't want to get caught unprepared by an early storm.

The coat had probably belonged to some up-town doorman. It was a faded navy blue with a double row of brass buttons. In truth, it looked quite silly out of context. But in its favor, it was thick and warm—genuine wool with a sturdy lining—and it had deep pockets both within and without. As the cold weather came on, Teddy began wearing it almost daily, and eventually, in the minds of his classmates, he and his coat became a cherished part of the Jacquard experience.

So too did Teddy's letter-writing. His classmates all favored cell phone calls, text messages, and tweets to stay in touch with friends and family. But Teddy didn't have a cell phone. It was an expense that neither he nor his mother had been able to afford. Yet Carla had drilled her son on the importance of good manners. If someone did something nice for you, you sent a thank-you note. If someone paid you a visit or called, you would return the favor. So Teddy wrote notes almost from the moment he arrived at school.

His first letter of thanks went to the man on the admissions committee. His second went to the committee in charge of financial aid. Next, Teddy wrote an effusive note of thanks to Doris, with a request that she'd extend his thanks to Betty as well. Then Teddy branched out.

He sent notes to all of his family members of course—newsy letters to catch them up on how he was doing. He always closed these missives with grateful acknowledgements of how much they'd all done to raise him and help him to get where he was today. By the end of first term, however, he was also sending notes to some of his professors. If one of them went the extra mile to explain some point of theory or to help Teddy in some way, that professor would find a folded piece of lined notebook paper in his hard-copy mailbox the next day.

At first, being New Yorkers, Teddy's professors were baffled by this behavior. One of them even asked his colleagues if Teddy might not be the most smarmy brown-noser that they'd ever taught. But soon, they came to realize that Teddy was just very polite and completely sincere. Thereafter, they came to welcome his correspondence as a refreshing change from the egotistical arrogance and air of entitlement displayed by other pupils in their charge.

In short, although other students might succumb to New York's influence and lose their way, Teddy managed to stay true to himself and his upbringing. He knew well what an amazing opportunity had come his way. So if he awoke in the middle of the night from some nightmare, or if he had trouble falling asleep in the first place due to the snores of his many roommates, he would lie awake meditating, reminding himself that, no matter how much he might be suffering in the moment, he was suffering for his art.

Then, one day, there came a turning point, a true breakthrough. Teddy and his classmates were given a year-end assignment. They were to compose a piece of music, either alone or with a partner, and then they were supposed to orchestrate it. Teddy raised his hand and asked if the partner had to be a current student at Jacquard. The professor said no, that someone from outside would be acceptable, and Teddy's heart began to race as he realized what he'd now be able to do. He'd be able to write down the composition that had been in his head as long as he could remember. He'd be able to complete and orchestrate the "Soul Rhapsody."

Teddy had retained a lot of memories from his past life as T-Bear—his name, his talents as a musician, and his belief that he'd once known true soul-mates. But the biggest, most complex, and most important memory of all had been the rhapsody—an intact composition that he'd produced with one of those soul-mates.

What had always frustrated him had been the fact that, during his reincarnation, he'd retained a vision of her face, but he could no longer recall her name. He wished intensely that he could give her proper credit on the assignment, but at the very least, he felt he owed it to both of them to record their work and keep it from being lost.

Teddy set to work immediately, and because he was capturing something known, not composing something new, he completed the first phase of his assignment in record time. Then he moved on to orchestrating the piece.

Meanwhile, up in Heaven, Nana was looking on with mounting alarm. She summoned her husband and her son to her side. As soon as they arrived, she told them, "It's just as Raphael feared. T-Bear is re-visiting the rhapsody."

Chet asked, "Why is this a bad thing?"

Albert tried to explain. "It isn't bad in and of itself. It's just that T-Bear's... Teddy's current job is to live his present life fully. The rhapsody is from his previous life, and if he dwells too much on his past, he'll compromise his spiritual success going forward."

Chet frowned in confusion. "You mean to tell me that my son has lived before?"

Albert nodded vigorously. "Yup! That's exactly what I'm saying."

Chet began to sputter. "But... but... how can that be?"

"Reincarnation," Nana's husband muttered. "But don't get the idea that he did something wrong in his past life. Through no fault of his own, he was, well, hijacked. We're just giving him the chance to live a complete life now, and what my wife is afraid of is that his past is leaking into his present, spoiling the whole thing."

Just then, Uriel came wandering by. He seemed surprised to see Albert and his family huddled together, and he drifted over to investigate. "Hello, how goes the watching?" he asked.

Still feeling distressed, Nana gestured to T-Bear, and then stood back. Uriel bent forward, frowning a bit in concentration. "Ah yes, the rhapsody... How delightful that it's being orchestrated at last, and by such a gifted mortal! I'm certain that he'll do a good job with it." Uriel straightened up and favored them all with his typical benign smile. Suddenly, none of them could quite remember what they'd been talking about before he came. "Well, lovely to see you all again," and Uriel drifted away.

After he was out of sight, Chet seemed to shake himself. "Who was that guy? Every time he shows up, it's like my brain goes hay-wire somehow."

Nana was smiling softly, her expression dreamy. "That's the Light of God. Won't it be wonderful when T-Bear finishes his assignment?"

Albert was nodding happily in agreement. "It always was a beautiful work. It could help transform countless lives for the better. I hope he presents it soon..."

5: T-Bear Looks for Answers...

Teddy finished orchestrating the rhapsody well before the deadline when he had to submit the work to his professor. He used the extra time to make two more complete copies—one to mail home to his mother for storage in his safe deposit box and one to keep on hand for his personal records. When he mailed the first copy, he did something that he'd never done before. With help from a clerk at the post office, he sent the package via certified mail with a return receipt request. When the green "proof of delivery" card arrived, Teddy felt a surge of relief. The longer he'd worked on the rhapsody, the more he'd become convinced that the piece was terribly important somehow and must be carefully protected from loss.

Finally, the day arrived when Teddy and his classmates had to turn in their compositions. Teddy handed the binder containing his sheet music to his professor and followed his fellow students out of the room. He didn't expect to hear anything further until final grades for the year were delivered. Teddy just prayed that, when his grades were posted, they'd be high enough across the board to enable him to retain his scholarship.

Many of Teddy's classmates would leave soon to go home for the summer, but Teddy would have to remain in New York to fulfill the terms of his employment. Six of his seven roommates were under similar financial aid obligations, so at least Teddy would still have a place to live. The rent would be higher for the next three months, but due to Teddy's thrifty behavior during the school year, he had the money to cover it.

So Teddy settled into a new routine. Every Monday morning, he went to Jacquard to pick up his schedule for the coming week—the times and locations of the auditions, recitals, and other events at which he must play. Every Friday evening, he stopped by Accounting to pick up his pay packet. From there, he went to the deli to stock up on food, and then he went home to give the lease-holder of record his share of the rent and get a receipt. It was a hand-to-mouth existence, but one that Teddy had come to find fulfilling. He didn't even mind the cockroaches and the crowded apartment anymore. He'd become used to them.

Then, about three weeks after Teddy's end of term, he got a surprise. That Monday, he went to Jacquard as usual, and there in his hard-copy mailbox was an envelope from Administration. Other students were standing around the mailboxes holding similar envelopes. As Teddy reached for his, one of his classmates said, "Grades are in!" Teddy withdrew his envelope and walked away to find some privacy. If the news was bad, he didn't want his classmates to see his reaction.

Teddy found a bench in the lobby, sat down, and tore open the envelope with trembling fingers. Inside, he found a transcript printed on pale-yellow paper. Swiftly he scanned his grades. He hadn't made top marks in every class, but he'd scored high enough in each one that his scholarship would be renewed the following year. Teddy heaved a sigh of relief.

Then he noticed that the envelope contained a second page, a letter printed on plain white bond paper. Teddy pulled it out, skimmed it, and then had to re-read it more carefully because he was so astonished by what it said. The man from the admissions committee wanted to meet with him. He should contact the man's secretary to set up an appointment right away.

In Teddy's mind, there was no time like the present, so he loped upstairs and entered Doris's office. She seemed pleased to see him. "Excellent! We were wondering how long it would take to reach you, Hon."

"Can you tell me why he wants to meet with me? I mean, he's in charge of admissions, and I'm already here. I hope there's no problem with my enrollment."

"Oh, heavens, no. Perish the thought. He and some colleagues just want to ask you some questions. That's all."

This answer did little to put Teddy's mind at ease. "Questions? What kind of questions?"

"Haven't the faintest notion... This is one time when he didn't confide in me. He just said, 'Find T-bear Sanchez. We want to talk with him.' So you know as much as I do."

"When does he want to meet with me?"

"As soon as he can get the rest of his party together. Would later on this morning work for you?"

"I don't know yet. I still have to pick up my work schedule for the week."

Doris turned to her computer and began typing and mousing rapidly. Then the printer in the corner came to life and spat out a sheet of paper. She gestured to the machine. "There's your schedule, Hon. You have nothing on the books until tomorrow morning, so a meeting either this morning or this afternoon should work fine. I've sent E-mail to his phone so that he can notify the other attendees and confirm the appointment. If you hang out here a few minutes more, I should be able to tell you all the particulars."

Teddy went over to the printer, picked up his schedule, folded the paper, and put it in his pocket. He was nervous, but good manners prevailed. "Thanks for the print-out, and thanks for helping me with the meeting."

"No problem, Hon. Oops, here's his reply." Doris resumed her mousing and typing. "Wow. He *really* must want to talk with you. He's set up the meeting for half an hour from now in the conference room across the hall. You might as well go there and take a seat. Do you have anything with you to keep you entertained while you wait?" She stared pointedly at the backpack slung over his shoulder.

"I guess I could get started on my lunch. It's early but..." Teddy shrugged.

Doris smiled. "Still living the nomadic life, I see."

Teddy smiled back. "Almost everything I own in the world is still at my family's house in Albuquerque. All I've got here is an old overcoat and my duffle bag full of clothes. They're sitting on a top bunk in that apartment you found for me. I really can't thank you enough for what you did for me that day. You saved my life."

Doris's smile broadened into a wry grin. "Was the apartment as much of a dump as I thought it would be?"

"Worse. A month after I moved in, we trapped a rat and kept it as a pet. His name is Willard. And every night before we can cook any food in the kitchen, we have to snap on the lights and then kill cockroaches like mad. The bathroom's in much better shape though. I told my roommates something they didn't know. You can use denture cleaner to remove rust stains on porcelain. One of my second cousins works as a maid, and she knows all the tricks."

Doris was shaking her head. "And yet apparently, you never looked for a better place."

Teddy grimaced. "You know what they say. In real estate, it's 'location, location, location.' You found me maybe the only place that I could afford within walking distance of the only place that I wanted to be. Enough said."

"Well, I'm happy that everything's working out for you. And now, as much as I've enjoyed seeing you again, I should get back to work. So if you wouldn't mind..."

Teddy smiled, stood up, left her office, and went to the conference room as she'd asked. There he placed his backpack on the table, sat down, unzipped a compartment, and began eating his sandwich. He'd barely consumed four bites before distinguished-looking professors began entering the room and seating themselves around the table. Embarrassed, Teddy quickly wrapped up his sandwich and thrust it back into its pocket.

Last to enter was Teddy's friend, the admissions committee member. He shut the door, took a seat at the head of the table, looked around the room at his fellows, and asked, "Shall we get started?" The others all nodded. Then the man turned to Teddy and said, "Thanks for responding so promptly to our invitation. I'm here simply to chair the meeting. They chose me because you and I have met in the past, and they thought that my presence would help you to feel more at ease."

Teddy nodded to show that he understood. He'd just noticed, however, that his music composition professor was one of the men in the room, so Teddy was feeling quite uneasy despite the precautions they'd taken. He cleared his throat nervously and asked, "How can I help you today?"

The professors all glanced at each other. Then his composition professor spoke. "I assume that you've already received your final grades?" Teddy nodded. "Then you know that you received top marks in my class." Teddy nodded again. "Your composition was remarkably beautiful and very sophisticated. Was it entirely your own work?"

Teddy shook his head. "You said it was OK to collaborate with someone who wasn't currently enrolled here. A partner and I composed the melodies together... all of the principal themes... Then I chose the order in which those themes were presented, and I did the orchestration all by myself."

"And what is your partner's name?"

Teddy felt as if the ground had just opened up beneath him. He swallowed hard. Her face was clear in his mind's eye, but... "I'm sorry. I don't know."

"You don't know? But that's absurd! How could you work together on something this complex and not know your collaborator's name?"

The admissions man cleared his throat to interrupt the tirade.

As soon as he did so, another man turned to address his colleague. "He said that they collaborated, but in today's world, that collaboration may not have occurred face-to-face. They could have met on the internet. They could have exchanged audio-files via E-mail or some other means. Collaboration doesn't always take place in real-time, you know. His partner may even have wanted to remain anonymous.

"A lot of internet commerce is conducted using user-names or other monikers. It may well be the case that all he ever knew was a social media handle like 'tunes-boy935.' And if that kind of ID is all he has, then it's not his fault that he can't give you what you want. You're the one who gave blanket permission to partner with others outside of our student body. You didn't say, 'Be sure to get the other guy's legal name.' " The speaker sat back in a huff.

Teddy's composition professor glared at the man. "Well all of that may be true, but it doesn't help us one bit in our current circumstances." He turned to Teddy. "Was that it? Did you meet your partner on the internet? Is that why you don't know his or her name?"

Teddy knew that they'd never believe the truth, so he simply nodded and then said a silent prayer to God, asking for forgiveness for lying so blatantly.

Everyone sat silent for a moment. Then Teddy thought to ask a question. "Why is it so important to know my partner's legal name?"

The admissions man spoke. "It's about time we explain, don't you think?" The others around the table all nodded. "We want to publish sheet music for your rhapsody—at least enough copies to present the fully orchestrated version at some concerts we plan to give. Before we can publish the work, however, we believe that we should help you to copyright it.

"Now, we could simply print a copyright message on each page that includes the year and your name, but legally, that message would be incomplete. If your partner learned of that message, he or she could sue for copyright infringement, and if he or she had prior work that proved there'd been a collaboration, then he or she would likely win the suit."

The admissions man gestured to a woman at the foot of the table. "Ms. Leichner here is from our legal department. She's been explaining the issues to us. She's the one who recommended that we get your partner's name and make sure that the copyright message is accurate and complete. Moreover, she recommends that we register the copyright with the federal government. Having a copyrighted work of this importance will look great on your résumé, especially if it's performed in public as per our plan, so it's in your best interest to help us. So what do you think? Will you try to find out your partner's name?"

Teddy didn't have much hope of success, but he wanted to learn his partner's name far more than they ever could, so he nodded again. "I'll do my best."

Ms. Leichner spoke. "Please do, and try to make it quick. What they still haven't told you is how soon they hope to go to press with your intellectual property." She gestured at the man seated next to her. "Dr. McHugh is in charge of event management and charitable solicitations. Please tell Mr. Sanchez what you have in mind."

Dr. McHugh cleared his throat. "As you know, your employment contract with us requires that you play at whatever events we specify, always assuming that you're physically able, that is. Heretofore, we've asked you to play accompaniments at venues here in town. For the rest of this year, however, we'd like you to play at concerts all over the eastern seaboard, predominantly throughout New England. The venues will mostly be private homes belonging to major Jacquard donors. The concerts will all be black-tie affairs—fund-raising opportunities staged to replenish our scholarship coffers and the building fund. Any questions?"

"Yes... First of all, how does this work? Do you advertise... put out invitations?... sell tickets?..."

"The donor whose house we'll be using invites other charitably-minded people that he or she knows. Those who accept attend in exchange for a minimum donation, often several thousand dollars per plate at dinner. People are free to donate more, of course—sometimes by paying to have an entire table reserved exclusively for their friends. During dinner, our students provide musical entertainment, and after dinner, we hold a concert of some kind. In the past, we've offered various soloists, choirs, chamber music groups, and now a full, if small, orchestra featuring you on piano. Anything else?"

"Yes, how do we get there, where do we stay, how will we be fed, and what do we wear?" Teddy heard the admissions man snort with suppressed laughter.

Dr. McHugh's face colored, but he answered as directly as he could. "Our staff and students travel by bus to the different locations. While there, depending on the size of the house, we stay either in the servants' quarters or in an inexpensive nearby hotel. You would undoubtedly call some of these homes mansions. They have more than a dozen bedrooms on the top floor, and by doubling up, we can usually accommodate everybody.

"As for food, our hosts provide three simple meals per day for the duration of our stay. We are aware that our students may still be paying rent and other expenses here in the city, so they may not be able to afford additional expenses on the road. As for what to wear, when students join one of our concert tours, we ask that they purchase at least two changes of suitable clothes—black skirts and white blouses for the women, and black suits with white shirts for the men. Naturally, all accessories like shoes and ties are black too. Have I addressed your questions?"

Teddy sighed. "I'm sorry to disappoint you again, but I can't afford to buy two suits, two dress shirts, and all those accessories you just mentioned. I can barely afford food."

The admissions man stepped in again. "Mr. Sanchez is one of our scholarship students. Given that we expect his composition and his performances to be a major draw, I'm sure that we can see our way clear to providing him with the necessary wardrobe. Does our representative from Financial Aid concur?" Teddy watched as the man directly across from him began to nod emphatically.

"OK then... It seems that we're all in agreement. Mr. Sanchez will do his utmost to learn the legal name of his partner so that we can publish his rhapsody and register the copyright. The school will provide Mr. Sanchez with the clothes he'll need for the tour. Our events manager will inform Mr. Sanchez of his new schedule, including the complete itinerary for the journey. And Accounting will prepare to receive our next influx of cash so that we can provide more scholarships to deserving students like the fine musician you see before you. Meeting adjourned..."

At that cue, everyone except Teddy stood up and left the room. Teddy stayed behind, his head filled with conflicting emotions and fragmentary thoughts. He took advantage of the time to finish his lunch. Then he went home, lay down on his bunk, and tried to think of some way that he could learn the name of his soul-mate and former partner. For without her name, the entire plan would come to naught, and Teddy's own name would be mud in the minds of his professors going forward.

*   *   *   *   *

Several hours later, Teddy awoke with a start. He'd been having one of his New York City nightmares—the one in which he ran terrified through an endless maze of sky-high concrete walls, pursued by a faceless crowd of thousands of hostile people. He tried to sit up, but when he did so, the room spun, and he was forced to lie back down again. He put a hand to his forehead and found that he was running a fever. He realized that it must be a high fever because his pillow was soaked in sweat and he was beginning to shake with chills despite the warmth of the room. As usual, the apartment's air conditioning was barely combatting the mid-June heat, but Teddy realized that, for once, that might be an advantage.

Teddy turned over his pillow, kicked off his shoes, and slid fully-clothed under the covers. He was still uncomfortable because of the duffle bag and overcoat at the foot of his bed, but at least his chills seemed to abate. He lay in the semi-darkness wondering what he should do. He knew he couldn't count on his roommates to take care of him, but neither could he afford to go to an emergency room. He had no health insurance. As had happened so many times before, Teddy felt a wave of homesickness wash over him. If he was at home, his mother Carla would sit at his bedside nursing him, and his grandmother Juanita would bring him bowls-ful of her chicken-tortilla soup.

Teddy decided that he'd just have to tough it out and take his chances. On the plus side, he was young and didn't have any underlying medical conditions. On the minus side however, for nearly a year, he'd been living in squalor on a bad diet under great stress. Teddy murmured a heart-felt prayer. "Dear God, please let me get well on my own, and if that's not possible, please let one of my roommates find me in time and call 911."

Teddy lay for a few minutes more considering alternatives. Then he threw back the covers, swung his feet out of bed, and dropped to the floor. The room spun again, and he had to cling to the side of the bunk bed to keep from falling. Fortunately, the dizzy spell was short-lived.

Teddy staggered to the kitchen and drank two glasses of water. Then he went to the bathroom and relieved himself. Next he filled his sports bottle with water from the tap so he'd have something to drink while in bed. He knew that, if he was going to fight this bug, he'd need to stay hydrated. As for food, he had a week's-worth in his duffle bag. He hoped that it would be enough. He hoped that he'd be able to get it down and keep it down. It was hardly the kind of fare that a sick man would need, but it was all he had.

Teddy returned to his bedroom feeling weak as a kitten. Getting back up onto his bunk was a struggle, but he made it. As a precaution, Teddy placed his water bottle beside him against the wall, and he pulled his duffle bag up to within arm's reach. Then he threw the covers over himself again, and for good measure, he added his overcoat over his legs and lower torso.

Teddy dozed fitfully for the rest of the afternoon and into the evening. Whenever he awoke, he'd eat a few bites and drink some water. At one point, when his bottle was empty, he forced himself to go refill it and use the restroom before returning to bed. But aside from that foray, he remained in his room trying to sleep, hoping that rest and time would allow him to recover.

Late that night, Teddy's roommates returned one by one. For a while, they made a lot of noise fixing and eating their dinners in the kitchen. Then when one of them walked into the bedroom where Teddy lay, he groaned, "Can't you hold it down? I feel terrible, and you're keeping me awake."

Alarmed, the man left the room and walked into the kitchen. "Dudes, T-Bear's sick. It might be bad. What do you think we should do?"

"I know what I'm going to do. I'm going to move my bedding out to the living room. I'm not going to take chances by crashing in the same room with a sick guy."

"Me too. Good thing George went home for the summer. I'm betting there's room for two mattresses on the floor out here, but no way is there room for three."

"But what should we *do?*"

"About T-Bear? Make sure he doesn't die on us of course. Can you imagine the hassle? We'll check on him every couple of hours, and if he begins to look really bad, we'll call 911. In the meantime, we can get him more water and stuff."

Teddy listened to this exchange with a sense of relief. Due to their enlightened self-interest, he was going to get at least some amount of care, so the second part of his prayer had been answered already. As he lay in the dark, he whispered under his breath, renewing the first. "Dear God, please help me to get well, and soon."

*   *   *   *   *

Up in Heaven, Nana had been very busy watching Janie and Suzy, but when Teddy uttered his first prayer, he caught her attention. She changed focus, looked in on him, and exclaimed in dismay. "Oh no... That meeting must have been too much for him. What if Raphael was right after all?"

Then Teddy uttered his second prayer. "This is terrible! He's coming down with pneumonia. There's already almost a twenty percent chance that he'll die of it. If he does, what will become of everything else that he was supposedly destined to do in his current life?" Nana frowned in resolve. "We've got to answer his prayer, and fast, but how?"

She thought hard. Technically, she was supposed to report this causality chain to her boss, the head watcher. But she was loath to do so. T-Bear's choice to keep the entire rhapsody from his past life had been very controversial. The Watchers reported up to Raphael, and Raphael had warned that dire consequences might result from T-Bear's decision. No, Nana needed to come up with a different approach. Then she thought of Uriel... of the many subtle and not-so-subtle ways in which he'd intervened thus far... and Nana began to smile a sly smile.

"Oh, Albert?" She called to her one-time son across the firmament, and although he was about to incarnate another human soul, he paused in his work and went to answer her.

"Hello, Nana, what's up?" Nana stepped aside and let him see for himself how sick Teddy was becoming. "Oh no... We can't let this happen!"

"I know. That's what I said. I don't suppose you have any ideas?" She regarded him speculatively as inspiration dawned in his face.

"As it happens, I do, but I don't think I should tell you what I have in mind—plausible deniability and all that..."

"Fine by me... I'm going to turn this whole situation over to you, at least for now, and you needn't tell me anything further about it if you don't want to... I trust your judgement. Do what you think best."

Albert kissed her on the cheek and then made an awkward attempt at vanishing. His form wavered in the air a moment before sublimating way. Nana shook her head fondly. Albert was still learning some of the tricks of the angel-trade, but he was getting better all the time, and one day, he might be able to simply wink out like his friend and mentor Uriel. Nana sighed and went back to work.

Meanwhile, Albert had returned to his work station. He glanced around him furtively to see if anyone might be watching, and then he bent over close to one of the portals. "Janie," he called softly. "Janie, please come. I need to speak with you."

Presently, he saw a bright brown eye peer at him through the minuscule crack he'd created by propping open her door. "What is it, Uncle Albert?"

"I need your help again, and because we got away with healing Suzy's mother, I'm fairly sure we'll get away with this miracle too."

"You need me to do another healing? How is this one different? As you know, I do a healing every day."

"Yes, but this one's for T-Bear. He's all alone in New York City, and he's very sick."

Albert heard Janie gasp. "But how can I find him in time? I was only able to find Suzy's mother through Suzy, and I was only able to find her because I'd searched the world for her for years. You've told me that T-Bear is in

New York, but the city is huge... absolutely millions of people... I would need some kind of help."

"If I understand correctly, T-Bear himself will help you. He's praying fervently that he'll get well. A prayer of that intensity is like a beacon. Cast your spiritual eye over the whole city and look for such prayers. I'm fairly confident that, by process of elimination, you'll be able to locate him before too long."

"OK, Uncle Albert, I'll give it a try, and I'll let you know if I succeed."

Janie extended her soul out of her body toward New York. It was literally a big stretch for her. She lived in the Los Angeles Basin, and her target was three thousand miles away. But as she'd told Albert, she'd searched the world for Suzy, so she had some prior relevant experience. The only reason she hadn't sought out T-Bear before was that Albert had explained the risks she'd be taking if she contacted her erstwhile soul-mates during their current lives. But now, he was asking her for the second time to put such risks aside. The cause was good, and she was intent on making the necessary connection.

As it happened, Albert was right. As soon as Janie could "see" the city, she observed hundreds of prayer beacons rising up to Heaven. All she had to do was listen to the different prayers, searching for T-Bear's particular request. The process was absolutely grueling—so many souls all suffering in their own disparate ways. But eventually, she discovered a young man in a tenement who was burning up with fever from a lung infection. Each time he regained consciousness, he sent forth another prayer. She touched his soul with hers, and she knew at once that she'd found her friend.

Janie tapped into Heaven's infinite ocean of healing energy and began pouring it into T-Bear. Moments into the process, he awoke, and clearly, he immediately became aware of Janie's spiritual touch. Although nearly overwhelmed by the healing experience, he managed to speak into the darkness. "Oh, is it you? It must be you! I've missed you so much... Thank you for coming. Thank you for making me well again... Please! Please tell me your name..."

Janie completed his healing. Mindful of Albert's past admonitions, she was about to terminate her soul's connection to T-Bear and simply return to her own body. But something plaintive, even desperate, in the way he spoke touched her heart. "It's Janie... Jane Marie Hanson..." and she severed their link and left.

Teddy lay in the dark savoring his renewed feeling of robust good health. "She came for me," he thought. "She answered my prayer and saved me. And now I even know her name... Jane Marie Hanson..." Teddy closed his eyes and fell into a deep refreshing sleep.

The next day, he got up, showered, dressed, and walked to Jacquard. He went straight to Doris's office. When she looked up from her computer monitor, he told her, "Jane Marie Hanson." A look of comprehension spread over her face, and she exclaimed, "Excellent, Mr. Sanchez. I'll let Legal know right away."

*   *   *   *   *

Within the week, Legal filed the necessary forms to register a joint copyright in Teddy's and Janie's names. Jacquard's publications department applied the copyright message to every page of the rhapsody's sheet music and then sent that music to be printed and bound. When the press delivered the finished books, Teddy's professors auditioned musicians, formed a small orchestra, and began rehearsing it all day every day. Teddy and his fellow performers learned to play several classical orchestral standards, and also the rhapsody, now christened "Innocence."

Within a month, the professors agreed that the orchestra was "ready for prime time." In other words, it could now be trusted to play its repertoire in concert, representing the school well to a potentially quite-critical audience.

G. C. Ellis

Teddy found himself standing up for a team of tailors. They'd been hired to sew a pair of black suits for him, suits that must not only look good... They must also allow him full range of motion so that he could play grand pianos with virtuoso skill. As soon as he was properly attired, he and the rest of the orchestra performed a dress rehearsal in Jacquard's auditorium in front of the entire staff and their guests. The rhapsody came last in the program, and as soon as the final notes died away, Teddy was stunned to hear the audience erupt into loud applause and cries of "Bravo! Encore!" Not since the talent shows of his elementary school days had he received such effusive acclaim, but now it was coming from professors at one of the finest performing arts schools in the world.

Teddy had little time to contemplate this event. Early the next morning, he and the orchestra boarded a bus to go on tour. A second bus would follow, carrying the tour's support staff, including the professor chosen to act as conductor. Teddy had felt a flutter of stage fright as he'd tossed his duffle bag into the bus's luggage compartment, but his stomach had settled down once he'd taken his seat and the bus had gotten underway. He was surrounded by people he'd come to know well during rehearsals, and apparently, they attributed their coming trip to him, a trip that they all seem inclined to regard as some kind of adventure.

So to Teddy's surprise, he found himself in the role of "first among equals," and as he'd never been on vacation in his life, he began to look forward to the experience too. The bus rolled down one highway after another, and Teddy soon lost himself in the scenic vistas outside his window.

In early afternoon, the buses pulled into a long private drive. It wound through rolling grassy hills and stands of tall trees. When the house finally came into view, Teddy gasped. It was indeed a mansion—one of those vast stone piles erected by robber barons during the last quarter of the 1800s. The buses pulled to a stop behind the house at the servants' entrance. Everyone piled out, and a haughty-looking man in a formal-dress uniform began calling directions to the orchestra's "roadies."

Teddy sought out the professor-conductor and whispered, "What's going on?"

The professor frowned. "The butler is giving us our instructions. Evidently, the caterers have already set up the tables and chairs for dinner in the ballroom. They left a space at one end of the room for our orchestra—the location where bands and chamber music groups typically sit. However, we've brought more musicians, so we need more space, plus apparently, no one told the man that we'd need the grand piano. He's going to have to move tables aside temporarily so that we can wheel the instrument into position from where it usually stays in the music room."

Teddy was aghast. "They have a ballroom *and* a music room?"

The professor gave him a lop-sided smile. "Watch and learn, sonny... Watch and learn." Just then, the professor noticed some error that needed his attention, and he rushed off to correct it. Teddy stayed behind taking in the implications. Certainly, he'd heard of such wealth before, but as he'd grown up largely without access to either films or television, he'd never actually seen it.

By nightfall, all was in readiness. Teddy and his fellow musicians ate an early dinner in the servants' dining hall. Then the housekeeper conducted them to their attic bedrooms where they changed into their clothes for the concert. Once ready, they soberly followed her downstairs and through the door that led out onto the ballroom's stage. Teddy's colleagues took their seats, briefly tuned their instruments, and then began playing the dinner music program.

Meanwhile, Teddy stood back stage, looking out from behind a heavy velvet curtain at the assembled guests. He'd never known that there could be so many fine dresses and glittering jewels together in one room at the same time. Moreover, the room itself was the perfect setting for all that splendor. The high roof was supported by marble columns. The polished floor was set with marquetry designs, and the walls were covered in panels of silk brocade and hung with elegant oil paintings. Add several enormous crystal chandeliers, and the place struck Teddy as being much more of a museum than a house.

Teddy was also impressed by the dinner itself. When the orchestra began playing, the guests had obviously just taken their seats. They were still sipping glasses of sherry, placing napkins in their laps, and gossiping among themselves, more or less oblivious of the orchestra's efforts in the background.

As Teddy watched, waiters in pristine white coats brought course after course to the pampered diners—hors d'oeuvres, soup, salad, fish, meat, fruit and cheese, dessert... each course accompanied naturally by its own wine or other beverage. By the end, Teddy couldn't help but hope that the attendees had paid dearly for their "plates and tables" because, otherwise, the cost of putting on this event would easily negate any profit that Jacquard might accrue.

Finally, all the plates were cleared away, the diners turned their seats around to face the orchestra, and it was time for the night's entertainment to begin in earnest. The professor-conductor emerged from behind the curtain at the other side of the stage. He bowed to the assembly and took his place at the podium to a polite scattering of applause. Then he gestured for Teddy to enter. As Teddy used to do in his school days, he walked straight to the piano and took his seat, avoiding looking at the audience as much as possible. The conductor raised his baton, the orchestra played the first bars of the first piece, and Teddy began to perform his part.

An hour later, the conductor waved his baton sharply, concluding the first half of the concert. The audience broke into much longer, louder, and more appreciative applause as the musicians put down their instruments and stood up to go on break. Teddy and the conductor followed them out of the room. After such a long day filled with so much that was unfamiliar, Teddy was already feeling tired, and he knew that he'd need to summon up more energy somehow if he was to do justice to the rhapsody when he returned. So he asked a passing servant for directions and then stepped out onto the terrace beside the house.

Teddy spent his break pacing up and down its flagstones—staring at the blazing arc of the Milky Way overhead. He used to be able to see such stars splashed across a midnight-blue sky back home in New Mexico. They were just one more thing that he'd missed terribly since he'd come to live in New York. In his twenty minutes of star-gazing, Teddy found what he'd sought. He knew that the rhapsody had originally come from Heaven, and the beauty of the heavens had given him back his spiritual strength.

Teddy returned to the house. He re-entered the ballroom just in time to see the orchestra take their seats and the conductor stand up at the podium. The conductor glanced his way, and Teddy crossed to the piano, sat down, and poised his hands above the keyboard. The conductor slashed downward with his baton, and Teddy played the opening notes with the combined passion and reverence that they deserved.

Thirty minutes later, Teddy and his colleagues concluded. The conductor put down his baton, turned around, and bowed to the audience. For a moment, there was absolute silence, and Teddy couldn't help but fear that the rhapsody had failed to connect. But then, all the people present rose to their feet and began clapping wildly. Even the wait-staff in the back of the room joined in, some of them dispensing with decorum to the extent that they whistled shrilly between two fingers or called out, "Way to go!"

The conductor gestured for Teddy to take a bow. He stepped forward and did so, but then, he politely indicated the rest of the orchestra, who rose and bowed in turn. The guests began to shout, "Encore! Encore!" But unfortunately, the orchestra hadn't prepared an encore number and couldn't oblige. The conductor looked to Teddy with a question in his eyes. Teddy nodded slightly, so the conductor stepped aside, gestured to the orchestra to resume their seats, and gave Teddy the floor.

Teddy sat back down at the piano, poised his hands above the keyboard, and began to play his old warm-up stand-by—Chopin's Minute Waltz in one minute. From there, he ségué-ed smoothly into one of the nocturnes, then into another and another... stitching them together with improvisational passages inspired by Chopin's other works. After playing for just under ten minutes, Teddy brought his performance to an end, stood up, bowed again, and ignoring the renewed applause, he left. The orchestra and conductor followed.

Now truly too tired to continue, Teddy headed upstairs to his assigned room, changed out of his suit, and fell into bed. He didn't hear about the concert's outcome until breakfast the next morning, by which time he'd already packed his duffle bag and slung it back into the luggage compartment on the bus.

As Teddy shoveled hot oatmeal into his mouth in the servant's dining hall, he listened to his fellow musicians gossip. "...best concert the school's ever given... invited back for a second engagement this same season!... never heard anything like it, not even from Bach or Beethoven... extraordinary talent, and certain to be world-famous as a performer very soon... exceeded our financial goal by a wide margin, largely due to additional donations at the end of the night..."

Teddy finished his breakfast, wiped his mouth clean on his napkin, stood up, and went out to board the bus. He was glad that their first event had been so successful, and that the rhapsody had been so well-received. But he was uncomfortable with the praise implicitly coming his way, and he was eager to make his escape.

That first concert became the template for all the rest. The mansions were built in different styles. The servants' quarters were sometimes replaced by clean, but modest hotels. The food they were served varied slightly from region to region. And after the second concert, the orchestra begin practicing additions to their repertoire—initially so that they *could* play encores, and later just to save their sanity as repetition began to wear them down. But for the most part, the concerts followed the same pattern, and in Teddy's mind, the days began to blur together.

Summer fled. Jacquard, hesitant to see the influx of money cease, granted the orchestra, including Teddy, leaves of absence good through Christmas. Teddy began to wonder how he'd ever manage to finish his education at that rate. For as time passed, his loneliness was becoming ever more acute, and he longed to graduate and go home, or at least go on to the next phase of his career.

Finally, Christmas came. As the buses pulled up behind the concert venue *du jour*, Teddy stared out the window in disbelief. Someone with more money than sense had apparently transplanted a large Medieval stone castle from Europe to the east coast of America. The building featured square stone towers topped with crenelated battlements and high connecting walls pierced by the same narrow windows that archers had once used as they shot arrows at invading armies. The preceding day had been the winter solstice, and darkness was already falling despite the early hour. So Teddy and his fellows made haste to fetch their luggage and go inside.

Fortunately, the building's interior afforded far more comforts and luxuries than its exterior had promised. Teddy was able to get a hot shower after dinner before he had to dress and go downstairs. The concert went as well as all of its predecessors. The hall turned out to have excellent acoustics. So as most of the guests took their leave, Teddy went upstairs to bed, happy in the knowledge that the tour was over at last and he'd be heading back to New York in the morning.

Perhaps he should have avoided that last thought. Hours later, at nearly 3:00 AM, he awoke with a start from one of his New York City nightmares—the first one he'd had since going on tour. Teddy tried to get back to sleep, but in vain. Finally, he got up. He dressed in jeans, a shirt, shoes, and his overcoat and went downstairs. He found a side-door that was easy to unlock, and he let himself outside.

Teddy wandered through the gardens, hoping to wear himself out so that he could get back to sleep. His breath came in plumes in the cold night air, and the deep blue of the sky worked on his psyche until he shivered from more than just the chill. He found a path that led down the cliff face below the house. He followed the path and soon found himself standing in a sea cove, listening to the boom and sigh of the waves on the shore. He walked out across the sand, being careful not to twist his ankle on the piles of cobble stones below the cliff. And as he'd done so many times in the past months, he stared up into the sky at the stars, trying to take comfort from their remote beauty.

Teddy had read somewhere that 3:00 AM was the midnight of the soul. He'd never known quite what the quotation meant until that moment. His body's forces were at their lowest ebb. He was weary, yet unable to sleep due to his recurring dreadful dream. His mind was barely able to hold onto a coherent thought, and he felt oppressed by the isolation of his surroundings and the loneliness of his circumstances.

He was about to return to a city where he had many acquaintances, some of them kind, but no true friends. He was approaching his twenty-first birthday—in American society, the traditional demarcation of adulthood—yet he lacked most of what adulthood was supposed to confer. He still needed to complete his education. He had yet to find a full-time job or start a career. Worst of all, he had never been in love. He'd found no one to marry, no one with whom he could start a family, and he knew that he was handicapped in that arena. For he remembered having true soul-mates, and he doubted that he'd ever be able to settle for anything less than that most intimate of spiritual connections.

Teddy sighed. He looked around him and concluded that he'd better be getting back to the house. The memory of his brush with pneumonia was still fresh in his mind. Janie had saved him once. But it didn't follow that she'd be able to come and save him again. He'd better get out of the dank cold air and go back to bed, even if he sat up awake for the rest of the night, plagued by insomnia.

* * * * *

On Teddy's first day back from touring, he went to his hard-copy mailbox at school and found it jam-packed. He pulled out the wad of papers it contained and began sorting through them. Most of them were flyers and announcements for long-past events. Those papers he dumped in the recycling bin beside the mailboxes. But one envelope was apparently new and addressed to him in Doris's flowing script. He opened it, and inside, he found a neatly typed letter asking that he come to her office and make an appointment for another meeting. "Here we go again," he thought. He stuffed the letter into his backpack, but he climbed the stairs and went to do as she'd asked.

That afternoon, he found himself cooling his heels in the conference room across the hall, waiting to see who else would attend. At the appointed hour, to his not very great surprise, the admissions man entered the room, followed by the man who planned events and handled charitable giving. Teddy glanced at the door, but evidently, this meeting wasn't going to be a "star chamber" like last time. The admissions man closed the door, and the two of them took their seats.

The admissions man led off. "Mr. Sanchez, we have some very good news for you. Something unusual has happened that could jump-start your career as a composer and as a pianist. During your recent house-concert tour, one of the guests was an agent and music producer. He's very successful and very reputable. He already represents a number of other famous artists." Here the man handed Teddy a piece of paper, and Teddy's eyebrows rose as he recognized name after name on the list.

Teddy handed back the paper. "Are you telling me that he's interested in me?"

The events coordinator spoke up. "Yes, and to create public demand for your future performances, he wants to start by having you record your rhapsody, backed by the New York Philharmonic Orchestra. The CD would be issued under their normal label, and you would get billing as both composer and featured guest artist." Teddy was feeling dazed. He looked from one man to the other. The events man continued. "What do you say? Would you like to meet him?"

"Yes... Yes, of course..."

The admissions man stood up, opened the door, and called, "OK, Doris, send him in."

A good-looking middle-aged man in a very expensive suit emerged from Doris's office, carrying a briefcase. He crossed the hall, entered the conference room, and closed the door behind him. He extended his hand to Teddy and said, "Good to see you again, young man. I think that, between the two of us, we can make you pretty rich and extremely famous."

Teddy swallowed hard. "OK, what do I need to do?"

All three men laughed. The admissions man said, "See? I told you he'd be really direct."

The agent placed his briefcase on the table, spun the tumblers, and clicked open the locks. "Well, for starters, you'll need to sign a couple of contracts. One authorizes me to act as your agent. For your protection, it includes a non-performance clause, just so you know. For another thing, you'll need to sign a second contract authorizing me to set up the CD deal. That one will spell out what the likely production costs will be, what percentage of the profits I'll get as producer, what percentage the orchestra will get, and what percentage you will get. I recommend that, before you sign either one, you have them looked over thoroughly by an attorney familiar with the arts and entertainment industry who specializes in contract law."

Teddy was shaking his head, his eyes wide with alarm. "I don't know anyone like that."

The events man put in his oar. "No, but Ms. Leichner does, and for the good of the school, I'm sure she can twist someone's arm to get you representation."

"Excellent." The agent grinned and pulled another paper out of his briefcase. "Next we need to get you started with some marketing and branding. What's your full name again, son?

"Theodore Bernardo Sanchez." The agent winced. "But everybody around here calls me T-Bear."

The agent frowned and rested his chin on his hand. "T-Bear... T-Bear... It's not bad—not great, but not bad. I can work with that, and the rhapsody's name is 'Innocence'?"

"Yes."

"So what you need is graphic design and illustration support that will make your CD package irresistible to your target market. You want these things to fly off the shelves in brick-and-mortar stores and catch the eye of buyers on the internet. If you can leverage elements of your packaging design for event announcements, posters, and so on too, well, so much the better."

"So who's my target market?"

"Normally, I'd say anyone sophisticated enough to appreciate classical music. But in your case, I'm guessing, anyone with good musical taste of any kind. In fact, that rhapsody of yours is so catchy and so pretty that I'll bet it would even appeal to kids. So here's what I'm thinking. We don't go with modern art. Your piece feels more traditional somehow. We get a famous illustrator, someone who's won a lot of awards, and we turn her loose to produce something that says 'tasteful,' something that says 'innocent'."

"You're saying 'she'. I take it that you already have someone in mind?"

"Allison Mason, and as luck would have it, she's in town right now, signing a contract for her next book series deal with a major publisher. I told her about you and your rhapsody, and she's eager to take a crack at it if you're willing to meet with her and brainstorm some ideas."

Teddy was sitting very still. He recognized the name Allison Mason. One of his little cousins back home had some books that she'd illustrated, and they were very beautiful. If she agreed to take on his project, he'd be working with top talent and no mistake. "When can I meet her?"

The agent glanced at his watch. "In about ten minutes if all goes as planned. In the meantime, let's discuss the process of making this recording." The agent swung into a lengthy description of where the orchestra typically recorded, how Teddy would go about rehearsing with them, and many other details of that kind. Before they'd covered even half of what Teddy wanted to know, he heard a tentative knock on the door, it opened, and in walked a tall, lovely woman with long auburn hair streaked with silver. Another woman followed her into the room, undoubtedly her daughter or granddaughter because, except for the difference in their ages, they could easily be twins.

The women sat down, and the elder one placed a laptop computer on the table. She smiled at Teddy and said, "Hi, call me Allison. I'm from the west coast, and we do things a lot more informally out there."

Teddy smiled shyly. "Pleased to meet you, and you are?"

He'd turned to the other, younger woman, but she just smiled softly and shook her head in a self-deprecating way. "Oh, I'm just here to take care of my mother in the wilds of New York. Don't mind me."

The agent cleared his throat and exclaimed, "OK, let's get started. First of all, could you show my prospective client some of the comps you've prepared?"

"Sure." Allison moused and typed a bit. Then she turned around the laptop so that Teddy could see some thumbnails on the screen.

Teddy drew the laptop across the table and studied the pictures carefully. He even enlarged the ones he liked best so that he could see them in more detail. All of the illustrations reminded him at least to some degree of the pictures he'd see in his cousin's books. They were elegant and visually rich—obviously consistent with Allison's style as an artist. Unfortunately, they weren't consistent with his own views of the rhapsody. Teddy began chewing his lower lip in dismay.

Teddy dreaded losing this opportunity by coming across as arrogant or entitled so early in the game. He racked his brain to come up with some way to show appreciation while still pursuing a different course. "These are all gorgeous" he said. "Do you have anything that fits more closely with the title 'Innocence'? Like pictures of little children perhaps?"

Allison and the younger woman glanced at each other. "I don't, but my daughter might have one painting that meets your criteria." Allison took back the laptop and did some more mousing and typing. Then she showed the result to the agent sitting beside her.

He took a quick look and pursed his lips as his eyebrows rose. "Impressive! I see that artistic talent definitely runs in your family."

For the second time, Allison turned the computer around so that Teddy could see it. He pulled the laptop across the table, took one look, and felt as if he was going to faint. For there on the screen was a painting of Janie as he had known her in his past life, and she'd been portrayed sitting beside a rag doll and a teddy bear. Teddy cleared his throat against a sudden constriction. "This is wonderful. Where did you get your inspiration?"

The young woman hesitated as if she was reluctant to divulge a secret, but then she confessed. "I saw the image in a dream."

Her mother turned to her. "You never told me that."

Teddy stood up, walked around the table, and extended his hand to her. "Hi, I'm Theodore Sanchez, but people call me T-Bear."

Teddy saw sudden tears well up in her eyes. "And I'm Suzanne Mason, Suzy for short."

Their hands clasped, and they both jumped slightly as if they'd received a static electric shock. They stood a moment, holding each other's hands and gazing into each other's eyes, with Suzy looking down into Teddy's because she stood half a head taller than he did. Then, he rose up on his toes, embraced her, and kissed her full on the lips.

"Whoa! What's going on here? What am I missing?" the agent exclaimed.

Teddy and Suzy pulled apart, both wearing expressions of pure joy. "It's a long story," Teddy said, "far too long to explain here. Suffice it to say, we're just really glad to have found each other."

The man from admissions laughed in delight as the others continued to sit and stare in consternation.

* * * * *

Up in Heaven, Uriel happened to be visiting with Albert and his family again. "Oh, look! Isn't that nice?" He gestured at Teddy and Suzy standing on Earth with their arms around each other.

Nana followed his gesture and cried, "Oh my Lord! How *ever* did that happen?"

Albert looked at the pair, feigning innocence. "Why I have no idea. But if it has happened, then it must be consistent with God's plan. Right?"

Chet grinned.

Uriel was nodding enthusiastically. "Yes indeed! Right you are! I wonder if they'll invite Janie to the wedding. She'll be thirty years old, the perfect age for a matron of honor..."

Albert's father began to sputter. "Gabriel and Raphael said that they're not supposed to consort with each other!"

Uriel bathed him in light to calm him down. "I always find that what Gabriel and Raphael don't know won't hurt us. Besides, I truly love a happy ending, don't you?" And with that, he winked at Albert and then vanished, leaving them all a lot happier—if a little bit confused.

Soul Rhapsody

About This Book

Dedication

For JSG, my beloved friend and companion, who happens to be the best test-reader I know...

And for MBH, who is now in Heaven with God and the angels, just as she has wanted to be for so long... We love you and will miss you everyday until we meet again.

Acknowledgements

Many thanks go to JSG, RLH, VJF, APolin, RCMcQ, JJB, TMcKalson, VHutchison, and LClow for the appreciation and encouragement they expressed during this project. A book is a big undertaking, and receiving that kind of feedback really helps one keep going.

As test-readers, they helped improve the quality of the story's plot, characters, and underlying context (not to mention my spelling). Some of them helped me to find additional test-readers. Many of them urged me to publish. Special thanks also go to several folks who taught me about EPUBs:

1. LClow and MLim told me about consumer expectations regarding the look, feel, and pricing of EPUBs.
2. SSelf described various on-line markets and viewers for EPUBs and other soft-copy formats.
3. M&LClow gave me technical guidance regarding publishing tools, the EPUB specification, cascading style sheets, and elements of good internal design for soft-copy documents.
4. KLi gave me a copy of a very-capable free-ware EPUB authoring tool that would run on my down-rev equipment.

5. Last but not least, JHarper provided expert support for the aging computers, peripherals, and software tools comprising my authoring environment.

I'm indebted to you all. I've done my best to learn from your input. As always, any short-comings reflected in the final work are solely my own.

Image Attributions

This book's front cover and main title page use digitally manipulated copies of photographs of three paintings. See below for image attributions regarding those paintings. All three photographs are in the public domain. The front cover and main title page also use a photograph of a full-color sunset. Per Google Images, that photo is offered by Freepik and Pngtree as being in the public domain, available for any personal or commercial use without any copyright or use restrictions.

This book's front cover and all title pages throughout the book use a digitally manipulated copy of the file **cirrus-clouds-clouds-blue-4b08d6-1024.jpg**. Per PICRYL, this image is a public domain stock photo, free of any copyright or use restrictions.

The title page background for novella 1, *Soul Source,* is a composite image derived from digitally manipulated copies of the following photographs:

☐ Google Images offered the following files free of any attribution or copyright restrictions, i.e., as being in the public domain: photo of a vintage Steiff teddy bear offered for sale, photo of a vintage rag doll offered for sale, and **grasslands-Prau.jpg**.

☐ **Nidzica, Zamek w Nidzicy.jpg**. This file was licensed by Wikimedia Commons, the free media repository, under the Creative Commons Attribution 3.0 Unported license. Under this license, users are free to **share** (copy, distribute, and transmit) and to **remix** (adapt) the work under the following conditions. **Attribution:** The user must give appropriate credit and indicate if changes were made. The user may do so in any reasonable manner, but not in any way that suggests the licensor endorses the user or the user's work. **Share-Alike:** If the user remixes, transforms, or builds upon the material, the user must distribute his or her contributions under the same or compatible license as the original.

The title page foreground image for novella 1, *Soul Source*, is a digitally manipulated photograph of the following painting: **"The Age of Innocence" by Joshua Reynolds dated 1785/8.** This painting is currently in The Tate Collection in Britain. The painting is in the public domain in its country of origin and other countries and areas where the copyright term is the author's life plus 100 years or fewer. This work is in the public domain in the United States because it was published (or registered with the U.S. Copyright Office) before January 1, 1924. Per Wikimedia Commons, the file used was a faithful photographic reproduction of a two-dimensional, public domain work of art. The photographic reproduction is therefore also considered to be in the public domain in the United States.

The title page background for novella 2, *Soul Survivor,* is a digitally manipulated copy of the following photograph: **Nidzica, Zamek w Nidzicy.jpg.** See above for terms and conditions of use.

The title page foreground image for novella 2, *Soul Survivor,* is a digitally manipulated photograph of the following painting: **"Alice" by Henry Tanworth Wells dated 1877.** This painting is currently in the Kunsthalle Hamburg Collection. The painting is in the public domain in its country of origin and other countries and areas where the copyright term is the author's life plus 100 years or fewer. This work is in the public domain in the United States because it was published (or registered with the U.S. Copyright Office) before January 1, 1924. Per Wikimedia

Commons, the file used was a faithful photographic reproduction of a two-dimensional, public domain work of art. The official position taken by the Wikimedia Foundation is that "faithful reproductions of two-dimensional public domain works of art are public domain." The photographic reproduction is therefore also considered to be in the public domain in the United States. (In other jurisdictions, re-use of this content may be restricted.) The file has been identified as being free of known restrictions under copyright law, including all related and neighboring rights.

The title page background for novella 3, *Midnight of the Soul,* is a digitally manipulated copy of the following photograph: **green-leaved-on-mountain-with-castle-3.jpg** This file has been provided to the public as a free stock photo by **pexels.com. pexels.com** has published this photo without any attribution or copyright information. Because the photo has been published without copyright information, it is assumed to be in the public domain, without any restrictions on attribution, sharing, remixing, or other use.

The title page foreground image for novella 3, *Midnight of the Soul,* is a digitally manipulated photograph of the following painting: **"Léon Riesener" by Eugene Delacroix dated 1835.** The painting is in the public domain in its country of origin and other countries and areas where the copyright term is the author's life plus 100 years or fewer. This work is in the public domain in the United States because it was published (or registered with the U.S. Copyright Office) before January 1, 1924. Per Wikiart.org, the file used was a faithful photographic reproduction of a two-dimensional, public domain work of art. The photographic reproduction is therefore also considered to be in the public domain in the United States.

The **background for title page #5 for** *Soul Rhapsody* is a composite image derived from digitally manipulated copies of the following photographs:
- Google Images offered the following three files free of any attribution or copyright restrictions, i.e., as being in the public domain: **sea greece finikounda holiday water sea view outlook-1217421.jpeg, grasslands-Prau.jpg,** and **grasslands-Midewin2.jpg.**
- **Audrey Jeffers Highway Trinidad.JPG**—See above for terms and conditions of use.

The foreground image for title page #5 for *Soul Rhapsody* is a digitally manipulated photograph of the following painting: **"The Young Shepherdess" by William-Adolphe Bouguereau dated 1885.** This painting is currently on display in The San Diego Museum of Art. The painting is in the public domain, and the photograph, a faithful reproduction of an artwork in the public domain, is also in the public domain.

About the Author

George Currer Ellis (known to colleagues as "G. C.") is author of *Immortal, Resident Alien, The Assassin's Bride, Soul Rhapsody, Sleeper Agent, 4 Horsemen,* and *Eternal Light,* as well as six "trunk books" that should probably never see the light of day. After a forty-year career as a publications professional in High Tech, he has found true happiness writing works of science fiction, horror, adventure, romance, fantasy, crime/mystery, and the supernatural.

Retired and retiring, Ellis lives in seclusion south of Los Angeles, but north of the Mexican border, with his life partner and three rambunctious rescue cats. He hopes to write more books in the future—probably in moments snatched from waiting on said cats and catering to their every whim.

No photograph of the author is available. His body casts no shadow, mirrors don't show his reflection, his image can't be captured on film, and in his presence, digital devices produce only static—a terrible inconvenience for friends who try to use their cell phones.

Book Summary

This book contains three related novellas—*Soul Source, Soul Survivor,* and *Midnight of the Soul*—unorthodox fantasies about how angels do "soul management" and the issues that can arise... The first tale is about a seemingly ordinary little girl who's blessed from birth with extraordinary abilities. She uses those powers for good and finds a way to end her loneliness by making friends—literally. The other two stories relate what happens to those friends.

Readers who like movies such as "It's a Wonderful Life" and "Heaven Can Wait" will like this book.

Reader Comments

Amazon Kindle Customer: 5 stars—A new view of the human spirit... Do you have a soul mate, be it [a] spouse or best friend? *Soul Rhapsody* envisions three lives forever intertwined by heaven's influence. Moving from light-hearted to serious, Ellis has created a very different vision of how we all get here. I like the way the book creates what amounts to a theological overlay. I had to go back and read up on my Archangels. The characters are compelling and the author has clearly utilized elements they know a lot about. I think you will have a lot of fun reading this [book] and come away thoughtful. (Reviewed in the U.S. on October 26, 2022)

Other 5-star reviews on Amazon: Wonderful story!... Loved the story so much!... A grand read!... Exciting read!... Master story-teller!...